PRAISE FOR

JACK 1939

"The pace is so propulsive that you'll re... ability to weave fact into her tale is nothing short of remarkable. . . . There are precious few entertainments this captivating."
—*The Washington Post*

"As Hitler begins his march across Europe, President Franklin D. Roosevelt enlists a young John F. Kennedy, a Harvard student, to be his spy on the continent while researching his thesis there about fascists. And so the dashing future president gallivants through Paris, Moscow, Danzig, Istanbul, and Prague, chasing down a Nazi plot to keep Roosevelt from winning another term, among other feats of derring-do. . . . Grounding her thriller in spycraft and historical detail, Ms. Mathews pulls it off. The gang's all here: Churchill, Reinhard Heydrich, J. Edgar Hoover, Joseph Kennedy (John's father), and Roosevelt himself."
—*The New York Times*

"A brisk thriller that defies the odds . . . It's no small feat to take a historic figure who looms as large in real life as John F. Kennedy, place him in an improbable fantasy, and not strain credulity. But in this case, Mathews has accomplished her mission."
—*USA Today*

"Francine Mathews has a way of making you believe that improbable situations just might be true. . . . *Jack 1939* is a complicated thriller, filled with trust and betrayal."
—*The Denver Post*

"Deliciously inventive."
—*MORE* Magazine

"A highly entertaining cocktail of twentieth-century political history and sexy-spy-novel tropes."
—*The Daily Beast*

"A rollicking adventure story . . . It is an awful lot of fun to see FDR, J. Edgar Hoover, and Winston Churchill pop up in the services of a plot straight out of a John Buchan novel."
—*Financial Times*

"Tautly written . . . thrilling, credible, and memorable."
—*The Historical Novel Society*

continued . . .

"Imaginative, well-researched . . . An intriguing look at pre-WWII politics, both in the United States and Europe, as well as a meticulous character study of the future president." —*Publishers Weekly*

"Complex and thrilling in equal parts."
—*Library Journal* (starred review)

"A thrilling premise . . . *Jack 1939* is a gripping novel you won't be able to put down. The perfect summer indulgence!"
—*Portland Book Review*

"Vivid and sexy . . . Mathews' strobe-light, fact-infused drama of covert pre-WWII operations is riveting." —*Booklist*

"Filled with memorable characters both fictional and historical; Mathews provides an edge-of-the-seat journey, filled with haunting images that readers won't soon forget. . . . Aficionados of espionage fiction, history, the Kennedy family, World War II, and seat-of-the-pants excitement will devour this book, a must-read story that stands out from the pack. It'll make you want to turn back to your history books once again." —*BookPage*

"A triumph: an exciting thriller, an intriguing exploration of a troubled time, and an absorbing take on the early history of one of America's most iconic figures. Highly recommended."
—Iain Pears, bestselling author of *An Instance of the Fingerpost*

"Francine Mathews delivers a marvel: a thriller with genuine heart. This is a delicious imagining of one of the twentieth century's most fascinating figures, wrapped up in a gripping story of espionage."
—Eleanor Brown, bestselling author of *The Weird Sisters*

"Like JFK himself, this book is smart, sexy, and unafraid of taking risks. With nimble prose and easy charm, Francine Mathews leads us beyond the frontiers of history to make us believe in her vision of a young Kennedy at large in a dark world of prewar spies and secrets."
—Dan Fesperman, author of *Lie in the Dark*

"A brilliantly conceived, riveting tightrope race across Europe in the predawn of World War II."
—Stephen White, author of *Line of Fire* and *The Last Lie*

JACK 1939

Francine Mathews

RIVERHEAD BOOKS NEW YORK

RIVERHEAD BOOKS
Published by the Penguin Group
Penguin Group (USA) Inc.
375 Hudson Street, New York, New York 10014, USA

USA | Canada | UK | Ireland | Australia | New Zealand | India | South Africa | China

Penguin Books Ltd., Registered Offices: 80 Strand, London WC2R 0RL, England
For more information about the Penguin Group, visit penguin.com.

The Library of Congress has catalogued the Riverhead hardcover edition as follows:

Mathews, Francine.
Jack 1939 / Francine Mathews.
p.   cm.
ISBN 978-1-59448-719-4
1. Kennedy, John F. (John Fitzgerald), 1917–1963—Travel—Europe—Fiction.
2. Roosevelt, Franklin D. (Franklin Delano), 1882–1945—Fiction.   3. Hitler, Adolf,
1889–1945—Fiction.   4. Espionage, American—Germany—Fiction.   I. Title.
II. Title: Jack Nineteen Thirty-nine.
PS3563.A8357J323   2012   2012006443
813'.54—dc23

First Riverhead hardcover edition: July 2012
First Riverhead trade paperback edition: July 2013
Riverhead trade paperback ISBN: 978-1-59463-144-3

PRINTED IN THE UNITED STATES OF AMERICA

10 9 8 7 6 5 4 3 2 1

Cover design by Wednesday Design
Cover photographs: Young JFK, Fox Photos / Stringer / Hulton Archives /
Getty Images; Eifel Tower, Devaney Collection / SuperStock / Getty Images
Book design by Amanda Dewey

For Sam

The Boy in Room 110

"*. . . patient's 6000 cell count at intake,*" Dr. George Taylor wrote, "*has dropped to 3500. The persistent loss of white blood cells may indicate septicemia. Color and texture of skin are suggestive of jaundice.*"

He didn't bother to note that if the count dropped to 1500, the patient would die. Any doctor reading the Mayo Clinic chart would know that.

Taylor rubbed his eyes; it was after eleven, and he'd been poring over these files for hours while a snowstorm raged beyond his office window. The black-and-white Minnesota landscape was desolate in early February. But in the quiet of the hospital he should have been able to figure out why a good-looking, privileged college kid was wasting away in a bed down the hall. The patient's charts and files told him little. Every doctor who'd dealt with the case over the past five years had been as baffled as he was. One man's handwriting broke off, and another's picked up, while the 1930s wore away. The boy waned and recovered, waned and recovered; but nobody could put a name to his illness—or explain his curious knack for survival.

"*Weight has dropped to 148 pounds, a loss of twelve pounds in six days, possibly due to eliminative diet of rice and potatoes."* Taylor had weaned the boy from wheat—it was just conceivable that he couldn't tolerate it—but there'd been no improvement in the painful stomach cramps that made most meals an agony. It wasn't bread that was killing his patient.

"Eight enemas have been administered in the previous twenty-four hours, and contents of the bowels examined; a significant quantity of blood is observable in the stool." Maybe it's a duodenal ulcer, Taylor thought. That could explain the drop in white blood cells. Or maybe it was simply acute colitis. A spastic colon, resulting in persistent diarrhea and the inevitable emaciation. Or even more worrying: What if the free fall in the boy's white blood cell count meant he had leukemia?

Taylor threw down his pen and thrust himself away from his desk. At this hour of the night, Mayo was a locked cloister; on their rubber-soled shoes the nurses were hushed as nuns. He didn't know what was wrong with the patient, but he knew he was missing a critical fact—the puzzle piece that would solve his problem. He was *missing* it.

He strode down the half-lit corridor, his heels clacking obscenely—a tall, stooping, hawk-nosed man with a thin carapace of black hair on his skull. His patient was invariably restless; a confirmed night owl, he'd still be awake. Taylor halted in the doorway of room 110.

"Jack."

"Hey, Doc!" The boy closed the book he was reading. "You're up way past your bedtime."

Taylor ran his eyes over the six-foot frame, cadaverously thin under the sheet. Sweat beaded Jack's upper lip, and his shock of unruly hair needed cutting. But his eyes were alight and a wave of energy seemed to flow from his body. It was uncanny, Taylor thought, how this sick boy could fill a room—even as he threatened to leave it behind forever.

The doctor cocked his head sideways to examine Jack's book. *Young Melbourne*, by somebody named David Cecil.

"What happened to *The Good Society*?"

"Finished it this afternoon." Jack tossed *Melbourne* aside. "So what'll it take to get me out of here?"

"A higher blood count."

Taylor shifted the pile of books at the foot of the bed, frowning at the titles. *History of Political Philosophy. Recent Political Thought. Dictatorship in the Modern World. Germany Enters the Third Reich.*

He hefted this last one in his hands. "You a Nazi fan?"

"Oh, that's from last year." Jack was a junior in college now. "But I'm planning to drive through Hitler's backyard in a few weeks. I figured I'd better reread it."

Taylor set the book down as though it burned his fingers. "About that trip—"

"The *Queen Mary*'s got a stateroom with my name on it, Doc. She sails February twenty-fourth." Jack's jaundiced face was suddenly flushed. "If you try to keep me here, I'll bring in the big guns. Which means my dad. He'll spring me from this place."

"It's a hospital, not a prison. We're trying to save your life."

"Sorry." Jack glanced away. "I just hate to be touched. Always have, ever since I was a kid. It drives me nuts when you guys turn me inside out and come up with nothing. Can't we just accept that nobody knows what's wrong?"

"Not if it means you die," Taylor said quietly. "What if you take a turn for the worse, all the way across the Atlantic?"

"My family's in London. So are a lot of doctors. I'll be fine."

Taylor doubted it. He'd never met Jack's parents, but their

lack of concern about him was legendary at Mayo. Neither his father nor mother had set foot in Rochester; they communicated with Jack's doctors by telegram. Taylor had never treated a kid who was so profoundly sick and so completely alone.

"Look," Jack persisted, "I've been sick all my life. You name it, I've had it. The last rites of the Catholic Church at age *two*. My body's screwed up every plan I've ever made. I'm not going to let it screw my senior thesis."

"That's why you're going to Europe?" Taylor was surprised. "To write a *thesis*?"

"Oh, there'll be some parties, too."

"Parties will kill you."

"I'm dying anyway." The boy gave a snort of laughter. "Don't worry. I'm more interested in research than booze."

Taylor sat down on the bed and looked at him. "If you remember, four years ago, after you graduated from boarding school, you took another boat to London."

"Yeah. I was supposed to study with Harold Laski at the London School of Economics."

"What happened?"

"I got sick." His eyes flicked uneasily away from Taylor's. "Had to come home."

"What was the diagnosis then?"

Jack shrugged. "Agranulo-something. I was supposed to shoot up a liver extract. But it was hard to find in London. By the time I got back to the States, my blood count was higher and I never took the stuff anyway."

"Agranulocytosis?" Taylor suggested, his thoughts racing. "Was that the word?"

"Could be."

Agranulocytosis was a disease of the bone marrow, akin to

leukemia; it would explain Jack's plummeting white blood cell count. It would explain a lot of things, in fact—his constant susceptibility to colds and infections, his sudden bouts of hives. The boy's immune system was shot to hell. "Who diagnosed it?"

"Some Harvard prof my dad telegrammed." Jack was studying Taylor's face curiously. "He didn't entirely trust British doctors, so he wired this guy named Murphy."

"*William* Murphy? The Nobel laureate?"

"I have no idea."

"That's not in your file," Taylor said irritably.

"Maybe Murphy doesn't write to Mayo."

Taylor stood up and began to pace along the side of Jack's bed, stepping carefully around the piles of books. He'd have to contact William Murphy and find out why he'd diagnosed agranulocytosis—but that could take weeks, and Jack didn't have that much time. Not with his white cell count dropping hourly.

"I think we need to deal with your problem colon first." Taylor was thinking out loud. "If we could get that under control, you might regain some strength—keep some food under your belt, keep some weight on—and then your white blood cell count might rise. Ever heard of DOCA?"

Jack shook his head.

"Desoxycorticosterone acetate," Taylor said. "It's an adrenal extract—highly experimental, like Murphy's liver dose. It seems to control a spastic colon. The problem is, you'd have to administer it yourself."

"In Europe, you mean?"

"Anywhere."

"I can do that." Jack sounded confident, but Taylor wasn't buying.

"You wouldn't do it four years ago, in London. Afraid of needles?"

"No!" He looked insulted. "I *told* you. The liver stuff was hard to find."

"I couldn't release you until I was sure the treatment was working."

"How long will that take?" Jack demanded.

Taylor considered. "Two or three days."

"If it means going to Europe, I'll stay another week."

There was so much hope in the boy's ravaged face that Taylor bit his lip.

"You'd have to keep in touch," he warned. "I'd need reports on your condition."

"My friends will tell you I'm a devoted correspondent."

It was true—the nurses were constantly mailing out reams of Jack's illegible handwriting. Letters, like books, seemed to keep his loneliness at bay.

"Roll up your pajama leg," Taylor said. "I'll be right back."

He almost ran from room 110. The idea was crazy; it was irresponsible; it might not even work.

When he got back, Jack's right leg, thin and vulnerable, was stretched nakedly on the bed.

"Play any sports?" Taylor asked as he readied his tools.

"I swim for Harvard." Jack sounded almost embarrassed; real men played football. "We went undefeated last year. And I box pretty well."

"Good." Taylor held a scalpel in front of Jack's nose. "I assume that means you don't faint at the sight of blood."

He grinned. "I had to get twenty-eight stitches once. Head-on collision between two bikes."

"What'd the other guy look like?"

"That'd be my brother. Not a scratch on him."

"You're going to have to cut yourself, Jack, if you want to go to Europe."

The smile faded slightly. "I can take it, Doc."

With a single quick movement, Taylor sliced open a quarter-inch flap of skin over the boy's right calf muscle.

A hiss of indrawn breath. But when Taylor glanced up, Jack's face betrayed nothing.

"See this?" The doctor held up a pellet.

"DOCA?"

"DOCA. You tuck it into the cut, Jack. Then cover it with a bandage. It should dissolve slowly into your system."

Jack nodded, his eyes fixed on Taylor's fingers. "How often should I do it?"

"We'll figure that out," the doctor said, "before you leave Rochester—"

"By how much my colon improves, or my blood count fluctuates over time?"

"Exactly." The kid wasn't stupid. He could analyze the data and draw his own conclusions. That might be a problem, Taylor thought, if the data worsened. . . .

"And if the DOCA doesn't help?"

Taylor avoided Jack's eye as he twisted the bandage around the wad of cotton. "Let's hope it will."

Part One

WINTER

ONE. PLATFORM 61

A BITTER COLD WEDNESDAY in February, nearly midnight. Jack strolled out of Grand Central Terminal and up Park Avenue to the Waldorf-Astoria, carrying his ancient suitcase. Seventeen hours on the 20th Century Limited, the most exclusive and luxurious train in America, and he felt as battered as if he'd traveled by camel. He hadn't eaten much more than a Parker House roll. He hadn't slept, either. His skin was drawn tight across his cheekbones and his eyes had the feeling of August on the Cape—too much sun and salt ripping across the Wianno's bow.

The hotel doorman was looking at him as though he were a Bowery bum in search of a heating grate. His clothes were a rumpled mess—they always were; his mother was constantly nagging him about it—but the Waldorf was Kennedy territory. His father had lived here for a year when Jack was a kid, and he still stayed at the hotel whenever he came to New York. His mother preferred the Plaza—and booked it whether Dad was at the Waldorf or not. It was a metaphor for their marriage. Never mind separate beds; Joe and Rose got separate *hotels*.

"Checking in, sir?" the doorman inquired frigidly.

Jack handed him the suitcase. The man's arm sagged from the weight of his books.

"I think my father already has a suite. Ambassador Kennedy?"

"Of course." The doorman snapped his fingers for a bellboy, his relief obvious. "Welcome to the Waldorf-Astoria."

"Thanks." He thought about tipping the guy, but before he could find a quarter in his pants pocket, a hand came down on his shoulder. A surprisingly heavy hand. Like a cop's.

"Mr. Kennedy?"

He turned around. "Yes?"

There were three of them—Foscarello, Casey, and Schwartz, as he would learn later. They wore trench coats and snap-brim fedoras, and although they bore no relation to one another, their faces had a blunt-featured sameness. Schwartz was in charge of this cutting-out expedition and it was he who'd clapped his hand on Jack's shoulder. He was four inches shorter than Jack but his hips and chest had the centered mass of a wrestler.

Jack could feel the doorman watching him; he saw the bellboy halt in his tracks. And so he flashed his smile at the men who were not cops, and said, "Gentlemen. What can I do for you?"

THE MAN IN THE WHEELCHAIR couldn't sleep, but that was nothing new. Because his days were filled with too much talk and competing bids for attention, he'd made a habit of insomnia; he thought more clearly in the emptiness of midnight. Four hours of peace were his as the train rolled north from Washington, and he'd spent some of it reading the manila file that Ed Hoover had sent over from the Bureau that morning. When his eyes grew tired, he stared blankly at the protective steel louvers that striped his private Pullman's windows, thinking. He was pulled up in the lee of a desk bolted to the train car's floor. It was covered with cables from Europe.

He had owned this job for nearly eight years now, and the insomnia was building with the threat of war, a continuous adrenaline feed into his bloodstream. It was sapping his strength and his life, but he could no more give it up—this excitement like a second pulse throbbing beneath his skin—than he could choose to walk again. He knew, better than any man in America, just how critical the work was and how little time he might have to control it. The work was more vital than legs or sleep or even living a few years longer. It was defining the shape of the coming world—*he* was defining the shape, he and a few other people on the opposite side of the ocean, and the crooks they tried to contain, and the sheer variability of facts and impulses that collided each day as randomly as a boy's marbles. He could not sleep because he could not stop watching the world as it gathered itself to explode.

A year ago—1938—Adolf Hitler had seized Austria, although the term he used was "annexed," without firing a shot. A few months later, he'd screamed for the German slice of Czechoslovakia, the Sudetenland, when what he really wanted was the country's munitions factories and uranium mines and a clear passage to the Russian border. Neville Chamberlain, the British Prime Minister, had flown to Germany twice to tell Hitler he was welcome to the Czechs, if only he'd leave England alone. Hitler had shaken on the deal and promised to be a good boy. The British public cheered with relief and called Chamberlain a savior.

The man in the wheelchair thought Chamberlain was an egotistical ass.

He squinted through his spectacles at the most recent cable—it was from Poland, the next prize in Hitler's sights—then set it down in favor of the manila file he'd practically memorized.

Believed to be dying at age seventeen . . . misdiagnosed with leukemia . . . possible blood or liver disease . . . damaged vertebrae while playing football at Harvard . . . spends several weeks each year at the Mayo Clinic, with additional tests at Brigham Hospital . . . medical consensus: unlikely to thrive . . .

A slight sound from the doorway drew his head around; Missy was leaning there, the perfect personal aide, a cup of tea in her hands.

"Like some?" she asked.

"Please." He took the cup from her, scenting the rum-spiked tea. As he drank, he tapped the manila file. "Ever meet this boy?"

She shook her head.

"Supposed to be a charmer." Roosevelt peered at her over his spectacles. "The Black Sheep of the family. Hang around and say hello, if you want."

Missy had a soft spot for black sheep. She came over to his chair and planted a kiss on his head. "My book's too good."

He eyed her critically. His wife would be reading an improving work filled with labor statistics. But Missy . . . "Is it something by Jane Austen?"

"Dashiell Hammett. Tell me about Jack in the morning."

THEY LED HIM THROUGH a part of the Waldorf few guests ever saw and exited a service door into the hotel garage, pulling up eventually before a freight elevator. By this time Schwartz had flipped open his badge.

"Secret Service," Jack mused. The Treasury department's special force. Which might mean he'd been dragged out of the lobby because Dad had overplayed the markets again. Why not talk to his father, then? Why buttonhole Jack? It was important, he figured, to look unconcerned. To stay calm, even if his heart was racing. His eyes met Schwartz's and held them.

"Is my father in some kind of trouble?"

He didn't need to remind the Secret Service that Joe Kennedy had made a fortune manipulating stock in ways the Treasury department had never been able to prosecute. Franklin Roosevelt had made Jack's father his first chairman of the Securities and Exchange Commission as a reward for his cunning. *Set a thief to catch a thief,* Roosevelt had said—or so Dad once told Jack, smiling his thin smile at the head of the dinner table. Dad found the President's cynicism funny. How could Treasury have caught up with Joe Kennedy *now*?

"Last I heard," the man named Foscarello said, "your old man was just swell. Out dancing with a hatcheck girl."

Jack flushed and almost went for Foscarello, but at that moment the doors of the freight elevator opened and Schwartz's hand was on his shoulder again, guiding him into the steel cage.

"Mr. Kennedy," Schwartz said soothingly, "we're President Roosevelt's bodyguards. He wants to see you. He's waiting below in his Pullman."

Foscarello stared at Jack without blinking and there was a definite challenge in the man's stolid face. The elevator lurched like a tin can on a string and Jack's stomach dropped sickly.

"Below?" he repeated. "The President's Pullman is in the hotel's basement?"

Schwartz sighed. "There's a track beneath us, Mr. Kennedy. The Waldorf was built over some old train yards connected to Grand Central. Platform 61 belongs to the hotel. Public trains don't stop here—you can't actually find the platform unless you know where to look. The President uses it on his way to Hyde Park."

Jack ran a hand tentatively over his hair. "You're sure Mr. Roosevelt didn't ask for *Joe* Kennedy?"

"He asked for Jack."

"How'd he know I'd be here tonight?"

Schwartz almost smiled. "I have no idea, Mr. Kennedy."

The elevator doors opened.

"Hey," Jack said urgently. "Anybody got a comb?"

ROOSEVELT WAS PRETENDING to read the file when the boy slid through the doorway, ducking his head in deference to the occasion, one finger working at his tie. His clothes were a mess; so was his hair. It was remarkable hair: springy and barely tamed with pomade that'd been applied a day and a half ago. Roosevelt dismissed Schwartz with a nod.

"Ah. Jack. Good of you to come. Sit down, won't you?"

"Mr. President."

It was all visitors ever said, as though the title implied whole layers of meaning—*I'm honored, I'm bewildered, I'm waiting to find out what I did wrong*—and for a moment Roosevelt was disappointed. He'd expected more from the Black Sheep.

"I didn't exactly have a choice," Jack went on, with a sudden grin. "Those boys of yours are very persuasive. But I like my nose unbroken. So I came along quietly."

There it was: The jauntiness. The inveterate curiosity. Roosevelt had guessed right about this one.

Jack sank into one of the Pullman's seats with unconscious grace. His face was gaunt, his frame as thin as a teenager's. But

Roosevelt caught a whiff of cordite on the air—the scent of a fired gun, a burnt match. It came from the kid in front of him. Jack crackled with energy.

J. Edgar Hoover thought the boy was an embarrassment, the expendable Kennedy.

He's the kind who never finishes anything, the FBI chief had insisted as he'd handed Roosevelt the file that morning. *The kid who comes in second, the one who drops out, who trades on his daddy's name. He was nearly expelled from Choate, for God's sake, he was such a discipline problem. He quit the London School of Economics.* And *Princeton.*

But Roosevelt never relied on a single source of information. He knew more about Jack than Hoover or his files would ever hold. Jack might be sick and his record might be checkered, but he was one of those rare souls completely at home in the world. It didn't matter that he was Irish or Catholic or that his father was regarded as an unprincipled cad; Jack slouched into the most breathless of WASP bastions in his careless clothes and threw his legs over armchairs like he'd owned them from birth. His ease was admired and slavishly imitated; his quips and sarcasm circulated like a kissing disease. He was voted into Harvard's exclusive Spee Club when no Kennedy had ever made a final club at Harvard before—because his friends categorically refused to join without him.

Hoover loved to tick off the ways Jack slid by: the standing account at the Hyannis Port gas station, where the convertible's tank was always filled and the owner never paid; the clothes strewn all over the floor of his college suite; the string of girls he picked up and dropped. But those things meant nothing to Franklin Roosevelt. He'd been privileged and young once, too. He was much more interested in the ways Jack *didn't* conform to type. His love of risk. His analytic brain. His need to argue. His willingness to ditch the pack and go it alone.

His refusal to admit he probably wouldn't see thirty.

The man in the wheelchair looked at Jack Kennedy, and saw something he recognized. Something he'd learned to respect. Something he was himself.

A survivor.

"YOU'RE WONDERING WHY you're here," the President said.

The smile flashed again. "I told Mr. Schwartz it was probably Dad you wanted to see."

"I saw your father in Washington. He's a fine man. I'm proud of the job he's doing for us over there in London."

Roosevelt kept his voice light as he mouthed the lies; nobody ever won a boy's heart by insulting his father. He disliked Joe Kennedy more than most of the men who hung on his coattails; and he'd never trusted him, even when Joe's money and Democratic contacts had helped win the '32 election. Roosevelt had sent Joe to London mostly to get him out of his hair. He preferred to leave the Atlantic between them; if Roosevelt had his way, Joe would stay in England until after the 1940 election.

"That's kind of you to say, sir." It was the correct response, of course—but Roosevelt saw Jack's slight frown; he was wary, now. He'd know, of course, that Roosevelt was forcing his father to return to London early—two weeks before Jack sailed—because he was fed up with Kennedy idling by his pool in Palm Beach, with his detective novels and his easy women and his fawning reporters drinking his whiskey, while they assessed Joe's chances of winning the presidency. Joe Kennedy *actually thought* he was Roosevelt's heir apparent. His ambition, Roosevelt thought, was childlike; for a crook he had very little guile. It was as though all his craftiness was reserved for making money. In the game of politics, Roosevelt could run circles around somebody like Joe. Even in a wheelchair.

He took a sip of Missy's tea. "You know I was a Harvard man, of course."

"Yes, sir."

"I put in a call today to Bruce Hopper. I believe you two are acquainted?"

Jack sat up, on alert. "Professor Hopper's my thesis adviser."

"He's a fine man. Fought in the War, you know."

"Have you heard his Armistice Day lecture?" the boy asked eagerly. "It's something I'll never forget."

"I've heard it. Hopper tells me you're taking the spring semester off, and sailing to Europe to research your senior thesis."

"Yes, sir. I leave in two weeks. Dad was supposed to travel with me, but—"

"I ordered him back to London." Roosevelt bared his teeth in a smile. "Hopper says you mean to tour Germany this spring. Aren't you afraid of heading into a war zone?"

"Begging your pardon, sir—but it's not my war."

"*Yet.*"

Again, a slight frown creased Jack's forehead.

"Dad says the American public will never accept another European war. The polls look pretty solid on that point."

"You care about polls?" Roosevelt asked genially.

Jack shrugged. "They're a moment frozen in time. One piece of information. And opinions change, of course."

"According to circumstances. If we were attacked, for instance. And had no choice but to go to war."

"Exactly. Dad insists we can simply *choose* to stay out."

"What do you think?"

"I'm not so sure." The boy studied Roosevelt. "My dad doesn't really understand politics, sir. I shouldn't say this, but—"

"No, no. Go ahead. Please."

"He understands business. Nobody makes money like he can. But he looks at the world as a series of markets—markets we have to protect. Markets we *need*, or don't. *The Germans are good trading partners. War is bad for business.* But the war that's coming, it has nothing to do with trade. On the German side it's about history—and revenge. For the rest of us, it's about standing up to bullies. Give Hitler the Czechs, and he'll take the Poles."

"And after the Poles?" Roosevelt asked softly.

"He'll take whomever he damn well pleases."

To Jack, it was obvious, Roosevelt thought—and yet most of the world refused to believe it. No wonder Professor Hopper had agreed to work with the boy. He could think for himself.

"Your father and Neville Chamberlain say Hitler's *reasonable*. Chamberlain thinks he can strike a deal."

"It won't be an honorable one. Do you know Winston Churchill, sir?" Jack asked suddenly.

"We've met." The question startled Roosevelt. Churchill was shunned by most people in power, including Joe Kennedy.

"He said something at the embassy's Fourth of July party last summer that I've never forgotten." The boy smiled crookedly. *"It seems we will be offered a choice between dishonor and war. I suspect we shall take dishonor—and get war afterward, as a kind of dessert."*

Roosevelt sighed. He would like to talk to Churchill—get a different picture of Britain than the one Joe Kennedy usually gave him—but Churchill was viewed as a warmonger in the United States, and Roosevelt had to distance himself. But Jack, now . . . that was why Jack was here.

"Is that how you intend to research this thesis— By talking to people?"

"If they'll make time for me. Sure."

"In London? Berlin?"

"I've got to get to Poland, too," Jack said thoughtfully. "Danzig is the next target. Hitler wants a North Sea port, and what he wants. . . . Have you heard Ray Buell talk about his new book *Poland—Key to Europe*? It's due out in a few months. Lays out the whole thing."

Roosevelt blinked. Raymond Leslie Buell was chairman of the Foreign Policy Association and an ardent interventionist. Not the sort of expert a Kennedy should admire. "I haven't had the pleasure."

"Most people haven't," Jack assured him kindly. "I've already got a copy of the book on order."

"And after Danzig?"

"Moscow, if I've got time. Mother expects me in Cannes for August."

Roosevelt conjured a picture of Rose Kennedy: her tight little figure, her tight little mouth. Her bottomless respect for rules and convention. *Mother expects me in Cannes for August.* Jack with his careless wit, dancing with debutantes. His frame too thin and his face too tan, thinking furiously about Danzig while he talked nonsense into the night.

"How will you travel?" Roosevelt demanded abruptly.

"I thought I'd drive."

Hoover's file noted that Jack was a wicked driver, with more traffic tickets in a month than most cops wrote in a year. Roosevelt could see it now: Jack alone at the wheel of an Austin or Lanchester, with only a diplomatic passport between himself and the Gestapo.

"Take a friend," he suggested, "and stay at our embassies. It'll be safer."

"Thank you, sir, but I've driven through Europe before. A few Panzers here or there won't make much difference."

Because if your days are numbered, you live every one, Roosevelt thought. *Risk doesn't scare you—it just makes death more interesting.*

He came to a decision.

"Professor Hopper says you have a first-class brain. That your writing is masterful and your analysis far more sophisticated than most men of your age. He says you're a rare bird at Harvard—an independent thinker. Is that true?"

Jack glanced away, suddenly embarrassed. Praise from Hopper was unexpected, and when delivered by the President, impossible to take. "I don't work *that* hard, sir. I mean, it's not like I'm a *grind*."

"Understood. But that's not what I asked."

Jack hesitated. "Of course I'm an independent thinker. What's the point of being anything else?"

"The world is full of men who repeat what they're told."

"I know! How do you *lead* a country like ours, sir?" Jack asked curiously. "Where most people don't read, and think even less? It's like living among the deaf and blind."

"I think I was deaf and blind myself when I was your age," Roosevelt said. "I had the use of my *legs* then. I took them—and everything else—for granted. Before I was forced to decide what to live for. Or whether to live at all."

It was far more than he'd intended to say. He stopped before he told the boy the unforgivable thing: that in his dreams at night, he walked tirelessly for miles down a thousand sidewalks, the campaign crowds awed to silence.

Jack was looking at him intently, his mobile features arrested. He was thinking about what Roosevelt had said; Roosevelt, knew, suddenly, that he understood it in his gut and in his blood, where his illness lived.

"Sir," Jack said carefully. "You still haven't told me why I'm here."

Franklin leaned toward him. "Can you keep a secret, Jack Kennedy?"

TWO. THE SPIDER

THE WOMAN PERCHED ON the black stool was perfectly dressed for the Stork Club, even if she was parked in the cloakroom instead of onstage. Silk draped the generous curves of her body, her platinum hair was swept high in a shining pouf, and her lips were painted crimson. Her name was Katie O'Donohue and she was twenty-six years old. She earned five dollars a week checking coats, and lived in a fourth-floor walkup somewhere in Hell's Kitchen.

Her teeth were sharp and white as a cat's, the man thought as he watched her from the curtained doorway. Her tongue darted over her painted red lips as though a drop of cream lingered there. The man read greed and lust in that tongue, Katie's chief weaknesses; he planned to capitalize on them tonight. He glanced at his watch, then back at the girl. Nearly two a.m., the end of her shift. It was time.

His gloved fingers tightened on the handle of the plain black satchel he held close to his coat. He stepped out of the shadows.

Her eyes widened as she saw him; her lips parted in a false smile. "You're making a late night of it, Mr. Saunders. Are you alone, or meeting someone?"

It was the prearranged code phrase and she had it down pat; but instead of answering her with the correct phrase—*Unfortu-*

nately I'm alone, Miss O'Donohue—he moved swiftly round the coat-check counter and swept her into his arms. The satchel dropped at his feet.

She stiffened beneath him, but when he kissed her roughly on the painted mouth something in her relaxed; Katie understood men and sex. That was her other weakness.

"Aren't we all hot and bothered tonight," she murmured, as he eased away from her.

"I am," he agreed. "Let us go. There is a back entrance, yes?"

"There is a back entrance, yes," she repeated, mocking his foreign accent. "What about your bag?"

He placed the satchel on the cloakroom's bottom shelf; it was empty, but Katie didn't need to know that. Her friend Jimmy Riordan had been picking the satchel's lock for the past three weeks, thinking nobody would notice. Jimmy was swimming in fifty feet of East River tonight, with a stone tied where his balls used to be.

Katie shrugged herself into a smart red coat.

"Don't button it," he said. "I want to be able to feel you."

Her false smile again; the catlike teeth. The orchestra surged from the dining room, a triumphal blast before the break—and he wanted the cover of noise. He'd have to move fast.

He grasped her arm and propelled her toward the rear door.

"Ow," she said irritably. "Hold your horses, Loverboy. What I've got'll keep."

The door gave out into darkness, a single streetlight shining where the alley met 53rd. He turned his back on it and stared down at Katie.

She slipped her arms around his neck, pressing against him. "Where were we?"

"You've been stealing from me," he said gently. "Haven't you?"

She stepped back, fear tightening her pretty face. "Never! I swear it!"

"Jimmy Riordan says otherwise."

"Jimmy Riordan's a stinking liar."

He pulled her close, his fingers firm on her ribs, feeling the silk dress slither over her delectable body. She was caught between his hands. He kissed her cat's mouth open and drank in the rush of surprised air as she gasped; tasted her moan of almost-pleasure as his knife slid wetly between her ribs.

She stiffened an instant, then collapsed to the street. She was dying at his feet, a stricken look on her face. He knelt down and peeled back one sleeve of her coat, one strap of her dress, exposing the creamy flesh of her breast. With the tip of his knife, he carved a crouching spider just above the nipple.

THREE. HATCHECK GIRL

THE BOOK TITLES displayed in the plate-glass window looked like tough times and February. *The Fashion in Shrouds*, by Margery Allingham. *Anthem* by Ayn Rand. And the latest Simon Templar novel, *Prelude for War*.

Jack studied the haloed stick drawing on the cover. The Saint wandered the world alone. He used his brains as much as his body. His charm was devastating to women. Jack was feeling a little like Simon Templar this morning, although sainthood had never been one of his ambitions.

I need an independent thinker.

He wandered down the aisle of the bookstore—Charles Scribner's Sons, his favorite haunt in New York, with its wood paneling and iron scrollwork over the soaring windows. His father had bought the Billy Whiskers stories here when Jack was about five years old. Rose said they were vulgar and should be given away, but Jack loved Billy Whiskers. Like him, the goat was always in trouble, and always butted his way out of it. He hid the books and read them alone, when he was sick.

Can you keep a secret, Jack Kennedy?

He had no intention of telling Dad about the midnight conference with FDR. He was hugging his knowledge to himself, well aware of the family betrayal implicit in his silence. He was serving the President and his country; Dad would be proud enough when it was all over. And if he wasn't . . . Jack shrugged slightly, his eyes roving among the stacked titles. He'd spent most of his life begging forgiveness instead of asking permission.

"YOU KNOW THAT IN THIS COUNTRY we've got no spies, Jack," Roosevelt had said in the silence of the Pullman, the circle of lamplight focused on the manila file in front of him. "We tried to get a network started once, after the last war when the whole Bolshevik thing blew up, but a horse's ass of the Grand Old School declared that *Gentlemen do not read each other's mail*, and as a result the spies were sent packing. We're heading into a hurricane now with our ears plugged and our eyes closed."

"That can't be good, Mr. President." Jack flushed; he sounded idiotic and young. But Roosevelt didn't notice.

"You're a sailor, Jack," he said. "Ever sail into a hurricane with your ears plugged and your eyes closed?"

"I hope I never have to, sir. But I understand you're a blue-water skipper to reckon with."

"That's something else we have in common, then."

"There are some tricky shoals off Hyannis," Jack admitted, "but they're nothing compared to Campobello."

Roosevelt lit a cheroot, his hands large-knuckled and veined in the flare of the lighter. "I suppose I've beaten the odds once or twice in my day."

Jack tried not to stare at the wheelchair. "Are you asking me to read someone else's mail while I'm in Europe?"

Had that been too blunt? Too lacking in finesse?

"I'm suggesting you take this trip of yours and keep your ears and eyes open." Smoke spiraled from Roosevelt's nostrils, veiling his face for an instant. "Talk to anyone who'll agree to see you, in London and Paris and Munich and Prague. Chat up Stalin himself and Hitler into the bargain, if you can pencil yourself onto their dance cards."

Jack nodded, but his brows pulled together slightly. "Forgive me, sir—but aren't dance cards my father's job?"

There was a silence, the heavy kind that falls over a chessboard when a player considers checkmate. There were a number of questions within Jack's question, a number of possible answers. The notion of loyalty—and of dividing it—hovered over their heads. Then Roosevelt smiled. It was, Jack thought, his characteristic smile—sharp enough to slit throats.

"Your father is tied down in London. You're a free agent. And to be honest, Jack . . . I can't trust the State department with this. It's a different kind of job."

And then the President lowered his voice and stabbed the desk in front of him with one long forefinger and took Jack into his confidence—right into his breast pocket.

"I've decided to run for a third term," he said.

Jack frowned. "Is that legal?"

"Of course. It's just never been done before."

"Bucking history, aren't you, sir?"

"—Because George Washington thought eight years should be enough for any man? He never met Hitler, Jack."

The conversation was increasingly unreal, as though his tiredness and the stale underground air of the Pullman were lulling him to sleep. He blinked at Roosevelt and tried to argue, but the President forestalled him.

"I'm afraid for this country. Afraid of what will happen if an isolationist gets his hands on power. Somebody who'll wash his hands of Europe and hope the Germans never come calling.

Somebody who'll hide his head in the sand until it's bombed out beneath him."

"An isolationist would be right up Hitler's alley," Jack agreed.

"That's why he's trying to buy one. To install in the White House."

He stared at Roosevelt. "What do you mean?"

"The Germans are flooding Democratic precincts all over the country with cold, hard, cash." Roosevelt smiled thinly. "Money that people need, money that Regular Joes can give their wives and children. Money to pay for coal and bread and a new pair of shoes. Provided they vote the way they're told. Which will certainly not be for me."

"How much money are we talking about?" Jack asked.

Roosevelt adjusted his spectacles, well aware that price tags never shocked a Kennedy.

"Ed Hoover puts it at about a hundred and fifty million."

"Marks?"

"Dollars."

Jack whistled thoughtfully. "He actually thinks he can *buy* an American election?"

The President's fingers fluttered. The cheroot's tip described a glowing arc. "You think it hasn't been done before?"

After that, Jack gave up questioning the strangeness of the night, his own exhaustion, the intimacy of the hidden train car, or the fact that several floors above him, people tossed restlessly in the Waldorf's beds. He was talking conspiracy with Franklin Roosevelt. He recognized some of the names the President dropped like cooling ash on his Pullman floor: Democratic labor leaders, union people, local bosses, state senators. Isolationists to a man. All ready enough to take a Nazi buck and kick the one guy willing to fight them out of power.

"We know Hermann Göring proposed the plan," Roosevelt was saying. "We know Hitler approved it. What we don't know is how a hundred and fifty million is getting into all these men's pockets, in Ohio and Pennsylvania and the coal mines of West Virginia. That's a hell of a lot of money, Jack, to send over from Germany in a diplomatic pouch. We have to find who's running the network—and how."

"When you say you can't trust the State department—"

"I mean I can't trust anybody right now. Particularly over at State. Cordell Hull's an excellent man, but those cookie-pushers of his think it's their job to swap stories at every cocktail party in Europe. Too many of my private conversations are finding their way into Hitler's office."

A *traitor*? In the State department?

Jack opened his mouth to ask another question, but Roosevelt's face had suddenly set in stone. There was a warning there; a limit, apparently, to what he would tell Jack.

Was *Dad* one of the people the President couldn't trust?

The thought wormed its way through Jack's tired brain but he dismissed it irritably. Roosevelt would hardly be talking to him if he had no confidence in his father.

"I've been turning it over in my mind, Jack—this trip of yours," the President was saying. "To the Nazis, you're just the American ambassador's son. But to me, you're a perfect spy. *My independent thinker*. Arriving in London with a fresh outlook and an unclouded mind. As far as the Nazis are concerned, you're clean as the driven snow. They know your dad and I don't always agree. They'll never expect you to be my man in Europe."

His man in Europe.

Despite his doubts and the lateness of the hour, or perhaps because of those things, Jack's breath caught in his throat. *Clean as the driven snow.* Like a boy on his First Communion day. Like the Innocent Lamb his mother had always wanted him to be.

"You'll have access to everybody," Roosevelt persisted. "Your father will see to that. You'll have a diplomatic passport and a hired car. Your own brand of guts. Your charm and your smile and your trick of making everybody underestimate you. You'll find the German network we're looking for, Jack—I know you will."

He didn't add that Jack had a body nobody could count on. Or that he would probably be sick more often than he was healthy.

And because infirmity and physical weakness meant nothing to Franklin Roosevelt, Jack Kennedy would have died for the man then and there if he'd asked.

HE CONCLUDED HIS BUSINESS with the Scribner's clerk.

"There's a book coming out in a few months. *Poland—Key to Europe*, by Raymond Leslie Buell."

"Yes, sir. Publication is scheduled for April."

"Soon as you've got a copy," he said, "I'd like one sent to a Mr. Sam Schwartz. I'll write out the address. Do you have a card I could enclose?"

I thought you might enjoy reading this, Mr. President, he wrote in his cramped, barely legible hand. *Perhaps we could discuss it after I've been to Danzig.*

Sincerely yours,
Jack Kennedy

P.S.: Please thank Mr. Casey for the use of his comb.

HE BOUGHT A COPY OF *Prelude for War* as a going-away present for his dad. Joe liked a good thriller; it would help kill the boredom of another Atlantic crossing. Even if he refused to admit war was coming.

They met for dinner that night at the Stork Club. Dad was boarding the *Queen Mary* in the morning and he wasn't happy about it. London was perpetually dark and chill in February and Rose was traveling through the Middle East. He'd wanted two more weeks of Palm Beach sun and Jack's company for the crossing. But Roosevelt had changed all that.

"Franklin's little joke," J.P. said with his tight smile. "I could buy and sell the bastard a hundred times over, so he reminds me every once in a while who runs the country. *This* year, at least."

Jack eyed his father, the way his chest swelled slightly as he boasted; he was such an innocuous-looking man, neat and trim from his wire-rimmed spectacles to his handmade shoes. Only something about his mouth, the way it twisted when he thought he'd been insulted—or maybe the coldness of those eyes he tried to mask with his round schoolboy glasses—suggested Joe Kennedy's ruthlessness. As long as he could remember, Jack had ached for his father's approval. And watched him toss it casually to his older brother instead.

There were some who called Joe Kennedy a crook to Jack's face, and others who hinted his dad's luck was too good to be true. But they never said it twice. Jack was a scrappy fighter. He didn't care if he nursed a shiner for a week; there were still such things in the world as honor. He had a pretty good idea how Dad had made his millions. But that was between Joe Kennedy and the Law—and the Law had caved.

He was realizing, however, that there were limits to his father's canniness, and they began and ended with Wall Street. How was it possible, Jack wondered, for Joe Kennedy—the Bronxville Shark, the Croesus of Hyannis Port—to believe all those reporters inflating his ego in Palm Beach? Did he seriously think he had a shot at the presidency? He dined with the King of England now, and his wife bought her clothes in Paris—but the rest of the world would never forget he was the son of a mick who'd owned a saloon. Nobody would be voting for Joe Kennedy, Jack thought—because FDR was running for president again, and apparently not even Joe Kennedy knew it.

He fingered his private knowledge like a smooth and shining pebble, hefting its weight. He was the Bearer of Secrets. He knew things his father did not know.

"Everything go okay out at Mayo?"

Mayo.

Jack's stomach turned over, the acid of his wine mixing unhappily with beef and potato.

"Mayo was swell," he said, scraping his fork through a pool of gravy. Dad would have read George Taylor's notes already. That's what Joe Kennedy paid the world for—advance notice of disaster.

"Does it hurt?" his father asked abruptly. "—cutting those pills into your leg?"

Jack glanced up. "No," he said.

"Think they help?"

"I'm here, aren't I?"

His father reached out and clapped him on the shoulder. "Attaboy. Can't keep a Kennedy down."

They lingered a moment in the club's foyer while the girl got their coats. J.P. was holding out a folded dollar and smiling at her in a way that made Jack uncomfortable. Foscarello's face rose suddenly in his mind. *Your old man's swell. Out dancing with a hatcheck girl.*

"Where's our Katie, then?"

The girl's dark eyes dropped to the counter. Her thin white hands rested there, trembling slightly, the nails painted blood red. "I couldn't say, sir."

His dad's smile grew more fixed. "Out on the town with some young man?"

"If you'll excuse me, sir—"

The girl disappeared behind the curtain.

"Didn't you read the paper this morning, Dad?"

Joe looked at him, perplexed.

"There was a murder out back in the alley last night. A hatcheck girl—stabbed to death."

"*Murdered?* Jesus, Mary, and Joseph—"

"Her name was Katie O'Donohue."

"I knew her people in Boston, Jack." His father looked white and shocked in the foyer's gentle light. "Truth be told—I got her this job."

Jack fished awkwardly in the pocket of his overcoat. "Here," he said, handing his dad the Simon Templar novel. "I got you this today. For the crossing."

Joe stared at the stick drawing of the haloed Saint. "Thanks. I haven't read this one."

"I didn't think you had."

"Little Katie," Joe murmured, his gaze sliding past Jack, to the shadows around the door. "It's a terrible world, you know that?"

"I'll get us a cab," Jack said.

FOUR. LOOSE ENDS

"TAKE A LOOK AT THIS." J. Edgar Hoover passed a folded square of newsprint to Roosevelt, who adjusted his glasses and peered at the black-and-white image of a Manhattan alley, police in the foreground. A shrouded form, humped and miserable, bisected the shot.

"That's the girl we were tailing. She was murdered the other night while you were in New York."

"Really?" Roosevelt glanced over the edge of the newspaper. "And your tail never saw me plunge my knife into her heart, Ed? You're slipping."

Hoover grimaced. "Mr. President, I never meant to imply—"

"Just a joke, Ed."

"The girl was *murdered*, Mr. President."

"Yes. Very sad. And she was how old?"

Hoover shrugged, unsettled. "Twenty-five, twenty-six. I don't know. She was just a hatcheck girl."

Typical, Roosevelt thought. Sanctimonious and callous in the space of a heartbeat. Hoover was an odd fellow—emotionally unstable, in Roosevelt's opinion; paranoiac and a hypocrite and quite probably a liar; but wickedly intelligent. He saw wheels within wheels. The trick lay in knowing when to stop listening.

"The point is," he was saying, "that Katie O'Donohue was a

lead in this German money case. And now she's gone. The mick she was dealing with has done a bunk, too. Nobody's seen him for days."

"Then he probably killed her and took the cash." Roosevelt sighed. "And your tail saw nothing?"

The FBI chief moved restlessly in his chair. "He was stationed in front of the Stork Club, waiting for her shift to end. She left by the back alley instead."

"Your tail would have recognized the . . . *mick*, as you put it? If he had entered the club by the front door?"

"Or even the alley. Sure. Hammond's a good op—he'd have picked up Jimmy Riordan right away. But the only guys Hammond saw were the usual types who hit the Stork. Well-dressed. Respectable. Walter Winchell and his crowd."

"And the cash hasn't surfaced?"

"Not yet."

"What about a personal motive? Love gone wrong?"

Hoover shook his head. "The wound's not the work of an amateur. It was a trained thrust, straight through the ribs to the heart. *Military*, one of our forensic boys said. And there's another thing: a swastika was cut into her left breast."

Roosevelt whistled faintly. "Hardly subtle."

"We think it's a deliberate warning." Hoover dropped his voice. "From the Germans. We think they know we're onto them—and they're rolling up the network."

"If German agents came all the way to New York to kill this girl," Roosevelt pointed out gently, "then someone at your shop has talked too much. This man Hammond, perhaps?"

"No." Hoover was emphatic. "Or *he'd* be the one with the knife through the heart. Maybe Katie talked—or had light fingers. A girl doesn't make much these days, checking hats."

"So what will Hitler do?" Roosevelt mused. "Silence a few more bagmen? Find another Katie? Or concede my third term?"

"Hitler's got eighteen months before the next election and plenty of cash to spend, Mr. President. He won't concede."

Roosevelt set the newspaper clipping on his desk. "Poor child. Why did you even notice her in the first place?"

"Because of the company she kept." Hoover smiled wolfishly. "She was one of Joe Kennedy's girls."

AFTER THE FBI CHIEF LEFT the White House, Roosevelt sat for a while staring at nothing. There were issues on his plate—he'd asked Congress for $525 million to buy planes and train pilots, but the Hill was taking its time. Nobody wanted to vote for defense and look like they were voting for war. He wanted to amend the Neutrality laws this term, so he could help France and Britain if Hitler turned west, but it was risky—the isolationists would eat him alive. And then there was *Eleanor*. His wife was demanding repeal of Jim Crow laws segregating blacks and whites in the South. He couldn't push the issue now and win reelection next year. He needed too many Southern Democratic votes.

So why, with so much to handle, was he obsessed with Hoover's parting words?

He rolled irritably across the uncarpeted floor. His study was oval in shape and next to his bedroom. By the connecting door was a table where he worked on his stamp collection—he was concentrating on Central and South America at the moment, but he was thinking of starting a special war album. Stamps of countries annexed by the German Reich, countries that would cease to exist by the end of the summer. How rare those stamps would be!

He had just picked up the envelope full of foreign mail the State department saved for him each week, so he could cull the stamps, when there was a knock on the door.

It was Sam Schwartz, the head of his Secret Service detail.

"Tell me something, Sam."

"Mr. President?"

"Did I, at any time, to the best of your recollection, require J. Edgar Hoover to investigate Joseph P. Kennedy, the ambassador to the Court of St. James's?"

"*Investigate* him, sir?" Schwartz looked puzzled. "You mean his manipulation of the stock market years ago? Our boys over at Treasury have turned that inside and out. We couldn't touch Kennedy. There weren't enough laws on the books then to cover what he did."

"Poking around in his private life, Sam. Following him off-hours. Checking up on the people he chooses to . . . *entertain*. That sort of thing."

"No, sir," Schwartz replied with distaste. "To my recollection, you have never asked the FBI to investigate Mr. Kennedy in that way. Perhaps Mr. Hoover . . . fell into it, when you asked for the background report on Mr. Kennedy's son."

"Charitable of you, Sam. But they're different people, surely? Edgar keeps files, you know. Secret ones. Full of scandalous information. He's very diligent in compiling them. A bit of black-mail will always be useful."

"That's not right, sir."

"Edgar doesn't waste time on what's right—he concentrates on what's legal. And in my experience, that's whatever the FBI *decides* is legal. Makes you wonder," Roosevelt added, "whether he has a file on you. Or my children. Or me."

"I doubt that, sir!"

"Why?" He eyed his bodyguard. "If he has the dirt on one of the wealthiest men in America, why not the President?"

Schwartz's stolid face was shocked. "*Because* you're the president!"

Roosevelt laughed mirthlessly. "I bet he tapped Kennedy's phones in Palm Beach. God, those transcripts would make some reading! Sam, I think it would be as well if you and Casey and Foscarello swept my bedroom for whatever it is that taps phones. Hell, sweep the whole White House for the damn things."

"Bugs, sir?"

"Bugs." The word delighted him; it suggested something telling about Hoover's mind.

He turned his wheelchair toward his desk and rolled slowly across the study floor. "Edgar thinks the Germans know we've discovered their secret cash network. And that they're shutting it down as a result."

"Hitler doesn't shut down, Mr. President."

"Agreed. You think Edgar's too eager to declare victory, Sam?"

"It'd serve his purpose."

"Which is?" Roosevelt demanded.

"To make himself indispensable. First he threatens you with a plot, then he blows it sky-high and calls himself a hero. Remember General Butler?"

"How could I forget?"

Major General Smedley Darlington Butler was a man Roosevelt admired. Once the youngest major general in the Marine Corps and twice a recipient of the Congressional Medal of Honor, he'd been forced to retire by Roosevelt's predecessor,

Herbert Hoover, for publicly denouncing Benito Mussolini as a "mad dog." When the Italian ambassador complained, then-president Hoover threatened the general with court-martial. Butler stood by his words—and was forcibly retired.

In 1934, Butler came to J. Edgar Hoover with a bizarre story: He'd been tapped by two prominent American Legion officials to lead an armed march of half a million veterans on Washington, protesting the New Deal. The men in question had just returned from Europe, where they'd been studying the formation of Germany's Nazi Party, the Italian Fascisti, and the French Croix de Feu. They were struck, Butler said, by the critical role army veterans had played in the founding of these political movements—and felt there was a place for such an organization in the United States. It would save America from the Communist Menace. If Roosevelt opposed them, he'd be removed by force, along with his cabinet.

Butler wanted no part of any plan to overthrow his own democratically elected government, but he played along with his contacts in order to learn who was financing them. They told him confidentially they were backed by a new organization: the American Liberty League.

The ALL's professed purpose was to oppose "radical" political movements. Among its members were the directors of some of the country's largest corporations—U.S. Steel, General Motors, Standard Oil, Montgomery Ward, Goodyear Tire. Alfred P. Sloan was a member, as were the Du Ponts. E. F. Hutton had joined. So had Elihu Root. Together, they controlled more than $37 billion in assets.

And they were gunning, Butler explained, for the overthrow of Franklin Delano Roosevelt.

Hoover refused to investigate the American Liberty League;

he told Roosevelt they'd violated no federal statute. The real reason Ed sat on his hands, Roosevelt knew, was that he would never cross the wealthiest men in the country. He handed that thorny problem directly to Roosevelt. The President tossed it to a private congressional subcommittee charged with investigating Nazi propaganda in the United States. In a closed session, they listened to Major General Butler and others who'd been offered leading roles in the putsch. Word of the plot leaked from the session and circulated in Washington and New York. Somebody wrote a news exposé about it. By the time Roosevelt ran for a second term in 1936, the American Liberty League was totally discredited. Most of its prominent backers had quit.

But the lesson remained. J. Edgar Hoover had prevented a conspiracy to overthrow the United States government. And he'd come to Roosevelt again, five years later, with evidence of the Nazi money network.

"The way he sees it, Boss, you owe him something now," Schwartz surmised.

"Spies," the President said thoughtfully. "That's what he wants, you know—his Bureau boys opening secret files all over the world. And a few spies would be useful in this coming war, God knows. But I hesitate to concentrate all my eggs in Edgar's basket, Sam."

Schwartz's lips compressed. Hoover's power grabs were old news. He even wanted Schwartz's job, and fought an ongoing battle with Henry Morgenthau, the treasury secretary, over Roosevelt's security detail. By hallowed tradition, guarding the president was the Secret Service's duty. Hoover thought his Bureau boys should take over the job, and he trotted out the slightest threat to the President as ammunition in his war. If Hoover could convince Roosevelt to place his life in the FBI's hands, Hoover's eyes and ears would be right there in the White House: recording the President's every thought and move. But to Schwartz's relief, Henry Morgenthau had crushed Hoover's bid. For now.

"I think we have to assume that Herr Hitler is as devoted as ever to removing me from office," Roosevelt was saying. "He'll barely break stride for the death of a hatcheck girl. Or an ambassador's son, if it comes to that. Could you get Jack Kennedy on the phone?"

JACK WAS IN THE HANDS of the bellman, his bill settled and his Boston train departing in half an hour, when the President's call came through. His hat was on his head and his coat slung over his arm; he was feeling well enough this morning to eye the girls walking through the hotel lobby. There was a real looker waiting demurely on a sofa, gloved hands folded over her handbag; a typist for hire, probably, with great legs beneath her narrow business suit.

"Long-distance call for you, Mr. Kennedy," the bellman said.

Jack dropped his hat and coat next to the typist, and walked over to the switchboard operator's desk. She offered him an earpiece.

"Jack? Roosevelt here."

His pulse accelerated. "Good morning, Mr. President."

"I guess your father sailed today?"

"He did, sir."

"We'll hope for fair winds and following seas, then. About that thesis research of yours . . . Sam and I were just saying that we think the level of *foreign interest* in your work has shot up."

Jack's fingers tightened on the black earpiece. "Is that so, Mr. President?"

"I want you to cable Sam if you need to talk things over. Your theories, for instance, or anything interesting you may find. Sam could be a great help."

"I'll keep that in mind, Mr. President."

"Better yet, Jack, take down this telephone number. Do you have a pencil?"

Jack fished frantically in his breast pocket. *Fuck.* He could never find anything when he needed it. He gestured wildly at the hotel operator, and she whipped a pencil out of her hair. The wood felt warm in his palm.

Roosevelt was dictating already. Jack scribbled numbers on the cuff of his dress shirt, hoping he'd got them right.

"That rings at my bedside. Call any time you'd like to chat. Just try to remember the time difference between Europe and Washington, all right?"

"I certainly will, Mr. President."

"And Jack?"

"Yes, sir?"

There was the slightest of pauses. "Take care of yourself, son. The Atlantic's rough this time of year."

FIVE. A HERO OF THE LAST WAR

JACK CAUGHT HIS TRAIN NORTH. There was a man he needed to see.

Bruce Hopper's office was in the Old Yard, but he was rarely there—too busy giving lectures to undergraduates or radio interviews on the Fascist threat. Jack tracked him that morning to a quiet bay in Widener Library. Hopper had commandeered an entire oak table, littered with books and papers in Cyrillic. He glanced up as Jack's thin shadow fell over him. Then he tossed aside his pen and eased back in his hard chair.

"Cheers, *mon brave*."

It was Hopper's classic greeting, reserved for the select group of souls he respected. As a freshman Jack had thought *mon brave* must be easier than attempting to remember a thousand names—but he learned quickly it was a prize to be won. He hadn't earned it until this year.

Hopper had flown aerial combat missions in France during the last war and all the Harvard men secretly idolized him. He'd won the Croix de Guerre and the Legion of Honor and some other decorations he didn't bother to mention; he'd been hurt badly in one crash, but lived to fly another day. When the war was over he'd stuck around Europe, studying at the Sorbonne and Oxford with the rest of the generation they called Lost. He didn't even look like a Government professor. His neat figure was pared down, stripped for action, ready for a fight.

Jack loved Hopper. He loved his stories of bumming around Burma and the Middle East during the twenties, stringing for newspapers. He loved listening in the lamplight of Hopper's seminar while he talked of samovars and cold and the hidden viciousness of Moscow, where he'd lived until the Crash of '29 put an end to his fellowship money. Hopper had come back to Harvard and settled down to teach. There was a Mrs. Hopper now. But in moments of abstraction, Jack saw how the professor's eyes searched the sky unconsciously for airplanes, the slightest hope of combat.

He shook Hopper's outstretched hand.

"Thought you'd sailed."

"I've still got two weeks."

"Then what the hell are you doing here? There must be a girl you could chase."

"I saw Roosevelt," Jack said quietly. "He told me he talked to you."

Hopper grunted. "So he did, *mon brave*. I've never had a telephone call from a president before. It caused quite a sensation. The switchboard operators chatter. Nothing in the Yard is private. Now the Dean wants to know when I'm leaving for Washington and what I possibly think I could add to FDR's Brain Trust. I told him Roosevelt couldn't care less about me. Shall we walk?"

THEY PULLED UP THEIR COLLARS against the wet cold of a Cambridge February and strolled down to where the crew shells were putting out into the Charles.

"What did he want?" Hopper asked.

Jack did not answer for a moment. He had come all this way for help because Hopper was the only man he really trusted, and now that he was here, the whole fantastic night—the Pullman hidden beneath New York, the Nazi funds, FDR's third term—seemed like a hallucination. Maybe it was the pellets he kept thrusting under his skin. Maybe DOCA made a guy crazy.

He shrugged. "He wants me to keep my eyes open while I'm traveling in Europe."

"Makes sense." Hopper fumbled in his coat pocket for a cigarette case and lighter. "You'll be on the ground in a potential combat zone. You'll glad-hand everybody and talk their ears off. That's what you *do*. Smoke?"

They lit up and exhaled, staring at the river. The shells moved with precision, eight oars lifting at the coxswain's count, eight backs bending. Jack recognized a guy who lived on his floor at Spee, mouth furled in anguish. He knew crew was hard as hell, but it looked beautiful from a distance and he wanted to remember it that way, even if inside the shell it was pure suffering.

"You told him I'm an independent thinker."

"You are. Is that a sin in the Kennedy household?"

Jack glanced at him. "Depends who's laying down the law."

"Joe, for instance." Hopper had taught Jack's older brother a few years ago. "But you're always arguing with Joe, and you're usually right."

"That's different from . . . *advising a president*. I mean, what if I don't see or hear anything special, Professor? Never mind what it means for my thesis. What if I . . ."

"Fail?"

Jack nodded.

"Do nothing, and you fail," Hopper said gently. "You've already chosen to act. You're leaving Harvard. You're going to Europe. *Jesus*, Jack—I'd leap at your chances! You get to watch the world blow up and figure out who lit the fuse."

"What," Jack deadpanned. "Teaching Government 1 to a bunch of Brahmins isn't enough for you anymore?"

"Look." Hopper turned toward him in exasperation. "You're *young*. You don't realize yet that there are only a few times in life when you get to test everything you've got—when the moment calls and you have to respond. Half these boys in the Yard are stone deaf as far as the world is concerned, but *you*—you were made to live by your wits and the seat of your pants and the dumb luck that's kept you going this long. *This is your moment, Jack*. Don't miss it. It comes around once or twice and never comes again. I know."

Jack heard the raw longing in Hopper's smoky voice and felt his pulse quicken. It was impossible not to feel a dangerous exhilaration. To want to fly straight into enemy gunfire.

"Is he looking for something specific?" Hopper asked tentatively. "Or just . . . general intelligence on the ground?"

Jack hesitated, his hands clenched inside his coat pockets.

"Never mind. I shouldn't have asked."

"Professor—"

"It's okay. You'll be in England for a while?"

"Most of March. Then I head to Paris. After that—" Jack grinned. "Summer, and Points East. I'd like to get to Moscow."

"Lord," Hopper sighed. "Youth is wasted on the young, you know that?"

Jack waited. Hopper was scanning the sky for wings.

"Right," he said at last. "Chamberlain runs the Tory Party the

way Mussolini runs his trains. Dissent is not tolerated; it's Neville's way or the highway. Agree with the Prime Minister, or be booted out of Parliament. Which means you've got to talk to Churchill, Jack. He's not afraid of Neville and he sees the coming mess for what it is."

"I met Churchill last summer. My dad says he's just a drunk."

"Oh, he drinks all day long. Whiskey in his bath, champagne at lunch, claret for dinner . . . To Churchill, drinking is good manners, not a disease."

"Dad says nobody listens to him anymore."

"I hope he didn't tell Roosevelt that."

"Why?"

"Because he'd be dead wrong. For years, Winston's been howling about German rearmament, while his own party hooted and jeered. But it turns out he's right, by God, and if Hitler grabs more than the Czechs, Neville Chamberlain will be out on his ear. Your dad's advice will be so much horseshit then. And whatever *you* can pick up in Europe will be pure gold." Hopper smiled at him crookedly. "No offense, but your old man has lousy political instincts, you know that?"

Jack kept his gaze on the crew shells knifing down the Charles. "Have you ever wanted to save a guy from himself, Professor, and been completely unable to do it?"

"Every day. I teach, remember?"

THEY PARTED AT THE DOORS of Widener. Hopper offered his hand.

"You'll write if you need anything?"

"I will. Thanks."

"I envy you, *mon brave*."

Jack merely nodded. Hopper's confidence should have been bracing. But he'd sought out the professor half convinced he was hallucinating. A jabbering product of DOCA pellets. And Hopper had confirmed that Jack was all too sane.

SIX. THE MARK

WHEN JACK LEFT CAMBRIDGE, he took Hopper's advice. He spent the last thirty-six hours before he boarded the *Queen Mary* chasing Frances Ann Cannon.

She was a peach of a girl, and it wasn't just her looks, which were fabulous and head-turning, or her money, which came from the Cannon family mills in North Carolina. Jack had always had money and he could whistle up good looks any night for a song. What he loved about Frances Ann was the way she talked, tilting her head to one side and letting the soft Southern words roll out like sheathed daggers. The things she said were intelligent and acute and detached and funny, and they enslaved him. When Frances Ann spoke, Jack listened, and he'd never really listened to any girl before, except his sister Kick, who was so much like himself it didn't count.

Frances Ann staved off the curtain that hovered just beyond Jack's sight, a kind of fog he thought of as Boredom or Death. He spent his days striding away from it, hands shoved in his pockets, jingling loose change. When Frances Ann tilted her head and opened her mouth the curtain lifted. He wanted her the way broken men wanted strong drink or sleep.

He flew to meet her in New Orleans and the two of them danced a conga line through Mardi Gras. She refused to go to bed with him; she was that kind of girl. Frances Ann understood something fundamental about Jack: It wasn't sex he really wanted, it was the chase—and because she was no dummy, she kept the chase alive. She mocked him and toyed with him and then, desolate at the airport, waved frantically through the terminal window, a red sweep of lipstick smearing her cheek, unshed tears in her eyes.

He had asked her to marry him. And she'd refused.

It was partly, Jack guessed, because he was an Irish Catholic and she was a WASP. And it was partly because he was Joe Kennedy's son. There was something not quite right about Joe Kennedy, in respectable American eyes; Frances Ann's parents did not approve.

It was just possible, Jack knew, that in her heart of hearts, Frances Ann did not approve, either. Jack was good enough for a few laughs and a swell time—but not good enough to marry.

He was sick at heart and angry as he flew back to New York. And ready to show the world he was good enough for anyone.

HE WAS STANDING ALONE in the rain now on the Promenade Deck, watching other people wave good-bye to figures on the pier. There were stevedores and there were umbrellas. There were excited women chattering idiotically, handbags suspended from gloved hands. Some of the well-wishers had come on board for a last drink, thousands of people, in fact, pushing past each other from First Class to Third, popping champagne corks and delivering baskets of fruit and flowers, getting drunk in the middle of the day because a friend was crossing to Europe. *Bon voyage.*

Jack crossed his arms and leaned on the rail, shoulders hunched, no particular party to attend. There was a telegram in his pocket from Frances Ann, deliberately gay; she'd signed it *Good-bye darling I love you*, but the words were meaningless now. She'd be relieved to put the Atlantic between them.

He'd brought a fedora but he wasn't wearing it. The rain settled in his hair, turning the careful pompadour to corkscrewed Irish. He debated the idea of the First Class lounge and a glass of Bourbon, which would wreak havoc with the ulcerated duodenum Taylor thought he had, but what the hell. The DOCA seemed to be working. He was able to keep some food down now and he thought he might have gained a pound or two. A shot of Bourbon wouldn't hurt. He was lonely and the curtain that was either Boredom or Death was hovering just off the port side.

And then she materialized beside him: cool and porcelain-faced, knees bound in a pencil skirt. Her fur was high-collared and ended abruptly at the waist. Her hat swept like a dove's wing over one cheek. It made her seem sly and seductive and unreachable as she stared thoughtfully at the pier. Where was her farewell party? Like Jack, she did not bother to wave. Like Jack, she crossed her arms and leaned on the rail, one shoulder grazing his. Her mouth was painted crimson. An unlit cigarette dangled from her lip.

He reached in his pocket. "Need a light?"

She bent toward the flame. As the cigarette caught, her chin lifted and she stared over his head, exhaling through the perfectly stained mouth. He could see that her hair was jet black and chin length, with a heavy fringe on the forehead; her black eyes had not the slightest bit of expression in them. *French*, he thought. His pulse quickened and the lit match burned his fingertips. He tossed it over the rail.

Only then did her gaze drift for an instant to his face.

"I'm Jack," he said, offering his hand.

He thought perhaps her lips quirked. Then she moved past him without a word, her hips swinging in the pencil skirt.

His head craned sideways to follow her.

THE MAN WHO HAD STUCK a knife into Katie O'Donohue's heart was several decks below, eyeing the people who jostled one another in Tourist Class. A glass of rye whiskey had been pressed into his hand by a whirling party girl already three sheets to the wind, and he'd accepted it gratefully as a God-given prop that suggested he had a reason to be there. He was almost out of time.

His gaze moved indifferently over the passing women. They had nothing he needed. He was searching for a man: one who looked like himself, one who was *not* going ashore when the shore whistle blew. He knew to the second when that whistle would sound, and what he must do under cover of its noise. But first he needed the mark.

"Hey, handsome," a girl crooned at his elbow. She rocked against him as though overbalanced by the motion of the boat. A redhead. She smelled unpleasantly of cigarettes and whiskey. "There's a swell party going on in D-13. That's my friend Darlene's cabin. It's got the sweetest little bunk imaginable."

"Excuse me." He could utter those two words without the slightest trace of accent. He disengaged his arm and edged past the girl. The drunken throng closed around him.

The first shore whistle blew.

Panic rose in his throat. He *must find* somebody. Five foot ten, blond, and hovering on the edge of thirty—

He raced through the crowd to the Tourist gangway, searching for one man who could be his savior.

And there, unbelievably, he was: a mild-faced fellow gripping a briefcase, with a good felt hat pushed back on his head, a wool scarf tucked into the collar of his somewhat shabby camel's hair coat.

The man with the knife surged forward, a smile of welcome on his face. Smiling made the scar on his upper lip sting.

"Here you are at last!" he cried. "I'd given up, my friend! Where is your berth? Allow me to help you. I *insist*."

He seized the bewildered traveler's bag. The man led him, protesting but polite, to his cabin. It was easy to thrust open the door, drop the bag inside, and shut the chaos behind them.

"I'm afraid there's been some mistake," his mark said, but he wasn't listening. He clapped his hand on the man's shoulder and muttered a few banal words. He had only seconds before the last shore whistle blew.

When the blast came, he slid his knife quickly between the fellow's ribs. A gasp of disbelief, a hand clutching at his sleeve— the eyes rolled backward. The face blanched. There was very little blood; he knew how to stop a heart.

Later, when it was dark, he would slip the body over the side. But first he needed the man's papers.

He pulled his knife from the body and wiped it clean. Then he turned back the lapels of the worn suit jacket, and slipped his hand into the breast pocket. The American passport was there, along with a wallet. He leafed through its contents. He had dollars and pounds. His name was now Charles Atwater. He was thirty-four years old and had a surprisingly pretty wife. His cabin was Tourist Class. Number D-15, next to . . . Darlene, wasn't it? With the sweetest little bunk imaginable?

He repeated the phrase; he liked to work on his English.

He felt a sharp need to touch the dead man's skin—to feel the muscle and bone beneath the starched white shirt. His fingers were trembling with sudden, overwhelming desire, and despite the sound of voices in the passage beyond the closed cabin door, despite the steward's knock and the shouted warning of *All ashore that's going ashore*, he slit the fabric roughly with the tip of his knife.

A pale white pectoral gleamed in the cabin light. With five deft strokes, he cut a crouching spider into the skin.

There were those in New York some days later who would insist that the mark was a swastika.

THE WHISTLE BLAST TORE like a shock wave through Jack's thin body as he leaned on the Promenade Deck's rail. The unwanted visitors were flying across the gangways, and the ship would soon be his own for six days. The unknown French woman—the unknown French woman had nothing to do with New York; she would certainly stay on board, and be traveling First Class.

He lifted his head into the rain as the tugs did their duty. The piers began to slide away. The grime of New York slipped to the stern. He breathed in the dusk's wetness.

Forget Death and Boredom and Frances Ann Cannon.

He was alone on the Atlantic. He was sailing to Europe with a beautiful girl. He had a president's secrets to keep.

He tossed his fedora over the rail and watched it vanish in the waves.

SEVEN. FELLOW TRAVELERS

IT WAS A STEWARD NAMED Robbie who told Jack the woman was anything but French, as he unpacked his luggage that evening.

The two of them became acquainted over a battered trunk and a five-dollar bill. Robbie had met J. P. Kennedy two weeks before on the same ship, and for the ambassador's son he ran through the passenger list as he moved about the cabin.

"Lord and Lady Kemsley—he's our British press baron, owns everything what old Beaverbrook didn't snap up first. Then there's Mrs. Sloan Colt and her daughter, Catherine—a very *nice* young lady, no more than eighteen, and quite under her mother's thumb."

Jack had met Cathy Colt at a deb ball or two—old New York railroad money. She was a shy girl with ballerina arms, prone to blushing; not his type.

"You might want to steer clear of Mrs. George Minart," Robbie persisted. "*And* her daughter. They've been hunting you the better part of a week, Mr. Jack—calling the Cunard offices to be sure you were on the passenger list, offering *insulting* sums to every steward in First Class so's to get a deck chair either side of you. Fortune hunting, the old bitch is."

"June Minart," Jack mused. She was in her last term at Radcliffe. "Who's The Looker, Robbie? Tall, black-haired, drop-dead gorgeous. Sable coat and a Robin Hood hat. Don't tell me she slipped off the boat before we put to sea."

Robbie closed his eyes, a priest in pain. "You *would*, Mr. Jack. You *would*."

Jack grinned. "Is she that bad? What's her name?"

"Diana Playfair. A mannequin, as I heard, or maybe an actress. *Or* something worse," the steward added darkly. "Not quite respectable, if you take my meaning, until the Honorable Denys Playfair went and married her."

"Ah. Didn't see the husband."

Robbie shook his head. "The Honorable Denys isn't aboard. Some say they're *estranged*."

"You lift my heart, Robbie, you really do." Jack held out a twenty-dollar bill. "Get me a deck chair near her. Please."

Robbie palmed the money with a dubious air. "Awfully cold in the North Atlantic, in Febr'y. Can't tell as there might not be *ice*. Captain says as how it's goin' ter be a filthy run. Storms, he says, off the coast of Greenland."

Jack offered him another twenty. "I've got to work on my tan, Robbie."

The steward sighed. "I'll do my best, sir. She's a looker, all right, our Diana. Though there's some," he added as an afterthought, "as don't hold with her politics."

"Why?"

"She's one of them *Fascists*," the steward said.

DIANA PLAYFAIR WAS NOT to be found among the paneled columns and deep armchairs of the First Class lounge, and she scorned the Captain's table that evening, where her seat was reserved among the select. This was a measure of her importance to the Cunard Line—Jack, as the British ambassador's son, had a place at the table along with Lord and Lady Kemsley. Mrs. Sloan Colt and her blushing daughter were there, too—Catherine seated conveniently next to Jack—but June Minart and her mother remained in exile. Presumably Mrs. Minart had failed to bribe the *Queen Mary's* captain.

Jack tried to talk to Cathy Colt while keeping one eye on the empty chair reserved for Diana Playfair. Maybe she was just chronically late. Dramatic entrances would suit her.

"I hear you're going to Sarah Lawrence in the fall," he said to the ballerina arms.

"Yes. I am."

"That should be swell. A girl I know had a great time at Sarah Lawrence. Frances Ann Cannon. You know Frances Ann?"

"No. I don't."

"My sister Kathleen is thinking about Sarah Lawrence. Ever met Kick? That's what we call my sister—Kick."

"No. I haven't."

Jack got the distinct impression that Catherine Colt found him as repulsive as a slug. She'd edged her chair away, and kept her eyes firmly on her plate. In different circumstances the girl's undisguised dislike might have piqued his interest—but not tonight. He had other game to hunt. He was hoping for what Robbie called Something Worse. He craned his head around the vast dining room, but Something Worse was not to be found.

When Catherine scurried off before dessert, pleading a headache, the man to her left—a German in his thirties—caught Jack's eye.

"You won't see the Fair Diana tonight," he said. "Seasickness. She's a martyr to it. Probably lying in her cabin with a compress on her head and her maid at her feet."

The Fair Diana. It was a deliberate play on her last name, one the German probably hadn't invented; but his English was good enough to halt Jack's darting mind.

"You know the lady," he said.

"Very well indeed."

There's some as don't hold with her politics. She's one of them Fascists.

"I don't believe we've met." Jack held out his hand.

"Willi Dobler." The German was dark and anything but Teutonic; a poor representative of the Aryan ideal. His clothes, however, had obviously been tailored in London; and he held his cigarette like a work of art. "You're the second son. *Jack* Kennedy."

"Guilty as charged."

Again, the faint smile that failed to reach Dobler's eyes. "We met at an embassy party last summer, but you wouldn't remember. I am with the German delegation in London, and your father . . . is so good as to meet with us, from time to time. I am also a little acquainted with your brother Joe."

Of course, Joe. He was done with Harvard, footloose and fancy-free, and he'd been working as Father's secretary in London for the past few months.

"He is . . . an uncomplicated young man, yes?"

Jack glanced at Dobler. "I'm not sure what you mean."

The diplomat shrugged. "The quintessential American. That is to say . . . not very complex in his observations or ideas. A black-and-white thinker, in fact."

"Joe would think *quintessential American* is a compliment." A waiter set a cup of coffee before him; Jack reached for a spoon. "But that's not how you intended it, is it?"

The hand holding the cigarette waved dismissively; a faint trail of smoke arabesqued in the candlelight. "You must forgive my appalling habit of summing up every dazzling star I meet. It's a habit acquired on the job."

"Which is?"

"Third political secretary."

Jack took a sip of coffee, bitter and dark. He unwrapped a cube of sugar and watched it float for an instant on the surface before sinking endwise, like the *Titanic*. Dobler was a diplomat; he'd just been to the United States. What if he'd carried a trunk-ful of deutschmarks with him?—And distributed them quietly in exchange for the right votes?

"I suppose you're a member of the Nazi Party," he said.

Dobler inclined his head. "It would be difficult—or should I say impossible?—to be anything else at the moment."

"If you want to work for the government. There must be other things you could do."

"But I quite like government work!" Dobler protested. "I was bred to it; my father was a diplomat before me. I joined the Party, yes. That doesn't mean I agree with everything they say."

"No," Jack mused. "You just have to push the Aryan Ideal. Look earnest and apologetic when somebody mentions the nasty Jew-bashing that's going on back home. And say 'Hiya Hitler' whenever you walk through your boss's door. That seems a fair trade for a few years in London."

"Have you been to Germany?" Dobler inhaled deeply, and allowed a thin trail of smoke to drift from his nostrils.

"Yes," Jack said drily. "Two summers ago. Before you gentle-men wandered into other people's backyards and claimed them for the Fatherland. I'll admit that your economy's thriving—jackboot production is way up—but I found the average Fritz less than welcoming. Apparently you regard the Irish as a mongrel race. I took it a little personally."

Dobler's lips compressed. "You have no idea how I regard much of anything, Herr Kennedy," he said. "I haven't told you."

There was a brief silence; Jack's eyes dropped to his cup. "Fair enough."

"It's not easy being German right now." Dobler stubbed out his Dunhill with precise and elegant fingers. "One is forced to choose one's battles. To live in the gray area of life. Unlike, for example, your brother."

"Joe again." Jack eased back in his chair. "My brother certainly seems to have seized your fancy."

He was deliberately insulting, as though to suggest that Dobler would like to bugger a big, healthy American boy now and then. He waited for the German to react.

The long fingers ground the cigarette to dust. "Your brother is universally admired in London—he treats the exclusive clubs as his playground, and the daughters of the best families as his private stable—but so far as quality of *mind* is concerned . . . I understand that you, Jack, are a very different sort of person from Joe."

This snare was allowed to drop neatly on the table between them.

Dobler dusted tobacco from his fingertips.

Jack turned the saucer of his coffee cup. It bought an instant of time.

He could stand up now, throw down his napkin, and avoid the German for the rest of the crossing. He could hotly declare that he was Joe Jr.'s twin, thank you very much, and thought and acted as he did in everything. Christ knew he'd spent enough time pretending as much.

But he could not expose his brother, or the multitude of things that divided them—had always divided them. He could not talk about the punches he'd taken in the gut, the blame he'd shouldered, the scalding misery of being judged less admirable, less successful, less *valuable* than Joe.

Or his brother's corrosive envy: That it was always Jack other people loved.

So instead he said softly, "Now who in the world would sell you a line of crap like that?"

"Our mutual friend." Dobler gave his stillborn smile and rose from the table. "Franklin Roosevelt."

EIGHT. TRAVELING TOURIST

THE CROSSING, as Robbie predicted, was filthy.

That first night out of New York the wind began to rise, and Jack, who'd had too much coffee and cigarette smoke and dark, wine-scented medallions of veal for his body to handle, curled in agony in his stateroom as the great ship heaved upward, a Coney Island ascent, then plunged ecstatically into the screaming trough of the next wave. He was a blue-water sailor by training and passion, but the *Queen Mary* was no trim little Wianno bucking whitecaps off the Cape; she was eighty thousand tons of heaving torture. Jack heaved with her. The groans of the riveted hull and the scream of the gale enfolded him in an iron fist. He tried once to stand, and cartwheeled in vertigo. At intervals, the steward Robbie's face loomed over his, a spoon of hot bouillon in a wavering hand.

Jack had never crossed the Atlantic in winter before.

Seventy-five hours after he left New York, he opened his eyes, saw that his cabin had stopped reeling, and said, *"Fuck."*

"Yes, Mr. Jack," Robbie replied from the service doorway, "it's no wonder the Good Lord preferred to *walk* on water. Would you be wanting that deck chair, and a cup of tea?"

———

HE LAY UNDER HEAVY BLANKETS, feet propped on cushions, while the tea cooled beside him. The neighboring chair cooled, too, without the benefit of Diana Playfair.

It was early morning, twenty-eight degrees Fahrenheit, with a weak ball of sun still low on the horizon. Jack's breath blew in a crystalline cloud; he kept his arms under cover and stared at the sea. Presently he would drink the tea and ask for some toast with it, which might give him energy enough to work his pocket knife into the flesh of his leg; he hadn't had a dose of DOCA in three days, and that was too long. But for now, the smell of salt and ice on the clean air was enough. Periodically a man or a woman he did not know would stroll past him on the First Class Promenade Deck, walking a terrier or pushing a child on a trike. They all looked cheerful and well-fed, as though the three-day gale had focused its rage on Jack's cabin and skipped the rest of the ship.

"Hey, sailor," said a languid voice off his starboard side. "Care to give a girl a light?"

He turned his head and met the green glare of June Minart's eyes. She was tricked out, head to toe, in fox furs and suede boots; a Cossack hat with a tassel perched rakishly over one eye.

"Miss Minart," he said. "Are you a sight for sore eyes! I heard a rumor you were on this tub."

"You've been hiding in that nasty old stateroom." She pretended to pout, and glided genteelly toward him. He saw, then, that part of her fur sleeve was in fact a tiny dog huddled close to her breast, ratlike and shivering. A pink bow was tied to its head. Jack was allergic to dogs.

June sank down on the deck chair beside him, a cigarette

poised in her gloved hand. He fumbled beneath the blankets and managed to locate his lighter. Another time, he'd have loomed over June, captivated her with a wisecrack and his famous smile, left her with quivering knees and a desperation to see him again— but today he felt too weak to bother. She was good at flirting— she was an artiste of the calculated come-on; and she thrust her round, ripe mouth right into Jack's face. She clearly expected a kiss.

He lit her cigarette.

"Why'd you leave Radcliffe in the middle of term?" he asked.

"Mother thought I needed to get away. Before the Germans make it impossible to meet *anybody* in England anymore. She's hoping your parents will introduce us to the right people in London. That's why she's been chasing you so hard."

"Ah." Jack was amused by June's frankness; he'd come to expect social climbing from the women he met. "I'll make sure Dad invites you to some parties."

"There's one tonight," June said brightly as she exhaled, "in the Tourist lounge. A girl I know's traveling cheap down there. You can pay a steward to let us through."

The Minarts specialized in paying stewards. Jack resigned himself to escorting June; if he refused, her mother would go back to New York and tear the Kennedys to shreds. It was a hobby in certain circles, only surpassed by trashing Roosevelt.

"Cocktails, or later?"

"Oh, they drink most of the day—but Mother's all over me like a wet slip until dinner."

A wet slip. *Really.* "Shall we say nine, then?"

"That'd be swell, Jack." She ground the cigarette under her heel. "Only don't call for me at my cabin—or Mother will never let us go. She'll do something silly, like offer you sherry. Mother's always silly where men are concerned."

"Let's meet at the head of the Tourist gangway at nine, Miss Minart."

"Oh, call me June, won't you? It's so much *friendlier*." She leaned toward him, her rat of a dog spilling onto the blankets. Jack sneezed.

TOURIST WAS A NICER NAME for what used to be called Third Class. Third Class, on the other hand, was what used to be called Steerage—a word so bitterly associated with impoverished immigration that no shipping line used it anymore.

The Tourist lounge was dense with smoke. Faces loomed through it like ghastly clowns in a funhouse. Jack was leading June through the murk. She teetered on high heels and he dodged a few bodies as they swayed to a Tommy Dorsey tune. He could feel sweat start up under his dinner jacket, and queasiness from the motion of the ship, more noticeable below the waterline. What had he eaten today? Jack tried not to think of it—or of the swaying bodies and the smell of June's perfume, which was heavy with jasmine. He hated jasmine. It smelled like death. One of the poker players at the end of the lounge had a cigar. The fumes of tobacco and cheap whiskey mingled with the smell of death. His stomach turned over.

"Hey, kid," he muttered, coming to a halt in the middle of the lounge. "D'ya see your friend? 'Cause if not, I'd like to get some air."

"Lorna! Lorna *Doone*!" June squealed, and dropped his hand.

She rushed in her full flounced skirt toward a girl Jack could barely make out, and there was a lot of hugging and more squealing. The ship rolled and he was thrust suddenly against a stranger—a guy slightly shorter than himself, but ten times more solid, with a chest like a brick wall. He met the man's cold blue eyes, registered blond hair, a scar bisecting the upper lip—and felt a hand close like a vise on his right arm. And then suddenly he was slugged, an iron hammer in the gut.

He doubled over, arms clutching his stomach. The vise loosened and he fell to his knees.

"Jack."

He could not stand up. The ship rolled and heaved. He was going to vomit. Right there in the middle of Tourist Class.

"Jack."

He opened his eyes. He was staring at a pair of knife-edged trousers. And he knew that voice.

"Dobler," he croaked. "How's tricks?"

The diplomat was lifting Jack now and urging him to move. *"Please.* Call me Willi. You are unwell?"

"I could use some air."

A dense crowd of churning bodies, the heat, the promiscuous smells. He managed to let go of his gut, shuffling in a half crouch toward the cooler air of the passage, breathing heavily. Pain shafted through his abdomen to his lungs. He was propelled up the gangway to the Second Class Promenade Deck and hung on the rail. He hated his bitch of a body.

He was desperately and wrenchingly sick over the side of the ship.

Bitter cold, sharp as glass. The brine wash of the salt sea, far below the canyon wall of the *Queen Mary*. His entire digestive tract felt like it was being tossed over the side and he was probably puking blood. He should have gotten the DOCA into his leg sooner. Damn the Atlantic in February—

"How old are you, then?" she asked. "Seventeen? Eighteen?"

He pulled his head up from the rail.

Not Dobler, but Diana Playfair, standing tall as a French tulip in a sheer silk gown the color and texture of champagne. There were black velvet bows looped in the champagne and the black jet of her hair fell like a curtain on her porcelain brow. Her arms were bare and the skin was shuddering with cold. He ought to do something about that. It wasn't right that she was freezing because somebody'd slugged him in the gut.

He fished a handkerchief from his pocket and wiped his mouth.

"Willi's gone for a glass of water. I said I'd stay."

"Willi got the better of that deal."

"He usually does." She was hugging herself now, her beautiful shoulders hunched in the frigid air. "He said you're one of Ambassador Kennedy's boys. What do they call you?"

"Jack."

"I'm Diana Playfair."

"I know." He shrugged out of his dinner jacket and draped it carefully over her shoulders. "I made a point of learning your name after I lit your cigarette."

"What cigarette?" Her fingers lifted his lapel, her shoulders relaxing a trifle in the jacket's warmth.

"The one you smoked as we pulled out of New York. In a pencil skirt and a swan of a hat."

"Ah. The Promenade Deck." The memory pleased her. Probably because she'd walked away from him so coolly.

"I had to know the name of something that beautiful. Before it vanished forever."

Arrested, she ran her eyes over his thin frame, the stark white of his dress shirt against the blackened sea. "Exactly how old are you, Jack Kennedy?"

He smiled crookedly. "Older than I look."

NINE. THE WARNING

THEY CARRIED HIM OFF to Diana's stateroom and watched while he swallowed a couple of aspirins with a snifter of brandy.

"You were *punched*?" Diana repeated. "By a complete stranger? The man must have been drunk."

She sank into a chair and crossed her legs. The champagne gown was slit to the thigh. Her pumps were black velvet. In between was a sleek expanse of skin.

"Don't ask." He dragged his eyes from Diana and set his brandy glass carefully on a table. The stateroom was far more feminine than his—a dressing gown was spread across the turned-down berth, a pair of gilt slippers perched beneath it. An elusive scent teased the air; the scent of Diana's skin, as he remembered her standing in darkness.

"What were you two doing down in Tourist anyway?"

She shrugged. "Looking for a bit of fun."

"And found me." His mouth twisted. "I'm grateful to you both. You turned up right before that joker decided to finish the job. I don't suppose you got a look at his face?"

Diana's gaze drifted from Jack to Dobler, who was leaning against the cabin door smoking pensively. The German sighed and slid into the remaining armchair. Jack waited while he arranged himself, his cigarette, the crease in his trousers. Then Dobler said, "I may have. Describe him, if you please."

Jack closed his eyes. The brandy was settling badly in his stomach. "He was shorter than I am, but about twice my weight. Not," he admitted, "that that's difficult. Chest like steel, a fist like a pile driver."

"Coloring? Features? . . . Nationality?"

Jack's eyes flickered open. Dobler's arm was bent upward at the elbow, the smoke from his Dunhill masking his face.

"You sound like a cop, Willi. Next you'll be asking for my driver's license."

"Was he blond? Brown-eyed? An Italian tough?"

"—Blue," Jack said sharply. "His eyes were blue and cold as ice. And yes, he was blond. Very . . . *Aryan*."

"Aryan," Dobler repeated evenly.

"You know the type."

"I do," the German agreed. "But are you suggesting he was German?"

"No idea. He didn't speak."

"Old? Young?"

"Late twenties, early thirties, I'd say. And he had an inch-long scar through his upper lip, like he'd been in a nasty knife fight once."

Dobler went very still, his eyes fixed on Jack as he exhaled a thin stream of smoke. Then he leaned forward and discarded his ash. There was a silence that was not entirely comfortable.

"Look—he probably *was* drunk," Jack said harshly. "Or he's just a thug who gets his kicks beating up complete strangers. It's not that uncommon. In Tourist Class."

Dobler glanced at Diana. "Have *you* run into his kind before, my dear?—In Tourist Class?"

She gazed at him blandly. "Give me a cigarette, Willi."

He tossed her a gold case and looked back at Jack. "You should be in bed. I'll walk with you."

"I can manage, thanks." Jack forced himself to his feet, pain creasing his abdomen.

"Still—I'll walk with you." Dobler bowed to Diana and kissed her hand. "Good night, *charmante*."

Jack simply stood, aware of a slight, singing tension in the air because she breathed it. She returned his dinner jacket, neatly folded. Her dark eyes met his, and a line of fire moved from his gut to his throat. It was impossible to speak; and he was never at a loss for words.

Dobler smiled faintly and steered him like a fractious child through the stateroom door.

"HOW DO YOU KNOW the Old Man?" Jack demanded abruptly as they made their way around the First Class deck toward his cabin. His was on the port side, Diana's was starboard. He'd made a point of memorizing her cabin number.

"Your father? I told you. I'm at the embassy."

"Not Dad. FDR."

There was a pause. "I do not think we should discuss such things out here in the open."

Jack laughed, then winced with pain. "It's the middle of the goddamn night, Willi. You think anybody's listening? Your Aryan friend with the ugly scar?"

Dobler's grip on his arm tightened. "If you hope to serve your president, Jack, learn when to shut your mouth."

"What do you know about my president?"

The German halted in front of Jack's cabin and waited while he searched for his key. When he'd found it, Dobler's hand grasped the knob. "Allow me."

The German's other hand was in his pocket, and with a sudden sense of unreality Jack knew he held a pistol. In sheer disbelief he stepped back as Dobler eased through the door.

"Christ," Jack muttered. "Who the hell *do* you work for?"

"It's all right," Dobler said. "There's no one here."

"I asked you a question."

The German smiled his thin smile. "I've already answered it. *I'm with the German embassy.* Come inside, Jack."

He obeyed. Dobler shut the stateroom door behind him.

"Today is the first of March," he said. "You know that we're scheduled to make Cherbourg and Southampton tomorrow?"

"Sure."

"I strongly suggest that you remain in your cabin until we do. Is someone meeting you at the dock?"

Jack shrugged. "Maybe Dad'll send a car. If not, I'll catch the London train. I'm a big boy, Willi."

"The White Spider is bigger."

"The *what*?"

"The man who punched you tonight. From your description, I think that's who it is. Although there's no one by his true name on the passenger list. I made sure of that before we sailed. Which means he's traveling on a false passport."

"He's a crook?"

"No, no. He's a killer." Dobler's gaze skimmed Jack's face, and then he chose his words carefully. "You are fortunate it was a fist he jammed into your stomach this evening. Usually it's a knife. I have seen a few of the bodies. He likes to cut his mark into his victim's chest—a crouching spider."

Jack said nothing for an instant, taking it in. "Are you trying to scare me?"

"Absolutely. *Yes.* You should be afraid of no one so much as this man."

"Then lock him up," Jack said brusquely.

"The White Spider has extremely influential friends. I could not touch him. I would die an unpleasant death if I tried."

Jack stared at Dobler, convinced he had stumbled into a movie. Something with Peter Lorre.

"I'm not lying to you," Dobler said gently.

"Why's he called the White Spider?"

Dobler was examining the stateroom's portholes, testing their bolts. He moved on to the door. "Because he survived it. It's an ice field high on the North Face of the Eiger. Hitler is determined that an Aryan youth must be the first to conquer the Eiger's North Face. It has never been done. He's thrown any number of boys to their deaths because of it."

"I remember now," Jack said. He slumped onto the end of his bed and unknotted his tie. "A whole bunch of Germans died on that mountain a few years back—in '36, wasn't it?"

"Yes. This man claims to have been with them, and to have reached the top. But as no one else lived to authenticate the climb. . . . Good night, Jack. Lock your door behind me. And do not open it until your steward comes in the morning."

"Where are you going?"

He sounded young and belligerent, even in his own ears.

"To find out why the Spider is on this ship. I thought he was in Poland."

IF YOU HOPE TO SERVE your president, Jack, learn when to shut your mouth.

So Willi knew Roosevelt had recruited him to spy. And when Jack pressed him about *how* he knew, he'd successfully changed the subject: telling bedtime stories about bogeymen in the mountains, who hid long knives up their sleeves.

He was very good, Willi; he'd obviously been at this game a long time.

Jack gave him ten minutes. Then he slipped through his cabin's service door and moved noiselessly down the passage.

TEN. ROPE

THE SERVICE PASSAGES that Robbie and the other stewards used to move invisibly about the *Queen Mary* were well lit, and at this hour of the night, completely empty. Passengers never entered them, if they even knew they existed; but Jack and his brother were old hands at navigating the interior of transatlantic liners. Service passages were escape routes, from the stuffiness of First Class to great parties belowdecks. During a previous crossing on the *Normandie*, Joe Kennedy had taken to locking the boys into their stateroom at bedtime. He had no idea they simply exited by the service door as soon as he turned the key.

Jack's instincts told him to strike upward tonight through the interior of the ship, not down into its bowels, where the kitchens and laundries and storerooms were housed. His target was the captain's bridge.

He passed through a bulkhead marked *Exit* and emerged cautiously onto the Promenade Deck. He glanced left and right, half expecting a man with a knife to be waiting in the shadows; and then shrugged off Willi Dobler's warning. He'd meant to scare Jack silly; he wanted him cowering in his stateroom. Which was reason enough to leave.

Jack vaulted over the chain that barred his access to the quarterdeck and bridge, and mounted the stairs two at a time.

"Oy, mate," said a caustic British voice as he attempted to slide through the bridge entrance, "Passengers *not* allowed."

"Evening. I'm Jack Kennedy." He held out his hand.

The sailor ignored it.

"I need to send a Morse signal. It's something of an emergency," he persisted. "Could you help me out?"

"A Morse signal," the sailor repeated in tones of disbelief. "You think the *Mary*'s bridge is a telegraph office?"

"I said it was an emergency."

"And I said yer a passenger," the sailor retorted.

"Captain Storrer," Jack called out. "Good evening, sir!"

The white-haired man standing at the helm turned his head to gaze at Jack. The last time they'd met he'd presided over a dinner table. There was an instant of silence. "Mr. Kennedy," he said. "Would you like to take the con?"

JUST SHY OF THREE O'CLOCK in the morning he descended the quarterdeck stairs. By seven, Storrer said, they would make Cherbourg. He'd allowed Jack thirty astounding seconds of guiding the *Queen*, all eighty thousand tons of her, through the North Atlantic winter—and then waved him off his bridge.

Jack's telegram was winging its way to Cunard's London shipping office, and from there by transatlantic cable to Sam Schwartz, Roosevelt's bodyguard. It was probable Schwartz would read the telegram in a few hours.

Confidential to the President: Please advise background one Wilhelm Dobler, Third Political Secretary German embassy London. Also one alias White Spider, believed Nazi agent. Both men traveling Queen Mary *and have made contact.*

It was easy to feel silly now that he'd sent the message, to imagine Willi Dobler laughing up his beautifully tailored sleeve. The whole White Spider tale could be just so much bullshit. Jack slouched toward his cabin without bothering with the service passages, suddenly exhausted to the bone. He was completely alone on the First Class deck, a vault of frigid stars overhead, a bitter wind keening from the bow. The DOCA he'd cut into his thigh before dinner was taking its own sweet time; he was cotton-mouthed, wavering, clammy with sweat.

And then, as he neared his berth, he glimpsed the bent figure—a darker bulk in the night's darkness. The gloved fingers were at the handle of the stateroom door, probing delicately at the lock. The man was so absorbed in his task that he did not catch Jack's faint footfalls above the wind.

The White Spider was breaking into his cabin.

He'd looked into the man's face only once, before the iron fist plunged into his gut; but he remembered the barrel chest, the broad shoulders. The thug's silhouette.

What the hell? Why is he after me?

Jack began to retreat, one silent foot behind the other. The whole night seemed suddenly unreal—the frigid vault of stars, the loneliness of the deck, Willi Dobler and the gun he'd carried in his perfect English suiting. This man who liked knives, kneeling at Jack's door.

The President wasn't kidding when he said Hitler wanted him out of power. That cultured, whipsaw voice on the telephone: *We think the level of foreign interest in your work has shot up.* Roosevelt had sent Jack off with a dangerous secret, German bribes for American votes. A secret somebody would kill to keep.

He made it to the far side of the deck and felt his way by instinct to a door he'd only seen once. *Her door.* He had a fleeting thought that he might find Dobler there and embarrass all three of them, but he was past caring. There was safety in numbers and he had nowhere else to go.

"Let me in," he whispered when Diana Playfair answered his knock. "For the love of Christ, let me in."

SHE WAS ALONE.

She put him in a chair and poured him a glass of whiskey.

"Scotch?" he asked as he took it.

"Irish," she said. "Suits you better."

The corner of his mouth crooked as he sipped; he liked a girl with a sense of humor. He liked everything about Diana, as a matter of fact: her silk charmeuse pajamas, and the way they clung to her body; her English accent, which fell somewhere between Robbie's and the Queen's; her black hair as shining and neat as though he hadn't just dragged her out of bed; the startling youth of her face stripped of its makeup. She looked canny and cool, as though she'd apprenticed as a gangster's moll and was accustomed to hysterics in the night.

She slung a leg over the armchair next to Jack's and clinked her glass against his. "Cheers."

And that quickly, the singing tension was back, the awareness of her throbbing in his veins. He fought the impulse to set down his drink and reach for her—slide the silk off her shoulders and his mouth along her collarbone—and remembered instead why he was there.

"The guy showed up," he said. "At my stateroom door."

"The chap who slugged you?"

"He's picking the lock. Probably inside by now."

"Then we must ring somebody." She stood up briskly and went for the steward's bell. "It's a crime, you know, to burgle a fellow passenger. They'll lock him up."

"*Don't.*" He grabbed her wrist.

"Don't what?"

"Call anybody."

"Why ever not?"

He groped for an answer. "Because I'm giving this guy rope. Playing it out. Seeing where it leads."

"—Until there's so much he hangs himself?"

"Something like that. If he's caught now, I may never know . . . what he was looking for."

She stared pointedly at the wrist he was still clutching. Her pulse was like a bird's wing, fluttering beneath his fingers. He grazed his thumb lightly over the vein, blue beneath her translucent skin, and she drew a sudden breath. Snatched her hand away. "You *are* a dark horse, aren't you?"

"I'm scared witless, to tell you the truth."

She sank down into her chair again, and reached for her drink. "Does Willi know? About the man?"

He hesitated. "I haven't told him. I don't know where Dobler . . . sleeps."

Her eyes narrowed. "As opposed to where his *stateroom* is, do you mean? Is that why you came here—because you expected to find Willi?"

"I came here because I hoped you would open your door."

"Yes. I rather expect you *did*.—Hoped I'd open everything else, too, on the strength of it," she said with acid amusement. "Arms, legs— How old *are* you, Jack?"

He downed his glass of whiskey. "Twenty-two this May."

"*Bully* for you. I'm twenty-nine and I've been married for ten years. I don't give party favors to children. And now, as it's nearly half three in the morning, I'm going to bed. You can doss on the couch if you like—though it's a bit short for your inches."

"Diana—"

She turned and looked at him.

Again, his throat constricted and it was impossible to speak; he swallowed hard, and managed it.

"Do you know you're the most beautiful thing I've ever seen?"

"You suggested as much. But I'm not a *thing*, Jack. Good night."

HE WOKE TO GRAY LIGHT seeping through a porthole, and an empty stillness. Diana and all her belongings were gone.

ELEVEN. INTELLIGENCE

"LORD LOVE YOU, MR. JACK, is this how you make yourself at home?"

Robbie was standing in a chaotic heap of Jack's clothes. Somebody had slashed all the upholstery, and a drift of white goose feathers covered the floor. A pungent odor of spilled aftershave and hair pomade permeated the room. Everything had been shaken, upended, torn to shreds—except the tray of coffee and eggs Robbie had carefully set down on Jack's nightstand.

"Doesn't matter," Jack muttered as he gathered his shirts and ties at random. "Robbie, have you seen Diana Playfair?"

"The Fair Diana got off at Cherbourg at least an hour ago." Willi Dobler was standing in the doorway, with a charcoal wool coat over his arm. His hat was in his hand. A leather case rested at his feet. He looked every inch the diplomat.

"Cherbourg?"

"She was bound for Paris, not London."

She'd never told him. He'd imagined breakfast this morning, the exchange of addresses as they waited for their trunks. The possibility of meeting in London.

But she would not be in London.

He felt a sudden blaze of desolation—utterly unlike the loss of Frances Ann Cannon, by at least an order of magnitude. It made no *sense*. He knew nothing about Diana Playfair. Except the quality of her voice. The darkness of her hair and eyes. That she did not give party favors to children.

"What happened here?" Dobler demanded. "And how, I wonder, did you survive it?"

"Our friend broke in last night." Jack snatched at a pair of pajamas, slit from waist to knee. He began to pile the ruined clothes in the center of the room, saving what he could. *Diana.* Her air of weighing him, and finding him wanting.

Robbie spluttered in outrage. "And you never *rang* for me, Mr. Jack?"

"He had a knife, Robbie. I didn't want to get you killed."

Dobler stepped gingerly through the doorway and glanced around. "You left by the steward's entrance, I suppose, as our man came through this door?"

"Actually, I wasn't here at the time."

"Ah." The German's eyes drifted coolly to Jack's face. "The expression, I believe, is that you *got lucky?*"

He was too clever not to intend the double entendre. Jack might have grinned, and tossed off a ribald comment of his own—but he was feeling empty and orphaned this morning and he was wary of the German's claims on Diana Playfair. It was none of Jack's business, of course. He would never see her again.

"Why Paris?" he demanded.

"Why *not* Paris?" Dobler fished in his pocket. "Captain Storrer asked me to give this to you."

It was a telegram. Jack perched on the back of his ruined sofa to tear open the envelope.

W.D. believed German Intelligence treat with caution STOP No information White Spider STOP Have ordered embassy car to Southampton do not take train STOP Schwartz

"Good news, I hope?"

Jack lifted his eyes to Dobler's face. "Yeah. My father's sent me a ride up to London."

"Wise man. We're coming into Southampton now."

W.D. believed German Intelligence.

Jack's fingers trembled slightly; the smell of coffee and eggs hit his nostrils sickly.

Everything Willi had done made a skewed sort of sense: Easing into Jack's confidence at the Captain's table; flattering him by disparaging his brother Joe; suggesting that he, Dobler, was intimate with Roosevelt; lecturing Jack on the finer points of espionage. *If you hope to serve your president. . . .*

Willi must have known about the midnight meeting on Platform 61. He was a *spy,* for chrissake, with traitors in every corner. What had Roosevelt said? *I can't trust the State department with this. I can't trust anybody right now.*

Jack tucked the telegram into his breast pocket, trying to mask the tremor in his fingers. Only a few people knew he'd met Roosevelt in the Pullman. Was it Casey? Foscarello? Somebody on the President's staff? Maybe Sam Schwartz was in Dobler's pocket—Schwartz was a German name, after all. But FDR had told Jack to work with Schwartz. He'd just sent the telegram he was fingering right now.

Dobler was the one to fear—rescuing Jack in Tourist Class, from a thug who was probably on Dobler's payroll. Walking Jack back to his stateroom, so he could tell the Spider which lock to pick. Snowing Jack with the Eiger story, to scare him silly.

He'd almost asked Willi for help last night. It might have got him killed.

Diana, he thought despairingly. She was a friend of Willi's. And a Fascist. Neither fact was good news.

Dobler settled his hat on his head with precise grace.

"Have you eaten?" he asked. "No? I suggest we carry that tray into the First Class lounge—and let your man here get on with the packing. You're making a bigger mess than the Spider."

He was a charming fellow, Willi, even if his looks would never fit Hitler's Aryan ideal.

Jack felt gauche and stupid. What the hell had FDR been thinking when he'd recruited him?

Your own brand of guts. Your charm and your smile and your trick of making everybody underestimate you. You'll find the network we're looking for, Jack. I know you will.

Roosevelt had guessed he'd be standing eventually in the ruins of some stateroom, wondering how to get out alive. He'd deliberately tossed Jack to the wolves—and would be wildly entertained if he survived.

He reached for his breakfast tray.

"You're a rock, Willi," he said with a smile. "Can I give you a lift to London in my Old Man's car?"

TWELVE. CONTEMPT

"**THE POOR FELLOW WAS PICKED UP** in the Hudson?" Roosevelt asked.

"Bobbing around in the shipping lanes," Hoover replied. "We figure he was dumped off a boat." He handed the President a black-and-white photograph of a white pectoral muscle. "The mark's somewhat faded after several days in the water, but you can make out the swastika if you look hard."

Roosevelt reached for the magnifying lens he kept with his stamp collection and held it to his eye. There it was—Hitler's juggernaut. A cartwheeling Black Widow. "You think there's a link to the hatcheck girl."

Hoover shrugged. "We kept the swastika *out* of the press accounts of Katie O'Donohue's murder. Which means this is not a copycat crime. It's the same killer. Same military thrust to the heart. Question is, who's the victim—and how does he fit into the Nazi cash network?"

"You haven't identified him?"

"No papers. Clean as a whistle. Even his tailor's marks were cut out of his clothes."

"And the quality of those clothes?" Roosevelt asked.

"Good. Wool suit, long-staple cotton shirt. Handmade leather shoes."

Roosevelt lowered his magnifying lens and studied the middle distance. "He'd been in the water several days."

"That's right."

"Transatlantic liners sail on Fridays and Saturdays."

"And the New York Harbor police found the corpse Monday. It was Wednesday before the coroner saw the swastika on the chest and figured something funny was going on. He called us. That's why I'm just talking to you now, on Thursday."

Jack's boat would have docked in Southampton today, Roosevelt thought. What had he cabled Schwartz? *Please advise background . . . one alias White Spider, believed Nazi agent.* White Spider. What if the cartwheeling mark Hoover called a swastika was in fact a *spider*? Not just a mark of German loyalty—but one particular killer's calling card?

The President steepled his fingers and tapped them lightly beneath his nose. Hoover was talking rapidly about something but he wasn't listening anymore, he was following a thread in his mind. A body with a possible spider cut into its flesh had been found in the shipping lanes. And Jack had said the White Spider made contact on the *Queen Mary*. Hoover's Nazi killer had almost certainly crossed the Atlantic on Jack's ship. They had missed the point of the swastika mark—but the boy knew better. The boy worked fast.

Roosevelt was disinclined to tell Hoover anything about Jack.

"Embarkation lists," he suggested vaguely. "Cross-checked against disembarkation lists, at the French and English ports."

"Beg pardon, Mr. President?"

Roosevelt sighed. "There are two possibilities, Ed. Either this corpse floating in the Hudson is one of the Nazis' bagmen, or he was an innocent who got in the way. If the latter, it's possible someone was meeting him in London. A business associate. A lover. But he hasn't arrived. Check the Missing Persons reports. Your corpse may be among them."

"I'll get on the horn to Southampton and Cherbourg."

Roosevelt turned his wheelchair, an implicit dismissal. Sam Schwartz had slipped noiselessly into the room. He was staring at Hoover with open contempt.

"Oh, and Ed," Roosevelt tossed over his shoulder, "Sam here has learned that there's a Nazi agent whose nom de guerre is the White Spider. It's possible that mark cut into the bodies isn't a swastika at all, but something more personal. One that could identify the killer.

Comprehension filled Hoover's face. "A spider."

"You might run the idea by Scotland Yard." Roosevelt paused for satiric effect. "If you can spare a minute from spying on my friends."

THIRTEEN. KICK

THE GIRL AT THE HEAD OF THE STAIRS was trying on a picture hat that tied under her ear with an enormous bow. She was frowning in the pier glass that hung between two marble pillars, obviously unhappy with what she saw—and Jack's greeting died on his lips. Even at nineteen, Kick would never be a beauty; she was too Kennedy for that, with a freckled face, a snub nose, and a square jaw. But she was shrewd and funny and her smile lit up a room; half of London was in love with her.

So why this desolate look?

She must have felt him watching, because she turned and caught him, awkward and alone, in the middle of the sweeping staircase. She shrieked and held out her hands.

"Hey, kid," she crowed. "What's the *sto-ory?*"

It was what she always said when he showed up out of the blue. Jack lifted her off her feet and swung her around. He could feel her thin frame through the silk of her dress. The London season had honed her curves. *Sharpened* her. He hadn't seen Kick since last September and it was this tightening of her bones that reminded him of how much time had passed. There was something painful about it. A childhood they'd lost.

"Gosh, you're a sight for sore eyes," she murmured. "I've *missed* you, Jack."

"You're looking snazzy, Kick. Where're you going?"

"Billy's taking me to a dress party." She glanced down the stairs, despair flooding her face again. "He'll be here soon."

He lifted her chin, stared into her eyes. "What's the *sto-ory*, kid?"

"It's just—*Billy*."

"Hartington?" He didn't really need to ask; there was only one Billy worth mentioning, in London.

"Marquis of," Kick added gloomily. She pulled off her hat and tossed it on the bench beneath the mirror, then sank down beside it. "Mother *hates* him, Jack. She's perfectly *polite*, but—"

Rose Kennedy's politeness was frigid enough to freeze the balls off a greater man than Billy, Marquis of Hartington. Who was heir to the Duke of Devonshire and his vast fortune, one of the most powerful men in England. Billy was the catch of the season, the Protestant Prince every British mother wanted. And Rose treated him like a chimney sweep. If she could have barred the ambassador's residence to Billy Hartington, that aristocratic despoiler of innocent Catholic girls, she'd have done it in a heartbeat. But Billy's family was too politically important to snub. So Rose settled for freezing off the poor guy's balls.

For the past year, the London papers had been full of Billy and Kick. They were caught in the glare of flashbulbs at race meetings and cricket matches and debutante balls and the wicked 400 Club, where Kick was forbidden to go.

"Mother's in Egypt," Jack said bracingly. "Who gives a damn what she thinks?"

"God, apparently. She's got a direct line to the Almighty, and He says I'm in mortal sin if I so much as *kiss* Billy."

"You already have."

Kick's dimples flashed. "How was Mayo?"

"Swell. Turned me inside out and found nothing."

"You look good. *Thin*—but . . . you're always thin."

"I like your hat." He tried it on. "Frames the face."

"You think so?" she asked anxiously. "You think Billy will like it? I never wore half so many hats in the States. I'm not used to it. I'm not very *good* at it, Jack. There's so much to learn, here. About dress—and . . . *parties*, and . . . the right way to act at weekends in the country. Sticking your shoes outside your bedroom door to be polished, like in a hotel. Tipping the servants. I'm always doing or saying the wrong thing."

"Which is why they love you, Kick. You're *real.*"

"I'd better get going." She grabbed her hat off his head and took one last look in the mirror.

"Is Dad here?" Jack asked quickly.

"Still at the embassy. Never home, really—always off holding Chamberlain's hand. Or some showgirl's tush."

There were no flies on Kick, Jack thought. She'd always known what their father was.

"You don't like Chamberlain?" he asked.

"Billy hates him," she said simply. "Thinks he's a coward. Flying off to see Hitler, with an umbrella in his hand and a bowler on his head, like something out of *Mary Poppins*. Billy says the Germans will never be satisfied with just the Sudetenland and it's only a matter of time before they roll into Prague and seize all of Czechoslovakia. And it'll be Chamberlain who gave them *permission*. As if they needed it. Billy says there's going to be war—"

Billy says. If Kick quoted Hartington every third sentence, no wonder Rose was worried.

"And Joe?" he asked.

"He's in Spain." She rolled her eyes in profound boredom. "He got all lofty and superior and called it a *Fact-Finding Mission*, but I think he's just sightseeing. Daddy was *furious* when he got off the boat and found out Joe had beat it for Madrid. He thinks he'll get shot or something. But I guess Joe was just fed up. Hanging around the 400 Club, getting tight, isn't terribly interesting when there's a fight going on somewhere."

That was Kick—offering up the Spanish Civil War as a cure for yesterday's hangover.

A bell sounded in the octagonal hallway below; an elderly butler moved in stately procession across the marble tiles. Number 14, Prince's Gate, was a whale of a house, with six storeys, thirty-six rooms, an elevator, and a staff of twenty-four. J. P. Morgan had owned it years ago; but J. P. Kennedy had spent a quarter of a million dollars redecorating it. Jack wondered which bedroom was his. The housekeeper would know.

He'd never really had a room of his own growing up, just temporary beds in a series of enormous houses. All the Kennedy kids lived like that—shuttled between boarding schools and whichever place their parents went next. Only Hyannis Port felt like *home*. Life was a suitcase.

"That'll be Billy," Kick said breathlessly. "I have to go. If Daddy asks, I'm out with *Debo Mitford*. Got it?"

"Sure I've got it." He looked at her quizzically. "You lie to Dad, too?"

"Where Billy's concerned, I'm lying about everything." Kick was taking the stairs two at a time, her voice trailing behind her. "Meet us at 400 around midnight. There's bound to be a girl you'll like."

A girl he'd like. When his whole heart ached for a woman run wild in Paris.

He could just see the top of Billy Hartington's head below; the British prince was dark and tall and was sure to have perfect manners. Kick ran to him, and his arm came around her waist.

Jack stared down at them. He'd never seen his little sister in love before.

HIS ROOM WAS THE SAME AS LAST SUMMER, a high-ceilinged space on the third floor with no closets and a couple of armoires, an en suite bath with pipes that banged terrifyingly, wide windows overlooking Hyde Park where society still rode on horseback each day.

Jack threw open his window and leaned out, the Portland cement of the sill snagging the sleeves of his wool jacket. He sniffed the brown coal smell of London. Lights were coming on, faint and sulfurous; and as his gaze drifted over Hyde Park, a sudden movement caught his eye.

A broad and compact figure in a camel's hair coat, a fedora pulled low on his brow. Impossible to see the hair or face, but something about the set of his shoulders screamed *thug.*

Jack leaned farther out, his gaze intent. The man was strolling along Kensington Road, which separated Prince's Gate terrace from Hyde Park. He stopped and looked up at number 14.

Their eyes met.

And Jack knew.

Willi Dobler was having him followed.

I would like nothing better than to ride up to London with you, in your father's car, Dobler had said as they parted on the Southampton dock, *but I do not wish to provoke an international inci-dent. Imagine the headlines, Jack.* "Ambassador's Son Befriends Hitler's Man in London . . ."

Dobler had walked Jack to the waiting embassy car, tipped his hat in farewell, and watched as the driver pulled away. Jack had been grinning to himself, alone in the backseat, convinced he'd called the German's bluff.

But he was beginning to realize that was tough to do.

He drew back from the window. Anger tightened in his chest. He would not let them *watch* him, like an animal in the zoo. He turned and raced from the room, down the broad flights of stairs to the entrance hall, and slid back the bolts of the heavy oak door.

Prince's Gate was almost empty at this hour, the early north-ern dark falling on pitched roofs. He turned east and pelted down the paving to the point where the street bent north, toward the park, and stopped short in Kensington Road. He craned in both directions for a glimpse of the Spider. Was that a camel's hair coat among the multitude of grays?

He began to run, his gait wavering from six days in rough seas, the hard surface of the sidewalk reeling up to meet his feet, his arms pumping and his breath tearing in his lungs. Years of sprinting down football fields and indoor pools could not com-pensate for weeks of lying at Mayo. The threat of sickness caught at his throat. The camel's hair coat was within yards now. Well-bred Englishmen spun out of his path. He thrust between two women and clapped his hand on the Spider.

The man whirled to face him.

Jack dropped into a boxer's crouch, fists clenched and mind turning over his coach's half-remembered lessons. *No gloves.* He'd break his hand on the Spider's jaw—

But it was not the Spider.

Of course it was not the Spider.

A middle-aged Englishman, with a look of terror on his face. He raised a furled umbrella against the coming annihilation.

Jack eased up. "Sorry," he gasped, his breath still ragged. "I thought you were somebody else."

"*Bloody* Americans," the women seethed behind him.

FOURTEEN. SINNERS AND SAINTS

JACK FOUND HIS LITTLE BROTHERS, Bobby and Teddy, established at one end of the long dining-room table while a woman he assumed was Teddy's latest nanny sat nearby, correcting the boy's use of fork and knife. Teddy had learned, in the past year, to hold the fork backward and shovel peas with the knife—Continental manners that would be punched out of him in boarding school back home, Jack thought. His little brother had just turned seven and was the baby of the family—sturdy and cheerful and prone to sliding down the banisters at Prince's Gate. Bobby was six years older, taciturn and nervy and often alone—a touchy kid, who lashed out bitterly when he was hurt, which seemed to be most of the time. Bobby hated his London school and had made no friends. Jack would have liked to have helped him somehow, but he barely knew either of the boys. They were a different generation, growing up behind his back.

Teddy prattled to the nanny as he ate and Bobby stewed in silence, his fork swirling aimlessly around his plate.

"Hey, brats." Jack tossed his hat down the table. It came to rest between the two of them. "How's tricks?"

"Jack!" Teddy ran to him, all draggled socks and scabby knees in his gray flannel shorts. "Daddy *said* you were coming today. I was going to wait up."

"Indeed you were not, Master Teddy," the nanny said.

"I was, too! There's *hours* before bed yet."

Jack lifted him a few inches off the floor in a hug. Teddy was as solid as a truck; Jack's back spasmed.

"You missed my birthday," the boy said accusingly.

"I was stuck on a ship. In the middle of the ocean."

"You could've sent a telegram. Birthday wishes. Did you bring me a present?"

"I thought we'd pick something out here. Your choice," Jack improvised.

"Take me to the zoo tomorrow! There's a baby elephant."

"*You're* a baby elephant," Bobby said scornfully. He'd risen from the table when Jack walked in and stood by his chair, the perfect diplomat's son. "Tomorrow's Friday. We've got school, and Jack'll be going to morning mass with Father."

Mass. Jack felt something tighten in his gut. He wasn't a bad Catholic but he wasn't an ardent one, either—he lived in the gray area of life too much to believe in the black-and-white world Rome and his mother painted. Sinners and Saints, when most of us were somewhere in between. The idea of Eternal Damnation was never something he'd been able to swallow. But Bobby was different—he *needed* belief, Jack thought. If there were no reward in Heaven, life would be just so much hell. There was a certain satisfaction, too, in all those rules, in telling everybody where they'd screwed up. Jack eyed Bobby's perfectly combed dark hair, the thin face that was too pale, the bitten fingernails. Bobby would probably end up a priest.

"Where's Jean?" he asked.

"School." Bobby shrugged slightly, as though he hadn't been missing his favorite sister. "Roehampton. The convent there. She's with Pat and Eunice. *You* know."

"And Rosie?"

Bobby frowned, and glanced swiftly at Teddy; but the little boy had gone back to sawing his beef happily again. "Some place where she's learning to be a teacher. Monty-something."

"Montessori?"

"That's it. I haven't seen her since Christmas."

Rosie fell between Jack and Kick in the family pecking order. She was the prettiest of the Kennedy girls—but slow. Very slow. Jack had once punched a kid on the playground for calling Rosie a moron and he dreaded the nights when his mother insisted her brothers take her to their parties. Jack would dance with Rosie and pass her off to Joe just to shield her from some guy who'd try to get her out into a car and lift up her dress. They all tried to shield Rosie. But it was getting tough. Kick had written to Jack a few months ago, worried sick. Rosie had taken to slipping out of Prince's Gate, and walking the streets of London at night, when everyone thought she was safe in bed. Probably why she'd been shipped off to this Montessori place.

"Have you eaten, sir?" the nanny asked.

"No," he admitted. He eyed the boys' congealing beef, the grayish peas flattened into gravy, the lumps of potato. English cooking at its finest. His bowel twisted suddenly and he grasped a chair, knuckles whitening. "I'm dining out this evening."

THE 400 CLUB WAS IN A BASEMENT in Leicester Square. Along with the Café de Paris, it catered to the wealthy twenty-some-things of London. It had a minuscule dance floor and an eigh-teen-piece orchestra. You could get food if you needed it, but there was no menu; you simply ordered what you wanted and somehow the kitchen delivered. Drinks were sold by the bottle, not the glass, and if you didn't finish the bottle the barman corked it and kept it until you returned the next night, or the next.

The practice was useless with champagne, and so a great deal was ordered and drunk to the dregs in the 400 Club.

Jack wasn't a member—admittance was by subscription only—but everyone he knew in London belonged, and he'd spent most of last summer in the club's perpetual gloom. Bert the Doorman, as he was affectionately called, would never turn a Kennedy away; Kick and Joe and Jack haunted the place. The dancing didn't stop until four o'clock in the morning, and if you were still there at dawn, they gave you breakfast.

Jack carelessly handed Bert a pound note and walked in. Tim Clayton's band was playing swing and half the room was dancing the big apple, one of the wildest things to cross the Atlantic in the past few years. The big apple was something like the Lindy and something like the jitterbug, and it was worth watching in Harlem or in a juke joint down Carolina way. But here in London? Jack stopped in the doorway, his eyes roving over the gilded youth of Mayfair as it kicked up its heels in a wavering circle. Trumpets squealed and a redheaded girl fell into somebody's lap.

His mother considered the big apple *vulgar*, probably because it looked like something cannibals danced before eating their supper. Kick was brilliant at it, drunk or sober; she could snap her fingers and shift her hips and smack her neighbor's ass with the best of them, her mouth open wide in a shriek of laughter.

Convinced he'd find his sister out on the floor instead of tucked into a corner with Billy Hartington, Jack searched among the dancers—and there she was, crying "Bumpsa-daisy!" as the big apple gyrated to a close. She swung her tush into the backside of the guy next to her.

But the guy was neither Billy nor his brother Andrew nor his friend David Ormsby-Gore, all men Jack would trust with Kick's life, but an iron-chested Aryan with massive shoulders and a suit that might have graced Al Capone. He was turning toward Kick, his arm coming up to steady her. He smiled at her glowing face and muttered something she seemed unable to hear. She was leaning toward him, attentive and earnest.

The White Spider. With his hand gripping Kick's arm.

Jesus. Jack shoved his way through the milling crowd, a tea-kettle whistle singing in his ears and the words *get away get away get away* pounding in his head, frantic and accelerating. Not a knife in an alley for the ambassador's son but a sacrificial lamb, a girl diabolically chosen, a strike at the Kennedy heart.

This was true fear and he felt it, now: fear not for himself but for the only thing he really loved, Kick with her monkey's smile. The Spider jerked her toward the door and she began to look uncertain, as though the script had changed. Then, as Jack watched, she raised her hand and slapped the man's cheek.

The Spider reared back and Jack swore aloud but the music started again and his obscenities were drowned in a swirl of sax. He shoved a middle-aged man aside. The Spider wasn't even aware of Jack; he was looking at Kick. Not with rage or violence, but overwhelming hunger. Because Kick had resisted? Because she'd slapped him?

The guy gets off on pain, Jack thought. And drove his fist into the Spider's gut.

The man's breath left his body in a whoosh as Jack connected. But he barely registered the punch; he smashed a right like an anvil into Jack's left cheekbone. Jack's head snapped back and he reeled, off balance, then put his shoulder down and executed a perfect Harvard tackle, bowling the Spider back against the wall. It didn't matter that he was a flyweight or that the man could snap his neck with his bare hands, because Jack was suddenly surrounded by Kick's friends—Billy and Andrew and David and even Bert the Doorman, whose refrain of *Now then, Gents, now then,* rattled in Jack's ears.

He righted himself, skull aching and wind tearing in his throat, his eyes fixed on the Spider. It was clear from the way the man stood that he could toss all of them in the air like cricket balls; but he was being careful now. He did not want more attention. What Jack knew and no one else could suspect was that the Spider was a German and a killer. He would not want to talk to the British police.

"Jack," Kick said worriedly. "Jack, you're bleeding."

He felt her butterfly fingers against his cheek.

"Somebody call the cops. Fast, you hear?"

"That's a little close to the knuckle, isn't it?" she murmured. "The guy didn't hurt me. He's just fresh, is all. And he could have you up for assault, kid."

Bert and Billy and Andrew hustled the German across the tiny dance floor.

"Call the police!" Jack yelled furiously. He thrust himself in front of them, blocking the way. The Spider's face was inches from his own. The scar bisecting his lip; the utter lack of expression in his flat blue eyes—

"Now, now, Mr. Kennedy," Bert said soothingly, "None of our young people want to talk to the bobbies tonight. I'm sure you'll agree, once you've had a breather."

They pulled the man away. Kick's hand was on his arm. "Jack—do you *know* that guy?"

He shook her off and pushed through the crowd, already dancing again, already singing the latest tune, and tumbled out into the street. *He had to catch him.*

But the Spider was gone.

FIFTEEN. DRESSING FOR AMERICA

"**JACK!**" His father looked up irritably from his desk. "That's a helluva shiner. And you haven't even been in London twenty-four hours, for chrissake."

It was the first time Jack had seen his dad since landing in Southampton. They'd both returned to Prince's Gate so late last night they'd missed each other at breakfast. But Joe Kennedy made no move to greet him. No bear hug or handshake from the Bronxville Shark. "The papers say you threw a punch at some poor bastard in the 400. What the hell were you thinking?"

"He . . . insulted Kick."

"Kick can take care of herself. Whereas *you* just embarrassed the whole family. A public brawl? From the American ambassador's son? You know what kind of damage that does to my reputation, Jack? They'll say it's because you're an Irish lout. No couth. No background. Most Brits are just *looking* for a reason to write us all off. And on your first night back in London, you gave them one." Joe whipped his wire-rimmed spectacles from his face and tossed them petulantly on his desk. "Your brother would never throw a punch in public, I can tell you that. He knows what he owes the Kennedy name."

A wave of heat rose in Jack's face, along with a memory—sharp as though etched in glass—of Joe systematically pummeling the face of Ritchie Sanborn in the dirt of the Dexter School playground while he took bets from the crowd of watching boys. Joe beat up somebody nearly every day and Jack made a fortune in marbles, the betting currency of nine-year-olds. Brawling was what the WASP kids expected from Joe, who was perpetually as tough and hearty as Jack was pale and ill. The other boys taunted and ridiculed the Irish Catholic Kennedys daily until the fighting began. Then they lined up to watch.

"I'm sorry if I let you down," he said.

"It's time to *grow up*, Jack." Joe shuffled some papers, refusing to meet his eyes. "We're all tired of your screwups. Joe's risking his life in Spain, you know—and doing *good work*. I read his reports to the folks at Nancy Astor's last weekend, and the Cliveden Set was mighty impressed, I can tell you. When Joe says this Franco's the only hope for pushing the Communist thugs out of town, high-level Brits sit up and take notice. And by high level, I mean Chamberlain's *cabinet*."

"You read Joe's letters to Chamberlain's cabinet?"

"Nancy thinks I should get them published," Joe retorted. "I'm working on Henry Luce over at *Time* right now. But as for you, son—straighten up and fly right. You can't be an embarrassment forever. Got it?"

"Got it," Jack said.

Joe nodded brusquely and reached for a file. Son dismissed. Jack stood there, awkward as only his father could make him.

"It's swell to be back. Not much has changed—except your walls, of course."

His father had inherited a large office on the American embassy's second floor, swathed in pale blue silk. He'd replaced what he contemptuously called "the fairy look" with oak paneling. The room overlooked Grosvenor Square, where already the gardens were being sacrificed to a British trench crew. There were trenches in Hyde Park, too, and the streetlamps were being painted black. London feared attack from the air, delivered without warning or a declaration of war.

His father glanced at him; something in his face softened. "Need a beefsteak for that eye?"

Jack's left socket was swollen, the skin every kind of color.

"It doesn't hurt anymore."

"I hope the other guy looks worse."

Jack smiled faintly. There was no way on earth he could begin to explain the White Spider to Joe Kennedy.

"How was your crossing?"

"Lousy. I spent most of it in bed."

"—And slept in everything you own." His father scanned him briefly. "Those clothes are a mess. Get down to Poole's right away and order some things that fit. You'll need lounge suits, morning dress, white tie and tails. And a pair of silk knee breeches."

"A pair of *what*?" Jack demanded, revolted.

His father's mouth twisted. "It's queer as hell, I know. But that's England all over. Tell Poole's you need everything by middle of next week—we're flying to Paris."

Paris. Jack's pulse quickened. *Diana.*

"I want to chat up Bill Bullitt on this Munich business—get the French view." Bullitt was Roosevelt's ambassador to France. "Then we're heading to Rome for the Pope."

"I thought he was dead."

"And his successor's about to be crowned," Joe said patiently. "Roosevelt's asked me to attend. I'm the most prominent Catholic in the diplomatic corps."

"Swell." A papal mass. At the Vatican. *That* would last the better part of an entire day. Standing and kneeling, standing and kneeling, while the incense settled in his hair.

"Your brothers and sisters are coming later, by train. Mother's flying in from Egypt."

"When's the . . . coronation?"

"Next Sunday. March twelfth."

"How long will we have in Paris?"

"A few days."

"And when will the rest of the family get there?"

His father shrugged. "Next Friday?" He leaned toward him conspiratorially. "How's about you and I paint Paris red? Folies Bergère? Or there's Josephine Baker. I hear she's something *else*."

"We ought to take Kick with us," Jack said suddenly. "On the plane. Instead of sending her with the kids."

Joe Kennedy frowned. "Put kind of a damper on the Folies Bergère, don't you think?"

"Well, maybe, but—"

How to say *I don't want to leave her alone*? He'd watched his little sister like a hawk last night, urging her whole glittering group of friends to abandon the 400 Club for the Café de Paris, glancing back through the black cab's rear window to make sure no blond-headed thug was following. He was terrified Kick would wander off, with only Billy between herself and a knife.

"She'd like a few days in Paris," he said lamely. "Shopping."

"Judging by the bills I've paid, she gets over there often enough." His father clapped him on the shoulder again. "This is a *stag* trip, Jack. Now get outta here and order your clothes. I don't want to see you again until you're presentable. You're dressing for *America*, remember?"

Jack went. Poole's was not all that far from the German embassy. He could look up Willi Dobler on his way.

———

A KID WITH A BLEMISHED FACE and a *feldgrau* Nazi uniform told him in heavily accented English that he was in the wrong building. This was the *embassy*, Number 9 Carlton Terrace. Herr Dobler worked in number 8.

Jack didn't ask what they called number 8. He thought he had a pretty good idea.

He gave his card to a bland individual in an impeccable suit, who eyed his wrinkled jacket dubiously. "May I ask why you wish to see Herr Dobler?"

The accent, this time, was Oxbridge; and the boredom in the drawl was familiar from a hundred London parties.

"We met on the *Queen Mary*. He suggested I stop by."

"Ah. You're one of *those*." The cool eyes surveyed him again; the lips quirked with amusement. "Aren't you Ambassador Kennedy's son?"

"He has a few." What did the guy mean, *you're one of those*? "Could you tell Herr Dobler I'm here?"

Jack waited while the man's shoes clicked down a marble hallway and disappeared through a door; number 8's business was conducted at the rear of the building. And probably, Jack thought, through antennae on the roof.

He shifted from one foot to another, his right thigh throbbing. The small pocket he'd carved in the muscle for his DOCA tablets was red now and sensitive to the touch; probably an infection. He'd have to abandon it and cut a new flap of skin elsewhere. In the meantime it was growing uncomfortable to stand. There were no chairs arranged before the reception desk; building number 8 discouraged visitors. But an Ionic column thoughtfully supported a corner of the foyer; Jack retreated and leaned against it. He glanced at his watch. How much time would his father mentally accord him for ordering clothes?

The door at the far end of the hall opened quietly. Willi Dobler strode toward him, neat and elegant; before he'd even reached the desk, his hand was extended.

"Jack! What an unexpected pleasure! Have you had luncheon yet?"

The languid Oxbridge man followed behind; the scent of his cigarette wafted across the foyer. Jack was conscious of him watching Dobler. Watching them both.

"I've barely had breakfast. I was out late last night—at the 400 Club. But you know that, don't you? Your friend the Spider probably reported already. He's stalking my sister."

A silence; Dobler's smile faded slightly; his eyes slid over Jack's bruises, slid away. Jack read something like nervousness in his face.

"I want his name," he said.

"Whose name, my dear fellow?"

"The Spider's. Because if I see him near my sister again—or anyone else in my family—I'm calling the police. I'll have him arrested for harassment. *Questioned* by people who count in the British government. Got it?"

His voice was rising and it echoed around the marble walls of Number 8 Carleton Terrace; Dobler glanced over his shoulder. The Oxbridge man eased around him and confronted Jack.

"Perhaps you should go, Mr. Kennedy. We wouldn't want another unpleasant . . . incident. On your first day in your father's service. You've done enough damage already."

They read the papers. They knew about the fight, of course. They'd like him to think they knew everything.

"Give me his name, goddamn you."

"Jack." Dobler slipped an arm casually around his shoulders, turned him toward the door. "You're under some sort of misapprehension, I'm afraid. Too much champagne at the club last night, yes? I'm sorry to hear your sister was . . . bothered, but I haven't the faintest idea what you're talking about, and I think my colleague is right. It's best that you leave. Sleep it off, hmm? Clear your head?"

"If I see him again," Jack muttered for Dobler's ears alone, "I go to the police. If he *touches* her, I'll kill him myself. Understand?"

"But of course!" Dobler cried. "I'll look forward to it, with pleasure!" He was smiling as he reached for the door, but Jack saw the strain in his eyes. Maybe he'd called the German's bluff. Maybe the Spider would disappear.

It was only when he reached Henry Poole & Company, in Savile Row, that he found the folded paper Willi had slipped into his pocket.

Rules, it said. *Seven o'clock.*

SIXTEEN. STRATEGIES AND REINFORCEMENTS

"HOOVER'S PUT A NAME to that corpse," Sam Schwartz said to the President. "He sent this over." He handed Roosevelt a manila envelope with *Urgent* stamped on it.

Roosevelt raised an eyebrow. "Is Ed avoiding me, Sam? Did my little barb about *friends* shoot home?"

"I couldn't say, sir."

"But you can think." His spatulate fingers fumbled with the red string sealing the buff-colored flap.

"Mr. Hoover may be devoting his time to legitimate business, sir. Now that Mr. Kennedy's back in London."

Roosevelt peered into the envelope and withdrew a sheaf of paper. "Good Lord. Ed has typed up everything there is to know about this poor man. Did you find any of his bugs, by the way?"

Schwartz's brown eyes shifted to his. His expression was carefully wooden. "Only one, sir. A wiretap on a telephone."

"Clever Edgar! In this office, I suppose?"

"No, sir. Next to Miss LeHand's bed."

The air in the room seemed to grow heavier. Roosevelt's fingers tightened on the arms of his wheelchair. Schwartz knew just how often he was with Missy. Neither of them had to discuss it. The damn phone probably had some kind of device that recorded pillow talk as well as Missy's calls. All of it set down in one of

Hoover's secret files. The man wanted an iron grip on Franklin Delano Roosevelt's neck.

"How offensive," he said at last. "And how consummately stupid."

"You could have him arrested. Section 605 of the 1934 Federal Communications Act explicitly states that *no person not being authorized by the sender shall intercept any communication and divulge or publish the existence, contents, substance, purpose, effect, or meaning of such intercepted communications—*"

"—to any person," Roosevelt finished. "Particularly Nazi agents."

What Schwartz did not know, the President reflected, was that he had played both sides of Section 605 himself, with Hoover as willing accomplice. Nearly three years ago he'd summoned the FBI director to the White House for a private chat about the investigation of "subversives," particularly Fascists and Communists. Ever since the American Liberty League had reared its ugly head, he'd wanted somebody monitoring political threats. He'd never have learned about Göring's cash network otherwise. He'd chosen not to ask how Hoover got his information.

"If I know Edgar," he said, "there will be no way in hell to link that wiretap to his shop. We'll never prove it in court. Gist the goddamn report he sent over, Sam."

Schwartz took the sheaf of paper. Roosevelt was aware of the keenness of his bodyguard's mind, the acuity of his focus. No hint of embarrassment about the distressing news he'd just conveyed. Schwartz was a professional, and his detachment was reassuring.

"Charles Atwater," he recited. "Manhattan attorney with a wife and two kids in Pelham. Thirty-four years old. Yale graduate. Reported missing by a business associate in London when he failed to arrive there March second. Embarked as a passenger on the *Queen Mary*—the February twenty-fourth sailing—and his Tourist Class ticket was stamped that day in New York. Bureau thinks he was knifed and thrown off the ship before it passed Ellis Island."

"Does the fellow have ties to Nazi Germany?"

Schwartz thumbed through the sheaf of paper. "Hoover's boys can't find any. None to Göring's cash network, either."

"In short, the man was killed for no reason."

"Everybody's killed for *something*." Schwartz glanced up. "This is odd, sir. A Charles Atwater also *dis*embarked at Southampton."

"Did he, indeed?"

"But the wife in Pelham has positively identified the corpse as her husband."

"How tragic for her," Roosevelt murmured. "This Spider fellow is very clever, Sam. Killed his man, tossed him overboard, and proceeded to travel to London in style as Atwater himself. He must look rather like the dead man—or close enough to survive passport inspection."

"Hoover's asked Scotland Yard to keep an eye out for Atwater's papers."

"Which our man will have tossed by now, of course. Someone else will have to die, if the White Spider needs to leave England." He met Sam's watchful eyes. "Let's hope it's not young Jack."

"He wouldn't kill the ambassador's son for his passport."

"He might do it for attention. Remember the mark cut into his victims' flesh. The signature. He likes attention." Roosevelt was silent an instant, thinking. "It's no coincidence this killer embarked on the *Queen Mary*. Hoover says he thinks the Nazis know the Bureau is on to their network—which is his way of telling me there's a Bureau leak, somewhere. And I'm beginning to think the leak extends to my office. The Spider knows I've recruited Jack. He intended to make contact with him on that ship."

"It's possible, sir."

"Then I've put the boy in considerably more danger than I meant to." His mouth set in a hard line. "Get me Wild Bill, Sam. We need to powwow. We need strategies and reinforcements."

"Yes, sir."

Wild Bill was General William J. Donovan, a retired war hero and Wall Street financier. He and Roosevelt were at opposite ends of the social and political spectrum—Donovan was Irish Catholic like J. P. Kennedy, a Republican who'd campaigned against FDR—but Wild Bill's friends were varied and useful. He knew people in British Intelligence. And the President was willing to use them.

"Tell me, Sam," Roosevelt was saying. "If nobody but Missy and my Secret Service detail knew about that meeting with Jack Kennedy beneath the Waldorf, how did the Nazis find out? We can't blame the State department this time."

Schwartz frowned. "Mr. President—I can vouch for myself and my men. None of us have been talking to German agents."

"But one of you might have talked to Ed Hoover, perhaps?"

"Not even Hoover's dough can buy him love, sir. The guy wants our jobs," Schwartz retorted contemptuously. "And Miss LeHand—"

"—Was tucked up in bed with Dashiell Hammett. Just out of curiosity, Sam, how much dough *has* Edgar offered you boys?"

"Never enough."

"Then he's getting his news the old-fashioned way."

"Eavesdropping? On the President of the United States?" Schwartz reddened. "That's *treason*."

"He'll make us prove it." Roosevelt flashed his shark's grin. "Let me think about Edgar, Sam. And in the meantime—check the Pullman for a wiretap. Perhaps we can use it to hang him."

SEVENTEEN. RULES

NOBODY AT PRINCE'S GATE OBJECTED when Jack said he was dining out again—with Rose away, Joe Kennedy was firmly pursuing other pleasures; and with Joe Jr. in Spain, Kick was triple-booked each evening. She moved constantly in a crowd of well-born Brits who did little besides dress, dance, and drink. The fear that a devastating war loomed made the partying more obsessive and extreme.

Jack invaded his sister's bedroom late that afternoon while she dressed for Debo Mitford's. Debo was one of Baron Redesdale's daughters; they lived around the corner from Prince's Gate. Kick liked her because she was in love with Billy's brother, Andrew, and because she was saner than any of her sisters. One of the Mitford girls was a Communist, and had eloped to join the Spanish Civil War cause; another had divorced her first husband to marry the British Fascist leader Oswald Mosley. A third sister—Unity Mitford—was rumored to be secretly engaged to Adolf Hitler, whom she adored. She could frequently be found taking tea with him in Berlin. Jack figured the Mitfords were fanatics and fanatics were dangerous; he stayed away from all of them except Debo.

"Promise me something," he said as he leaned over Kick's chair.

"Anything—if you'll fasten my pearls."

She handed him the necklace and he fumbled with the catch. Beneath the heavy fall of her auburn hair, which she always wore down in a shoulder-grazing bob, her neck felt childish and vulnerable.

"Don't run off alone with Billy tonight."

"Gosh, kid—you sound like Mother." She swiveled in her seat and offered a saintly expression. "I'm not one of those girls you invite up to Harvard. *I'm* saving it for marriage."

"What do you know about my girls?" he demanded.

"Joe told me everything." She turned back to the mirror, adjusting the pearls. "Apparently you've left him holding the baby one too many times. He says you've got so many girls on the string, you can't remember their names—so you call them all *kid* just to be safe. Joe says you drop invitations all over the East Coast, and then promptly forget about them. He's had to meet girls' trains, find hotel rooms, *and* take them dancing more weekends than he can count. While you're off hooking other fish to fry."

"At least he's had a few dates," Jack protested. "Besides, that was years ago. Before Joe graduated. I've reformed since then."

"Frances Ann?" she suggested knowledgeably.

He felt his stomach knot. "*Frances Ann.* She was the one, Kick. Until she turned me down flat right before I left New York."

Kick's mouth formed a surprised O in the mirror.

"I'm too young to get married," he said hurriedly. "And her parents don't like Catholics."

"Jack—" Kick grabbed his hand with both of hers and gripped it tightly. "Is that why you don't want me disappearing with Billy? Because *his* parents don't like Catholics?"

"It's one reason."

Her eyes were too bright, suddenly. "I didn't know you'd proposed. I could slap Frances Ann silly. You're worth ten of her."

"I like to think I'm worth a hundred, myself," he said awkwardly. "But *promise* me, Kick. Stay with your friends. This town's gotten rough. And there's safety in numbers."

She studied him coolly. "This is about the fight last night at the 400. Isn't it?"

"Yes."

"That man was just a *cad*. I've run into his kind before."

Her insouciance troubled him. "What did he say to you?"

"Before you slugged him, you mean? That I had *beautiful breasts*." She looked slightly nauseated. "That—that he'd like to—*touch* them—"

"—So you slapped him silly," Jack concluded. "Good girl. But stay with Debo and Andrew tonight, Kick. Just to make your big brother happy."

"I will, Jack," she said clearly.

He kissed her cheek and left her.

RULES WAS THE OLDEST RESTAURANT in London. It sat in Maiden Lane, and its privacy and discretion were legendary.

Jack arrived at five minutes past seven. Dobler was nowhere in sight. A waiter led him to a banquette in an alcove. He ordered a glass of Bourbon on the rocks and glanced at his watch for the next eighteen minutes. Then he paid for the drink and left.

It was dark when he stepped out into Maiden Lane, gas lights burning low in their painted lanterns. A black London cab pulled up alongside him. The rear door swung open.

"Good evening, Jack."

"Evening, Willi," he said.

"A thousand pardons for keeping you waiting. Would you get into the car, please?"

There was another man seated in the shadows of the cab. Jack figured getting in was a mistake; they weren't far from the Thames. As good a place as any to dump a body.

"I'll walk back, thanks," he said.

The cab rolled alongside him.

"Jack," Dobler said patiently, "I must talk to you, and I don't wish to be seen. Dinner is impossible but a cab ride is not. I've brought a friend from the British Foreign Office to vouch for me. You know his name, I think. Denys Playfair."

Playfair. Diana's husband.

Jack stopped short. So did the cab.

"Caution is all very well in its way," Playfair drawled from the depths of the car, "but I'm beginning to find you a crashing bore."

He got in.

"DENYS PLAYFAIR, JACK KENNEDY—Jack, Denys," Willi said as the cab dove into the traffic around Trafalgar Square. "I've already explained how we met on the *Queen Mary*. And that you know Mrs. Playfair, of course."

Mrs. Playfair. He'd tried not to think of her that way.

Diana's husband had fine, long-fingered hands and an aquiline nose. His pale hair was slicked back like a parrot's poll; there was something remote and indifferent about him that Jack did not immediately understand. He was staring through the cab window at the lights of Piccadilly as though he were alone.

Jack perched on one of the jump seats facing the two men, his knees almost touching theirs. He felt like a piece of baggage or a child. The lurch of the cab as it rounded corners threw him off balance; he resisted clutching the ceiling strap. There was a glass partition between passengers and driver; Willi seemed to regard it as soundproof. Jack kept his voice low all the same.

"Give me the Spider's name, and I'll get out at the next corner," he suggested.

"But I have a good deal to say to you," Dobler objected, "and not much time in which to say it."

They were heading west now, toward Mayfair. Jack supposed it was preferable to the river but he was still uneasy. Playfair turned his head and studied him, expressionless; then his lips quirked. "You've *scared* him, Willi. He's convinced all Germans wear jackboots."

"I'm a European first, Jack," Dobler said, "and only then a German. That may sound fatuous to you—a distinction without a difference—but to me it represents an ideal."

"Deutschland über alles?" Jack suggested.

"Not at all. Deutschland as part of a unified Europe with common aims. A Europe at peace with itself and the world. The United States could be our model."

"It's not your boss's."

"My boss," Dobler said carefully, "is Admiral Wilhelm Canaris, head of the Abwehr—our military intelligence service—and his goals have little to do with Hitler's."

"Even though he's Hitler's top spy?" Jack glanced at Playfair; none of this was news to the Foreign Office.

"Particularly *because* he's Hitler's top spy." Dobler reached into his jacket for his gold cigarette case; he offered it to Jack, who shook his head.

Playfair took a smoke and leaned over Dobler's hand. The flame showed his skin dead white, his eyes a faint green.

"I'm here in London for one reason," Dobler continued. "To *prevent war*, if I can. That's also why I met with your Franklin Roosevelt in New York three weeks ago." He snapped the lighter shut. "We spoke the day after your conversation in the Pullman beneath the Waldorf-Astoria, and then again, later, at the White House. He is a charming fellow, is he not? One has the constant impression of a sheathed sword."

The cab pulled up suddenly before a town house facing Cavendish Square: tall windows, swagged draperies, box topiary in tubs beside the door.

"This is where I leave you," Playfair said courteously, and extended his hand. "Good hunting."

Jack's eyes followed him as he got out of the cab and sauntered up the flagged walk: indolent, faintly theatrical, one hand in his trouser pocket. The odd figure went perfectly with the stage set of the house; but where did Diana fit? What role was she playing?

"YOU REALLY DON'T WANT TO TELL ME the Spider's name, do you?" Jack said as the cab entered Hyde Park and slowed to a crawl.

"Hans Obst," Dobler said indifferently. "His name is Hans Obst. He's thirty-three years old, five feet eleven inches tall, two hundred and twenty pounds, and a native of Munich. He has no family—the rumor is that he murdered his father—and works exclusively for Reinhard Heydrich, Hitler's golden boy."

"I've heard of him."

Willi smiled bleakly. "Then you're unusual. Heydrich cultivates secrecy. He trained under my boss, Wilhelm Canaris, before he was cashiered from the navy. Now he could have Canaris's head and the Abwehr, too."

Jack frowned. "That's a lot of power. How'd he get it?"

"By killing people," Dobler said, "although he'd probably call it *liquidating threats to the Reich*. He runs the Gestapo, Jack, among other things. Obst is one of Heydrich's freelancers. The kind who kicks down doors in the night."

"Why are you telling me this, Willi?"

"Because I want you to understand something." Dobler drew on his cigarette. "The White Spider is not after you or your family. He's *following* you," he added quickly as Jack protested, "but *I'm* the one he wants."

"Really? Then why's he dancing with my sister?"

"I made the mistake of contacting you on the *Queen Mary*. That was stupid; but I had no idea the Spider was on board. Obst noticed you because *I* noticed you. He thinks you're part of my plans. Hence the surveillance. Of your home—and your sister . . ."

"If it keeps up, he'll discover two can play at his game. So what *are* these secret plans of yours, Willi?"

Dobler ignored the question. "Obst's presence on the *Queen Mary* means that Heydrich knew about my trip to New York. He may know of my meeting with Roosevelt. That's unfortunate."

"Because?"

Dobler studied him quizzically. "Because I'm working *against* Heydrich, of course. If he's put Obst on my tail, then my work and that of my superiors—Admiral Canaris, and the handful of people he trusts—is in danger."

"I don't particularly care about internal Nazi squabbles or what kind of work you do," Jack said evenly. "I just want Obst called off."

Dobler concentrated on his cigarette. The tip glowed red in the car's shadows. "He's not my dog to call."

Jack considered this. He knew too little about Dobler's world to sift the truth from the lies. Instead he posed another question. "Tell me something, Willi. Why would the President of the United States talk to *you*? I mean, don't get me wrong, you're a real prince of a Nazi—but you're not exactly on Franklin's level."

"Neither are you, Jack."

"I'm the son of the ambassador to England, not a Nazi spy."

Dobler scowled at his repeated use of the word. "I joined the Party in order to work against it. It's called *cover*."

"I thought it was called treason," Jack said blandly.

"Now *that* is truly *scheisse*." Dobler's dark eyes were snapping. "Adolf Hitler is exceedingly dangerous, for Germany and the rest of the world. As an Oxford-educated man who believes deeply in peace and the rule of law, I have a duty to save my country from madness. That's not treason, Jack, that's patriotism."

"Heydrich would disagree."

"Do you know how many people have disappeared, simply because Heydrich ordered it? He keeps thousands of dossiers, full of names and personal information. Reasons to kill. The victims' families learn nothing of their fate—until an urn full of ashes is delivered to the door. There is no recourse in the courts, Jack. No place to appeal. The Gestapo simply forget the people they torture and kill."

"So why don't you run for it?" Jack's leg was aching again and his patience was wearing thin. "Abandon the Fatherland. Ask Roosevelt for a job."

"Because more people will die," Dobler said simply. "Could you live with yourself, knowing what I know? Could you just walk away?"

"The question doesn't arise. This isn't my war."

"It will be," Dobler said soberly.

"Is that what Roosevelt told you?"

"I went to him with an offer." Dobler ground out his cigarette, eyes averted. "Canaris is secretly passing information to certain individuals in the British government."

"Playfair," Jack suggested.

"Playfair, certainly."

"Even though his wife's a Fascist?"

"Many things make excellent cover."

Jack held Dobler's gaze. *Was he suggesting that Diana was a spy, too?*

"I offered to pass the same information to Mr. Roosevelt. The private truth behind Hitler's public lies. Whatever the Abwehr knows of his plans of attack. And there *are* plans."

"Which is why the Spider should be in Poland," Jack said thoughtfully. "Poland's next, isn't it?"

"Of course."

"What did Roosevelt say to your . . . proposition?"

"He was intrigued," Dobler said. "You Americans have no intelligence service. That kind of innocence brings tears to my eyes. You're like Eve in the garden, before the snake appears."

We're heading into a hurricane with our ears plugged and our eyes closed, Jack. A horse's ass of the Grand Old School declared that Gentlemen do not read each other's mail . . .

He could imagine FDR weighing Willi's sincerity against the likelihood of a Nazi trap—one that would pull him into a war the country didn't want, and scuttle his third term. Was Willi a threat? Or a gift in the battle against Hitler?

The cab had reached the southern end of Hyde Park and

eased left into Regent Street; Jack could just see the lights of Prince's Gate.

"Mr. Roosevelt thought it best if I passed my intelligence through friends, not government channels," Dobler said.

Of course. *I can't trust the State department with this.*

"Have you got any friends, Willi?" Jack wondered. "—Besides Playfair and that guy at work who watches your every move?"

"Friendships are born in surprising places."

"Like back alleys," he suggested. "Or foxholes."

The cab pulled up before his door.

"Will you work with me, Jack?" Dobler asked quietly.

He weighed the German for a long moment. "Give me a reason to, Willi."

EIGHTEEN. TRAFFIC

"LOOKING FOR SOMEBODY?"

Jack paused in the doorway of the embassy's telegraph room. There was only one code clerk there at 8:45 on Saturday morning: a slight man with hunched shoulders and hair as glossy as a mink's. "I'd like to send a transatlantic cable."

"Clear text or coded?"

"Coded."

"Who do you want to reach?"

"A man named Sam Schwartz."

"The President's bodyguard?"

Jack handed him the sheet of paper he'd carefully printed.

PLEASE VERIFY DESIRED RELATIONS WITH W.D. STOP CHECK BACKGROUND ONE HANS OBST ALSO SR. MARY JOSEPH LITTLE SISTERS OF CLEMENCY ROME STOP BEST JACK.

"Thanks," he said from the doorway, but the clerk was already tapping the keys of his machine, and didn't answer.

SISTER MARY JOSEPH *of the Little Sisters of Clemency,* Dobler had murmured last night as Jack got out of the cab.

"Sister Mary Who?"

"Joseph. She runs a charity network in Rome. You're attending the Pope's coronation, I believe?"

"Next week."

"She'll be there. Ask where she gets her donations—and where they're going. A bit of research for your *senior thesis.*"

It was Willi's first tidbit of intelligence. Jack would have liked to ask some questions, but he was standing in the street, completely exposed. Dobler had chosen the moment for that reason. He'd thrown Jack a teaser, like a girl shimmying, her skirt high on her leg as she danced the big apple.

Jack pushed the German out of his mind now and knocked on the door of his father's office.

"What are you doing here on Saturday?" Joe Kennedy asked. "You should be keeping an eye on Kick. She spends too much time with Billy Hartington."

"He's a nice fella, Dad. Kick could do worse."

"She's risking her immortal soul."

Jack's eyebrows shot up. "Sounds like Mother talking."

"By trunk call, every day. From *Egypt.*" His father looked strained and mulish. Rose usually had that effect. "You know what she's costing me?"

"I didn't know Egypt had telephones." He leaned casually against his father's desk "Need any help around here?"

"You could drop my weekly report at the code clerk's office." He tossed some paper across his polished desk. "Not that Franklin reads it."

"I'm sure he does," Jack said absently.

"He never takes my advice." J.P.'s voice was rough with resentment. "In my last cable, I *told* him Chamberlain's stock was on the rise, and we needed to keep our distance from the Jewish lobby agitating about Munich. If Chamberlain says Hitler's satisfied with the Sudetenland, who are we to argue? It's not like we've talked to the Führer. Ever since Franklin recalled Ambassador Wilson to protest Kristallnacht, our relations with the Germans have gone straight downhill."

"These cables," Jack said. "Your secretary just hands them to the code clerk, whichever one happens to be there, and he sends them?"

"Sure," his father said.

"And you don't mind him reading your reports? Everything private about the British government—you've written for Roosevelt's eyes alone?"

"I'm not sure those guys can read," Joe said mildly. "Besides, I don't have any choice. I can't work a Morse key, much less an encoding machine."

"What do you know about the clerks?"

"They're vetted by State. That's good enough for me."

What had Roosevelt said? *Too many of my private conversations are finding their way into Hitler's office.*

Jack stared at his father's report. He couldn't send Willi Dobler's intelligence through State department clerks. He might get Willi killed.

"Some things you just have to take on faith, son," his father said. "Now, could you run that report downstairs? I'd like Franklin to see it before bedtime."

THE LONDON SOCIAL SEASON didn't truly begin until Easter, and most of the West End stage was still dark; but that night Jack dined with Kick at the Mitfords' and then took in a musical called *Magyar Melody* at His Majesty's Theatre. It was a sappy play about an Englishman in love with a wild Hungarian maiden, a romanticized vision of Eastern Europe that firmly ignored Hitler's plans for it; the audience applauded when love triumphed, but Jack left feeling vaguely unsettled, as though he'd been treated to a child's bedtime story. He glanced at every stranger's face as they left the theater, looking for a man with the build of a halfback and a scar bisecting his lip. Killers like the Spider didn't just give up.

"Coming to the 400, Jack?" Kick asked.

"I don't feel like it tonight. How about we get up a dance back at the house? I brought some new records from New York. Dad'll be out."

"He always is." Kick frowned at him in perplexity, and seemed about to ask why he was so reluctant to drink in their favorite watering hole, but Debo Mitford interrupted. "Oh, Jack—tell me you've got that new tune by the Ink Spots!"

"'If I Didn't Care'?" he suggested. "You bet. Sitting right there in the stack, on my bedroom dresser."

"It's supposed to be divine, but nobody in London has heard it yet."

He raised his eyebrow at Kick, and she shrugged a little, reconciled. It took three cabs to get all of them back to Prince's Gate.

A GREAT DEAL OF GIN WAS DRUNK and the armchairs of Rose's formal salon pulled back against the wall to make room for a game of touch football, but since only Jack and Kick fully understood the rules, the others danced the big apple in a ring around them. A girl named Sally Norton, rangy as a Thoroughbred and in love, Jack thought, with Billy Hartington, raced hilariously across Regent Street at two o'clock in the morning and plunged into Hyde Park's frigid Serpentine.

It was Jack, not Billy, who dove in to save her.

He didn't mind the shock of the water or the mess it made of his clothes. Sally and her games had kept Kick occupied for one more night, safe from the White Spider.

NINETEEN. PRAYER

SUNDAY MORNING. The Spider sat in the rear of the Brompton Oratory unmoved by the vastness of the dome, the way the light cascaded from its clerestory windows even in the depths of March. The exalted trebles of the choir reached his ears without penetrating them. He could command stillness from his body—it was his tool to use and he had mastered it long ago—but his pulse was throbbing chaotically. His eyes were fixed on a girl some distance in front of him, near the transept. She was kneeling there in the midst of her family, gloved hands folded like a dove's wings. Her head was bowed. A lace veil covered her tumult of auburn hair. He could almost feel her breast rise and fall with each breath she drew, each prayer she murmured. So pure. So impossibly white. He wanted to take her there and cut his mark into her flesh—make her his own. But she was denied him. He closed his eyes and bit down on his lip until he tasted blood.

The Latin mass eddied around him. He did not move, though his rootedness in the pew was unusual, the mark of the unbeliever. It was only when the final benediction came and the congregation rose that he abruptly thrust his blunt body out into the side aisle, head down. The priest and his acolytes passed, crucifix high. He followed.

From a doorway across the Brompton Road he watched them leave the oratory. She was laughing as she slipped into the chauffeured car. Her brother did not even look in his direction. The Spider felt their indifference like a slap in the face. *What fools, to slap him.* His hand tightened lovingly on his knife.

TWENTY. COLONEL GUBBINS

EVERYONE AT PRINCE'S GATE ate dinner in their pajamas Sunday night—a Kennedy tradition when Rose was away—and the sight of Kick with her hair tied up in curl-papers, casually filing her nails, was a relief. Jack hadn't realized how tense he'd become, waiting for the Spider's next move.

He read about it after the fact, on Monday morning. In a small headline on a back page of the London *Times*.

East End Girl Murdered.

Her name was Sadie Mullins and she'd been found in an alley near the docks. A child, really; only fifteen. She'd been knifed in the heart, and a crude mark cut into her breast. It looked, the reporter said, like a carnival wheel—or a swastika. . . .

Jack studied the newsprint, remembering something Willi had said. *He likes to cut his mark into his victim's chest—a crouching spider.*

He tore out the article and stuffed it in his pocket.

HE ROAMED HIS FATHER'S OFFICE after the ten o'clock staff meeting like a restless cat, leafing through books and a bundle of week-old newspapers from the States. He was waiting for an answer to the cable he'd sent Schwartz.

"Mr. Kennedy?"

He turned, dropping a stack of *Time* magazines, and saw the code clerk with the sleek black hair. "Yes?"

"Cable for you."

"Thanks." He took it eagerly from the man's hands.

The clerk lingered, watching him. "The message is a little odd, I have to say."

Jack glanced at him. So J.P. was wrong—the code clerks *could* read. And pass judgment on the cables they encrypted.

"What's your name?" he asked the man suddenly.

The cool gray eyes held his own. "Tyler Gatewood Kent. Princeton '32."

"Good man. I spent some time at Old Nassau. Before I transferred to Harvard."

"I know," Kent said. His lips quirked in something that was almost a sneer.

Jack flushed. He didn't broadcast the details of his Mystery Disease, so any number of people thought he'd flunked out of Princeton. Tyler Kent must be one of them. The clerk wanted to unsettle him. Suggest that he'd read Jack's dossier behind his back. Have some fun with the ambassador's son. J.P. was not terribly popular with career State department people—and a few took it out on his kids.

Jack grasped the edge of the office door as though he were about to close it. He wanted to read the cable and he had no interest in an audience.

"Thanks again," he said.

Kent saluted sardonically and drifted away.

Jack shut the door and threw himself into one of his dad's easy chairs.

IT IS RARE TO HAVE SNOW IN MARCH STOP BUT NOT ENTIRELY UNKNOWN IN LONDON STOP SCHWARTZ

What?

He read the infuriating phrases through a second time, and then a third. Nothing about Willi Dobler or Roosevelt's desire for intelligence; nothing about the Little Sisters of Clemency. Was this Schwartz's attempt at a joke?

"WHERE ARE YOUR NEW CLOTHES?" his father demanded at lunch. "You're still a mess. And that shiner's taking its own sweet time to heal."

"I have a fitting this afternoon."

He couldn't care less about his face or the state of his wardrobe. He was still annoyed about Schwartz's cable. Didn't the guy take German agents seriously? Maybe knives in the dark were all in a day's work for the Secret Service.

His father looked him up and down. "Please, Jack. We leave for Paris in a week. Get your ass down to Poole's right now."

SAVILE ROW WAS A QUIET STREET lined with what looked like gentlemen's clubs. The tailors who ruled it didn't need to advertise; their clothes spoke for them. There was Gieves, whose original founders had dressed Victoria's court and military men for generations; Anderson & Sheppard, who specialized in Hollywood movie stars; Kilgour, French & Stanbury, who enjoyed a Mayfair patronage; and Henry Poole & Company. The latter was known for serving the diplomatic corps.

Benton, who greeted clients as they stepped into Poole's foyer, remembered Jack from his previous visit. He took his coat and hat without commenting on their New York labels and led him to a leather chair by a gas fire.

"May I offer you coffee, sir? Or perhaps a sherry?"

"What I'd really like is a fitting," Jack replied. "I've got an appointment for two o'clock, but I have to leave town Thursday morning and I'm worried my clothes won't be done."

"I'll inform Mr. Rathbone," Benton murmured.

Jack waited. He assessed his reflection in one of the tall mirrors. His cheeks were still too hollow and his skin too white. Except where it was bruised and green. Mother would not be pleased when she saw him in Rome. But he thought the DOCA was working. His nausea and diarrhea were diminishing. He'd written to Mayo to let George Taylor know.

"If you would come this way, Mr. Kennedy—"

He followed Benton into another room. More sumptuous carpet, glass-fronted cabinets displaying wool samples; Georgian side chairs. Rathbone, with a measuring tape and chalk.

He'd ordered three lounge suits at sixteen guineas apiece, an overcoat, a dinner jacket, morning dress, evening dress, court dress, and white tie at twenty guineas apiece. There were incidentals like shirts, ties, hats, and flannel trousers to add into the mix, but Jack had lost track of the total cost. Somewhere in the neighborhood of his Harvard tuition, he suspected.

Rathbone and his retinue led him to a fitting room and handed him a pieced version of one of his suits. He eased himself into it, trying not to strain the white tacking stitches. It hung baggily on his skeletal body, a pinstriped shroud.

"You're remarkably slender, sir, for one of your height," Rathbone commented. "A true whipcord frame."

"We Americans like a lean and hungry look."

The tailor's gaze drifted impassively over Jack's bruised cheekbone. "No doubt, sir."

Much turning and chalking on a dais before a three-way mirror. The waistband of his trousers sagged. He had no ass to speak of. Deft fingers pleated and pinned the wool. At least his shoulders would never shame him.

An hour into it, they reached the court knee breeches. The tailors worked quickly and efficiently, in the process outlining his crotch in a way that fascinated and repelled him. He glanced at his thighs in the skintight breeches, a Regency figure straight out of Cecil's *Young Melbourne*, and thought derisively of how his Harvard friends would laugh. Jack Kennedy as Lord Byron—if he could gain thirty pounds to pad his "whipcord" frame.

"Ah, Colonel Gubbins," Rathbone murmured, with a nod to a short, trim, military man who strode briskly into the fitting room. "I hope you won't mind sharing the mirror with Mr. Kennedy. He is somewhat pressed for time."

"Not at all," Gubbins said. "I came about that tweed jacket, Rathbone. Though I doubt I shall wear it soon; shouldn't wonder if we have snow before the week is out."

"Surely not in March," Rathbone replied.

Jack glanced at the stranger. Gubbins wore a red carnation in his buttonhole; a black homburg dangled from his hand. The perfect clubman, indistinguishable from a thousand others. Why did talk of snow bother Jack? *Schwartz's cable.* It sounded like Schwartz's goddamn cable.

Gubbins met his gaze in the three-sided mirror.

Jack's heart began to thud. "It is rare to have snow in March."

"But not entirely unknown in London." The colonel smiled. "What about that jacket, Rathbone?"

WHEN ALL THE POKING and prodding was done, Gubbins politely held Poole's door for Jack, who gestured him through it.

"Pleasure making your acquaintance, Mr. Kennedy," the colonel said, offering his card. "Do look me up sometime—I should be honored if you'd join me at my club."

"That'd be swell," Jack said.

Ten minutes later, he stepped into the Lyons Corner House in the Tottenham Court Road, and took a table upstairs, near a window. The place was full of clerks and secretaries wolfing olive-colored peas and gray meat. The air was stale with the smell of boiled cabbage and wet mackintoshes. His gorge rose and he swallowed convulsively. He drew the card from his pocket.

Colonel Colin M. Gubbins, Royal Artillery, it said. The address was a mews off St. James Street.

On the reverse, in a minute hand, was written *4 o'clock. Make sure you aren't followed.*

HE DROPPED DOWN INTO the Tube at Victoria Station and rode it to Greenwich, where he strolled through the halls of the Maritime Museum. It had opened only two years before and this was Jack's first visit. He was a passionate sailor and it was an enjoyable place to kill an hour. At a quarter past three he was back in the Underground. The station closest to Gubbins's was Green Park, but Jack rode on to Oxford Street, and began a leisurely saunter among the shop windows. He studied his reflection as he browsed; no scarred lip leered behind him, no camel's hair coat halted when he did. Perhaps the Spider's latest murder had made him cautious.

The address in St. James was a second-floor walk-up. A girl in dark red lipstick and a cashmere sweater answered his knock. He paused a moment to appreciate her curves.

"Good afternoon," she said coolly, and stepped back to admit him.

The room was filled with women's lingerie.

TWENTY-ONE. TRICKS OF THE TRADE

"I MUST BE IN the wrong place," Jack said.

"Depends what you're looking for." The girl was fair-haired and delicate, but for the crimson mouth. "A gift for a lady friend, perhaps?"

He wanted to ask if she knew Gubbins, but something stopped him. If he was *not to be followed* to the place, he shouldn't ask stupid questions either. He said tentatively, "I doubt you've got anything warm enough. The weather's getting nasty."

"It is rare to have snow in March," the girl observed.

"But not unknown in London."

She turned abruptly. "We keep all the flannels back here."

He followed her between displays of girdles and brassieres, garter belts and negligees. A mental picture of Diana flitted through his mind, in silk charmeuse, her sharp fall of black hair. He should have kissed her that last night on the *Queen Mary*, when he had the chance.

The girl knocked twice on a door, then once more. A buzzer sounded and he heard a bolt snap back.

"The door's wired?"

Her mouth quirked at the corners but she said nothing.

"Thank you, Matilda," Gubbins called.

The door closed behind him.

GUBBINS WAS IN his shirtsleeves.

"Ah, Jack," he said warmly, rising from a desk to extend his hand. "I value punctuality in a man. I may call you Jack?"

"Everybody does."

"—Unless they call you Ken."

Jack's brow rose slightly; only a few people in the world used that nickname. He'd met most of them at Choate when he was thirteen.

"Quite the black eye you're sporting, lad. I understand you acquired it at the 400?"

"Forgive me, Colonel—but who are you, and why the hell am I here?"

"Because you chose to come," Gubbins said crisply. "As for myself . . . I've given you my card. My name is quite genuine, I assure you."

Jack glanced around the room. It was windowless. But the fact of the wired door made him realize that other things could be wired as well. "Can we talk freely here?"

"Of course."

"And I should trust what you say because . . . ?"

"You received a cable from your president this morning. I received a similar one. Not, I may say, from Mr. Roosevelt. Both cables contained phrases intended for mutual identification."

"It is rare to have snow in March."

"Exactly. We call those *bona fides* in my current line of work."

"You're a spy?"

"No, no, dear chap—just an old artilleryman." Gubbins smiled bracingly. "I putter about on odd jobs for the Foreign Office now and again. I've been asked to help you with your thesis research."

"My *thesis*?" Jack repeated incredulously.

"Yes. Please—do sit down."

Jack took the only available chair.

"I understand you're traveling about Europe in the coming months. Interviewing sources for your . . . study."

"Well—"

"And given the uncertainties of travel, the general upheaval caused by the sudden incursion of Panzers, the potential for wholesale destruction of various electrical grids, and so forth— you will require a secure and portable means of communication." Gubbins paused. "One that is independent of embassies and code clerks."

The colonel reached under the desk and produced a black suitcase. He turned it neatly to face Jack, and snapped open the lid. Silk slips, panties, a corset or two. Beneath them was a tangle of electronics and wire. "Our latest model of shortwave wireless radio. With a Morse key."

Jack leaned closer and examined the thing. Knobs and dials, like the cockpit of a plane. Wires and tubes. All chockablock in a leather case eighteen inches by twenty-four.

He poked a tentative finger at a dial, then looked up at Gubbins. The colonel's brown eyes were exuberant. A Santa who'd just dropped a splendid toy in Jack's stocking.

"Ever had a go?"

Jack shook his head.

"I'll show you, of course. This kit only has a range of five hundred miles, so the transmission must be relayed—but don't worry about that; our network will take care of it."

"Your network?"

"Our shortwave relay network. Your man Schwartz is familiar with it. Are you acquainted, by any chance, with General Donovan? Wild Bill?"

"I've heard the name. You want me to encode and transmit my own messages?"

"No, no, dear chap," Gubbins protested. "*I* don't come into it at all. It's your president who's requested this back channel. He broached the matter to my superiors. And they contacted *me*. Back channels being rather a specialty of mine."

"Got it." Jack eyed the colonel dubiously. *Was* he a colonel? Was he even British? Handing Jack a shortwave radio and the code to use it would be a brilliant way for the Germans to capture everything he sent home. But there was the fact of the bona fides . . . and no harm in prolonging the conversation. Provided, of course, that he could exit the room quickly. His glance strayed to the door Matilda had pulled closed behind her. It probably locked automatically. . . .

"Nothing could be easier or more efficient," Gubbins was saying with pride. "This little chap runs on batteries. You charge them with a simple lead from your car. Only *think* how useful, in the wilds of Poland or Latvia!"

"With my kind of talent, I'll fry us both."

"Not once I'm done with you," Gubbins said cheerfully, and clapped Jack on the back. Jack felt the blow through his entire frame. "Let's get started, shall we?"

He began to shove his desk toward the rear wall. Jack took the other end and helped him. Set into the floorboards beneath the desk was a trapdoor.

Gubbins lifted it. A set of stairs led down into darkness.

———

THE COLONEL'S WORKSHOP held a number of secrets.

There was a kind of paper he'd made from rice instead of cotton, so his men could eat their instructions; and invisible ink. The words appeared when heat was applied.

"Useful if you'd like to jot down the odd note for Hopper," Gubbins observed, as he presented Jack with one of his pens. "And you can use your own urine, in a pinch."

"You know Professor Hopper?"

"Met him in the last war," Gubbins said briefly. "First-rate man. You're fortunate to work with him. I should assume anything you send him, Jack, no matter how academic, will be intercepted by the enemy and read. He's being watched."

"Because of *me*?"

"Because of your president's interest in you. And Hopper's supervision of your . . . thesis. Both facts are known—the world's really a very small place, my dear fellow. And at the moment, ridiculously crowded with *Germans*. Try to bear that in mind."

He proceeded to teach Jack the rudiments of frequencies, Morse code, call signs, and five-letter group transmission. Jack found that the shortwave radio and its Morse key demanded intense concentration on his part. His face was beaded with sweat after the first half hour and after the second, his hands shook; but Gubbins pronounced him *good enough to go on with*.

"Send your first burst tonight, to let your contact know you're up to speed. Don't forget the call sign, to signal you're live, and repeat the transmission every fifteen minutes until it's acknowledged. Given the distance your message must travel, acknowledgment will take a while. In the field, you'll want to move about a bit between repeats—confuses the enemy and keeps them off your back. Tonight, however, I should use the roof of number 14. The house runs to six storeys, I believe?"

"Yes, but . . ." He had no idea how to get out on the roof.

"And this," Gubbins added, "is the poem you're to use as your encoding key."

"The *what*?"

"Old college cheer. Mr. Roosevelt chose it."

He was handing Jack a sheet of paper with "Ten Thousand Men of Harvard" typed on it. Including the dog-Latin first verse. Jack skimmed the words, a familiar tune humming through his mind.

> *Illegitimum Non Carborundum;*
> *Domine salvum fac.*
> *Illegitimum Non Carborundum;*
> *Domine salvum fac.*
> *Gaudeamus igitur!*
> *Veritas non sequitur?*
> *Illegitimum non Carborundum—ipso facto!*
> *Ten thousand men of Harvard want vict'ry today,*
> *For they know that o'er old Eli*
> *Fair Harvard holds sway.*
> *So then we'll conquer all old Eli's men*
> *And when the game ends, we'll sing again:*
> *Ten thousand men of Harvard gained vict'ry today!*

"I have no idea what to do with this."

Gubbins frowned. "It's a simple substitution cipher, Jack. Choose a phrase from the song, write it down, and then string your message beneath. Substitute the song's letters for yours, and you've got a *code*. You must number each word in the song *first*, of course. Before transmitting the encoded message, you must send the *numbers* that correspond to your cipher words. Understand? Your receiver will have numbered his copy of this charming little ditty as well, and will know that 3, 7, 12, 18, and 24 are the words he must use to *decode* your transmission."

"You've thought of everything."

"I try," Gubbins said modestly. "Sticking one's head in the sand won't stop Hitler. I've written a few manuals, you know—*not* in general circulation. If you'd care to have them."

"I would," Jack said. "Very much."

"You won't need *The Housewife's ABC of Home-Made Explosives*, I imagine," Gubbins mused, "but *The Art of Guerrilla Warfare* should be dead useful."

"Give me the *ABC*, too."

"Really?" He shrugged. "Best have *The Partisan Leader's Handbook* as well. We expect that one to do very well in Poland in the coming months. Very well indeed."

Jack managed to fit the pamphlets into the breast pocket of his suit jacket. His fingers grazed a torn edge of newspaper; the article he'd found in the *Times* that morning.

It seemed as good a way of testing Gubbins's bona fides as any.

"Would you do something for me?" he asked.

"Something *else*, you mean?" Gubbins asked drily.

Jack handed him the article. "The man who knifed this girl is a German agent. Hans Obst, alias the Spider. That mark he cut into her skin—it's not a swastika. It's his calling card. Scotland Yard should be told."

Gubbins raised shrewd brown eyes to Jack's own. "I won't ask how you know. *Right*. I'll pass the word to my friends at the Yard."

HE KNEW THEY MUST BE LOOKING for him, but he lingered in Wapping anyway, a blunt shadow in the alleys running down to the river. He felt at home among the gasworks and power generators and heaps of coal slag, the chandlers' shops and whorehouses and pubs. The smell of blood was lost in the reek of the East End.

He systematically rifled the dead merchant seaman's pockets, his mind focused as it had not been for days. The pain he'd inflicted on the fragile child last night had eased his need, but he awoke to the knowledge that he'd risked too much. He had to get out of London. For that, he needed a passport.

A seaman was the obvious mark. Not a navy man, because sailors were accountable to their commanders and pursued when missed. What he wanted was an ordinary vagabond, a rat of the world's shipping. Somebody who slipped into the Port of London one day, the Port of Marseille the next. Who was cursed and forgotten when he failed to report for duty.

He wandered the streets near the river with his hat pulled down and his hands shoved into his pockets, fingering his knife. It was after eleven before a squat Pole, hair the color of straw, reeled drunkenly into the alley where the Spider waited.

He nearly laughed aloud now as he fingered his new papers.

Jan Komorowski from Danzig. Heydrich himself might have sent this tarred angel to deliver his man from evil.

He sliced a vicious spider into an exposed pectoral, then cleaned his knife on the corpse's trousers. In the act of turning away, he stopped suddenly and considered the Pole's clothes. No merchant seaman wore camel's hair.

He shrugged himself into the dark wool peacoat, which smelled not unpleasantly of tobacco, and closed the wide lapels around his throat. He glanced up at the starless sky. A ship's horn blasted in the distance. The Spider began to move.

HE TRUSTED HIS LEGS MORE than trains or automobiles. His legs would never lose an engine or run out of petrol miles before the border. He'd walked the breadth of Germany in his day and the distance from Wapping to Westminster was nothing to it. He was carrying only the clothes on his back and some cash in his pocket. He was *Jan Komorowski of Gdańsk.* He would make his way to Dover and cross the Channel in the morning—just another Pole headed in the wrong direction.

The white face of a clock tower rose above him, the peaked mass of Parliament below. He stood on Westminster Bridge and watched as Charles Atwater's passport and papers floated down the Thames.

The clock hands met at twelve. Big Ben boomed. He should have left London hours ago, but his desire for the girl with the auburn hair was suddenly overwhelming. He'd tried to slake it on the one he'd snatched from the shadows last night, but it hadn't worked. He still saw the Kennedy girl in his mind whenever he closed his eyes.

He reached for his knife, stroking the shaft. Then he walked deliberately away from the train he should be taking, and toward Prince's Gate.

THERE WERE LIGHTS burning in the house's third-floor windows.

He stood on the lawn sloping down from the back terrace. Behind, Kensington Road and Hyde Park. In front, a row of French doors. He walked noiselessly toward a pair of these and paused, his eyes straining in the darkness. A house with so many servants would be careless about bolting every door. Careless, too, about investigating noises—there were too many children, too many comings and goings, for anybody to care.

He tried the handles of three pairs of doors before one gave beneath his hand. He eased it open, felt the panel push back against heavy drapes, and slid through the space into a ground-floor reception room.

The house was still as a tomb.

His heart raced. That pale perfection of a girl was somewhere above, in her dressing gown, maybe, as she brushed her hair before a mirror. Or she might be sprawled in bed with a book, breasts softly outlined in silk—

He crept noiselessly around the dim furniture, just visible in the glow from the French windows, to the darker passage beyond.

"WHERE ARE YOU GOING, Jack? Can I come?"

Teddy's voice piped through the silence of the upper hall. Jack jumped, nearly dropping the suitcase he carried.

"Jesus, Brat," he said. "You scared the hell out of me. What're you doing up?"

Teddy, sturdy as a caboose, was standing before the elevator door in his bathrobe and slippers. His hair was tousled and his full cheeks flushed. "I'm hungry," he said.

"You're always hungry." Bobby emerged, scowling at the light, from the room the boys shared. There were basset hounds with red bows all over his flannel pajamas.

"That's because I'm *growing*," Teddy protested.

"Sideways, maybe. Get back in bed."

"I want some milk. And some of Banksie's custard."

"Okay by me," Jack said, eyeing them both. "Can't sleep if you're hungry."

"Mother wouldn't like it," Bobby said.

"Mother's not here."

"What's the suitcase for?" Bobby's attention was suddenly focused; he stepped tentatively forward. "You running away?"

"To Rome," Jack said soothingly. "Remember? Dad and I leave before you do. I'm packing now."

He was not about to admit to Gubbins's radio transmitter. Or tell them he'd just come down from the roof. It had been chilly work and his fingers were numb, but he'd managed to find the frequency Gubbins had specified and send something like an encoded transmission. He'd been agonizingly slow. An hour of work with the Harvard fight song, for a few bursts of Morse code. *Special to Schwartz. Have received radio and cipher. Will cultivate WD as instructed.*

He'd waited twenty minutes in the freezing attic for an answering burst, but none had come. He'd try again tomorrow.

The elevator door opened and Teddy skedaddled into it, intent on the kitchen and food. With a shriek of protest about raids on the pantry, Bobby followed. Jack waited until the elevator door closed before heading for his room. He was faintly exhilarated at having dodged the kids' inspection. Nazis had nothing on Bobby.

THE SPIDER STOOD MOTIONLESS in the shadows of the staircase as the conversation between brothers played out above. *Children. Custard.* He could hear the elevator car descending and for an instant he considered waiting for it to open, the boys emerging one after the other straight onto his knife. Then a key was thrust into the front door's lock and his head turned swiftly. The sound carried across the octagonal marble foyer; someone had come home.

He raced past the elevator door just as the car bumped to the ground floor. He skittered down a back passage, the sound of his running feet masked by the iron rattle of the elevator sliding open, the fluster of arrival in the front hall. A girl's rich laugh drifted to his ears. "Oh, come *on*, kid. It's not like I'm moving in with Mussolini. I'll see you when I get back from Rome."

It was she. He would know that voice anywhere. But he could not have her tonight—she was too exposed, he would not risk it.

He slipped through the salon's French doors, which gave out onto the north-facing terrace, and ran pell-mell down the lawn to the Kensington Road.

Rome, she had said. It was as good a destination as any.

FROM HIS THIRD-FLOOR bedroom window, Jack glimpsed the dark shape of a man pelting from the terrace across the lawns. He did not need to ask himself what sort of predator fled the dreaming ranks of Prince's Gate in the dead of night; he could trace the

Spider's outline in his sleep. His eyes strained to follow the figure until the deep black of Hyde Park swallowed it whole. Impossible to give chase at night. He slammed his window frame with his fists in frustration. *The killer had entered his house. Where his family slept.* This could not be allowed to continue. He sprinted down the hallway to the telephone closet, and put through a transatlantic call to the United States.

He'd memorized the number he'd scrawled on his shirt cuff in the Waldorf-Astoria weeks ago. It should be close to dinnertime in Washington.

"ROOSEVELT HERE." The connection was very bad, with a constant swooshing sound as of wind or water, the sea washing over the transatlantic cable. But the President's voice was high and thin and clear, familiar from a hundred fireside chats.

"Mr. President. It's Jack Kennedy, in London."

"Jack! How are you, my boy? I received your message. Well done."

So it was Roosevelt, not Schwartz, who was decoding his bursts. There was no one between the President and himself. The President and *his man in Europe.* Jack's pulse accelerated. "I'm sorry to disturb you, Mr. President—"

"Not at all. I'm free as a bird."

"—but I thought you should know—or Mr. Schwartz should know—that the White Spider broke into our house tonight."

"The Spider?" Roosevelt repeated.

Was that complete ignorance, or mild concern? Did he think Jack was babbling nonsense?

"He's a very dangerous fellow, Jack," Roosevelt said.

A wave of relief washed over him. "You know."

"Indeed. He's got two victims this side of the Atlantic to his credit, and I assume he's killed a few more on yours. He cuts a spider into the corpse. But you know this. He crossed with you, didn't he, on the *Queen Mary*?"

"Yes, sir."

"Sam and I have been talking to Ed Hoover. He thinks the Germans are rolling up that network we discussed. The girl who was killed in New York a few weeks ago, at the Stork Club—"

"Not Katie O'Donohue?" Jack said, his bowel twisting. *Little Katie. I knew her people in Boston.*

There was an infinitesimal pause on Roosevelt's end. "You're familiar with the name?"

"She was murdered the night we met on the Pullman," he said quickly. "I saw the papers the next morning. But I didn't know the Spider killed her." *Shit.*

"Ah." Roosevelt digested this. If he thought it strange that Jack should remember a name from a minor article read nearly a month ago, he refrained from questioning it. Roosevelt ignored tangents, Jack realized; he kept to the facts. It was probably the only way to organize the flood of information constantly sweeping over him.

"We think it's possible this man is after *you*," he continued. "That he knows what I've asked you to do, and that he means to stop it. You must be very careful."

"I realize that, sir." He'd been lying to his father for weeks, saying nothing about his job for Roosevelt, and now he was lying to the President of the United States, too—keeping Dad and the hatcheck girl to himself, the fact that his father had gotten Katie the job at the Stork Club. She was dead and the Spider had killed her, which could look pretty lousy for Dad if the FBI found out. And they were bound to find out.

"Do you think," he said, clutching wildly at straws, "that

under the circumstances of the break-in tonight, I ought to tell my father?"

There was a pause. "About the Spider?"

"Yes, sir."

"Jack . . . do you consider your father . . . a man of considerable courage?"

He took a deep breath to calm himself. Joe Kennedy was a born gambler. His risks and his instincts usually paid off. But was he *brave*, exactly? He'd refused to enlist for the last war, in 1917. If told that a Nazi assassin was prowling around, he'd mount full-time guards or move his kids into a Mayfair hotel. Joe was no warrior, no Bruce Hopper scanning the sky in the hope of enemy fire.

"Not really," he said.

"Then let's keep this between ourselves. We don't want to alarm your dad—his work's too important right now. We need Joe firing on all Chamberlain's cylinders."

"Yes, sir," Jack muttered. So he would go on lying to them both. "What do you want me to do?"

"Research your thesis," Roosevelt said. "If you leave London—perhaps the Spider will follow. And then you won't have to worry anymore about putting your family in danger."

Jack thought of Kick—of Teddy and Bobby—with rising hope. If he could lure the Spider to Europe . . .

"And Jack?" The distant voice was speaking again, very faintly in his ear. "A suggestion from Professor Bruce Hopper. We spoke the other day."

"How is he, sir?"

"Quite well. But he thinks you ought to buy a gun."

"A gun?" Jack repeated, startled.

"And learn how to use it," Roosevelt said.

Part Two

SPRING

TWENTY-THREE. CLEMENCY

"JA-A-ACK," Rose called in her grating Boston drawl. "You've *arrived*, then. *Darling*."

She was leaning in the doorway of his hotel room in Rome, arms crossed protectively over her chest.

"Mother," he said. "You look well. How was Egypt?"

"*Thrilling*. Nothing compared to Jerusalem, of course—the site of Our Lord's Passion. You simply *must* get there one day."

Never mind that it had been nine months since they'd met; Rose kept a safe distance. Not for her the joyous embrace, the kisses showered on her boy. When he'd been dying that one winter at Choate, possibly from leukemia but probably from the Mystery Disease, it was the headmaster's wife who had played gin rummy and gramophone records by his hospital bed in New Haven; the headmaster's wife who summoned a Catholic priest in the middle of the night. Mrs. St. John had written letter after letter to Rose, detailing Jack's illness—how worried all his friends were and how he was remembered daily at morning prayers, even though he was Catholic and Choate emphatically was not.

Rose's secretary replied to the letters on engraved stationery: Mrs. Kennedy was too busy with the younger children to leave

Palm Beach. She was sure that with God's help and the ministra-
tions of the doctors, Jack would pull through.

Jack knew his deteriorating body was a reproach to Rose, a
public suggestion she'd failed as a mother. Failure was a judgment from God, and judgment terrified her. She firmly ignored
Jack's disease and Rosie's vacuity and Eunice's nightmares and
Bobby's loneliness. As long as her children looked presentable
and didn't embarrass their parents in public, Rose had nothing
more to ask. The same rule applied to her husband.

She surveyed Jack critically now. "You're still too thin. You
were supposed to *gain* weight this winter, Jack. Get *stronger*.
Have you been eating your ice cream?"

"I have," he said hurriedly. "I just had a rough crossing,
and—well . . . it was hard to keep much down." Sweet Jesus, he
was glad his bruises had finally faded. She'd have suggested he
borrow Kick's face powder, probably, to disguise them.

"Your clothes fit, thank heaven," she persisted. "Poole's, I
suppose?"

"I'm on a last-name basis with the staff."

His joke didn't work with his mother. His humor never did.
"That won't do," she said swiftly. "It's bad form to hobnob with
the serving class. You know that. The British already despise us
because we're Catholics." Not to mention American Irish.

Jack tried to change the subject. "I like what you've done
with your hair," he offered. "Very Wallis Simpson."

"It's the *Duchess of Windsor*, Jack," she said impatiently. "And
don't *speak* of that dreadful woman again. She's done more damage to Americans—a divorcée, forcing the King to abdicate! It's
all I can do to hold up my head when she's mentioned."

Although Rose held it up fast enough, Jack thought, when
the Duchess came to her summer parties in Cannes.

"Dinner's at eight," Rose called over her shoulder as she left. "*Evening* dress for the dining room, of course."

"And morning dress in the morning," he muttered as she swung down the hall. Just for once he'd like to show up in his underwear and shock Rose silly.

He glanced at his watch. Time to get out while he still could.

THE HOTEL D'INGHILTERRA sat in the Via Bocca di Leoni, a few blocks from the Piazza di Spagna. Jack had some idea of strolling along the Via dei Condotti in search of a quick drink, something to calm his rage at being treated like a schoolboy. As he approached the square he glanced up the Spanish Steps: the Swiss-run Hotel Hassler was at the top of them, and half the dignitaries who'd descended for the Pope's coronation were staying there. The other half were in Jack's hotel. The steps were a tourist magnet, a wide sweep of stone that twisted and turned up the hillside. It seemed to Jack as though half the city—regular Romans, intimate knots of lovers, the old and young—had found a seat there, sprawled in the kind of carefree abandon his mother deplored. He might as well sit down on the steps, too, and gaze out over Rome.

He picked his way through the crowd, listening to the lilting Italian voices. It was a chewable language; it rolled like wine on the tongue. After dinner, when he'd shaken off his parents, he'd grab Kick and come down here.

He reached the first landing, then the next. The climb was exhilarating after the long ride in the train from Paris, far preferable to sitting, so he kept going, his gaze fixed on the top of the Spanish Steps and the haze of green from the Villa Borghese beyond them.

Then he saw Diana.

She was leaving the Hotel Hassler. He knew that blunt sweep of black hair and porcelain chin beneath the upturned hat. Kick had taught him enough about clothes to recognize Chanel, and he guessed Diana's had been acquired quite recently in the Place Vendôme. He stopped dead on the paving and stared, trying to convince himself that she was any other woman. A beautiful Italian, intent on a glass of prosecco at Antico Caffè Greco. But he failed; there was only one Diana.

He had looked for her everywhere two days ago on the streets of Paris while his father wasted an afternoon with Bill Bullitt. There were women enough to rivet Jack's eye—blondes in stilettos and pencil skirts, girls with perfect complexions and slanting black eyeliner, red mouths begging to be kissed. He'd bought a champagne cocktail for a great pair of fishnet stockings in the Ritz Bar, but his French had always been lousy and the girl spoke not a word of English. Diana was not in the Ritz Bar. She was in Rome. He hadn't expected that.

A black-shirted Fascist was standing with a gun not ten yards away, a self-appointed guard of public decency. Such thugs were everywhere in Mussolini's capital, but Jack had seen their kind before. Besides, he carried a diplomatic passport.

He continued climbing, intending to intercept Diana, but halfway down the top section of the Spanish Steps she turned fluidly into the archway of a neighboring building, and vanished.

He took the risers two at a time, dodging tourists and loiterers lounging on the stone. There was a shout behind him. The Blackshirt with the gun. Apparently it was no longer permitted to run in public; that kind of haste suggested violence, fear, the vulnerabilities Fascisti tracked like bloodhounds. Jack ignored the shout and ducked into the passage Diana had taken. It was an ancient little alleyway of the kind that riddled Rome, called a *vicolo*, the buildings on either side leaning toward one another from age and inclination. He could just glimpse her hat ahead, descending another flight of stairs.

A clatter of feet behind him; the man with the gun. Jack spun around to face him. He could whip his passport from his pocket but the Blackshirt was just as likely to keep it as not, and then he'd be at a standstill; he was supposed to have left it at the hotel's front desk, and Dad would be furious if he lost it. Jack let the guy pound up to him, a belligerent look on his face and a torrent of Italian on his lips. A short man, but solid, in his midthirties. A cut to the chin might knock him backward, but it wouldn't deck him. Jack went for his stomach, a powerful Harvard right the Blackshirt never saw coming. He doubled over with a *whoof*, completely winded, and dropped to his knees. Shaking his fingers painfully, Jack took off.

The stairs at the far end of the alley curved left and ended in another narrow passage. He skittered past two people, craning for a glimpse of Diana—and saw her step into a taxi. He sprinted the last hundred yards and emerged onto the Via dei Condotti, hand raised and eyes searching for another cab.

SHE LED HIM SOUTH AND WEST at the racketing pace of Rome, which suited Jack fine. He hung on to the edge of the open car window, his progress heralded by a snarl of horns and shouted curses, exhilaration flooding his veins, and urged the cabbie repeatedly in his lousy French not to lose her. They roared through the Piazza Navona and sailed by the Palazzo Farnese. The Tiber was very close, and St. Peter's dome loomed across the river.

Diana's car dove left into Via Giulia and pulled up before an ancient building—one of many—in the quiet street. The only entrance was through massive double doors, barred to the world, with a smaller door cut into them.

"*Arrêtez,*" Jack said, and tossed the cabbie some lire. The clear note of a bell split the evening air.

Diana stood before the entrance, waiting. She looked remarkably composed, her gloved hands folded on the strap of her purse. It was she who'd rung the bell; it was still vibrating in its bracket. Jack hesitated, just looking at her. The Chanel was demure and in excellent taste but her long legs betrayed her—there was a dancer, a siren, an intoxicating power beneath that black and petal-pink sheath.

She was still the most beautiful thing he had ever seen and yes, the word was an insult when applied to Diana. Jack had grabbed *things* all his life; he used and discarded them as soon as he was bored. He wanted Diana now as he'd never wanted any woman before, but he knew the danger of boredom, and he feared the eventual discarding. She had Willi and sleek Denys and her house in Mayfair. She did not give a damn about him anyway.

The smaller door cut into the massive gates opened.

A nun stepped out, hand extended.

To Jack's shock, Diana bowed her head like a supplicant.

The nun drew her inside. The door closed.

He left the cab and walked slowly toward the barred gates. A small bronze plaque was mounted on the wall, just below the bell, which still trembled from the pleasure of Diana's touch.

Piccole Sorelle di Clemenza, it read.

The Little Sisters of Clemency.

TWENTY-FOUR. THE CLOISTER

IT WAS NEARLY AN HOUR before Diana emerged from the convent, and Jack had burned through three cigarettes as he strolled the length of the Via Giulia, trying to look like an indolent tourist interested in ancient buildings. He was a good two hundred yards away when the small door in the gate creaked open, and the slim figure slipped through it.

She led him on foot to the Campo dei Fiori, a dusty little square given over to the flower sellers and a single café where nobody fashionable drank. When the waiter had brought her Campari and Diana had drawn her cigarette case from her handbag, Jack sauntered over. He grabbed a chair and straddled it backward, ever the casual American.

"Hello, gorgeous."

She'd ignored his approaching steps as only Diana could, but at his words she glanced up and treated him to her thousand-mile stare. The same one she'd used on the Promenade Deck as the *Queen Mary* pulled out of New York. Then the penny dropped.

"Jack!"

"Mrs. Playfair." He grinned and saluted. "Fancy meeting you in Rome. But I hear all roads lead to it."

"You're here for the Pope's do, I suppose."

"With family in tow. Mother, Father, and assorted brats whose names I can never keep straight. The Kennedys have nailed down an entire floor of the Hotel d'Inghilterra. How about you?"

"I'm at the Hassler."

"I didn't think you were Catholic."

"Good Lord—I'm *not*. I've no intention of fighting the Vatican crowds tomorrow." She took a sip of her drink, buying time. "I'm here to see an old friend. We were at school together, ages ago—only I had the stupidity to get married, while she entered a convent."

Oh, Diana, he thought, *you're goddamn brilliant.* Admit the convent and supply a plausible reason for being there. Just in case he'd seen her in the Via Giulia.

"Now, what could you two ever have had in common?" he wondered. "A taste for priests?"

"For stealing cold pudding from the school larder in the dead of night," she said. "We were both nearly given the boot more times than I like to count. But I daresay the Head needed our school fees. And some sort of piety must have rubbed off— witness Daisy's pending sainthood. I drop over from time to time in the hope she'll save my soul. If there's anything left to save."

She'd meant it as a joke. Yet Jack heard unintentional bitterness.

"Wind whistling over your grave, Diana?"

"Of course not." She forced a smile. "It's just that life is so *bloody*, isn't it? Particularly now."

"Talking to a guy you thought you ditched ten days ago?"

She smiled. "*Jack.* I meant all these . . . men in black shirts. Guns at every corner. The sheer ugliness of it all."

"I thought you liked Fascists."

She flipped open her gold case and chose a cigarette. He fished in his pocket for his lighter. It was the replaying of a familiar scene; only this time he knew her better. Her face was deliberately blank; she hadn't liked his barb. He remembered Dobler saying something about Diana and fascism and *cover*. Was she a spy? For us—or them?

He rocked his chair forward, excitement surging in him. He wanted to take Diana's helmet of hair in his hands and kiss her crimson mouth.

"Fascists dress so much better than Communists," she offered indifferently.

"Except when they dress in black."

She expelled a cloud of smoke over his shoulder. "I understand the American ambassador in London is rather keen on them as well."

Jack went still. When he spoke he tried to match Diana's tone, but there was an edge to it. "People have been lying about my father for most of his life. He's used to it."

"Are you?"

No. "I happen to know the truth."

"Which is?"

"That Dad hates war. If talking to the Nazis will buy us some time and some peace—then I guess he's buying."

"Yes, I rather imagine that's how your typical American would see it," she said thoughtfully. "Hitler as just another nuisance to be bought off. Is that why Mr. Kennedy lunched with Wohlthat in Paris?"

Jack frowned. "Who?"

"Helmuth Wohlthat. Göring's private banker. I saw him with your father at Tour d'Argent two days ago."

Göring's private banker. Jack's mind turned like a cornered dog. "Dad lunched with Bullitt at the embassy."

"Then he ate twice."

A meeting with Göring's banker? *One hundred and fifty million dollars . . . we know Göring proposed it and Hitler approved it. . . .*

"I wonder what Wohlthat wanted, Jack. Stock tips?" Diana smiled lazily. "It's unfortunate your father's such a fool. Given how much of Neville Chamberlain's ear he's got. Between the two of them, they'll *buy* our way right into Hitler's hands."

She was being consciously cold. Insulting, even. Because he'd seen her in the Via Giulia? Or because she couldn't be bothered with a raw and boring kid?

He stood up and righted his chair.

"Sorry I bothered you, Mrs. Playfair. Give my regards to the Little Sisters of Clemency."

Her cigarette was beautifully balanced in her gloved hand, her dark eyes fixed on his face. But at his final words her fingers trembled a little, and the ash fell into her Campari.

FOR JACK THE CORONATION BEGAN at seven-thirty the next morning, with a convoy of cars flying American and papal flags. Seventy thousand people filled the vast St. Peter's Basilica; Count Ciano, Mussolini's son-in-law, had reserved places for Joe and Rose directly in front of the altar. Joe grabbed an extra eight seats for his kids. Pushy and ungracious. Typical of an *americano*.

Jack was bleary-eyed from a late night wandering the streets with Kick. He'd been in raging high spirits, despite the way Diana had treated him. After he'd had a few drinks with Kick at the Antico Caffè Greco, he was ready to breach the Hassler itself—push his way up to Diana's room and thrust her lovely shoulders against the wall. Force her to tell him the truth. Explain her insinuations. Confess where her loyalties lay and what Dobler meant to her. Why she'd married that sleek Whitehall Denys.

"I think the Chianti went to your head," Kick muttered as she steered him toward the d'Inghilterra. "It's not as hard as you think, kid."

"It's swell. I'm grand! I'm Black Jack Ken." He shook off Kick's hand and lurched determinedly toward the Piazza di Spagna. He would hurtle up the Spanish Steps and dive off the top. Launch himself spectacularly over Roma. Diana would see from her hotel window and be astounded by his strength and vigor. Except that he tripped on an uneven stone and his feet went out from under him. He fell hard, spread-eagled on the steps.

"Jack!"

Kick grasped his shoulders and rolled him over. Her tousled curls hovered above his face; the globe of a streetlamp loomed beyond. A man loitered near it, barrel-chested in the light. Jack sat up so abruptly his forehead bumped Kick's.

"Hey!" she snorted, her hands on his chest. "Slow down, cowboy. You've done enough damage tonight. I'm going to get you home."

"Home's a suitcase." He struggled to his feet, swaying slightly. Tried to focus his swimming vision on the figure beneath the streetlamp. But the Spider—*was* it the Spider?—was gone.

"I'm drunk as a skunk." He said each word distinctly, to prove he could.

"Nah. You had skunks beat a couple of hours ago."

"It's because I'm in love with her." He swooned toward Kick.

"And she thinks I'm a *bug*. Terrible thing, love. Rips the heart right out of your body."

"She's not worth it, Jack."

He shook his head miserably. "Not worthy of *her*."

"Sure you are, kid. Worth a hundred, remember? Said so yourself."

Kick wrapped her arm around his waist. They wove slowly back toward the Hotel d'Inghilterra.

The next morning, sober, Jack realized they'd been talking about completely different women.

HIS LEFT LEG THROBBED NOW, painful from the cut in his calf where he'd thrust a DOCA pill. He was using one every two days, which George Taylor had estimated was about right, but something—the food or the water or something in Rome—wasn't agreeing with him. It was a sin to eat before mass so at least his stomach was empty; he'd snuck a little black coffee just to slap himself awake. He was sweating in his morning suit, despite a wave of chills running over his frame. He closed his eyes and gave himself up to the strains of the Sistine Choir.

The Latin mass was endless.

When the kneeling and the standing and the anointing were over, when the thousands upon thousands had shuffled down the aisle to take the Bread of Christ from the ranks of cardinals, when the new pope had been proclaimed again—Pius XII—Jack emerged into the misty gray sunlight of a Roman noon in March with the musk of incense clouding his nostrils. He came to a dead halt as the multitude of people poured past him down the steps—a flood of bodies and smells and heat and oppressive contact, coats and hats brushing his sleeve, crushing his shoulder. *He hated to be touched.* The bodies swam before his eyes. He shuddered convulsively.

"You okay, kid?"

Kick wore a black lace veil over her hair; hung over and without makeup, she looked sorrowful and mourning. As though the Pope had died instead of coming into his Kingdom.

"Ja-a-ack," his mother said. She was dressed in black, too, only her veil had a diamond tiara underneath. She'd adopted tiaras lately. The ambassador's wife as Princess Rose.

He bent over and was wretchedly sick.

"JACK'S LITTLE TUMMY," as Rose called it, turned out to be a godsend. He was allowed to skip the official celebratory five-course meal hosted by the American embassy and lie down in his room, with a cup of bouillon on a tray. His morning suit was taken away to be cleaned and pressed. He wore an open-necked shirt and a pullover sweater with his flannels, the most comfortable clothes he'd had on in a week.

He took a spoonful of bouillon. It had cooled, and tasted of kitchens and metal. It smelled vaguely like semen. He tossed back half a glass of water, wondering which ancient sewer it came from. *Wohlthat. Göring's banker. Hitler just another nuisance he could buy off.* His stomach twisted again.

It was time, Jack decided, to see the Little Sisters of Clemency for himself.

HE PREPARED WHAT HE'D SAY, all the way to the Via Giulia. He'd send in his card to Sister Mary Joseph—the name Willi Dobler had given him. If he was lucky, the name was real. If he was lucky, the order wasn't a cloistered one and they would let a man through the door. Jack wasn't feeling particularly lucky today, but anything was better than drinking semen-scented soup in his hotel room.

When his cab pulled up before the convent entrance, he saw that the double doors were already thrown wide open to the street.

He paid the cabbie and walked through the gates. The sound of wailing met his ears.

TWENTY-FIVE. A GIRL NAMED DAISY

THE GATEWAY WAS WIDE ENOUGH to admit a truck. In the past it had probably allowed the passage of carts full of supplies, or a dignitary's coach. Today it had opened for the morgue.

Jack stopped short in the convent courtyard as he registered the black van. It had slewed crazily sideways before the arched colonnade that ran around the building. Like the courtyard, it was empty. But the wailing he'd heard grew steadily louder, and with it came the clatter of poorly fitted shoes. A moment later a figure in a long black habit hurtled down a flight of stairs opposite Jack and turned abruptly to her right, running full tilt toward a door at the far end of the colonnade. Her fists were pressed to her red cheeks and her mouth was open in a continuous scream.

The sound of her wooden heels echoed around the stone walls; then the nun pushed wildly through the door and disappeared into darkness.

Jack drew a deep breath and walked past the black van, toward the stairs.

As he mounted the last step, his foot slid out unexpectedly. He clutched for a banister, saved himself from falling, and glanced down.

He was standing in a pool of blood.

———————

THE WOMAN WHOSE LIFE had dripped away on the paving of the corridor was rather young, he thought. She lay as she fell, on her back, her arms flung wide, as if in supplication. Her eyes stared upward, searching for God. Her fingers were slightly cupped, her lips parted. Her habit had been cut to the waist, and her left breast glowed like a perfect pearl against the black serge. Perfect but for the crouching spider.

Blood crusted blackly along the lines sketched by the knife.

Jack's vision blurred and he felt his throat convulse; he turned away, forcing himself to master the sickness. A knot of people—more nuns, the men from the black van—were moving toward him, their voices raised in rapid and questioning Italian. He could not understand a word of it. Somebody grasped his arm and started to pull him back down the stairs but he managed to say something. The only Italian phrase he knew.

"Parla inglese?"

"I speak English." One of the nuns—no longer young, with snapping black eyes and a hooked nose—stepped forward and stared at him. "You are not welcome. It is not convenient."

"Sister Mary Joseph," he said, shaking the whirling haze out of his eyes. "I must speak to Sister Mary Joseph."

Her mouth tightened. *"Idiota!* You see what has happened—the . . . the *sacrilege . . ."*

It was the same word in both languages.

Jack took a step forward and stared down at the dead girl. A Little Sister of Clemency. The Spider had shown her none.

"What do you want with her?"

Another voice this time; a second nun came forward. Older, more stately, with a simple silver cross at her neck.

"You're Sister Mary Joseph?"

"I am the Mother Superior." Her eyes strayed to the body at their feet. "*This* is Sister Mary Joseph."

Of course it was.

Jack scrounged in his jacket for his card, the one with the London embassy's address, and handed it to the Mother Superior. "I'd like to talk to you. I think I know who killed her."

The nun held his card at arm's length, the better to read the fine writing. "Ken-ne-dy," she said. "You will be some relation of the famous ambassador from America?"

"His son."

"A good Catholic boy." She nodded once to convince herself. As if she really knew. "I will see you. But first, I think, you must talk to *la polizia*."

THE POLICE WERE TWO SMALL dark men in well-tailored uniforms. Neither of them spoke English. Jack's grudging translator—whose name, he learned, was Sister Immaculata—agreed with a sigh to lend her services while the men from the morgue took the corpse away.

She led them back downstairs to the courtyard, where they sat on one of the hard wooden benches that lined the colonnade. And watched Sister Mary Joseph as she was loaded into the van.

"Don't you bury her on the convent grounds?" Jack asked.

"She is not Italian," Sister Immaculata said indifferently. "She will be given a mass, of course, and sent home to her people. Once the police are done with her."

There was no love lost between Sister Immaculata and Sister Mary Joseph, it seemed. Jack would liked to have asked why, but one of the policemen—he had a stripe of authority on his shoulder—was peppering him with impatient Italian, and the nun was gesturing ferociously with her hands. Then she turned to Jack.

"He asks why you are here. An American. A stranger. A *man* in the holy convent of holy women."

"I came to see Sister Mary Joseph."

This time, the policeman didn't wait for Immaculata's translation. He grabbed the front of Jack's sweater and twisted it menacingly.

"To see her—or to *kill* her?" Immaculata supplied helpfully. "*Il ispettore* wishes to know who you are, *immediatamente*, and why we found you with the murdered sister."

"I told you—I'm Jack Kennedy. My father is the American ambassador to England. *Joseph* Kennedy. Look, here's my passport." He rose abruptly from the bench, shaking free of the inspector. *He hated to be touched.* Alarmed, the man pulled a truncheon out of his belt.

"Easy." Jack raised his hands in the universal sign of surrender. "I was just going for my passport. So you can see for yourself who I am."

The nun muttered to the policeman and after an instant, he nodded grudgingly. With careful slowness, Jack eased his right hand into the back pocket of his flannels and withdrew his passport. The inspector took it. His colleague seized the moment to frisk Jack in a style he could only have learned from a gangster movie.

"You've got the wrong guy, mister," Jack said. "No bloody knife in my pocket, I promise you. I didn't even know the dead woman. And the murderer's getting away while you're wasting my time."

Immaculata frowned at him menacingly. "A little respect, if

you know what is good for you, *idiota*," she hissed. "The inspector asks why you came to the Via Giulia, asking for Sister Mary Joseph, if you did not know her?"

"A mutual friend from the States asked me to drop by. She went to school with the sister many years ago."

"The name of this friend?" his translator demanded.

"Eileen Dunne," he improvised, his eyes on the inspector. "From Boston. I'm in college there. At Harvard. You've heard of Harvard?"

The policeman was studying the photograph. Comparing it to Jack's face.

"He asks," Immaculata said, "why you are in Rome."

"I'm working as my father-the-ambassador's secretary in London," Jack said swiftly. "My father is President Franklin Roosevelt's official representative to the Pope's coronation."

"*Il ispettore* wishes to know of your movements today. Did you go to St. Peter's alone?"

Jack frowned. "No, I was with *my father the ambassador*. And the rest of my family. There are ten of us. We swiped Count Ciano's seats, if you want to know."

At the mention of Mussolini's son-in-law, the policeman's face hardened. He spat in the courtyard dirt. "Ciano!"

Immaculata shrugged her contempt. "Ciano is a violator of women and of Mother Church. When did you leave St. Peter's?"

"At noon. I was driven in an official embassy car with four of my brothers and sisters straight to the Hotel d'Inghilterra, where my family is staying."

"And then you came here? Why?"

"I told you—to pay a visit to Sister Mary Joseph."

"And you came alone? Nobody saw you?"

Jack gave an exasperated sigh. "My cabdriver dropped me

outside a minute before you found me at the top of the stairs. I doubt we'll be able to find him. But *I didn't kill Sister Mary Joseph*. How could I? I didn't even know what she looked like!"

"There is only your word for this."

The policeman conferred with his subordinate. Sister Immaculata yawned.

"Look," Jack suggested. "You can talk to my father. Ambassador Kennedy. He'll tell you I was with him all day. Ask Ciano himself if I was at the Vatican, for chrissake."

Immaculata hissed again at his sacrilege.

Unexpectedly, the police inspector said in perfect English, "You have something to tell us, signore?"

"I do." He eyed the man with renewed interest. "The mark cut into the nun's breast."

"The . . ." the inspector halted, confounded by the word.

"It looks like a spider," Jack said helpfully. "There are a string of bodies from New York to London with the same mark. The killer's a German named Hans Obst."

"How you know this?" the policeman demanded.

"I read the newspapers. But you might want to call Scotland Yard. They'll be able to help. Could I talk to the Mother Superior now, please?"

HE'D NEVER BEEN TAUGHT BY NUNS, as most Catholic boys growing up in America were. His father's social and political ambitions demanded that Jack and his brothers fight for an equal place in America's power structure—and that meant shedding the appearance of a Boston mick and graduating from the right WASP schools. Kennedy money bought them berths at Choate, and then Harvard, where the Irish was almost scrubbed out of them. Jack's brother Joe was a rousing success at Choate and won its coveted Harvard Trophy; a football star with perfect features, he was always better at looking the part of Brahmin than Jack. But despite his privileged education, Jack was no stranger to convents; his sisters spent most of their lives in schools like this. Only J. P. Kennedy's *boys* got the best education money could buy. The girls were simply expected to marry well—and marry Catholics.

Jack followed Sister Immaculata's swaying black gown along the colonnade to the far door—the one the screaming nun had vanished through—and into the heart of the building.

It was probably several hundred years old. The stone walls were roughly plastered and the hallways smelled of wax. They smelled, too, of linen pressed under hot irons; disinfecting soap; and ancient drains. As Jack passed certain closed doors he thought he could smell sickness—of body or mind. It was not, after all, very different from Mayo.

He hadn't thought of the pain in his leg since he'd paid off the taxi. That was what the nuns would call a blessing. He wasn't sure what he'd call it.

Sister Immaculata stopped before a thick oak door and rapped sharply on it.

"*Entrato.*"

They went in.

The Mother Superior was just rising from her knees. Had she been praying for the soul of the departed, or for herself?

"Mr. Ken-ne-dy," she said. "Please. Sit down. You may leave us, Sister Immaculata."

The nun bowed her head and vanished through the door—

but not before throwing a malevolent look at Jack. She suspected him of something. If not murder, then every one of the other deadly sins in the book.

"You have seen *la polizia*. You have told them what you know."

"Yes."

"Good." She settled herself behind a handsome desk: a wide-hipped, large-featured woman of middle years, with liquid black eyes. She was studying him frankly, and Jack schooled himself not to look away. "It is a horrible thing, this kind of death. A violence without reason. She was a good girl."

"You have my deepest sympathy," Jack said. "But how was she murdered? This place"—he glanced around the windowless room—"seems tough to break into. Did anybody see what happened?"

"Nobody saw nothing," the Mother Superior said with a grand indifference to English grammar. "She was alone. She must have opened the outer door to the one who killed her. Perhaps she tried to run away—she reached the upper floor—but after that . . ."

He could imagine it: The Spider at the small entrance cut into the gate; the bell ringing as it had for Diana yesterday; the bulky shape forcing an entry—the terrified woman tripping in her long skirts—and then the knife. . . .

"We found her when we returned from the coronation," the Mother Superior said matter-of-factly, "and it was terrible. Sister Agnes Ruth had the hysterics. One had to slap her. And still she screamed. One cannot blame her."

"Why didn't Sister Mary Joseph attend?"

"She had much to do. The packing of the baggage and the writing of letters. She was to travel to Paris tomorrow."

"Paris?" He was startled.

"*Certamente*, Paris." The Mother Superior scrutinized him. "The head of our charity is there. Herr Helmuth Wohlthat."

Göring's banker. Helmuth Wohlthat, who liked to dine at the Tour d'Argent with men who were supposed to be elsewhere.

"What is your interest in Sister Mary Joseph?"

Jack fell back on his first lie, with variations.

"I'm in Rome for a few days for the Pope's coronation. A friend asked me to visit."

The Mother Superior nodded. "Mary Joseph had many friends, no? She came to us only a year ago, from Boston in America."

Jesus. He'd guessed right.

And with the thought came uneasiness. The dead hatcheck girl had been from Boston, too. *Little Katie . . .*

"Her body must be sent there," the Mother Superior observed. "You will help us, perhaps?"

"I could," Jack said slowly. "My father's dining with Bill Phillips—he's our ambassador here in Rome—right now. I can make a phone call to the embassy. The consular section will have to get the paperwork rolling. But I'd need Sister Mary Joseph's *original* name—before she took vows."

"That is most necessary, I comprehend." The Mother Superior rose and went to a cabinet in the corner of the room, where she kept her files. A drawer slid open; her fingers shifted among the documents. "Such a strange and lovely name. *Daisy.* Daisy Corcoran. She was only twenty-seven."

Jack's heart seemed to stop for an instant; then resumed its beating with a painful thud. The Corcoran name was common enough in Boston. But that wasn't why it had sputtered his pulse.

What had Diana said, after calling in the Via Giulia yesterday? *Witness Daisy's pending sainthood. I drop over from time to time in the hope she'll save my soul.*

The murdered nun was Diana's childhood friend.

"What were Sister Mary Joseph's duties, Mother Superior," he managed, "for your charity organization in Paris?"

"She was our *contabile*. How do you say? She made the accounts," the nun replied as she closed her files. "And carried the money to Paris, of course."

"The money?"

"Donations," she corrected. "The Little Sisters of Clemency are in Rome, you see, because it is the center of the Catholic world. The Faithful bring alms for the poor. Sister Mary Joseph made certain it reached them. She took the money to Herr Wohlthat. It was all this she packed while the rest of us went to St. Peter's this morning."

Jack rose. "Have you checked her baggage?"

Something in the Mother Superior's face changed. With swiftness surprising in one so large, she surged to the door.

Jack followed.

THE POLICE INSPECTOR and his colleague were already in possession of Daisy's room, which was so tiny and so painfully neat that it was obvious it contained little more than the narrow wooden bench on which she slept, the single small table and wooden chair positioned beneath the slit of a window, and three pegs at shoulder height in the wall. There was no mirror and no basin; but an earthenware ewer was half full of water, and a worn leather satchel rested near the door. The cell was so orderly, in fact, that Jack felt a spark of hope as he and the Mother Superior came to a halt before the open doorway: The White Spider *couldn't* have been here. It looked nothing like the chaos of his stateroom, after the killer had ransacked it.

The inspector was lifting a prayer book and what Jack guessed was a habit from the satchel with hands already encased in gloves. The Mother Superior uttered a sharp question in Italian and the policeman answered, his eyes on her face.

"What is it?" Jack asked.

She ignored him and strode instead into the center of the tiny room, glancing distractedly from one corner to the other.

"Mother Superior," he said gently.

"There was another *borsa*." She gestured frantically at the leather satchel. "A black one, you understand. With the account book and the *donazione* inside." She threw up her hands. "*Il dio mio*, Mr. Ken-ne-dy! She must have died for it. The *borsa* is gone."

TWENTY-SIX. CRUMBLE TO BLACK

THE JOURNEY TO THE ROOF of the White House was too pain-ful for a man in a wheelchair; and it would attract the wrong kind of attention. Roosevelt kept the radio receiver Wild Bill Donovan had given him in his bedroom, on the lower shelf of the table that stood next to his white iron cot, with a heavy flan-nel shawl thrown over it. Eleanor had her own room down the hall and nobody disturbed his. The last thing he did before turn-ing off his reading lamp each night was tune the radio to Jack's special frequency, the whistling and static from the ether almost soothing to his fitful sleep. Schwartz had instructed the boy to transmit, when possible, between ten and eleven o'clock in the morning, European time. The signal would reach Roosevelt as he waited restlessly for dawn.

When the click-clicking of the Morse keys broke into his sleep that morning, a few minutes past five, he awoke instantly. He'd learned Morse during the last war, when he was secretary of the navy, but it had taken Bruce Hopper nearly an hour to train him on the receiver and substitution code during the professor's last visit. Hopper was an old army intelligence hand, and he knew some of the same people Wild Bill Donovan knew. Be-tween them, the two men had arranged the secret session in the lingerie shop and Jack's back channel commo link. Roosevelt was adamant: Nobody connected to the State department—particularly Jack's father—must know about it.

Ciphers intrigued and excited him. They were a foray into the lost country of childhood, a Rudyard Kipling world, and the President insisted on receiving Jack's messages himself. He trusted Sam Schwartz; but he was selfish about sharing the fun—and the burden—of espionage.

He dragged himself upright against his pillows and reached for a pad and pencil. His white bedside table was cluttered with several telephones, scraps of paper, pencil stubs, a bottle of nose drops, an ash tray, cigarettes, and a bottle of aspirin. He knew Jack was supposed to repeat his radio transmission until its receipt was confirmed. He'd missed the first few letter groups, but he could pick them up on the second round. He switched on his reading lamp and began to scribble down the Morse.

Twenty minutes later, Missy tapped on his door and entered in her bathrobe, a cup of coffee in her hand. She set it on the bedside table. He reached for her, pulled her onto his lap, and held her there for an instant, the decoded message discarded at his side. She'd been with him as friend and secretary and lover for twenty years, through his failed vice-presidential campaign, his governorship, his polio therapy at Warm Springs, and now the White House. She was forty years old and her hair was turning gray in his service. Her face, however, was still as sweet and unlined as when they'd first met. She smelled of flannel nightgowns and linen-closet lavender and the warmth of nighttime. He thought of the wiretap on her phone and blasphemed violently in his mind.

"You're up early," she said. "Did you sleep?"

"Couple of hours." He reached for his coffee and drank some. "Listen, Miss—you're Catholic, aren't you? Who do you know in the Church hierarchy?"

She crowed with laughter. "Nobody at all."

"Do you know anything about the Little Sisters of Clemency?"

"Never heard of them. What do they do—teach? Nurse? Or just pray?"

"I think they do a bit more than that," he said easily. "The order's name came up in conversation a few days ago. I'd like to know more about them—where they're based, how they're run, who supports them financially, that sort of thing."

"Part of your drive to build community service?"

"Exactly. So many small organizations have sprung up in this terrible Depression, and few of them get enough recognition. But I don't want to flutter the dovecot with a premature call from the White House. Think you could ask around, and tell me what you learn?"

"Eleanor's much better at that sort of thing than I am."

"But everything Eleanor says or does is front-page news."

"And you'd like to sound out the Little Sisters before you burden them with presidential notice. I get it." She sprang off his lap and padded in her slippers to the door. "You've got Henry Morgenthau at ten o'clock, don't forget."

"I won't."

"You might shave this time."

"I might."

When she'd gone, he picked up the discarded pad. *Spider strikes in Rome STOP Sister Mary Joseph nee Daisy Corcoran American citizen killed STOP Little Sisters of Clemency records and cash stolen presumably by Spider STOP Suggest you investigate activity of Sisters stateside STOP Am proceeding to Paris STOP Jack*

And so it has begun, Roosevelt thought: the boy's wandering. He thinks the Spider is following him. He'll keep moving—keep asking questions—maybe even keep one step ahead of the killer. And what will he learn, in the end? Something worse than a stab in the gut?

Roosevelt reached for his lighter, lit a flame under the deciphered note, and watched it crumble to black in the ashtray.

TWENTY-SEVEN. CHARITY

JACK SAT AND STOOD AND KNELT with the reflexive habit of ten thousand masses—Teddy was receiving his First Communion from Pope Pius XII this Monday morning. But Jack could not get the cloister in Via Giulia out of his mind. The sacred hush of the Vatican chapel echoed with a woman's wailing.

She's dead, he'd told Diana when he'd found her last night in the Hassler's dining room, seated unfashionably early at a table. She was eating alone.

"Who's dead?"

"Your friend Daisy. The one who had the smarts to enter a convent. Marriage is looking better and better, isn't it?"

Her fingers went slack and her wineglass slipped out of her hand, shattering against a silver ewer of hyacinths in the center of the table.

A waiter sprang into action, mopping up the wine, but Diana said, "Never mind. I'll have a whiskey." Her expression hadn't changed; she sat erect and elegant; but when the whiskey came, she tossed it back neat. "How?" she finally asked.

"Stabbed to the heart by the Nazi thug from the *Queen Mary*."

"You can't know that."

"I saw the body."

"You can't know that it was . . . that man."

"I saw the body."

"What do you mean?" She shoved the whiskey glass aside and gripped the edge of the table. "Tell me."

"He cuts a spider into the breast of each of his victims. Daisy got one this morning."

She thrust her index finger between her teeth and bit down, hard. Her eyes welled but she did not cry. No tears ever trailed down Diana's marble cheek.

No mercy, Jack thought. *No quarter.* "Did you tell him where to find her?"

"What?"

"The White Spider. That's his nickname, isn't it?"

"Jack, I—"

"Is he a friend of yours, Diana? Somebody to dance with, when you drop in on Berlin?"

Her face hardened. "I don't dance with Heydrich's killers."

"Few girls do, and live to brag about it. So you know he works for Heydrich. We're getting somewhere. Did you tell the Spider that Sister Mary Joseph would be alone this morning— she needed to get out of town fast and was taking the account books and the bag of cash with her? Is that why you went to see her Saturday, Diana—to get the details right?"

She stood up and tossed her napkin on the chair behind her. Without a word she slid past the table and made for the door.

Rage flooded over him suddenly, unexpectedly, at the way he could not break her—could not penetrate that sleek mask she kept wrapped around her body and mind. He shoved his chair away from the table, heedless of the shocked faces of the few diners scattered about the room, and ran after her.

He knew what they'd be muttering. *Americano.*

He caught up with her in the doorway and grabbed her arm.

She was wearing something light and silken; chiffon, probably. Kick would know. She felt as fragile as a length of birch. She drew back, resisting him.

"Sir," a waiter attempted.

"You're going to talk to me," Jack muttered, "or I swear to God, Diana, *I will hurt you*. Understand?"

"It's all right," she told the waiter. "My little brother's had too much to drink. May I have my coat and hat?"

Jack pulled her out into the Hassler lobby and across the marble floor. The waiter ran after them with her things. Jack grabbed them impatiently and dragged her out the door to the sloping pavement beyond, the sharp descent of the Spanish Steps. Dusk was falling. The scent of lime blossom filled the air. He dropped her coat and hat in the street and pulled her roughly into his arms, careless of the world's gaze. He kissed her hard and viciously, biting at her mouth, lashing her with his rage. She was fighting him and he could feel her anger like a coiled spring, a punch she wanted to throw. He kissed her chin and her arched throat and pulled his hands through her black hair saying *God damn you, Diana. God damn you.*

Her breath was coming in faint sobs, of fury or fear or passion he couldn't tell. She strained against him, arching backward, hands pushing against his chest. Her hip bones grazed his groin and, that quickly, he stiffened beneath her, his hand sliding to the small of her back. Holding her against the sudden hardness. She sighed into his mouth. He wanted to rip her dress from her body. He wanted to eat her alive.

"Jack." She clutched his shoulders. "Are you going to take me right here on the street?"

"Hell, yes."

They were exposed to every tourist mouthing papal pieties, every Fascist ready to beat them for indecency. *Indecency.* He could think of a hundred ways to practice it on Diana's supple body.

He broke away, his breathing ragged, and saw the anguish in her eyes. Something to do with Daisy, he thought—not this vortex between them. She was grieving for the dead woman on the convent floor with the obscenity cut into her skin. Her knees gave way and she sank down with him, the two of them huddled on the Spanish Steps.

"Blimey," she said shakily. "That's how you get a girl to *talk*?"

He fingered her fragile neck. "Tell me I'm not your little brother," he said.

HER STORY WAS SIMPLE AND CLEAR. Jack wasn't sure he believed it—there were too many loose ends she refused to tie—but the bare outline was plausible enough. He did not expect Diana to trust him with the entire truth. He wondered if there was anyone she *did* trust. Whitehall Denys?

She'd never been to school with Daisy Corcoran, of course. Daisy had grown up in Boston and Diana in Liverpool. They'd met in the chorus of a West End musical when Diana was nineteen and Daisy was pretending to be. One of the principal actors got Daisy pregnant. Diana helped her get the abortion from a woman who operated illegally in Spitalfields.

"Daisy turned religious, afterward. Kept talking about mortal sin and the damnation of her eternal soul. She disappeared one day, without a word—and it was only after I married that she wrote. She'd seen something in the papers. *The Honourable Denys.* Has a taste for showy hoofers, has Denys."

Hoofers. Jack thought of Diana's long, luminous legs in fishnet and heels, and closed his eyes.

"Anyway, Daisy had turned into Sister Mary Joseph. She was working with a charity order, trying to atone for what we'd done. She told me she didn't blame me for my part in it—good of her, I suppose. She said she prayed for me. *Christ.*"

"Did you write back?"

"Not right away." She shrugged. "What was there to say, after all? Our lives were so different. I sent fifty quid to her charity. I suppose it was a lot of money, to Daisy."

There were families in London that lived for months on fifty quid, Jack thought. It would be a lot to anybody.

"Anyway—she kept me in mind. Whenever her charity needed . . . help in some way." Diana laughed bitterly. "It wasn't exactly blackmail, but it wasn't innocent, either. Daisy believed in Sin. Hers *and* mine. Asking for cash was a way to remind me. *I found the abortionist.*"

"She made her own choices," Jack said. "Some women would have thanked you for what you did."

"Not Daisy."

He thought of Kick. Rose insisting that if she married Billy, she'd be damned forever. The desperate sadness of his sister's expression, that first afternoon he'd arrived in London, as she adjusted her hat in the mirror. Jack knew there was such a thing as being *too* Catholic.

"Is that why you stopped by the convent yesterday? To give her cash?"

"The charitable works sort of . . . evolved." Diana was looking at her fingers, which she'd laced through Jack's. "By this time, Daisy was managing a relief network for refugees—Czechs displaced from the Sudetenland—and coordinating it out of

Rome. The thought being that if the refugees aren't *miserable*, they won't make life difficult for the rest of us."

"Chamberlain's theory," Jack mused. "Keep Hitler happy, and maybe he'll go home."

"Yes. I took up a collection among some people I know— Nancy Astor, Oswald Mosley, the Mitfords. Other people, in New York. It was enough cash that I thought I'd better deliver it myself. I went to Paris, but Daisy'd left. I might have sent her a check, I suppose, but I don't trust Mussolini's mails. So I came on to Rome."

She gazed at him steadily, her black eyes serene; she had spoken her piece clearly and well.

No, he didn't believe much of it, Jack decided. The White Spider had no reason to kill a nun, much less steal her books. Unless the charity was funding something far different from Sudeten Czechs.

Did Diana know that?

How much had she lied to him?

The answers, he thought, were in Paris. Daisy had been packing for Paris when she died; and Göring's banker might still be waiting there. It was time to conduct some thesis research, Jack thought. He would leave for Paris tomorrow.

He smoothed Diana's black hair from her brow, then lifted her to her feet. Her coat and bag were still lying where they'd fallen, haphazardly on the Spanish Steps.

"I've made you conspicuous," he said. "In the middle of Rome."

"Good of you. I usually manage that all by myself."

"Be careful." He grasped her wrist and shook it lightly. "Daisy's killer is still loose."

"What could one of Heydrich's thugs possibly want with me?"

"What did he want with Daisy, if it comes to that? What possible threat did a nun pose to the Gestapo?"

She stared at him, arrested. He had asked the unforgivable question, the one to which she had no answer. Her eyes narrowed. "We'll never know, will we?"

"Oh, yes, Diana. We'll know. I'm going to find out."

The air between them chilled. She stepped back. "Don't be a *bloody fool*, Jack. It's nothing to do with you."

"Sure about that?"

There would be no more confidences tonight.

She was definitely *not* going to invite him up.

Jack stood awkwardly while Diana smoothed her dress. He'd crushed it, kissing her, and the sight of the creases felt as intimate to him as the sheets of a tumbled bed. Desire twisted in his groin, unreasoning and overwhelming; but she was not for him, anymore. He was going to Paris. And he had no intention of telling her.

"Until tomorrow, then," he said.

She waved a cool good-bye. Already thinking of something else. Or *someone* else.

The Hassler's glittering doors closed behind her.

He walked back alone to the Hotel d'Inghilterra, looking for Spiders in the dusk.

TWENTY-EIGHT. GÖRING'S BANKER

THE MAN HAD LAID HIS HOMBURG and briefcase, his furled umbrella and decent coat on the seat beside him, so that nobody would sit down. It was his favorite corner of the Hotel Crillon lobby in Paris; he'd erected a copy of *Le Monde* like a shield in front of him. The newspaper was blessedly free of the disaster that blared from every radio—its presses had stopped before Hitler's tanks rolled into Prague that morning. March 15, 1939. As he sat in the comfortable chair, scanning the racing columns and considering his dinner, he knew that people were dying all over Europe in senseless and hideous ways. He adjusted a cushion against the small of his back.

He could detect a change in the attitude of some of the Crillon staff: they no longer made eye contact. They pocketed his tips with distaste. It didn't matter that his business was finance, the complicated relationships of debt and interest, gold reserves and loans, or that he had been educated in the United States and was an internationalist at heart. Helmuth Wohlthat was German— and therefore someone to despise. As of today, someone to fear.

A strange hand grasped his briefcase; his hat and coat were tossed carelessly onto an adjacent chair. Wohlthat crumpled his newspaper irritably and stared at the fellow who'd presumed to move his things.

"*Qu'est-ce que vous faites?*" he demanded. "*Qu'est-ce que vous voulez?*"

The man answered in German. "I want to talk to you." He sank down next to him. "Herr Wohlthat."

"How do you know my name?"

The man smiled. It did nothing to warm his eyes, which were the color of the North Sea in winter; but it sharpened the inch-long scar that bisected his lip. Early thirties, Wohlthat decided; ex-military or possibly plainclothes security man. He was sitting far too close; a threatening move. Wohlthat tried to put some distance between them.

"I serve Reinhard Heydrich. He knows everyone's name."

Wohlthat's throat constricted. "What does General Heydrich want with me?"

"You set up a certain network for your friend Göring, using your contacts in Europe and the United States. That network has been thoroughly and hopelessly penetrated. It is in the process of being liquidated, as I'm sure you know."

Wohlthat's mouth fell open. He tried to speak, but no sound came from his lips.

Heydrich's thug put his hand on Wohlthat's knee and squeezed. "You must see that as the architect of the network, you inevitably fall under suspicion."

"Of what?" Wohlthat whispered.

"Betraying it, of course."

The pressure of those blunt fingers increased. Wohlthat twitched irritably but the hand remained fastened around his knee. "Why should I betray my own network?"

"Why, indeed?" The thug's smile widened. "We considered recalling you to Berlin to answer that question. Although it's possible you would never arrive. The world is such a dangerous place—so many people die for stupid reasons."

"Are you *threatening* me?" Wohlthat tried to stand. But those hard fingers pinned him to his seat. And suddenly he saw—with utter disbelief—that Heydrich's thug held a knife in his other hand, as thoughtlessly as if it were a child's toy.

Wohlthat drew a panicked breath. "I don't understand."

"There was a nun in Rome. She was supposed to meet you."

"Sister Mary Joseph. *Yes*. I've been here three days and she hasn't shown up."

"You can stop waiting. She cut herself."

He fingered the knife casually, and in that second, Wohlthat understood. He stared at the bland face before him, the blunt fingers rolling the deadly toy.

"Happily for you, the account book is safe."

Safe.

Every detail of Göring's network. *In this man's hands.*

Which meant they would soon be in Heydrich's.

Wohlthat's mind darted hopelessly, a bird battering against a windowpane. All those names. . . . Donors, lists of funds, the people who'd trusted him on two continents. Vulnerable, now, to the deadliest man in the Gestapo.

"You understand that this is extremely serious," the creature was saying. "Your *entire network*, penetrated by the American security forces—exposed and humiliated—liquidated one by one. Failure, Wohlthat. *Failure*. Someone must be blamed."

The words were uttered so softly that they seemed like a vicious lullaby. Wohlthat was no fool. He remembered the Night of the Long Knives, when Heydrich had seized power for himself and taken the Gestapo—Göring's vicious creation—under his sole control. The two men hated each other. Given half a chance, Heydrich would see Göring killed, and pop champagne as he died. Wohlthat knew he was being set up to betray Göring; but it didn't matter. There was little to choose between the man and Heydrich. And he was alone with a killer who held a knife.

He swallowed convulsively. "So I'll shoulder the blame. Return to Berlin immediately. I don't tolerate failure either, Herr . . ."

"Too late." The fingers gave his knee a painful squeeze.

"Then what . . . ?"

He would not put the thought into words. He would not betray his fear of death and particularly of the knife.

"Heydrich has a suggestion—if you want to make amends." The blond head bent close. "You know Kennedy."

Whatever he had expected, it was hardly this. "Of course. I—"

"Heydrich wants you to cultivate him. Tell him how badly the German economy is suffering. As only you, a banker connected to the Reichsbank, could know."

"But the economy is *not* suffering—"

"You'll tell Kennedy, when you see him, that Hitler's mad rearmament plans are crippling us. That financial disaster looms. That we can't go on much longer."

"But—"

Wohlthat reared back. The knife point was thrust against his abdomen; his abdomen tensed, recoiling from pain.

"Are you incredibly stupid, Herr Wohlthat?"

Wohlthat said nothing, his teeth clenched, fighting for control.

Heydrich's man rose to his feet, the sinister blade disappearing into his sleeve like a conjurer's trick.

Wohlthat touched his fingers to his starched white shirt. A

drop of blood blossomed on the fabric. He looked up, aghast. He never felt the knife's blade.

"Go on about your life," the man said benignly. "I'll find you when I need you. And try, Herr Wohlthat, to be a *little* smarter. The knife can always go deeper."

TWENTY-NINE. THE EXPRESS

"BY ROLLING INTO PRAGUE, Hitler's broken at least seven promises he gave Chamberlain at Munich," Joe Kennedy said, "and you know what that means."

"Yeah. Chamberlain's an idiot."

"You don't know what the hell you're talking about, Jack. You just mouth these . . . warmongering platitudes . . . you've picked up at Harvard."

"You can't negotiate peace, Dad, with a guy who wants to make war." Jack threw a wrinkled tie into his suitcase.

"I've got to get back to London immediately," Joe persisted, "and I've hired a plane. You're coming with me."

"I'm going to Paris."

"You should be home."

"London isn't home. You just want to think I'm safe. But nobody's *safe* anymore, Dad. You just refuse to admit it."

His father spun him around by the shoulder. "I've pledged nine hostages to fortune, Jack—bringing you kids to Europe when it's about to commit suicide. Just because Roosevelt conferred his *goddamn honor* on me and your mother decided it was the bees' knees to swan around London. If I had a particle of sense I'd pack you all off to New York on the next ship that sails."

Jack's brow furrowed. There was active fear in his father's voice he couldn't understand. They were such different people—Joe was terrified of death, whereas Jack had always taken it for granted. The only question was how and when it happened.

"I'm going to Paris." He snapped the brass clips on his suitcase. "I've got a thesis to research and write."

"It's not gonna happen, son," Joe said roughly. "You're too damn sick. Even your mother can see that, and she never sees anything. You're yellow with jaundice and you're clammy with sweat. I heard you retching last night."

"Something in the Roman water doesn't agree with me."

"Something in the *world* doesn't agree with you, Jack. You look like walking death."

They confronted his reflection together in the hotel mirror. There was, Jack had to admit, a faintly yellow tinge to his skin. Nothing a little sun wouldn't take care of. His eyes were sunken. His cheekbones were as prominent as a skull's and his forehead looked a bit moist. "I just need some sleep. I've been burning the candle at both ends this week."

"You can sleep in London."

He grasped his suitcase. "I'll wire when I get to Paris."

"I'm not funding this fool's errand," Joe said querulously, suddenly aware that his grown son wasn't obeying him. "You won't get a dime from me."

His last trick: playing the poverty card.

"That's okay, Dad." Jack fleetingly calculated his loose change and few bills. "I'll manage." *Without you.*

Ten minutes later, as his taxi pulled away from the curb, his father ran after it, swearing a blue streak—with a wad of cash in his outstretched hand.

THE ROME EXPRESS was a sumptuous Wagon-Lit train that would get him to Paris midmorning. Jack had a luxury sleeper to himself and the rest of *Melbourne* to finish; but he was lonelier tonight than he could remember being. He ached for Diana. She'd checked out of the Hassler Monday while Teddy took First Communion from the Pope. She'd left no forwarding address.

Jack shivered. Chills ran the length of his body and he was sweating again. He mopped his forehead with a handkerchief, tossed his suit jacket on the rack with his luggage, and pulled a blanket from his berth.

His leg throbbed and his entrails no longer behaved. He'd lied when he'd told Dad he was okay; he was a rambling wreck again, but nothing would force him to admit it. *He would not let Roosevelt down.* Even though he'd been too sick to transmit this morning, and had nothing new to report. Maybe he should use the DOCA once a day. But his supply of pellets was dwindling and he would not experiment on his body while traveling alone.

As night fell, he stared out at the Italian countryside. Lombardy poplars, hills the color of wheat, the odd punctuation of ocher roofs. He could not decide where Diana's loyalties lay. She'd ridiculed his father and called Chamberlain a fool; did that mean she *wasn't* a Fascist? Cover, Dobler had called it. But cover could mean many things. Her story about Daisy Corcoran, for instance. How much could he believe? What if she'd gone to Paris last week to warn Wohlthat that Jack was nosing around Göring's network?

And had gotten Daisy killed?

He didn't know how to read Diana. She'd called him a teenager and a little brother Sunday night, then shuddered in his arms. Jack knew he was charming—charm was the most reliable weapon in his arsenal—but Diana had the pick of male Europe at her feet. Swooning over a college kid didn't make sense.

Leaving without a word the next morning did.

It was painful to remember the way he'd felt on the Spanish Steps, touching Diana's body—like he was drowning in it. Painful to recall the smell and feel of her skin, the taste of her mouth. For a few seconds he'd felt like he owned her, body and soul—that she was his for the asking—but she'd fooled him again and skipped town without a word. He suspected both Diana and her friend Willi Dobler had been playing him for weeks. They'd set him up from the moment he'd boarded the *Queen Mary*: offering a drink when he'd been sucker-punched; offering information when they knew—as Willi clearly did—that he'd been sent out by his president in search of it. Play Jack, they must have figured, and they'd play Roosevelt, too.

And yet—and yet . . . Dobler had told him about the Little Sisters of Clemency.

And Diana had lost her balance completely on the Spanish Steps.

His lip curled bitterly. He had as much of a problem with trust as she did.

What if they're both legit? his mind protested. *What if Willi and Diana are on my side?*

As the swaying train climbed steadily north, Jack closed his eyes.

Not even a college kid could be that gullible.

THIRTY. NOTHING LIKE JOE

JACK WAS SICKER THAN A DOG by the time he reached Paris.

Alerted by a cable from J. P. Kennedy, Carmel Offie met the Rome train that morning. The vice-consul took one look at Jack's face and threw his arm over his shoulder. Together, they staggered off the platform. Offie was short and Jack was tall and they made an odd couple, but Jack was too weak to protest. He'd spent most of the night vomiting.

"Tummy troubles?" Offie inquired sympathetically. "That *wretched* Roman water."

Offie was what Joe Kennedy called *queer*; but Jack liked the little man, who'd grown up poor in an industrial town in western Pennsylvania, and had worked his way up to the highest levels of diplomatic service. He let Offie grasp his waist and pour him into the back of Bill Bullitt's official car and speed through the streets to the ambassador's residence on the Right Bank.

"I need to send a telegram," he said hoarsely as Offie helped him into the foyer. "To my doctor. George Taylor."

He was prostrate for the better part of a week in the Beaux Arts monstrosity Bullitt called home. It was lined with marble and echoed with emptiness. Bullitt lived there with two dozen servants; but in the summer months he moved to the Château de St. Firmin, a lovely mansion in the park surrounding the Château de Chantilly. Bullitt was a natural aristocrat, the master of the grand gesture; he pursued dangerous women, entertained lavishly, never considered cost, and drank as determinedly as Winston Churchill. With the nightingales singing in the woods, his string of horses stabled nearby, and the gurgle of water from a torrent behind St. Firmin, the peace of Chantilly was overwhelming.

He took Jack to convalesce there. Jack implored Bullitt to say nothing to his father, and the ambassador—who had mixed feelings about Joe Kennedy—did as he asked. In return for silence, Bullitt demanded Jack see his doctor, but the man was bewildered by Jack's symptoms and could prescribe only *tisanes* and red wine. Jack puked up both. It was a telegram from Taylor, offering the name of a specialist, that saved him.

Dr. LaSalle was a researcher in endocrinology at the Sorbonne. An embassy car whisked him to Chantilly, where he examined Jack and injected him with a needleful of DOCA.

"While you remain in France, I will visit you every few days for these injections, *hein*?" he said.

"What's wrong with my pellets?" Jack asked warily.

"You used them too infrequently, *mon ami*, and now you are very ill. When you are better, we shall see if the pellets may be resumed," LaSalle said serenely.

"Why do I need the stuff so much?"

The Frenchman's brows lifted in faint surprise. "Monsieur le Docteur Taylor did not explain?"

"Not really."

"DOCA is an adrenal hormone, monsieur. In normal cases, such things are secreted by the adrenal glands, you comprehend. But in your case . . ."

"My adrenal glands don't work?"

The doctor shrugged. "I cannot possibly say, monsieur. I am merely doing as I am instructed by Monsieur le Docteur Taylor. As to the reasons for his treatment, I can give you no *véritable* information. I assumed the matter was understood."

"What do adrenal hormones do?"

LaSalle compressed his lips. "How to say in English? They conduct the salts in your blood."

"Salt?" Jack forced himself upright in bed, his head swimming. "That's it? I just need to eat more *salt*?"

The doctor shook his head. "I regret, no. Hardly so simple. You must discuss with Monsieur le Docteur, yes?"

JACK IMPROVED. HIS HIVES ABATED, his sweating diminished, and after LaSalle's third injection he could approach a dinner table without bolting for the bathroom. But he'd lost precious time; it was the end of March before he walked into the embassy.

He toured the beautiful old building on the Place de la Concorde, shook hands with Robert Murphy, Bullitt's chargé d'affaires, and allowed La Belle Offlet, as he privately called Carmel Offie, to find him an unused desk. While the vice-consul fussed over the correct chair for a man of Jack's height, Jack wandered through the embassy's Cultural section.

"Helmuth Wohlthat? He's that German economist who runs a charity organization, right?" Nancy Morgan was a French major two years out of Bryn Mawr who'd jilted her Yale man for a wilder life in Paris. She took dictation and organized Bullitt's lavish parties and she had superb legs, Jack noticed. She was perched on her desktop with her ankles crossed, an hourglass figure in cashmere.

"You've met him?"

"Sure. We get people asking about him all the time—American Catholics coming through town. His nuns get a lot of money from the States."

"So you know where he lives?"

"Berlin, I think. But when he's in Paris, he stays at the Crillon. It's just across the Rue Boissy d'Anglas from us."

"I know."

She gave him a smile that entirely reached her brown eyes.

"Your brother was here a few months ago. He took me to Le Mirabeau for dinner. That's in the Sixteenth. *Very* top drawer."

"Impressive. He usually prefers the bottom bunk. I'll give him your regards the next time I see him."

Nancy grinned to show she could take an off-color joke. "Beats me what a girl sees in a convent. I'd go stark raving mad without a man in my life."

"Got one?" he couldn't resist asking.

"Not at the moment. Charlie was shipped off to Moscow two months ago."

"Communist?"

"First Political Officer."

"Either way, he's happy. Is Wohlthat in town?"

She draped a hand on her hip. "What's it worth to you?"

Christ, he thought. He was beginning to feel tired. It was his first day out of a sickbed. "A drink at the Crillon. I'm headed over there now."

Her smile faded. "I can order one of those any day."

"Then I won't waste your time."

"Wohlthat's not at the Crillon," Nancy said coyly, as he turned toward the door. "It's nearly Easter. He always spends the holiday skiing—at Val d'Isère."

"Thanks," he said. *Val d'Isère*. He'd have to figure out where that was. Offie would know.

"Boy, were the guys in the Political Section ever *wrong*," she called petulantly after him. "They said you were a dead ringer for your brother. But you're nothing like Joe at all."

He was smiling faintly as he left. It was good to know *some* girls could tell the difference between them.

THE NEXT MORNING AFTER BREAKFAST, Jack found his way to Bullitt's mansard roof. An arc of pale blue sky canopied Chantilly as he tapped out his cipher message to Roosevelt; the world in spring had never looked so beautiful.

Suggest you find all available information on Wohlthat Helmuth German banker STOP Göring associate STOP Believed funneling money through Little Sisters charity network STOP am tracking now STOP CRIMSON

He liked the codename he'd chosen. CRIMSON. It made him feel like an honest-to-God spy.

THIRTY-ONE. POWER

FRANKLIN ROOSEVELT LIFTED HIS magnifying lens to examine a rare Seebeck reprint—a Nicaraguan 1893 stamp—he'd recently purchased at auction. Or rather, Sam Schwartz had purchased for him. It was a lovely thing, pale purple, with a glorious figure of a woman rising from a swirl of drapery.

He wasn't thinking about Seebeck's engraving, however.

He'd deciphered Jack's latest transmission early that morning. And compared it to Ambassador Joe Kennedy's most recent cable. The latter was written in Papa Joe's usual aw-shucks style.

I thought I ought to tell you that Jim Mooney—head of General Motors over here in Europe—is convinced I should meet with a Dr. Helmuth Wohlthat. He's connected to the Reichsbank, works with international loans and finance, and has some sort of deal he wants to propose for your consideration. Mooney hinted it might just resolve the whole Hitler mess. Why he thinks I'd make a good intermediary between you two I don't know—maybe I'm known for sizing up a money guy from my Wall Street and SEC days. At any rate, if it's all right with you, I'll fly over to Paris and meet Wohlthat there—or someplace quietly here, whenever he's next in London. I'd like to pick his brain about Hitler.

The coincidence—if coincidence it was—intrigued Roosevelt. Father and son had stumbled on the same German, for wildly different reasons.

"Franklin."

He set down his magnifying lens and twisted around in his chair; then held out his hand to Missy. She slipped her own into it. "Look at this beauty."

"The girl, or the stamp she's printed on?"

"You've known me long enough to answer that."

"Not if I live to be a hundred."

He slipped his arm around her waist. "You didn't come up here to look at stamps."

"Or girls. *No.* I'm reporting for duty."

He studied her quizzically.

"The Little Sisters of Clemency. You inquired."

"So I did."

"I was the soul of tact," she said briskly, "but I think I'll have to go to confession, now I'm done. Tact is hardly honesty."

"I should say it's usually the opposite," he agreed. "What'd you find out?"

"They've been operating all over the East Coast for the past thirty years—but the bulk of the work is in New York. They run a soup kitchen for Bowery bums and trot over to Ellis Island once a week, ministering to disoriented immigrants as they beat on America's doors."

"Nothing else?"

"Nope. A few relief places in Philadelphia and Boston. I understand they do much the same sort of thing in Europe."

"No fancy patron saint with deep pockets?"

"Lots of 'em. All signing themselves *Anonymous.* I guess giving away a boatload of cash in the middle of a Depression makes some people bashful."

"Not so shy they'll skip the tax deduction," Roosevelt said drily. He patted Missy absentmindedly in dismissal. She rose without a word, handed him his stamp tweezers, and left.

Roosevelt stared blindly at the album sheets scattered over his table, his mind focused instead on a scene played out in this very room a few hours before.

William Rhodes Davis, Hoover had said. *You know him?*

"Of course," Roosevelt replied. "Oil man. Persuaded the Mexican government to sell millions of dollars' worth of oil to Germany. The State department thinks he's a Nazi agent." He didn't add that State had been keeping a file on Davis's movements since 1928.

"He's taking money from Göring," Hoover replied. "A hundred and sixty thousand dollars so far, near as we can tell. Delivered by the Germany embassy's chargé d'affaires—one Hans Thomsen." The FBI director had paused. "We're just not sure, yet, who Davis is paying."

Edgar was a master, Roosevelt thought, of the partial disclosure. The tantalizing tidbit. He'd drop enough cards on the table to catch your eye, then fold his hand close to his chest and wait for your answering bid. He knew the mere mention of Davis—a white-haired Southern gentleman of considerable charm—would send Roosevelt's anxiety soaring. Davis was close to John L. Lewis, the powerful labor organizer. Whose union votes were essential to electing any Democratic president. If Davis's Nazi cash was buying labor votes for Roosevelt's rivals . . .

"Then I hope you're watching the man," Roosevelt had told Hoover genially. "I look forward to your next report."

He set down the tweezers and thrust his chair back from the table with a single forceful turn of the wheels. Damn J. Edgar

Hoover and his throttle-hold on facts! Roosevelt was beginning to feel manipulated. *Managed.* Dare he say it—trapped?

He needed something to barter with Ed Hoover. A chip to toss on the green baize table. An independent source of information. And the Little Sisters of Clemency's donor list just might provide it.

Hoover, Roosevelt could tell, had no inkling of the thread Jack Kennedy was following through Europe. It was purely conjecture, at the moment—but if Jack was right, and Göring's banker was using a Catholic charity as a front—and Roosevelt could get the names of his American donors without having to ask Hoover for help, without having to *depend* on FBI favors—

He took a deep breath and spun his wheelchair around. Rolled back to his stamp table and grasped a corner of the 1893 Nicaraguan delicately with his tweezers. With infinite care and steady hands, he placed it in the precise spot he'd reserved for it in his album.

He would cable J. P. Kennedy in London and order him *not* to meet with Göring's banker. He'd let Jack learn what he could about Wohlthat, instead.

He reached for a small hand bell and rang it.

Sam Schwartz stuck his head in the door.

"Sam," Roosevelt said. "Did you sweep my Pullman?"

The Secret Service man compressed his lips. "I did, sir."

"And you found?"

"A listening device in the portable phone."

The portable phone was an ingenious thing, developed at Roosevelt's instigation. It drew power from the Pullman's electrical system, and though useless while the train car rolled down the tracks, could be attached to a telephone cable by extension cords whenever the President halted at a station. As he had been halted, that Wednesday night when he'd chatted with Jack, beneath the Waldorf-Astoria.

—As he had been halted a hundred times in the past year, immersed in secret conversations, the painstaking detail of which had undoubtedly landed deep in J. Edgar Hoover's files.

If you can't trust him further than you can throw him, his wife's voice argued in his mind, *why not fire the dirty bastard?*

Dear Eleanor. Always so forthright and practical. Without a particle of political sense.

The answer, quite simply, was he could not end Hoover's reign without terrible risk. When he tried to tally how many secrets the man possessed—how many lives he could take down with him, in the ruin of his public career—Roosevelt's mind boggled. There had been so many private conversations, on so many perilous topics, in the Pullman over the past several years; and it now seemed likely that Hoover had a record of all of them. He beat his hands futilely on the arms of his wheelchair while Sam Schwartz watched. He could not begin to calculate what Hoover's files contained. Ignorance was mortally dangerous.

For as long as Roosevelt held the White House, he would have to hold Ed Hoover at bay. And for now—even though it was patently clear the FBI knew he had recruited young Jack Kennedy, because they had listened to him do it—Roosevelt's army of personal spies in Europe was his most useful weapon. They were beyond Hoover's reach.

He stilled his restless fists and glanced at Schwartz.

"I want you to talk to your friends over at Treasury, Sam. Very quietly, mind."

"Yes, Mr. President?"

"I need the tax records of a certain charity. The Little Sisters of Clemency."

THIRTY-TWO. THE ACCOUNTING

MARCH THIRTY-FIRST, Neville Chamberlain took the first bold step of his life, and declared that Britain would stand with France to save the Poles if they were invaded.

Nobody believed him.

Hitler answered Chamberlain by annexing the Lithuanian port of Memel, on the Baltic Sea, without a shot being fired.

The next day, April first, the Spanish Civil War officially ended—with another Fascist dictator, Francisco Franco, in power.

April seventh—Good Friday—Mussolini's Italian army invaded Albania.

The following Thursday, Neville Chamberlain announced that Britain would guarantee the borders of Rumania, Greece, and Turkey against possible Italian attack.

As dark was falling on that spring afternoon, Jack pulled into Val d'Isère.

It was the newest and most remote ski station in the French Alps, a tiny clutch of buildings with an octagonal stone church, one good hotel, and a single drag lift. The great Bellevarde peak dominated the lower valley. High above, near the Italian border, glaciers gleamed in the dying light. Somebody was attempting to build a cable car up a mountain face, but the work looked half-hearted and drifted in snow.

Val d'Isère sat on the highest pass in France. The Col d'Iseran had opened only the year before and Jack had never driven anything so treacherous in his life. It was twisting and narrow and punctured unexpectedly by falls of ice and rock. It had taken him three days from Paris, and another two to crawl the last hundred miles.

The valley was known for deadly avalanches, for ten-foot falls of snow, for the strange and brusque peasantry that had changed little in the past thousand years, and for ski terrain unmatched in Europe. Rose Kennedy might prefer the glamour of St. Moritz, and the Rothschilds had built Megève; but Jack stepped out of his hired car that night, gulped the bitter, clear air, and felt his heart soar. He was wrapped in absolute silence. The lonely cliffs held something he recognized, akin to blue water and a blowing gale—a challenge to the reckless, who sailed alone.

He had no skis and his only experience of the sport was years ago, in Vermont. His memory of that country was gentle and rolling, but the ground he stood on now was harsh. Treeless. Corniced by wind. He remembered vaguely that his brother Joe had broken his arm at St. Moritz this past Christmas. But what the hell. He carried his bags into the Hotel de Paris. It had sloping roofs with flat stone tiles quarried from the living rock; a beamed ceiling blackened by wood smoke; a platter of bread and cheese melting on the hearth; and a dimpled young girl in blond plaits who spoke not a word of English. Nobody in the Hotel de Paris, it turned out, spoke English. But they gave him a room when he asked for one in his halting French. There were only a handful of people staying there, the girl said.

Dinner was a fixed menu, in the room with the fire, in half an hour.

Jack felt almost giddy as he followed her up the narrow wooden stairs. Perhaps it was the altitude. Or his sudden sense of invisibility. He was utterly unknown, lost in the high wilderness—and nobody in Val d'Isère would lift an eyebrow at the name Kennedy. Maybe he'd be snowed in and could trade skiing for a good book and mulled wine.

But when he descended a bit later for dinner, in his flannel shirt and corduroys and heavy Nordic sweater, his plans changed. Somebody else had claimed the chair near the fire. A pale blond head with an aquiline nose and an expression of boredom in his green eyes.

Denys Playfair. Beside him sat Diana.

DID YOU FOLLOW ME HERE? she would ask him later, in an accusatory whisper, as they shivered in the chill drafts of the upper hall at midnight; and he would tell her what she expected to hear because he did not trust her with the Wohlthat story, not yet, not after the butchery on the convent floor. He told her that he could not forget the feel of her hair clenched in his fists or the velvet of her tongue, that he would follow her to hell and back if she chose to take him. She kept a wary distance there in the hall, conscious of Denys sleeping in one room and Dobler in another. Because Dobler was with them, of course—the Playfairs never went anywhere without Dobler.

What is he to you? Jack wanted to ask, but he said nothing then and had asked nothing earlier when Willi appeared at the dinner table, sleek from his bath and a day of wind on the *pistes*. He seemed unfazed by Jack's sudden appearance in Val d'Isère.

When Willi gestured with his head toward a gray-haired figure seated alone in a corner, engrossed by his pipe and his book, Jack understood why.

"Helmuth Wohlthat," Dobler said. "Near the end of his stay, I believe. Have you met before? No? I shall have to introduce you. Before he slips through your fingers."

Jack eyed Göring's banker as he consumed his beef stew. An invisible man in his own right, nondescript and even boring. Jack had expected a criminal mastermind. Wohlthat disappointed.

The Playfair table included him as a matter of course. It was no accident they were gathered here, Jack and Willi and Diana and Denys, in the remotest valley of Europe, while the logs settled and the frigid drafts of spring winds circled their ankles like hungry dogs. Secrets had drawn them. Tension, voiced and unspoken, ricocheted around the room.

Jack felt certain that something violent was about to happen. Playfair had a trick of watching him sidelong and Diana would not meet his eyes. Only Willi was composed.

Adrenaline sang in Jack's veins.

"AND HOW WAS YOUR SPORT TODAY, Herr Wohlthat?"

The phrase rang out in English, but Dobler switched abruptly to German as he strolled toward the middle-aged man seated alone in the corner. There followed a badinage in heavy consonants. Playfair's eyes did not follow Willi but the bored expression left his face, to be replaced by one of alertness as he drew patterns on the jacquard tablecloth with the tip of his knife. Jack knew then that he spoke German and was listening.

"Have you skied the French Alps before?"

This, from Diana.

"No," Jack said. "You have, I gather."

"For years," she murmured. "But never this station. Too remote. Too uncomfortable. Until the road went in. It brought electricity to the valley."

"You'll want a guide," Playfair said suddenly. It was the first remark he'd directed to Jack. "It's unsafe to ski alone. Picard might find you one."

Picard was the father of the blond plaits.

"I'm going to bed," Diana said. "Willi," she called. "Aren't you *tired*, darling?"

It seemed a deliberate provocation. Jack's hackles rose. But he said nothing to her and looked instead at her husband, who merely discarded his ash.

Willi was returning indolently from his chat with Wohlthat. He smiled faintly at the Playfairs, his dark eyes opaque and unreadable, as if he loved them both too much to choose.

"Come along, children," he said. "Until tomorrow, Jack."

And thus was Jack Kennedy left alone with Göring's banker.

THE MAN SEEMED INCLINED to let him make the first move. He remained in his chair, tamping tobacco into the bowl of his pipe with sharp, erratic movements.

Jack rose casually from the table and approached the fire; he held out his hands to the embers. Aware of the weight of cold beyond these walls; of Diana, undressing upstairs; of this silent man in his chair.

"You are Mr. Kennedy," the German said softly after a while. "The ambassador's son."

"I'd hoped my name wouldn't mean a thing here." *Strike the note of self-mockery. Two men of the world, who understand the value of honesty, stuck in the snow.* What had Dobler told Wohlthat, in that short incomprehensible exchange? He possessed a smattering of French and he'd wasted years in compulsory Latin; neither of them was of the slightest use in hunting Nazis. Ignorance lay like a mortar in his path, but he'd come all this way. He'd have to risk something. The image of Daisy Corcoran's brutalized breast rose in his mind.

He offered his hand. "Jack Kennedy."

"Helmuth Wohlthat. Please, young man. Sit."

He drew up a chair. "I've heard your name somewhere before. You're a friend of the Little Sisters, aren't you?"

"Gott im Himmel," Wohlthat breathed, "what a disaster, no? Sister Mary Joseph! The account book! My God, the account book! Your father has some message for me?"

Jack's hands clenched but he managed to keep his expression vacant. *Your father.* Wohlthat could call him that, they were such pals. What to say to the guy? *Nothing definite. Buy time.* "He was hoping you had one for him, sir."

Wohlthat put his head in his hands. "What can I do but beg his forgiveness? An unmitigated disaster! All those names—your father's, his friends, the most important people in England and America—in Heydrich's clutches!"

Jack sat back in his chair, staring at the banker's face.

Parsing out the words. Rejecting their meaning.

Parsing them again.

Sickness rising in his throat.

Dad's name was in the stolen account books. Joe Kennedy, ambassador to the Court of St. James's. Along with others—the power structure of two continents, probably. Men and women who'd tried to buy an election for Hitler. Who'd committed a crime. Roosevelt would call it *treason—*

They executed for treason.

"This'll break him," Jack muttered. "Destroy him completely. Everything he's worked for." He thrust his hands through his hair, kicked free of the chair, and began to pace before the fire. "Hell, this'll screw all of us. Once the press gets wind of it—the whole world knows—*Roosevelt's ambassador on Hitler's payroll . . .*"

And then a random thought stopped him dead.

What if Roosevelt already suspected Dad of disloyalty? And had sent Jack himself out on the hunt?

It was no secret the two men did not see eye-to-eye. Or that Jack's father was considering a run for the White House in 1940. What if Roosevelt *intended* to destroy Joe Kennedy with the crime Jack was unearthing? He could simultaneously gut his rival, and use the evidence of Hitler's plot to convince America to enter the coming war. Once the voters knew the Nazis had tried to buy an American election, it would be a patriotic duty to vote for Roosevelt—and do whatever he asked to halt the Fascist menace.

But in that case, Jack's flailing mind insisted, *you'd be the very last person FDR would recruit. Your loyalties are too divided. Between Dad and the man you wanted to serve. God help you, the man whose respect you craved . . .*

He had to protect his father. Fail, and he'd bring his whole family down.

He faced Wohlthat. "You're sure Heydrich has the book?"

"That creature took it. He told me so."

"The Spider? You *talked* to Hans Obst?"

Wohlthat shuddered. "He never said his name. He merely delivered a message: Heydrich wants me to *cultivate* your father. I know what that means. He's going to blackmail us both."

"But how can Heydrich blackmail you? You're one of them."

Wohlthat shook his head. "I work with Göring. Heydrich hates him. He deliberately compromised my network to bring Göring down." The bowl of his pipe glowed red. "I'm expected to betray my old friend—I'm afraid of knives, you see."

Jack stared at him numbly. "And my father?"

"I think he's meant for something special. Something involving *money*. And the embarrassment of your president, of course. Heydrich will hold the account book over Mr. Kennedy until he does what Heydrich says."

"No," Jack said fiercely. "He can deny all knowledge of it. Call Heydrich a liar. Say the account book's fake."

"Then both of us will die," Wohlthat said simply. "In horrible ways. The Spider will hunt your father down, and your family also."

"No."

The banker studied him implacably. "Heydrich knows how to use fear, Mr. Kennedy. *Vulnerability.* There's no escape, once his hand is at your neck."

Jack just stood there, thinking. This beaten man was of no use to him; he'd given up and given in. He would do whatever Heydrich asked. *There must be some way he could get the account book back—*

"I'm sorry," Wohlthat said.

THIRTY-THREE. CROSSING THE BORDER

WOHLTHAT WENT TO BED.

Jack sat up in the empty room and stared at the dying fire.

His father was a traitor to the president they both served.

There was written proof of it, and a vicious man would use that proof.

The room lurched crazily whenever he moved his head; blood pounded in his ears.

He could not choose whom to fail. Roosevelt, or Dad.

In Jack's world, that was no choice at all.

He worried his lip until it bled, thinking of the man in the wheelchair and how much he'd yearned to live up to his expectations. To be *Roosevelt's man in Europe.* There'd been honor and purpose and excitement in the idea. He'd felt different, tapped by the President. *Valued.* An independent thinker—which was much more than the screwball his family usually thought he was.

There'd be no more ciphers from the roof, no confidential phone calls. And no explanation he could offer. He could not breathe a word of his dad's treason to FDR, so his radio would have to fall silent. While he waited for the truth to blow up in his face.

Did Dad know what was coming?

He doubled over, hugging his rib cage, while pain scissored through his entrails.

He should have stuck some DOCA in his leg hours ago.

How could he possibly explain his silence to Roosevelt?

He could say he was ill. Jesus—he *was* ill! Nobody would think twice. He could take a boat home and check back into Mayo and write a bunch of crap for his senior thesis, and only Bruce Hopper would know what a failure he really was.

And himself, of course. He'd have to live with himself. While Franklin Roosevelt dismantled the Kennedy family in public, piece by piece.

Maybe Jack would be lucky, and die in the war.

"Jack."

It was her voice, whispered behind him; the scent of her skin on the air. He turned and looked at her with hollow eyes.

"What is it?" she asked. *"What is it?"*

"Nothing you can fix," he said, and walked away from the dying fire.

BECAUSE HE COULD NOT TRUST DIANA, they played out their scene in the chilly hallway, the other men sleeping behind their bedroom doors.

Did you follow me here?

Yes. No.

Desire. Despair.

The center had dropped out of his world. He hated to be touched but he needed to be held. He wanted this woman, whom he could tell nothing. It was too much, and in the end he left her standing in the upper hall, arms folded like iron bars across her chest.

He closed his bedroom door on his pain and lay down in the dark, knowing he should find the DOCA pellets and use them.

What had his father done?

Treason—or murder?

Words and pictures whirled through his exhausted brain. A dead hatcheck girl in the alley behind the Stork Club. *I knew her people in Boston, Jack. Truth be told, I got her this job.* Sister Mary Joseph's blood spilled at his feet. Spiders cut into pale flesh. Göring's banker, the man who was afraid of knives. Roosevelt in his Pullman. *A hundred and fifty million dollars, Hoover says.* The thug with the scar on his lip. *Diana.*

His door opened.

"Wohlthat's upset you, hasn't he?"

The door clicked shut. She came toward him slowly. The shiver of silk charmeuse in the dark.

He swung his legs over the side of the bed and waited. Words were not safe. He could not trust himself to speak.

Her fingers slid through his hair. She was whispering something. *Poor jack poor jack poor jack.*

He pressed his forehead against the flat plane of her stomach and closed his eyes. She was cradling his head and murmuring softly but it wasn't a nanny he needed now. He slid his hands beneath the silk and pulled her down against him. Covered her sudden gasp with his mouth. And then she was beneath him, that fragile birch-twig body and the hoofer's legs, sleek beneath his hands.

He lifted the silk over her head. She wore a diamond solitaire at her neck. It flashed in the moonlight slanting through his window. He took the rock between his teeth.

She held his face in her hands. "We'll have to be quiet," she breathed. "The others—"

Because he hated to be touched, sex was usually something furtive and quick. It was more about release and triumph than anguish or need, but this was Diana, and he tried to remember she was no Radcliffe virgin. He tried to give as well as take. Circled her nipple with his tongue until she cried out and arched beneath him; swept his deft sailor's hands along her inner thighs. He pinned her arms above her head and kissed the valley between her breasts, the dip of her navel. Traced each knob of her spine, delicate as a nautilus, and the sweet tendon behind her knee. As he buried his face in her sex, she gasped like a woman rising from deep water, legs pirouetting over his shoulders.

Somewhere in the night he found he was weeping as she surged above him, her head thrown back and that diamond glinting in the moonlight. Her flesh tightened around him like a current, some memory of the sea. He did not fear drowning. He feared loss, himself marooned on an empty stretch of beach. He clung to the jetsam of her body and took the wave.

"Why did you marry him?" he asked her near dawn. "Willi called it *cover*. Are you in love with either of them?"

She snorted into the crease of his elbow, her hair flung over his arm. "They're in love with themselves. Ever since they met at Oxford. Denys and Willi. Willi and Denys. It's been that way for years."

He thought of Carmel Offie and his best friend Lem who'd made a pass at him at Princeton. Of the two men side by side in a black London taxi while he swayed alone on the jump seat. He thought of Dobler's colleague at Number 8 Carlton House Terrace. *You're one of* those. He should have seen it all before, but jealousy had blinded him.

He'd seen only Diana.

"In England it's tolerated but still a crime," she was saying.

"In Germany they give you a pink triangle or hang you with piano wire."

He lifted her onto his chest and she rested there like a sphinx. He shook her gently. "Why did you marry him?"

"Willi's life is at risk. And I've grown fond of him. Denys is vulnerable to *politics*. Sheer bloody malice. They turn a blind eye at the Foreign Office as long as he does what he's told—but he could be crushed at any time. They both *need* me, Jack. The sensational wife. The insouciant mistress. I'm plausible deniability. I draw enemy fire."

"And what do *you* get out of that deal, Diana?"

Her eyes slid away. "A name. *Position*. More money than I could ever spend."

"And a hell of a lot of loneliness."

She pressed her body the length of his. "I seize my moments."

HOURS LATER, after she left him, he cut a DOCA pellet into his thigh and slept for a while. His dreams were tinged with fever and he tossed beneath sweat-soaked sheets.

When he awoke, it was after nine and the alpine sun was well into the sky. He knew now what he had to do.

HE FOUND WILLI DOBLER at the breakfast table draining the last of his coffee. He was dressed in loose woolen pants, leather boots, a heavy sweater. A pair of skis was propped near the door.

"You're up early," Willi said. "Or didn't you sleep?"

Jack ignored the jibe. He pulled out a chair and reached for the coffeepot. "If I wanted to find the White Spider, I'd have to find Reinhard Heydrich first. Right?"

"It's a logical conclusion. But you don't, Jack. *Want* to find the Spider."

Jack took a sip of coffee. "Fair enough. I want to find something he stole. From a nun he knifed to death in Rome."

There was a silence. "Sister Mary Joseph. Diana told me."

"Did she mention the charity's account book is missing?"

Dobler shook his head. "She was more concerned about the loss of her friend. I take it you talked to Wohlthat."

"And he to me. Told me more than I wanted to know."

"You scared him to death. He left this morning at first light." Dobler eased back in his chair and studied Jack. "What insanity are you contemplating, my friend?"

"You said something once. About walking away from the mess Hitler's made of Germany."

"I told you I couldn't do it. Because people would die."

"Yeah." Jack swallowed some tepid coffee. "There are a number of ways to die, Willi. One of them is a spiritual kind of murder. The body lives on, but the soul's gone out of it. That's what my family's facing. A public humiliation. The ruin of all our lives. I can't shrug off the problem, Willi—I can't quit the game this time. I have to find the Spider before he gives Reinhard Heydrich the means to blackmail my father. And he has almost a month's start on me."

"Less," Dobler corrected. "He was in Paris the middle of March. Wohlthat said so. It will take him weeks to work his way across Europe. Police *somewhere* must be after him."

"He won't waste time with the account book. He'll take it straight to his master. So tell me, Willi—where's Heydrich right now? Berlin? Prague? Danzig?"

"If I were near an embassy—I could answer you in five minutes. As it is . . ."

"Come on, Willi. You know everything. Before it happens."

The German sighed. "Even if I *did* know, I'm not sure I'd tell you. I've no desire to send you to your death, Jack."

"That's touching, Willi. Thanks. But it's not your decision to make."

After an instant, Dobler nodded. "Then start with Berlin. It has the advantage of being closest. If Heydrich's there, you'll know soon enough. You can work your back channels. Ask the American chargé to arrange an interview for your . . . *thesis*."

"And then rob the Gestapo chief."

"If you want to put it that simply." Dobler's voice was flat. "You're talking about the most dangerous man in Europe, Jack."

"Including Hitler?"

"Including Hitler."

Jack lifted his eyebrows and waited.

"Do you have a gun?" Willi asked.

He shook his head regretfully. "Roosevelt said I needed one."

"—*And?* You couldn't ask the little man in the lingerie shop to help you?"

Jack laughed out loud. "Is there anything you *don't* know, Willi?"

"Not much. Wait a moment."

He left the table and headed upstairs, taking the narrow wooden stairs at a bound, and Jack heard the sound of his boots tramping across the ceiling. When Dobler returned, he carried a flannel-wrapped package.

"*Si vis pacem, para bellum,*" he said softly, and handed the thing to Jack.

It seemed there was a use for Jack's Latin after all.

If you want peace, prepare for war.

Jack unwrapped the piece of flannel. It had lovingly concealed a Luger P08 semiautomatic pistol, the Parabellum. The German army's sidearm of preference for the past forty years. It was a thing of beauty, Jack thought, in the strangest of possible ways—with its slim barrel, elegant as a cigarette, and its grip canted at a fifty-five-degree angle. A semiautomatic, recoil-operated pistol, it had a toggle lock and took eight 9-millimeter bullets in its magazine. The bullet shells ejected once they were fired.

"Ever use one of these?" Dobler asked.

Ever? Jack had never used any kind of gun at all.

Dobler glanced out the window. "It's high time we woke Val d'Isère. Get your coat."

HE WORKED WITH THE PISTOL for nearly an hour, under Willi's patient tutelage. Learned to load it, and to steady it in both hands, held straight out like a shot-putter; to correct for the inevitable recoil; to correct for the vagaries of sight and nerve. He fired into snowbanks. He fired at trees. Purely by accident, he fired at Willi—and missed. For that he got a lecture on gun safety.

They drew a crowd of three silent Frenchmen, and as a gesture of goodwill Willi let them hold the Luger.

"De la guerre," one said. And the others gazed at Willi with sudden mistrust.

"Come along, old chap," he muttered as he threw an arm over Jack's shoulders and turned him toward the inn. "My father used this at Verdun. And the French have long memories."

JACK SETTLED HIS BILL and tucked his bags into the hired car. He would be driving higher on the Col d'Iseran, to the Italian border, then turning north to Germany.

"When you reach your embassy in Berlin," Dobler said, "send Denys a telegram. He'll be back at Whitehall the end of this week. We'll all want to know how you are."

Jack shook his hand. He got into the car and put it in gear. Dobler stepped back onto the steps of the Hotel de Paris and lifted his hand in farewell. It was an English gesture, nothing like the Nazi salute. Jack glanced over his shoulder as he wheeled the car around and caught a clouded glimpse of Diana's face.

She had appeared out of nowhere and was standing at Dobler's elbow. She was wrapped in furs. A suitcase sat at her feet.

"Jack," she called.

He stopped the car.

Dobler stepped through the inn's doorway and disappeared.

Diana leaned into his side window. *"Jack."*

She was fumbling at the door handle.

"Diana, I have to go."

"Take me with you."

"I have to go."

He was reaching for the passenger lock to slam it home when she opened the door and slid into the seat.

His hand fell instead onto her shoulder.

She stared at him, her black eyes unreadable.

"Don't do this, Diana."

Her lips compressed. She busied herself with settling her luggage. For a woman of fashion she had brought surprisingly little.

"This isn't a vacation. It'll be dangerous."

"And I know everybody in the Nazi hierarchy in Berlin, Prague, and Poland," she snapped. "You'll find I'm useful, Jack Kennedy. You'll find you can't manage without me. You'll wonder how you ever *dared*."

"I thought Willi could be trusted."

She shook her head. "Don't blame him. I know nothing, really. It's all a guess. But you *need* me, Jack."

He did not ask what she needed from him.

Her lips were swollen from his urgency the night before and the mere sense of her beside him made his head swim.

"Denys," he muttered.

"—Has other distractions. And he has been left before."

He leaned into the fur collar and kissed her.

THIRTY-FOUR. RESEARCH

THEY LURCHED UP THE COL D'ISERAN toward the Italian border and did not look back.

Later, Jack would remember these days imperfectly, the way he remembered dreams. Fragments of images slid through his mind, some heavy with meaning and some inexplicable. The way the country spread like an antique map at their feet as they descended from the mountains. The way April turned green again as they left the snows behind. Lambs in the fields. Lamb for dinner. Diana lying naked on a bed, a glass of red wine in her hand. Diana stalking angrily through an olive grove, clutching her suitcase, while he drove alongside, urging her back into the car. He could not remember what they had argued about. Something trivial. Nothing compared to the blood sports that would divide them later.

He admitted her to the secret of DOCA and she revealed herself as a competent nurse, swabbing the gash in his thigh with iodine. Somewhere she bought gauze and insisted on dressing the wound. After that, she studied him covertly for signs of fever, and strangely Jack did not mind. With every passing hour he let her further into his life, and this was part of the dreamlike quality of those days. He never let women come so close.

"Tell me," he urged, running his hand up her silk-clad leg to the garter's clasp. "Tell me who you are. Where you come from. How you got here, Diana."

She would not look at him. She was annoyed. His fingers slid beneath the garter and caressed her thigh. Slid deeper, to the wet heat between her legs. She drew a sharp breath, her knees convulsive. With his other hand he held the steering wheel of the small French car and the road was very narrow and very fast. Diana liked it dangerous.

"Tell me." His fingers fluttering. *"Tell me."*

But she refused, her head thrown back, taking her wordless pleasure from his hand and the speed. He pulled the car to the verge beneath a tree and rucked her skirt to her waist and thrust himself between her legs. He meant to punish her for all she refused to say but instead felt only this passion, the certainty of losing himself, the conviction that he would never come to the end of Diana. She was too strong. She held too much back. He wanted all of it, forever.

"She was in service," she said finally, as he sprawled in the wreck of her stockings and clothes. "My mother. She was a cook. Her fingers smelled of onions. My father was an actor who came through town. He left, of course, and went on to the next one. She boarded me with her sister and worked her fingers to the bone. At night, after I'd gone to bed, she'd come in and stroke my hair. All I remember is the onion smell. I ran off when I was fifteen."

He waited until he was sure she was done talking. Then he said: "My mother never sat by my bed in her life. Or stroked my hair. Not even when I was supposed to be dying."

She gave a bark of laughter. "You've nothing to envy, Jack."

Diana was her daddy's girl, a wandering trouper, her roles so fabulously layered it was impossible to know what was real and what was legerdemain. Jack took the fables she told as warnings. She could not be trusted. Only admired for her perfect pitch.

Three days out of France they reached the American consulate in Milan. Jack presumed upon his diplomatic status long enough to send two telegrams: one to Offie in Paris explaining where he'd gone, and another to his father in London. *Getting some interesting thesis material,* he wrote. *Headed east over next few weeks.*

Before he left Milan, the consul sent Joe Kennedy's reply to Jack's hotel.

Get your ass back here by 22 June for Eunice's debut party.

From this, Jack concluded his father had no idea their lives were as good as over.

"WHAT IS IT YOU'RE AFTER?" Diana asked him as they drove north toward Lake Como. "If I'm to help you, I should know."

He'd been agonizing over exactly this point throughout the journey. From selfishness and desire he'd allowed her to join a hopeless quest. He might have to use her Fascist contacts to locate Heydrich, once they got to Berlin. But he could not trust her *because* she had Fascist contacts.

How far did this "cover" of hers extend? Was Diana's Nazi pose purely personal, for the better protection of Denys and Willi—or was it political, too? Was she a Fascist by convenience—or conviction?

"Tell me who you're working for," he suggested. "Then I'll decide what I can share."

She glanced over at him, her eyes invisible behind dark glasses. "Can't," she said.

"Can't, or won't?"

"Both, I suppose." Her gaze drifted back out to the landscape. "The less you know, the safer we both are."

"That cuts both ways."

"I don't doubt it. But the fact remains: You're hunting something. I'm offering you my help. The offer's useless unless I know what to look for."

What if you're nothing but a beautiful lie? he asked himself. *The most beautiful lie I've ever wanted to believe?*

He had been asking this question about women, more or less, all his life.

He drove on toward the Swiss border.

Their lovemaking that night was a pitched battle. Neither took prisoners.

They climbed north through Switzerland and crossed into Germany a week after leaving France.

Jack's diplomatic passport drew immediate attention from the border guard across the river from Stein am Rhein, the picturesque Swiss hamlet they'd abandoned for the Reich. The boy in the field gray uniform—he was years younger, Jack guessed, than himself—was immediately suspicious and uncertain, as though advance notice of an American's official travel should have been wired to every German checkpoint. The guard had no instructions regarding Mr. John Kennedy. No real proof that he was a diplomat at all. And he claimed to be driving to Berlin, on official business? Why had he not traveled by train, with a secretary, like a proper American? The fact that Diana, a British subject with entirely different papers, was traveling with Jack was even worse. How to account for such a companion, other than by scandal? Diana sat in the open car doorway, her long, silk-clad legs crossed at the ankles, smoking a cigarette with obvious boredom. Jack peppered the tight-lipped boy in ever-louder English, all flattened vowels and drawling consonants, his Boston patrimony, of which the guard understood perhaps one word in ten.

When the boy moved to his pillbox, determined to call Berlin, Diana barked out a few phrases in German.

The guard froze. His expression, Jack saw with fascination, was abject when he looked at her. Diana made a business of crushing out her cigarette and dusting ash from her fingers. The passports were suddenly stamped and returned, the crossing bars lifted from the lonely roadway.

"What did you say to him?" Jack demanded as they drove past the rigid boy. "And where did you learn to say it?"

Diana blew the guard a kiss. Waggled her fingers. "I told him when his call was done I wished to borrow his telephone. I had come expressly from London to introduce *Herr Kennedy* to my esteemed friend, the Führer—and I felt he ought to be warned of our delay."

THREE DAYS LATER, they were standing in Berlin's Adlon Hotel on Pariser Platz.

Jack booked two rooms. The U.S. embassy was across the square, to the right of the horses topping the Brandenburg Gate, and he was afraid a well-meaning diplomat might cable his dad about the gorgeous woman he'd shacked up with.

The embassy was old General Blücher's palace, he of Waterloo fame. The staffers hated the location because the Nazi Party paraded through Pariser Platz whenever they needed to whip up a frenzy. Noise was a constant irritant. Roosevelt had recalled his ambassador the year before, to protest the atrocities of Kristallnacht, and relations between the two countries were deteriorating. Roosevelt had rebuked the Germans for seizing Czechoslovakia and Hitler had snarled in reply.

A chargé d'affaires named Alexander Kirk ran the embassy, a suave and elegant friend of Carmel Offie's who seemed to share La Belle Offlet's sexual proclivities. He cared deeply about antiques, entertaining, and food, in that order, and assured Jack that while he did his best to keep his finger on the Führer's pulse, he had no idea whether Reinhard Heydrich was in town. Kirk personally made it a point, he confided, to keep out of the Nazi security chief's way.

"Scary fellow," he said. "*Odd.* Just looking at him gives me the heebie-jeebies. That incredibly high forehead. Those close-set eyes. The *nose*. You might talk to the commercial attaché, Sam Woods. He knows a good deal about friend Reinhard."

Kirk leaned conspiratorially toward Jack. "Woods reports directly to Roosevelt. Bypasses State completely. The President had him transferred here from Prague, before the Czech show blew up. Knows everything there is to know about this new physics business. *Atoms.* Woods is the man you want."

But Sam Woods had already left for the day, so Jack carried Diana off to a cabaret. She wore the nude chiffon with the black velvet bows that had entranced him on the *Queen Mary*. Her eyes were narrowed and her lips half parted and her foot tapped as she watched the dancers; and Jack sensed a bit of what she'd lost to her respectable marriage. Diana was dying to be on stage, shoulders bared and pelvis thrusting. She craved risk the way other women craved affection.

This was something they had in common, Diana and Jack: They didn't care if they died, or how. They were simply determined to *live* first. He'd never known a woman so much like himself and the knowledge made him hungry for her. He devoured Diana that night in her sanctified separate hotel room, his mouth roaming over her thighs, her breasts, her sex, until she knotted her fingers in his hair and swore.

THE NEXT MORNING JACK knocked on Sam Woods's door.

The commercial attaché worked in a windowless room deep in the Blücher Palace, surrounded by posters of smiling American housewives and glossy American Buicks. He glanced up as Jack hovered in the doorway and said, "You're the Kennedy boy. Kirk said you were in town. College junket?"

"That's about the size of it," Jack agreed. He shook Sam Woods's hand. "I'm researching my senior thesis. 'Security in the Age of Fascism.' It'll be embarrassingly incomplete without the Reich Main Security Office. I was hoping you could get my foot in the door. Mr. Kirk says you follow Heydrich."

"Oh, I follow him, all right," Woods said drily. He tossed a packet of what looked like financial data to one side of his desk. "Through half of Europe, these days."

Jack was tempted to ask why a commercial secretary was interested in the head of the Nazi secret police, but he stopped himself. *Woods reports directly to Roosevelt . . . knows everything there is to know about this new physics business.* Jack was looking at another of the President's spies.

"I can't get you in to talk to Heydrich," the attaché was saying, "but I can find somebody who'll give you an hour. Got your dip passport with you?"

Jack showed it to him. Woods made a few phones calls. He spoke impressive German. Not for the last time, Jack wished he did.

"I've got to go send a cable to the White House now," the attaché said, "but I've gotten you into Heydrich's shop. Be outside the embassy in ten minutes. You won't need pen or paper for notes, by the way. The Gestapo give nothing away."

JACK WAS DRIVEN IN an official car to Prinz Albrechtstrasse 8, a five-story Beaux Arts building, the Gestapo's home. Hitler's security services took up most of the block, stretching around the corner to Wilhelmstrasse. If Jack could just get inside, he'd figure out what to do next.

"Could you begin," he asked the bland figure in the perfectly tailored SS uniform who'd ushered him into an office, "by explaining the difference between these forces—the Kripo, the Gestapo, the SD? None of them existed before the Nazi Party came to power, right?"

"The degeneracy of recent governments, and the chaos in civil society they encouraged, led to a general lawlessness that required a firm response," his handler said in dispassionate English. His name was Storck. "The German crisis demanded innovative methods. Disciplined personnel and clear penalties. Examples the general populace could understand. We are now a model of civic order envied throughout Europe."

"It's pretty confusing," Jack said. "All these police groups, all run by the same person—General Heydrich. He has quite a grip on the reins of power, doesn't he?"

Storck smiled thinly.

"I don't suppose he's around? Willing to talk to a visiting American?"

"The *Obergruppenführer* will be desolated when he learns he has missed your visit, Herr Kennedy," Storck replied, "but he is occupied with pressing duties. There is never so much time as the *Obergruppenführer* would wish. Your question is an excellent one, however, and I shall attempt to answer it. *Kripo* is the name of the Reich criminal police . . ."

Jack listened to a disquisition on Nazi repression for roughly twenty minutes before Storck deemed he'd said enough. Then he was turned over to a pair of Gestapo men and marched to the entrance of the Albrechtstrasse building. The corridors were wide and vaulted like a church and populated by SS and Gestapo uniforms. Guards were posted every few feet. They eyed Jack as though he were a prisoner bound for interrogation. There was no chance of finding Heydrich's office in this fortress. If the White Spider had already delivered Göring's account book, Jack would never retrieve it. He felt like a fool.

He bought himself a drink in the Adlon bar and stared moodily through the plate-glass window at Pariser Platz. He rolled the whiskey around his mouth and thought about his final year at Harvard, once his dad was exposed as a traitor. He'd be shunned. A pariah. Could they kick him *out* of Spee Club? His brother Joe would be furious—he was starting Harvard Law in the fall, and his whole life was about running for president one day. *That* plan wasn't looking good. Kick's romance with Billy would come to a screeching halt as well. Eunice's debut would end in a public shaming. At least he, Jack, only wanted to wander the world as a foreign correspondent. There were still remote places where nobody'd ever heard of the Kennedys.

Somebody slid onto the neighboring bar stool and propped a handbag on the counter.

"He's in Poland," Diana said crisply. "Danzig, to be exact. Probably plotting how best to steal it. Buy me a cognac? We ought to toast something."

He ordered the drink, grasped her gently by the arm, and led her to a cocktail table. She shrugged her furs off her shoulders and pecked him on the cheek. "You look tired."

"It's been a tough day." He kept his voice deliberately low, as though he were talking smut. Diana smelled divinely of cold air and lilies of the valley. "How did you find out?"

"I rang up his wife." She held her drink aloft and said, "The Thousand Year Reich."

"*Heydrich's* wife?"

"Of course. She's a sad sort of cow, pathetically eager for chat—he married her years ago to advance his career, and barely spares her a thought. Keeps a string of mistresses without the courtesy of *hiding* it. You know the sort."

He did. He thought of Gloria Swanson and Clare Booth Luce and pushed his father out of his mind.

"Anyway, she invited me to tea while you were storming Albrechtstrasse."

"Speak softer," Jack murmured in her ear. "People listen. Especially to English."

"Sorry. It's been rather a . . . *trying* . . . afternoon." She downed the cognac neat. "Unity Mitford was there. Know her?"

"I like her sister Debo better."

"Unity came over for the Führer's birthday last week. She gave him a *present*. From her smug expression, I assume it was her virginity." She motioned to the waiter. "Another cognac, please. Then I promise I'll *stop*."

The man smiled at Diana. Her color was high.

"Heydrich's been gone for weeks," she murmured into her glass. "Prague, of course, and Warsaw, and some filthy little town on the Czech-Polish border I couldn't possibly pronounce. Planning something. War with us, probably."

"Thank you, Diana," Jack whispered.

"We should leave for Danzig tonight. Whatever you're looking for, it won't be here. He'll carry it with him. He trusts nothing and nobody."

Jack lifted her chin and stared into her black eyes. "I'm hunting for Daisy's account book."

"You said the Spider took it. When he killed her."

"My father's name is in it."

"The charity wasn't a charity," she said slowly.

"It's a Nazi front," Jack agreed. "Hitler's trying to buy the next American election. Roosevelt's running for a third term, and Hitler wants him to lose. He wants an isolationist in the White House, so that the United States will turn its back on Britain and everybody else in Europe whenever he decides to attack. He wants the vast firepower of America neutralized, Diana—and he found a willing bunch of isolationists and appeasers, in my country and yours, to fund his operation."

"I bloody well did *my* bit," she whispered. "I collected for Daisy. Begged alms from the Mitfords. And Lady Astor. The whole Cliveden House set— Good God . . ." Something in her expression sharpened. "Did Daisy . . . ?"

"—Know? I think so."

"But your father . . . he was just giving alms . . . I mean, he *is* Catholic—"

"He's ambitious." Jack looked down at his hands. They were clasped in his lap and his leg was throbbing. "He wants the White House, too. Even if it takes Nazi money to get it."

"He *admitted* to . . . to . . ."

"Treason? I haven't confronted him yet."

"Then you can't be sure. You can't be *sure*, Jack."

"That's a luxury I can't wait for. Wohlthat expects Heydrich to blackmail him—and my father as well. That's why the Spider killed Daisy for the account book, and risked everything to get it to Berlin—that's why it's so precious. Consider the possibilities, Diana, in all those names! Heydrich will threaten each of them, one by one, with public exposure, unless they do what he asks. Linchpins of the American and British establishment, terrified of the charge of treason. They'll fall over themselves to do his bidding—little things, nothing important at all, really, that determine the fate of England. The alternative being unthinkable to each and every one of them."

"Is it so unthinkable to your father, Jack?—Accepting responsibility, I mean? Taking whatever comes with *admitting* to what he's done?"

"That'd be what you people call *cricket*." He glanced away from the intensity of her face. "God forgive me, I wish I could believe old J.P. capable of that kind of courage—but he's never been a courageous man, Diana. He'll tell himself he can't ruin his kids' lives. My future and my brother Joe's. He'll say he's doing it for my mother. *Christ*, that's rich! And if he caves to Heydrich . . . *when* he caves . . . *The U.S. ambassador to England* will be under the Gestapo's thumb. My father has been Roosevelt's principal liaison with Neville Chamberlain, Diana. Chamberlain trusts my dad. That could give Heydrich enormous influence over England's future . . ."

"So you're off to save your father from himself," she said acidly, "or die trying."

"You don't have to come."

"*Jack*."

He looked at her. She was more than annoyed, now. She was blazingly furious.

"Get me another drink. If I order it, the waiter will call me *ein Lügner*."

"I don't speak German, Diana."

"A liar," she said.

THIRTY-FIVE. BACK CHANNELS

*. . . **AN IMPROVED MODEL** of the coding machine is presently being constructed at several factories on the Czech-Polish border, and is confirmed to be Heydrich's pet project.*

"How convenient for the sake of Herr Heydrich's pet project," Roosevelt sighed as he studied the document in his hands, "that the Nazis now control the entire Czech border. I wonder if Mr. Chamberlain knew how useful he would be, when he graciously invited the Führer to take the place."

Sam Woods, the commercial attaché at the American embassy, Berlin, had sent his latest cable to the President; and the President was assiduously reading it. Woods was a highly trained engineer by education, a scientist first and a diplomat by only a distant second. His report did not deal with the "new physics," as the chargé, Mr. Kirk, might have assumed; but it dealt with something equally interesting—something Roosevelt had specifically asked Woods to investigate, when the President arranged for the engineer's transfer from Prague to Berlin: the newest form of encrypted communications currently under development by the German military. Roosevelt's ad hoc adviser on all things espionage, General William J. Donovan, had suggested communications would be mortally important in the coming months.

The "Heydrich-Enigma," as it is known, improves on the commercial version first developed after the last war. Sources say the new machine will replace all existing communications equipment throughout Nazi Germany. Heydrich is convinced the coming war will be won by unbreakable encrypted communication. The Polish Intelligence service has been breaking Enigma codes for the past six or seven years. This new machine is Heydrich's response.

A knock on the door broke Roosevelt's concentration. Sam Schwartz stuck his head around the jamb. "News from Scotland Yard, sir."

"Tell me they nabbed the Spider, Sam."

"He's been traced. Seems a body was found last month near the Thames shipyards, with a spider cut into its chest."

"Last *month*?"

"It took the Brits a while to identify the corpse, sir. The victim was a Polish merchant seaman—the Yard had to wire his ship for confirmation, which was halfway around the world by then. The man's papers were subsequently passed in Italy and France."

"Italy, and *then* France?" Roosevelt repeated. "The killer went east, and then doubled back?"

"Yes, sir."

Roosevelt stared thoughtfully through his office window, which was streaming with spring rain. Jack had gone to Italy, and then France.

As if reading his thoughts, Schwartz said: "Any news of young Mr. Kennedy, sir?"

"He's in Berlin." Roosevelt didn't add that young Mr. Kennedy had piqued the attaché Sam Woods's interest with a few choice questions about Reinhard Heydrich. Or that Woods had arranged for Jack to interview the Gestapo.

Why was Jack on the scent of the most vicious man in Europe?

And why hadn't he communicated with Roosevelt in weeks?

THIRTY-SIX. CONTACT

THE FREE CITY OF DANZIG was an anomaly in the heart of Europe, an ancient trading port on the Baltic Sea that acknowledged no overlord. It had once been part of the Teutonic Order and the Hanseatic League; but these were commercial ventures Danzig understood. It abhorred political ones, which had brought it only trouble. With its beautiful old medieval halls and red-tiled roofs, Danzig reminded Jack of Amsterdam or Prague; but its piratical merchant's heart conjured Venice and Constantinople.

Every ambitious warrior in history had fought for Danzig, including Napoleon. Prussia and Poland had played tug-of-war with it for centuries, but Danzig's people hailed from all over. There were Scotsmen and Russians, Dutchmen and Jews. Danzig had its own parliament and currency. Its own anthem and flag. Its own post office and stamps.

Its own immensely lucrative shipyards.

The city was dominated by Poland to the south, which needed it for access to the sea. Ninety percent of Danzig's population, however, identified itself as *German*. German territory bracketed the city east and west. And therein lay Danzig's fate: Hitler was screaming for it. What he really hoped was that the Free City would skip joyfully into the Reich of its own accord, just as Austria had done the year before. Then he could cut off Poland's trade and its navy's sole port.

Reinhard Heydrich and his secret police were in Danzig, Jack assumed, to make sure the spontaneous revolt went exactly as Hitler planned.

It was two hundred fifty miles from Berlin to the Free City, but Jack and Diana had set out in the late afternoon and the roads were so poor their progress was slow. Jack found his way into the heart of Danzig a few minutes past ten o'clock at night on May first. He was tired and suspected he had a fever. Spots were dancing before his eyes. He ignored them because the chance of finding somebody like Mayo's George Taylor or even the Sorbonne's Dr. LaSalle, with his convenient hypodermics, was extremely remote on the Baltic Sea. Jack's DOCA regimen wasn't quite working at the moment but he would simply have to gut out the Mystery Disease. His family's salvation depended upon it.

The ancient city's streets were extremely narrow and cobblestoned. When the signs weren't written in Polish they were written in German, which made Jack swear at his misspent youth. Diana guided him by instinct, holding her lighter over a map and turning it around and around in her hands. They were reduced to shouting two words through the open window: *American embassy*. A series of gestures from brusque strangers showed them where to go.

The American legation was housed in a narrow, high-storied building that might have been five hundred years old. At this hour, all but one of the windows were dark. Jack pummeled on the front door. Diana sat in the car, flicking her lighter.

A night duty officer named Russell let them in.

He was only slightly older than Jack himself, and he flushed

embarrassingly every time his eyes met Diana's. With one impe-
rious glance she succeeded in reducing poor Russell to speech-
lessness; he gabbled a little, offered a light when she reached for a
cigarette, and swallowed hard as he tumbled to the fact of the
Kennedy name.

"The place for you is the Kasino-Hotel." Russell plucked a
handkerchief from his breast pocket. Jack waited while he dabbed
his forehead miserably. "It's ideal, really, under the circumstances—just a few miles up the coast, in the direction of Gdynia.
It's a smashing place, with its own beach. Tennis courts. The
longest wooden pier in Europe, stretching right out into the bay.
They call it the Monte Carlo of the Baltic."

"I'd prefer to be—" Jack began, but Diana cut him off.

"There's a spa there, isn't there?—Massage?"

"Dancing, too," Russell replied happily. "And a decent dining room—although the cuisine is rather *German*. Most of the
patrons are, too."

"German?" Jack repeated.

"Ribbentrop and Göring have stayed there. I guess they like
to roll the dice now and again." At this feeble joke, Russell emit-
ted a high cackle of laughter.

Jack glanced at Diana. She was smiling her Cheshire-
cat smile.

"Gimme directions," he said.

THE BUILDING WAS MASSIVE under moonlight. An avenue led
to the front portico. Jack received a dim impression of a surfeit of
staff, obsequiously bowing; of Art Deco armchairs; of the sea not
far away. They took two rooms.

He awoke aware that he'd been sweating in the night. His

mouth tasted of cotton and sewage. He'd administered some DOCA before bed, but he inserted a second pellet now, hoping to avoid disaster. His supply of the drug was rapidly dwindling. He considered the problem for a moment, frowning, then threw on his clothes. They were profoundly wrinkled. He knocked on Diana's door.

She was breakfasting in bed, a picture of luxurious contentment, and waved him away. He descended to the dining room alert for the sight of a German uniform.

By day, the Kasino-Hotel was monumental. Perched on its stretch of beach, it suggested a banker intent on a dirty weekend. Jack strolled toward the wide French doors opening onto the terrace. The day was cloudy, and a brisk wind whipped the bay to white; not a bad day for sailing. He wondered idly if someone there rented boats. A few people were trekking the length of the pier, leaning into the wind; somewhere, he caught the popping sound of tennis racquets. The combined effect transported him instantly to his father's house in Palm Beach. He went in search of the dining room.

It was immense and sparsely populated. Sporadic figures stretched into the distance, isolated at tables. Most were men. There was a definite haze in the air of Nazi gray.

He was led half the length of the room before they halted at his own little island. He'd been placed well away from the German officers, who had been given the best tables near the windows fronting on the sea. Jack hesitated, then shook his head. "I'd like to be over there," he said firmly, pointing at the exclusive scattering of uniforms.

The maitre d'hotel gazed at him stolidly. Breakfast would be on his terms or not at all. Jack sat where he was told, and was handed a linen napkin for good behavior.

Coffee arrived immediately. The menu, he saw to his relief, was written in German, Polish, and *French*. He could read enough of the latter to survive. The meal ordered, he lit a cigarette and glanced casually at the distant Germans as he smoked it. Heydrich had a high forehead and small eyes, closely set, he remembered. Kirk, the Berlin chargé, had said so. He saw nobody he could identify as the man, but several had their backs to him. He looked next at his neighbors.

There was a white-haired Continental with a dramatic mustache. Two elderly German women in impassioned but whispered conversation, their lips trembling. And a neat, dark-haired, compact fellow with distinctly English tailoring and a vaguely military bearing, who had finished his meal and was in the act of quitting his table—

Gubbins.

Jack was on the point of rising and hailing the ex–colonel of artillery—inquiring after business in the lingerie shop—when something in the man's air stopped him. Gubbins was quite deliberately avoiding Jack's eye.

He followed the trim figure until it disappeared. His cigarette burnt down to his fingertips and he ground it in an ashtray.

A plate of fried eggs and wurst was placed before him. Jack ate half of it, his stomach cramping viciously. *Damn his bitch of a body. And damn the lousy food.*

He stopped at reception before heading back upstairs.

"What room is Colonel Gubbins in?"

The clerk consulted his register. "We have no one staying with us by that name, sir."

"I see."

His Majesty's spies moved with craft and stealth. And traveled under aliases.

He felt his pulse quicken. It would be a definite mistake to push further, to describe the man who'd just eaten breakfast and attempt to learn his name. He jingled the change in his pockets and turned away.

"Mr. Kennedy—"

He turned back.

The clerk presented an envelope.

He recognized at a glance the colonel's spare handwriting. With a casual air, he tore open the flap as he strolled toward the elevator, and withdrew the single sheet of stationery.

Meet me at the end of the pier at ten o'clock, the note read. *Come alone.*

THIRTY-SEVEN. GAMBLERS

IT TOOK A WHILE TO WALK to the end of the pier. Jack figured it was about six football fields in length, maybe longer, and as he trudged farther out into the bay the wind picked up and the temperature dropped. He kept his hands thrust into his overcoat pockets and felt the heavy wooden trusses sway beneath his feet. There were small food concessions and gaming stalls and the occasional photographer's booth, most of them boarded up and empty of life; it was only May, and the summer season came late to the Baltic. In August there would be an orchestra and a dance floor and colored lights strung along the pier, if the Nazis hadn't bombed it by then.

Most of the people strolling alongside him turned back well before the pier's end. Jack could just make out a solitary figure etched against the blustery sky; in a close-fitting dark coat and a tweed cap, it seemed contained enough to be Gubbins.

And if it wasn't?

If he'd been set up, and a knife waited at the end of the walk?

It would be a long swim back to the beach.

The man turned as he approached. On three sides, the sea; on this rocking platform, only the two of them.

Jack held out his hand. "How's business in brassieres these days?" he asked.

GUBBINS OFFERED JACK A LIGHTER and his pack of Player's. They drew smoke for a few seconds, staring out at the bay, and then the colonel said, "Thesis research, I take it?"

Jack nodded. "And you?"

"A sudden urge to see the Free City before it is no longer free."

"There's a hell of lot of gray uniforms in that hotel."

"They're likely to increase this summer."

Jack looked at him. "You think they'll take Danzig?"

"And all of Poland."

"That's why you're here, isn't it?"

Gubbins smiled. "Why are *you* here, Jack?"

He hesitated. He had no idea who gave Gubbins orders, but he trusted the colonel. He badly needed advice in this country where he knew nobody, didn't speak the language, and was determined to try to rob the Gestapo.

"I heard Heydrich was in town."

Gubbins's right eyebrow rose. "I watched him play roulette last night. For very high stakes. You're hoping to interview him?"

"—Or the man he pays to knife people. I told you about him once. Hans Obst. He's sometimes called the White Spider."

The Englishman tossed his cigarette violently into the sea. "Blond, blue-eyed, medium build, with the body of a wrestler and an inch-long scar bisecting his upper lip?"

"That's our Hans."

"He shadows Heydrich like a Rottweiler."

Jack's pulse quickened. If both Obst and his master were in the Kasino-Hotel, the account book must be in one of their rooms.

"Obst must be feeling safe, surrounded by so much gray," he

said. "No fear of his crimes catching up with him. That's good. It'd be a problem if he decided to hole up in his room."

Gubbins looked at him. "You'll have to find out which one it is, first. I don't think he's registered under Obst."

"You're not registered under Gubbins."

A faint smile. "When traveling in the lingerie trade," the colonel said carefully, "I am known as McVean. It's a family name, of Scots descent. When this war is done I shall retire to Scotland, and take up the ancestral family profession."

"Which is?"

"Killing invaders. Do you have a car, Jack?"

"A hired one. With French plates."

"And a diplomatic passport, courtesy of your father?"

"Of course."

"Excellent. It's just possible I'll need your help one night soon." Gubbins gathered his coat collar about his chin. "Delightful to chat with you, but I'm chilled to the bone. I'll start back. Give me five minutes before you follow. You'll forgive me if I treat you as a stranger in public."

"And in return for my help?" Jack asked suddenly. "You'll find Obst's room?"

Gubbins glanced at him. "In exchange for your help, I'll kill the blighter if I have to."

Jack stood for what felt like an age, his body shuddering in the wind. He counted five German planes in the sky over Danzig while the minutes ticked by. Bruce Hopper would have loved it.

DIANA WAS MAGNIFICENT THAT NIGHT, supple from massage, her hair freshly coiffed, her face dewy and her beautiful body sheathed in a narrow slip of gun-metal gray. She carried an evening bag Jack had bought as a Danzig souvenir, and it dangled from a steel chain on her wrist. She radiated a cold and terrifying sort of charm and within seconds of her arrival in the casino, she was surrounded by Germans. There were other women in the room but none to equal Diana.

Jack watched her dip her cigarette holder in a flame. Watched her lips encircle the smoke. She wore elbow-length black gloves, and gave the impression of wearing very little else. She had lined her eyes in black and the effect was exotic and intimidating. The diamond solitaire at her throat winked enticingly. He could not imagine that he had ever possessed the strength to touch her, or that she had ever allowed it. She'd told him that night to leave her alone—she wanted to work the crowd, learn what she could, be a free agent. Jack fought the impulse to drag her from the room by her hair.

He ordered a glass of whiskey and carried it to the *caisse*, where he tried to buy a rouleau of chips. There was a delay. A whispered consultation. Eventually an imposing figure attached to the hotel—security? management?—came out of the *caisse* and asked him, in heavily accented English: "How old you are, boy?"

Jack felt the blood rush to his face. Wordlessly, he drew his passport from his coat and showed it to the man. It was a night of familiar humiliations.

When he looked next for Diana, the crowd of gray had parted, and somebody was bowing over her hand.

The high, domed forehead. The eyes, almond-shaped and narrow. A long, aquiline nose. Surprisingly full lips; everything of the sensualist in them. The ears perfectly molded and set close to the skull. The lean figure in the tailored uniform. Two lozenges of oak leaves on the lapels. The eagle and swastika on the arms. Gold braid at the shoulders.

I rang up his wife, she'd said in Berlin.

She and Heydrich had met before, it was clear.

He led her out onto the dance floor and she turned in a waltz as though his hand at her back was intoxicating. Jack watched her murmur in his ear.

He keeps a string of mistresses without the courtesy of hiding it.

Jack's pulse was pounding in his head. With effort, he looked away. This was no sock hop in Hyannis, no Harvard Smoker. He searched the casino for other faces intent on roulette and dice, blackjack and chemin de fer. Gubbins was seated alone with a fatuous expression Jack mistrusted completely. He allowed his gaze to drift without recognition over the colonel, and come to rest on Hans Obst.

The White Spider was standing against the opposite wall. He wore a black Gestapo uniform and his eyes were locked on Heydrich as he moved around the dance floor. Jack had no idea whether Obst had noticed him. Was it possible the man could follow him across the Atlantic, through London, even to Rome— and not give a damn that he was in Danzig?

Then the Spider looked directly at him and lifted his glass in a mocking salute. *Don't worry,* the gesture seemed to say. *You're on my turf, now. I'll kill you whenever I choose.*

Jack saluted back. He was feeling just that reckless. With Heydrich leading Diana to an intimate table away from the gamblers, he needed a good brawl.

And then somebody jostled him and Gubbins's voice exclaimed *so terribly sorry,* as his handkerchief swabbed ineffectually at the drink he'd spilled all over Jack's evening clothes.

"Unforgivably clumsy," the colonel fussed. "I've *spoilt* your evening. You'll want to get out of those, I expect."

"It's okay." Jack lifted his whiskey-stained shirt from his chest with his thumb and his forefinger.

"My name's McVean," Gubbins said, beaming. "Allow me to give you my card—I *insist* upon taking care of the cleaning."

"In that case," Jack said, pocketing the square of cardboard, "I accept."

"Jolly good. Feel such a fool. Hope to make amends."

The card, when Jack looked at it, offered little to the imagination. *James C. McVean, Painter in Oils.*

HE STUDIED IT FOR A FEW SECONDS, frowning, and then remembered something Gubbins had told him in the secret room behind the lingerie shop.

He made his way to the men's room, and waited for the two Germans in uniform to finish their business at the urinals while he commandeered a stall. His trousers pooled at his feet for convincing effect, he pulled out his cigarette lighter and held the flame near the card. In a few seconds, words appeared, tiny but unmistakably Gubbins's.

Car in 10 min. Stop end of drive.

The colonel had written the message, Jack suspected, with Scotch.

THIRTY-EIGHT. THE BAKER STREET IRREGULARS

"I DON'T KNOW THE ROADS or the language," Jack said.

"Perfect." Gubbins slid into the car. He'd been waiting among the trees that lined the avenue to the hotel, another shadow among shadows. "I've got a smattering of both, as it happens. Head out of town and drive south for a bit. I'll tell you where to turn."

He settled into the passenger seat, his collar turned up, his trilby pulled down. It was, Jack thought, like having a complete stranger beside him. And it occurred to him then that he knew nothing about Colonel Colin Gubbins. Even less about James McVean, Painter in Oils.

The car bucketed over an enormous pothole and they lurched toward the windshield like rag dolls.

"Have a care," Gubbins murmured. "Get a puncture here, and the whole evening will be spoilt."

"You sound like a girl with a new party dress."

"Something like," Gubbins agreed. "That's what we'll tell them, when they ask—we were bound for an evening party. At your diplomatic legation. Only we got lost and never found it. And then, God help us, we couldn't find our way back to the hotel. Two hapless English speakers, lost in the wilds of Poland—perhaps we really *will* puncture the tire for verisimilitude."

Jack wanted to ask where they were going and why. But he held his tongue. It was like a birthday surprise. Knowing what was in the box would ruin it. He badly needed suspense tonight. Anything to banish the memory of Diana in Heydrich's arms.

They left the town of Sopot with its lights and its restaurants and its glittering vitrines behind them. The darkness of the Polish countryside closed around the car. The road unspooled before Jack's hood like a ribbon; he was heading south, into the Corridor—the strip of land connecting Danzig to Poland.

"That siren you unleashed on the casino," Gubbins said casually when they'd driven in silence for nearly fifteen minutes. "She wouldn't be Denys Playfair's *wife*, would she?"

"At the moment," Jack said abruptly.

"Jolly good. Smashing girl. Has her wits about her, has Diana. Just give her a free hand—she'll turn up trumps for you. Now," Gubbins said in a voice that signaled they were done with social chat and were about to attend to business, "slow down. You'll want to turn into that side road to the left—it's unmarked, barely visible, but believe it or not that is a *direct* route from the Polish-Czech border, or direct as these execrable roads ever get. Veritable death traps for anything on four wheels—but that's exactly what we want, tonight."

His voice was so thoroughly amiable that Jack ignored the warning implicit in the words and turned obediently to the left, from one unlit road to another. Ahead lay a darker smudge that might be a storm or a mountain. He could not see beyond his headlights. No other beams knifed through the black.

Perhaps ten or twelve minutes passed. There were fields and

the occasional glow from a lone farmhouse window. And then the looming smudge resolved itself into woods. Jack plunged into them.

The road bucked and curved through the trees. He slowed to a crawl. And then suddenly one of the trees was lying directly across the road and he could go no farther. It was a massive thing. It appeared to have been blown directly in his path by an epic storm; an entire canopy of roots loomed to the left.

"I suggest we stop here," Gubbins said.

"Or turn around and go back to the hotel."

"And miss all the fun? No, no, dear chap. It's almost *time*."

Jack threw the car into reverse.

"Perhaps a little farther from the tree," Gubbins murmured. "I should leave at least a hundred yards."

Jack did as he was told and killed the engine.

"Well, come *on*," Gubbins said, and shoved his door. "Chilly in the Baltic region in May, what?"

Jack got out and went around the hood of the car. "Have you been drinking?"

"Not so's you'd notice."

"What the hell are we doing?"

"Pulling Herr Heydrich's leg." Gubbins glanced at his watch. "You were rather slow over that last bit of ruts they call a road. *Hurry*."

He sprinted toward the fallen tree and began to haul himself over the trunk. Jack could just see, through the tangle of branches, the pale glow of approaching lights. Gubbins ignored them. Jack ran after him, grasped a branch, and climbed upward, wishing he was wearing anything but evening clothes. Gloves, for instance, would've been nice. He vaulted over the tree, looking for Gubbins. Landed hard on his left leg, the thigh throbbing viciously in protest. He could hear the approaching vehicle now; a heavy engine, whining with speed, probably some kind of truck.

"Over here!" the colonel hissed.

He was crouched in the brush at the road's inner curve.

Jack joined him.

They waited. The sound of the engine grew louder. Twin beams arced suddenly over the trees, sharp as searchlights, and then the monster was upon them.

Jack drew a deep breath. There was a hideous squealing of brakes. A crash of gears as the truck tried to avoid the massive tree directly in its path. The engine howled. And then an enormous shape, square and shrouded in tarpaulin, seemed to double over on itself—somersault past them—in a shriek of gravel as Jack clutched Gubbins's arm. It hit with a violence that shoved the fallen tree trunk sideways, as easily as though it were a discarded broom, branches and roots catapulting over and over with the truck somewhere in between. The whole tangled mess skittered down the dark road and Jack suddenly found his voice.

"My car!"

"Should be all right," Gubbins said, rising to his feet and pulling Jack along with him.

At that moment, the smashed truck burst into flames.

They both ran toward it, Gubbins drawing a gun. Other figures emerged from the woods—dark figures, unidentifiable, in shapeless clothes. A dozen? Half a dozen? They moved so swiftly it was impossible to know. They ignored the cab, where there was certain to be men trapped by fire, maybe dead already from the crash; Jack hoped so. Gubbins made a dash for the rear of the truck and somebody fired a gun at the hasp that secured the doors. They swung open.

Gubbins was shouting in a language Jack recognized as Polish and two other men vaulted into the rear of the truck, canted crazily on its side. They tossed boxes out into the road in a kind of frenzy. Everyone ignored the boxes. Two limp figures in gray uniforms hung halfway out of the truck and Jack knew suddenly that they were German soldiers—this was a German army truck—and he wanted to ask whether the soldiers were dead or just unconscious, and what would happen to them now. But there was no one to ask. He stood in the middle of the road, feeling the heat of the burning engine and aware that the gas tank could explode in a matter of seconds. Gubbins was shouting and waving everyone back to where Jack stood, but the men wouldn't move. And then a figure appeared in the canted truck doorway—stepped over the bodies lying there—and jumped to the ground. He was sprinting toward Gubbins.

There was a sucking sensation in the night, as though a giant had drawn breath, and then the concussion.

Jack was blown backward, falling hard to the surface of the road. Flames shot above him as he struggled to his feet. Men pounded past through the darkness. One of them was Gubbins. He was shouting in Jack's face.

"We'll have to work our way round to your car. *Quickly.*"

He plunged into the brush at the side of the road and Jack followed jerkily, his legs almost refusing to obey his screaming mind. Gubbins was scrambling up the bank, reaching for low-hanging branches, hauling himself into the cover of the trees. Jack stumbled after the colonel as he flitted among the trunks. Then down the bank and out onto the road, the burning truck with its charred human flesh behind them.

His car was still sitting where he'd left it.

He pulled open the driver's door and almost fell behind the wheel.

"Shall I drive back, then?" Gubbins asked anxiously.

Jack shook his head. He fumbled in his jacket for his keys. They were still there.

Gubbins reached into his coat and withdrew a flask.

"Here," he said, passing it to Jack.

The word had all the force of an order.

Jack took a swig, and felt the liquor burn its way down his throat. He closed his eyes on the rawness of it.

Then he shoved the keys in the ignition and the engine coughed to life. He backed down the road blindly, a sheet of flame from the burning truck soaring in front of him. He found room to turn the car. And sped away from the place as though the Gestapo were on his tail.

"IF ANYBODY ASKS WHERE we were tonight," Gubbins was saying calmly as they reached the turning for the Sopot road, "I should use the story about that party at your legation. And losing our way. Forget the punctured tire; that's something that can be checked."

"One of them already has a repaired puncture," Jack said mechanically, "so that's all right."

"Oh, you noticed that, did you? You're starting to think like a saboteur, Jack Kennedy. Been reading my manuals, haven't you? *The Partisan Leader's Handbook.* Jolly good. Changing a tire might explain the wreck of your clothes."

Jack turned the car toward Sopot, a glow on the horizon. "Those men were Polish."

"Yes."

"And the truck was German."

"Got it in one."

"What were they stealing?"

Gubbins sighed. He smoothed his mustache with one hand, as though listening to internal argument.

"You borrowed my car," Jack pointed out. "Hell—you borrowed *me*."

"So I did," Gubbins agreed. "And I'm damn grateful. You've got diplomatic immunity, d'you see. They wouldn't prosecute you, Jack, if we'd been found at the scene. A Painter in Oils has less pull than Ambassador Joseph P. Kennedy's son."

"Christ," Jack said tensely.

Gubbins was willing to toss him to the Gestapo.

Christ.

"They were stealing a wireless transmitter," the colonel was saying. "Heydrich's latest model of something called the Enigma. The Polish Intelligence service has been breaking German codes for years, Jack, but Heydrich has tumbled to the fact and changed the game. The Germans are perfecting a new machine, far more complex, and rumored to be unbreakable. The Poles badly wanted one so they can take it apart, figure out how it works. They'll need as much advance warning of Hitler's invasion as they can get—and the Führer's orders will be transmitted through the Heydrich-Enigma."

"He found it," Jack said suddenly. "The guy who jumped out of the truck, right before it blew."

"Yes. We'd learned a model was being sent from a factory on the Czech-Polish border straight to a Gestapo unit embedded near Danzig. There were several routes it could take from the border, but only one into Danzig itself—so we advised the Poles they'd best sabotage the truck here, under Heydrich's nose. And make it jolly well look like an accident," Gubbins added reflectively. "I think they succeeded."

"Who's *we*?"

"Beg pardon?"

"*We*. You keep saying *we learned* and *we advised*. Who's we? You and the partisans in the woods back there?"

Gubbins shrugged. "I've learned a lot from the Poles. They're clever chaps and exceedingly resourceful—that's what comes from being sandwiched forever between Russia and Germany. But no, Jack—my employers, such as they are, are known informally as . . . BSI."

Jack thought about it. "British Secret Intelligence?"

Gubbins laughed out loud. "Hardly so exalted, my dear chap! It's for Baker Street Irregulars. After Sherlock Holmes's gang of boys. Our offices are around the corner from Baker Street, in fact."

"I thought Britain had military intelligence. MI being the acronym."

"*That* would be Mr. Chamberlain's service," Gubbins said comfortably. "And I'm afraid, Jack, he's not inclined to use it. Has more faith in his ability to *reason* with the enemy. He thinks spying isn't *cricket*. We've had to work around him."

We, again.

"Nobody ambushes a Gestapo truck for the sake of friendship," Jack said, "no matter how much you've learned from the Poles. The risks are too high. What's in it for BSI?"

"The Enigma, of course. Our friends in the woods have a few months, perhaps, to tinker with the model we helped them nick—but if Hitler rolls the Poles as easily as he's rolled the Austrians and Czechs, their work will be shut down. And then *we* shall have to undertake it."

"Figuring out how the Heydrich-Enigma works? Breaking the German codes?"

"Yes. We'll have to smuggle the machine out of Warsaw—it's already on its way to Polish Intelligence headquarters there—and carry on the work in England. You realize, Jack, that once Poland falls, Hitler's encrypted communications will be directed against *us*. England has pledged to defend Poland, after all, and that will mean war once Hitler invades."

"England can't save the Poles?"

Gubbins sighed. "With Mr. Chamberlain in office? We shall hardly save ourselves."

"He knows nothing about what happened tonight, does he? Or this Enigma machine?"

"Really, Jack. Would *you* tell him?"

Jack had a haunting suspicion he'd thrown in his lot with a gang of extragovernmental criminals, and for an instant he wanted to stop the car and kick Gubbins out. But he remembered, then, the cable sent by Sam Schwartz with the curious bona fides, and the unquestioning assistance he'd received in the cupboard beneath the trapdoor in Gubbins's office.

Roosevelt knew the Irregulars existed. Jack had been deliberately handed to them.

"One more thing," he said. They were back in Sopot now, and the Kasino-Hotel loomed before them.

"What's that?"

"Our deal. My quid for your quo."

Gubbins smiled. "The Spider sleeps in room 5101, directly next door to Heydrich. Have you got a gun, dear boy?"

THIRTY-NINE. THE DUMBWAITER

AS THEY DREW UP UNDER the portico of the hotel they saw a crowd of German officers waiting in the night. One of them was Reinhard Heydrich.

Gubbins said under his breath, "They'll have heard about the truck. Whatever happens, don't argue."

And then Jack's door was flung open and he was pulled from the car. A Nazi with a death's-head patch on his collar—which meant that he was SS—jumped behind the wheel. Another held open the rear door for Heydrich to get in; apparently an *Obergruppenführer* never sat in front. Gubbins was already standing on the pavement with a sardonic look on his face. The motor gunned. Jack's car sped off.

"Hey!" he shouted after it furiously.

"I gather we've been *commandeered*, old chap," Gubbins drawled. "Wonder what's got these chaps in such a snit? Two o'clock in the morning, no less! A man can't even have his *nightcap* in peace."

He strolled nonchalantly through the crowd of officers and into the lobby. As Jack followed, five cars roared up to the entry. The Germans piled into them with a barrage of orders that fell on his ears like machine-gun fire.

In a few seconds the cars had disappeared in a line of red taillights, and the portico was silent again—but for the panting breath of a valet, who'd run for a car and been punched by an irate German for his efforts.

Jack stood there a moment as quiet descended, taking deep breaths to calm his erratic pulse. *Heydrich was racing to the scene of the ambush.* He'd figure out pretty quickly it wasn't a simple accident—wouldn't he? Gubbins was insane to think a handful of crazy Poles could pull off a stunt like that, under the very nose of the Gestapo. The Nazis would return in a few hours and start rounding up the innocent. Shooting people. And it was Jack's fault because he'd driven Gubbins in his car. Heydrich would remember that—the two of them driving up to the entrance with exquisite timing. They'd be interrogated, of course. Their story about a legation party and a flat tire, a pathetic joke under the circumstances.

Jack was swept with a wave of exhaustion so profound he swayed where he stood. He pulled a handful of Danzig currency from his pocket and gave it to the only other person still lingering by the hotel entrance in the waning night—the valet who'd taken a punch in the gut. He was a slight young man in a dark uniform who looked as spent as Jack felt. Jack figured he wouldn't need much cash, once Heydrich was done with him.

THE CASINO WAS EMPTY and there was no sign of Diana. He let the elevator carry him to the third floor, and hesitated outside her door. There was no light or sound within. He glanced down at himself. His evening clothes were a mess. Dirt and gravel were smeared along his trousers and he smelled of creosote and fire. He'd have to get rid of the suit. These were the evening clothes he'd had tailored at Poole's, but he couldn't risk keeping them.

He let himself into his room and stopped short, appalled.

It had been so thoroughly ransacked it rivaled the chaos of his *Queen Mary* stateroom. Obst and his picklocks, again.

"Fuck." He slammed the door. Torn books, spilled shaving kit. The contents of his suitcase dumped on the floor.

He crossed immediately to the room's sole window, a tall, imposing affair heavily draped and canopied against the wind off the Gdańsk Bay. The drapes had been drawn at dusk by the maid. Jack twitched them aside and reached up with his right hand, feeling along the interior wooden frame of the canopy. He'd hidden Willi's Luger there.

And the Spider had missed it.

He pulled the gun from its hiding place and looked at it, gleaming blue in the overhead light.

If you want peace, prepare for war.

He glanced around the savaged room. What else was precious? The books could be replaced. He'd had his passport and money with him. No letters from the family, nothing that could—

And then he went cold. *His radio.*

He sank down onto the carpet and huddled there, crosslegged, his head in his hands. He'd left the suitcase with the radio set locked in the trunk of his car. He had no real use for it, now that he was ignoring Roosevelt, and it seemed silly to lug the thing into every hotel along the road from Val d'Isère.

But Heydrich himself was riding in the car and either he or his driver might just use the trunk key Jack had left behind when they'd tossed him to the curb.

His first impulse was to get to the American legation and hole up until he could be sent home by plane or boat.

His second thought, which seemed saner than the first, was to find Gubbins.

He changed his clothes, stuffed his acrid-smelling dress suit in the hotel's linen laundry bag, and slipped out of his room. At the far end of the silent corridor there would be the inevitable service pantry: shelves piled with linens, butler's carts, supplies of soap and towels. He prayed the door was never locked and that nobody was awake at this hour of the morning.

He was lucky on both counts. The pantry door opened at his turn of the knob.

A dangling string grazed his face—the light switch. He shut the door behind him and reached for it in the dark. The sudden electric glare revealed what he was looking for: the trash chute leading directly to the hotel incinerator. It ran alongside a much larger shaft that accommodated a dumbwaiter. There would be openings for both on every floor.

He dumped his damning clothes down the trash chute. There was a faint roar as the incinerator yawned far below, then closed on Savile Row's finest tailoring.

"I SHOULDN'T LEAVE JUST YET, old chap," Gubbins said thoughtfully as he offered his hip flask to Jack. It was nearly three, now, and Gubbins had clearly enjoyed a bath while Jack was burning his evidence; no hint of what the colonel would call *petrol* lingered in the room. He wore a correct navy dressing gown that would not have been out of place at a Pall Mall club, and his face shone pinkly from his ablutions. "Might put the wind up the Gestapo. Turn their thoughts in an unpleasant di-rection. Best appear at your table this morning and tuck into a tidy breakfast of bacon and eggs. Engross the attention of that charming mistress of yours. Ten to one Heydrich will think the truck met with an unfortunate accident—and friend Death Head will never have opened your boot."

"And if you're wrong?"

Gubbins shrugged. "Call your diplomatic representatives. Or I will, if you're in jug."

"Jug?"

"Deprived of liberty. Rendered *incommunicado*."

"Thanks." Jack took a swig from Gubbins's flask. His forehead was clammy and chills were running up his spine.

"Has it occurred to you," the colonel said diffidently, "that you could put the wee hours of morning to better use?"

"I know. I look like hell. I should be in bed."

"Not at all, dear chap. Quite the contrary. If Heydrich and every other Jerry has gone to the scene of mayhem—stands to reason the Spider's room is empty. He's searched *yours*. Might as well return the favor."

Jack stared at him. He'd wondered before if Gubbins was drunk or mad. "I don't know how to pick a lock."

Gubbins's teeth flashed. He produced something narrow and black from his dressing gown pocket. "This is a *hotel*, Jack. A simple hairpin should do it."

TWENTY MINUTES LATER JACK was standing in the middle of number 5101, which reminded him strangely of Mayo. The Spider had left no trace in the room; it was sterile as a hospital ward.

Gubbins had lent Jack gloves and told him to leave his shoes by the door to avoid footprints. So here he was, with a black balaclava over his face. It itched unmercifully and Jack was sure he was allergic to whatever it was made of. Merino. Angora. An animal never intended to touch the face of a guy who broke out in hives whenever he petted a dog.

"The Poles *swear* by these when they're getting up to a spot of mischief," the colonel had said. "You could do a hell of a lot worse than learn from the Poles. They've managed, after all, to retain *some* national dignity, despite being conquered by every egotist with an army over the past thousand years. The jokes people make about them are *grossly* unfair."

He'd clapped Jack on the back and gone down to the lobby in the guise of a genial insomniac searching for company and perhaps a drink. Determined to know exactly when Heydrich returned. Gubbins as Spotter and Lookout.

Quickly. He had to move quickly.

Jack opened the Spider's closet. A set of street clothes, a strange navy peacoat beside them. He'd expected camel's hair. For an instant he was sure he'd broken into the wrong room. But Gubbins didn't make mistakes. Did he?

He ran his hand over the shelf above the hanging rod; nothing but an extra blanket. He unfolded it in case Daisy Corcoran's account book was tucked inside. Nothing. He put the blanket back, his neck prickling.

He got down on his knees and ran his hands under the Spider's mattress. He'd liked to have tossed the whole thing off the frame, but Gubbins's voice in his head stopped him. *Leave no trace.* The bedside table had a Lutheran missal, printed in German. And a New Testament in Polish.

No briefcase. No book. No personal papers. No piece of stationery missing from the supply in the desk. He checked beneath the armchair cushions. He ran his gloved hands along the window canopy. If the Spider hadn't thought to look there in Jack's room, he hadn't used it in his own.

There was a washbasin with a shaving kit on the shelf above. Nothing else.

The account book wasn't there.

For a wild moment, he thought: He doesn't have it. *We're safe.*

And then he thought: *It's in fucking Heydrich's room.*

A shaft of vertigo sliced through him. He would have to break into the room next door.

He went for his shoes—and heard faint footfalls from the carpeted corridor outside.

Someone was coming.

He jabbed at the light switch, plunging the room in darkness. He thrust his feet into his shoes, not bothering with the laces. His blood was pounding in his ears.

The footsteps halted at the Spider's door.

How the hell had Gubbins missed him?

There was a pale chink of light where the corridor's glow seeped through the keyhole. Jack watched as it was blotted out by the key. In a second the Spider would know that the door was already unlocked. He might even have sensed Jack's breathing.

Gubbins missed him because he didn't come through the front lobby. He wasn't with Heydrich. He never left the hotel. He'd been searching my room when they got the news about the truck.

Jack went hot and then cold. He'd coolly picked the man's door, thinking he was thirty miles away in the smouldering woods. When all the time he was having a last drink. Or screwing a maid. Carving his mark into the girl's breast—

The Spider kicked in the door with smashing violence.

If Jack had been behind it, he'd have been crushed against

the wall with a broken nose. But instead he'd stood on the opposite side, and the second Obst appeared, he fired the Luger blindly. Striking before he could be struck.

Force propelled the massive shape into the room, stumbling, until the Spider let out an animal grunt and rolled to his knees. One arm clutched his chest and the other swept out, desperate to stab; Jack slipped past the writhing man and bolted through the open door.

What had he done?

A guttural, inhuman roar filled the air behind him. That and the gunshot would be enough to sound an alarm.

Jack ran straight down the empty fifth-floor corridor, shoving the hot muzzle of the gun into his waistband, burning the skin above his navel. He was still wearing the balaclava. He was fleeing like a thief in the night. Such obvious stupidity, if anybody saw. If a single bedroom door opened. There must be a service pantry at the end of this corridor. They would start looking at the other end, near the elevator.

He pulled open the pantry door and shut it behind him. Standing in total darkness, he stuffed the balaclava down the incinerator, then pressed the button that summoned the dumbwaiter.

It might have been forty seconds while the dumbwaiter lumbered five stories up, while doors opened, feet pounded, voices shouted in horror. Was the Spider dead? Or was he heaving himself painfully, arm over arm, through a pool of his own blood? Jack's legs shook. He held down the call button savagely, urging the dumbwaiter to hurry. He prayed the Spider could not tell them which way he'd run.

The dumbwaiter rose slowly into view. A forgotten chafing

dish, a few napkins, a pot of stale coffee were still inside. Jack swung himself carefully on top, testing whether it would bear his weight. It swayed and held.

He forced himself to keep his mind on survival. Forget the five-story drop. He reached for the pulley that supported the wooden carrier, and began to work the cables by hand. He and Joe had done this when they were kids. Loads of times. There was a dumbwaiter in the Bronxville house and they used to scare the hell out of the kitchen staff when they burst through the door. There was a dumbwaiter at Prince's Gate, too. He'd have to show Teddy the trick sometime. If he lived long enough.

He was still wearing his gloves and he was thankful for the thin protection they offered between himself and the cable. He lowered the dumbwaiter by degrees, hand over hand, until a break in the shaft told him he'd reached the fourth floor. He could hear nothing of the world beyond his vertical tunnel but he was conscious of squeaking, something weary and habitual in the mechanism, a clear signal to anybody listening that the dumbwaiter was in use at half past three in the morning. He was sweating and yet clammy with chills. He was afraid he would vomit. But it didn't matter if he puked. Nothing mattered. The third-floor hatch was coming nearer. He could swing himself out and be safe—or stare down the barrel of a gun.

He halted the dumbwaiter a few feet above the third floor. No light. No movement. Just a current of air betrayed where the shaft opened into the service pantry. He lowered himself the last small distance and swung through the opening.

A hand grasped his arm. Another went over his mouth, stifling his scream of panic.

"Got you," Gubbins whispered.

THE COLONEL SAID THEY SHOULD brazen it out, so Jack folded himself onto the bottom of a butler's cart while Gubbins draped a piece of linen over it. He took the dirty dishes from the dumb-waiter and arranged them attractively on the cart. Then he rolled through the pantry door and went whistling down the third-floor corridor, oblivious to the mayhem all around.

Jack could just see through a narrow gap at floor level. Black boots rushed past. They were searching the entire hotel for the Spider's killer. They were searching for *him*. And the Luger was still tucked into his waistband. If they found him, no dip pass-port or famous name would save him.

A harsh splutter of German broke out above his head and the cart was suddenly reeling sideways, thrust along with Gubbins against the wall. Jack clung by his fingertips to the shelf, terrified one of his legs would swing out and betray him, aware as if from a great distance that Gubbins was snarling something in Polish, the perfect reaction of an abused waiter; and in an instant, the cart had righted itself and rolled on.

He closed his eyes. Gubbins stopped at his door, pounded on it with his fist, called out something that must be *Room Service* in Polish—and thrust a hairpin deftly into the lock.

The cart glided into the sanctuary of Jack's bedroom and he heard the door slam closed behind them. He slid to the floor and lay there an instant, staring at Gubbins's shoes.

"Now," the colonel said, "get into pajamas. They'll search every room—and you'll want to look plausible. Where's the gun?"

Jack pulled it from his waistband.

"A Luger. *Clever*, that. If they bother to check the Spider's wound ballistics, they'll think another German did it. Lord knows *some* of that cretin's friends must want him dead. Put it away safe. And for the love of Christ *get off the floor.*"

Jack scrambled to his feet. Gubbins was already at the door, with his cart full of dirty dishes.

"Did you find what you were after?"

Jack shook his head.

"Pity," Gubbins said, and backed his cart out into the hall.

FORTY. LOVE AND WAR

HE WOKE TO THE COOL TOUCH of Diana's hand on his face and the knowledge that he was sick again.

The ceiling lurched through his fever. Someone had told him he must be careful and stay in bed. He had killed a man. He heard himself ask what time it was.

"Five o'clock," Diana soothed. He tried to focus on her face and caught only a blurred outline. "Friday evening. There's a doctor come to see you, Jack. Can you sit up?"

He sat up, trying to pin down *Friday*. They had reached Danzig the first of May. Monday night. And later he had shot the Spider.

A man with gray hair and ridiculous glasses hanging from a chain was easing him forward so that he could press a stethoscope to Jack's back. The man wore a plaid wool waistcoat as though it were winter. "Breathe," the man said. Jack breathed. He closed his eyes. His mouth was dry as sandpaper. The man was speaking German. Diana was speaking German. He wondered again where she'd learned it.

The sound of abrupt consonants tossed his memory back, suddenly, to an oblong of light falling into the corridor, Diana fierce in a filmy wrapper, her face lifted to a Nazi's, her voice insisting angrily *He's ill can't you see how ill he is. My God he can't even stand you will not search his room—*

And now it was Friday.

"May fifth," he said, working it out.

"Yes," Diana replied. "Dr. Groenig wants to see your leg. The one where you put the pellets."

"*Der* pellets also," the doctor interjected ponderously.

He was German but he did not wear his death's-head on his sleeve. Jack wanted to ask Diana what had happened to Obst but Gubbins's voice in his fevered brain said *Don't mention it, old boy.* He lifted the sheet from his thigh and slumped back against the pillows.

Groenig probed the reddened gash. Jack groaned.

"Where are the pellets, Jack," Diana asked clearly.

He managed, this time, to focus on her face. "Shaving kit." She rose and went into the bath. Then handed the bottle to Groenig, who furrowed his brows as he read the label.

"*Ach.*" The doctor studied him over his glasses. "You are very ill boy." He directed a spate of German to Diana.

"He wants to give you an injection, Jack."

This was how they'd execute him for murder. With a needle. *Ambassador Kennedy we regret to inform you that your son John Fitzgerald passed away after a short—*

He shook his head violently and the room whirled. "*No.*"

"Jack—" Diana took his face between her cool hands and forced him to look at her. "Do as he says. He's a good doctor. He came to treat that poor fellow who was shot the other night."

She said it casually enough, but he caught the warning in her voice. It focused him.

"What fellow?"

"One of the German soldiers. Dr. Groenig very kindly agreed to examine you today, once he'd checked the other chap."

"Chap's alive?"

"Yes. Shot through the lung. Weeks, probably, before he recovers."

Relief flooded over Jack. They wouldn't execute him for a lung. But he had stopped the Spider for a while, and right now that was enough.

Groenig was swabbing his arm with alcohol.

"They think it was a Pole who shot him," Diana said conversationally as the needle plunged into Jack's thin bicep. "They've been rounding up Poles for days, poor blighters."

THE DOCTOR RETURNED ON SATURDAY and gave him another injection while Diana fed him lukewarm tea. She read to him from the only English novel she could find, Du Maurier's bestseller. *Last night I dreamt I went to Manderley again.* Jack dreamt of monsters coming through the door, hulking black shapes that exploded in petrol fire.

The next time he woke it was Gubbins who sat by his bed, dressed in tennis whites. He'd been down to the courts, he told Jack; a glorious day. He might even take out his easel and capture some views of the Bay. Gubbins made a point of introducing himself as *James McVean, Painter in Oils*, to Dr. Groenig who'd returned for the third day in a row, hypodermic in hand. It was unclear how well the doctor understood English but Gubbins kept up a soothing patter while Groenig was there. Once the doctor left, Gubbins reached for a bowl of soup and raised a spoonful to Jack's mouth.

"Your car's back, by the way," he said easily. "All serene, as far as I can tell. No disturbance to the boot. The keys are on your dresser."

"Thanks," Jack said. His mind was clearer. "What day is it?"

"Sunday, old man. Have another spot of soup."

"Is Diana okay?"

Gubbins's gaze shifted fractionally. "Saw her playing tennis. Seemed in good form. Dashed competent backhand."

"Tennis? With who?"

"*Whom*. Heydrich, of course. She doesn't waste her chances, Diana."

"No." Jack closed his eyes. *Heydrich*. "If you see her—"

"I'll tell her you'll be on your feet in no time."

HE NEVER KNEW WHETHER Gubbins gave Diana his message, because by the time he dressed and came downstairs—Monday afternoon, May eighth—both of them had left the Kasino-Hotel.

There was a note from Gubbins waiting in his pigeonhole. *Delightful to have struck up an acquaintance, old chap,* it read. *Do look me up at my club once you're back in Town.*

He'd signed it James McVean and enclosed his card. On the back was a handwritten address in Baker Street.

Diana's letter had been shoved under his door that morning while he still slept.

He's asked me to go with him to Moscow. We must assume he has what we want. You know that we both need to find it. Other names beside your father's are in those pages.

Don't hate me, darling.

He had read and reread this note, his knees propped up beneath the sheets, his fever for the first time gone cold. He could feel the shape of the Luger hidden beneath his pillow.

We both need to find it. Other names beside your father's . . .

English names, presumably. Ones too vulnerable to blackmail. Had she known what Daisy's accounts were really for, all along? Did she get into his car at Val d'Isère because she was under *orders* to find the network's records before he did? Had Diana slid into his bed with the same calculation as she did Reinhard Heydrich's?

She doesn't waste her chances, Diana.

Or was she just determined to do what he was too weak to accomplish?

Don't hate me, darling.

But in that moment he did. Diana was like every other woman he'd ever allowed himself to love. His mother, long ago when he was kid. Frances Ann, just last winter. Women had a way of taking his deepest feelings and twisting them into a noose around his neck.

Diana. He was hanging here, twisting.

FOUR HOURS LATER, Jack was on the road to Moscow.

He stopped only once on his way out of Poland, pulling into a dirt track that led through a wood. He unpacked the radio transmitter and ran a lead from the car battery as Gubbins had taught him. If he could not save his father's carcass, he might at least do something for the man fighting this war before it even began. He encoded his message with a few words of the Harvard fight song and sent it into the ether.

Polish Intelligence ambushed Heydrich-Enigma five days ago with British help STOP New cipher machine deemed unbreakable now being assessed STOP Gestapo embedded in Danzig possibly preparatory to invasion STOP Inform FBI White Spider recovering gunshot wound Kasino-Hotel Sopot STOP Am following Heydrich to Moscow STOP CRIMSON

FORTY-ONE. SOURCES

"CAN YOU TRUST THIS INFORMATION?" General Bill Donovan asked.

"I believe so."

"I won't ask who Crimson is."

"I wouldn't answer if you did." Roosevelt toyed with the hideous lunch on his plate; he noticed Wild Bill hadn't bothered to eat a bite of it. The White House's housekeeper, Mrs. Nesbitt, was fond of prunes; she thought they were good for a paralytic's digestion. Also liver. There were weeks where she served Franklin liver and prunes every single day. Eleanor wouldn't hear a word against her.

"It tallies with London's reporting," Donovan was saying. "My contacts think the Heydrich-Enigma is much more complex than anything we've seen. They'd love to get their hands on one, but it's the Poles' baby right now, and God knows the poor bastards need it. Time's running out for them."

Wild Bill had an informal army of spies in a number of countries, which was one reason Roosevelt invited him to lunch. "What else is London telling you?" he asked.

"Something funny, actually." Donovan pushed his chair back from the table and reached for his coffee cup. "Joe Kennedy had dinner on May ninth with Göring's banker. A man named

Helmuth Wohlthat. He sat down in a private room at the Berkeley Hotel in London and listened to Wohlthat's pitch. I guess you'll hear about it from Kennedy soon."

"I already have."

Wild Bill's expression changed.

"Wohlthat offered German disarmament and clear steps toward peace," Roosevelt said neutrally, "if Old Joe could get me to pony up a billion-dollar loan from gold reserves. I'm supposed to sell the idea to the Brits. Then we put our hands in each other's pockets and turn over the cash to Hitler."

"A *billion* dollars." Donovan sipped the lousy coffee from the White House kitchens and grimaced. "Give us your gold so we can pump up our economy?"

"—Give us your gold so we can take over Europe," Roosevelt said.

"Did Kennedy really think you'd buy it?"

"I don't know." Roosevelt shrugged. "Joe has always confused business and politics, Bill. In his mind, this was a friendly conversation about a *loan*. The international power play behind it would be completely lost on him. I should add that I expressly forbade him to meet with Wohlthat. And that he went against my orders."

They were silent a moment. Then Roosevelt said, "I expect your friends in England are watching Joe Kennedy."

Donovan's gaze never wavered; it was a habit Roosevelt valued. "They don't trust Joe in the slightest. Think he's a defeatist and an appeaser. It wouldn't surprise me if the embassy's bugged."

Which meant that Donovan knew it was.

"You should recall him," Wild Bill urged. "If he's lost your confidence *and* the Brits', he's no use to you in London."

"He's safer there."

Through the open window, Roosevelt could hear the high, birdlike call of his grandson as he ran across the White House lawn. The memory of former springs, of his young body running through fresh grass on a May morning, flooded his mind. With effort, he turned from that lost brightness.

"Joe stays across the Atlantic until after the next election."

"You'll have to work around him."

Roosevelt's eyes strayed to Jack's Danzig transmission. "I already am," he said.

Part Three

SUMMER

FORTY-TWO. A WILDERNESS OF MIRRORS

AS ORDERED, Jack arrived back at Prince's Gate on June twenty-first, the day before Eunice's coming-out party.

He had been all over Europe since Danzig. There was Moscow, of course—by way of Memel and Riga and Leningrad. Heydrich didn't stop anywhere longer than a night and Jack retained a hazy impression of each of the old Baltic towns, a kaleidoscope of crumbling buildings and rivers swollen with spring, of gray-clad people made furtive by his English, of rundown hotels and the residue of brown coal soot deposited on his car with the sudden rains. But in Moscow Heydrich lingered for nearly five days, taking over the German ambassador's residence; he spent nearly all his daylight hours closeted with the new Soviet foreign minister, Molotov, at the Kremlin. Which meant that Jack saw Diana again.

As an American staying at Spaso House, the glorious neoclassical mansion that was both embassy and residence in Moscow, he was constantly under surveillance. Diana, too, was hedged in on all sides—by Stalin's people and Heydrich's. If he hadn't understood that she was Heydrich's prisoner—a bird who'd flown straight into a steel cage—Jack learned the truth in Moscow. Diana was immured behind the German embassy walls, hustled into official cars, flanked by officers whenever she appeared in public. He had no idea whether it pleased or infuriated her that he was following, or whether she even knew he was there. He could not turn his back on Diana, although the knowledge that Heydrich touched her burned bleakly in his brain.

There was no American ambassador in Moscow at the moment, and the harassed chargé d'affaires was electrified by the sudden appearance of Reinhard Heydrich in Stalin's backyard. It was an accepted fact that Communists and Nazis abhorred each other. The chargé, a man named Manson, was frantic for an explanation. He needed a fly on the wall of the conference room. He had none.

"Where does he eat?" Jack asked idly one afternoon, as Manson was ringing his hands over yet another cable.

"Eat? Who?"

"*Heydrich.* You can't tell me Molotov sends him back to the German embassy for dinner every night. That's no way to parade the Soviet miracle. Molotov wants to impress the man. Show him how Stalin's big boys *live.* So where's he taking him?"

"I don't know." Manson stared at Jack. "The Metropol. Or the Savoy. They're the most European hotels Moscow's got."

"So send one of your staff to the dining room with a bribe. What would it be? A fistful of dollars?"

"Fresh beef," Manson said quickly. "Hasn't been seen on the streets of Moscow in months. Bananas. Single-malt Scotch. We get all of them shipped over and hoard them like gold."

"Bribe somebody at both hotels. Find out whether Heydrich's at the Savoy or the Metropol tonight. Then bribe them again to get a table. We'll make a party of it. My treat. We'll invite a couple of girls. One should speak German."

"Kitty Walker," Manson suggested. "In Records. Her last posting was Berlin."

"Then we'll seat her closest to Heydrich. Is she a looker?"

"She's forty-three, twice divorced, and hard as nails," Manson said.

"Perfect. He won't give her a second glance. Where do you keep the Scotch?"

BEFORE THE REVOLUTION, the Savoy had been the meeting place of poets and dreamers. Now it was the playground of the Soviet elite, and had suffered from the change. It felt, Jack imagined, as Al Capone's dining room might have, if furnished by William Randolph Hearst.

What he would remember forever was the sudden dilation of Diana's pupils as she entered the room and saw him. It was clear she hadn't known he was pursuing her. From the slope of her shoulders and the faint ducking motion of her head, he guessed she was dying a little. His recklessness surged.

Heydrich was studying every stranger, asking an aide why the Savoy wasn't closed to the public tonight. The aide was soothing him, one hand hovering over his sleeve.

They sat down.

Diana's clothes were new. She was wearing some sort of stole around her white shoulders and he wanted to graze her skin with his teeth. She was too thin and there were hollows beneath her eyes, but she would never be less than magnificent. Heydrich knew it. He was sleek with the power of possessing her.

In one jeweled hand Diana clutched the bag Jack had given her in Danzig.

He dragged his attention from Heydrich's table and said something meaningless to Kitty Walker. She had long red nails and brassy hair and a magnificent pair of breasts that had probably won her attention for most of her life. She was offering them now to Jack, purely from a sense of habit. He lit her cigarette and asked how she'd come to work for State.

"Desperation," she said frankly. "I hate to be tied down. The department lets me move every few years. No regrets. No obligations. No messy . . . *heartache*. You want me to eavesdrop on the table behind us, correct? Any particular fella in mind?"

"The one you can't miss," Jack murmured, blowing smoke over her head. "With the high forehead and the Asian eyes."

"The Golden Boy. Heydrich."

"You know him."

"I lived in Berlin for three years. He's a sadist."

Her eyes were a brilliant cornflower blue. They were the most authentic thing about her. Jack smiled into them and slid an ashtray toward her. She'd brought a younger, blonder friend to dinner but Jack wasn't interested and Manson definitely was.

"Try to hear everything Heydrich says."

"He's with Molotov. They've got an interpreter."

Jack reached for Kitty's hand. Over her head he could see Diana. Glancing at him. Glancing away.

"They're planning to split Poland," Kitty said through her smile, and managed a frivolous laugh as though Jack were flirting. "Raped from both sides."

"Have they mentioned any dates?"

Heydrich's fingers ran the length of Diana's arm, as though it were a keyboard and he heard a peculiar music. *He's a sadist.* Diana, his plaything.

"No dates," Kitty breathed. "Just who'll get what. The Russians can have the Baltics, but they both want Danzig."

"Keep listening," Jack said, and extinguished his cigarette. "They've got to talk dates sometime."

TWO HOURS LATER, Kitty Walker excused herself to the ladies' room. Manson's blonde followed. Heydrich was no longer speaking at the neighboring table and an air of satiety prevailed. Manson eased back in his chair while Jack signaled for the bill and talked nonsense about his thesis. He was conscious of Diana's empty place, of a vacuum where she had been. He was deathly tired and his forehead was sweating. The Savoy's food was abominable, but tonight the Scotch was good.

"I can't cable this to Hull," Manson murmured. Cordell Hull was Roosevelt's secretary of state. "It's not verifiable. A *Nazi-Soviet Pact.* Ribbentrop is Hitler's foreign policy man, not Heydrich. And it's absurd. Stalin in bed with Hitler? I'd be laughed out of town."

Jack shrugged and glanced toward the ladies' room. If the Nazis wanted Russian ass, Heydrich was the perfect pimp. He'd appeal to Molotov's instincts. Stimulate his greed.

Kitty Walker was returning. Her wrap was tossed over her shoulder like a sumo wrestler's and her hips swayed. She was an attention-grabber, Jack thought, determined to live on her own terms. He raised his Scotch glass in salute and grinned; she dropped a kiss, surprisingly, on his head.

"Such a sweet boy," she murmured. "You could be my son. If I'd been less careful."

She slipped a matchbook onto his lap.

He palmed it with his eyes still fixed on Kitty. It would hold her address in neat, schoolgirl script, he thought. An invitation worthy of Mae West: *Come up and see me sometime.* But when he flipped open the matchbook cover later in the privacy of his bedroom at Spaso House, he found Diana's handwriting.

Ladies' room Met 9 p.m. tomorrow.

———

"IT'S THE ONLY PLACE I'm ever alone," she told him when he slid through the bathroom door the following night. "He's got no female bodyguards, you see."

Jack had intended to lash her with words for leaving him in Danzig—had meant to strip her bare with his hurt and his anger until she pleaded for forgiveness—but that was senseless now and his mouth was on hers almost before she stopped speaking. It was there again, the vortex between them, draining his mind of reason. Enough to taste her. Enough to stop time for a little while. To forget the monstrous things waiting just beyond the door.

She was stiff with what he guessed was self-loathing. Her scent overwhelmed him. For an instant he considered smashing a window and hauling her out into the night. But she was fragile. She might break.

He loosened his hold and cradled her, whispering her name. Smoothed his hand over her cap of black hair as though she were a cat. She softened a little and leaned into him, the man who hated to be touched. It was the strangest love scene he'd ever played, both of them reflected infinitely in the Metropol's mirrors.

He'd stationed Kitty Walker outside to fend off all comers. Kitty powdered her nose from a gold compact and insisted a woman was ill in the bathroom. Too much vodka. The usual story.

"I've seen the account book," Diana said hurriedly, pushing him away. "It'd fit in your breast-coat pocket. Black leather cover, ruled pages. The list of names is dreadful. The Duke of Windsor. Wallis Simpson. Your father, of course. And poor Winston."

"*Churchill?* Holy shit."

"That'll be Unity's fault—Unity Mitford. She's a cousin to Winston's wife, and probably begged a contribution to her pet charity. He'd have no idea what it was really for, of course, poor lamb."

"Churchill should have asked. She drinks tea with Hitler."

"You don't understand, Jack. Unity may be mad, but to Winston she's family."

"Where does Heydrich keep the book?"

"In a strongbox. He left it open on his desk when I was supposed to be sleeping."

Jack saw it then, the bedroom at night, Diana like a swan beneath the sheets, Heydrich repellent in a dressing gown.

"He was called away by a trunk call from the Führer—never takes them where I might overhear. I had three minutes at most. Nipped over to the strongbox and leafed through the pages. I had to be sure the book was Daisy's. I know her handwriting, you see. Then he came back. I was nearly caught."

Jack did not ask what happened when Heydrich came back. *He's a sadist.* What did the man do in bed? What were his obsessions? It was worse to imagine than to know.

"I'm racking my brains for a way to steal it," Diana said.

He glanced away. "You'll have to take the whole damn box."

"I'd never get out alive. It weighs a ton. Two men are responsible for *carrying* it when we move. Killers like Obst."

"I'll think of something." Jack gripped the bathroom counter to keep from gripping Diana. "A false alarm that gets everybody out on the street. Smoke. Fire."

"No." The word ricocheted between them like a bullet. "You've got to leave Moscow and leave *now*. He recognized you, Jack—last night. He remembered you from Danzig. I ran a terrible risk asking you here—when he's right outside—"

"I don't care. You're not safe. It's hell thinking of you with him. The book's not worth it, Diana."

"It is," she said quietly.

"Walk out of here with me now." He took her face between his hands. "I'll fly you out on the next plane."

"Jack." She grasped his wrists, freed herself. "Heydrich will use that list. Hundreds of names from both sides of the Atlantic. We've got to get that dirty little book back, and I'm the only one who can do it. I'm *inside.* Go back to London."

"I can't."

"He'll have you killed."

"I'm dying already."

He lost control of his hands then. They roamed over her rib cage and circled her waist, pulled her pelvis toward his. The hollow at the base of her neck was mesmerizing. Her skin shuddered beneath his mouth and she curled into him, sighing. He slid the strap of her evening gown from her shoulder. His fingers traced the swell of her breast.

"We can't do this," she whispered. "He'll send someone soon."

Then she was clutching his hair and he was lifting her to the counter and her legs were around his waist. He felt the keen curve of her hip bones beneath his palms and her fingers on his trousers and then suddenly he was inside her, where he was meant to be, his heart pounding. She bit down hard to keep from crying out and held on to him as he plunged. As though it were possible he might save her.

"I love you," he muttered against her ear. *"I love you."*

"Hurry," she said.

FORTY-THREE

ON CHARLES BRIDGE

JACK WAS THE LAST OF the Kennedy children to arrive back in London that third week in June. The younger girls were set free from their schooling at Sacred Heart, and Rosie was done with her Montessori course. Teddy pounded up and down the stairs in short pants and stout shoes, his knees perpetually muddy. Kick was consumed with a round of race meetings and country-house parties, debutante balls, and fittings in Paris—the high tide of the London season.

And Joe was finally home, fresh from one of his "fact-finding missions," this time in Vienna and Berlin. It had been a year since Jack had seen his big brother, and he felt a simple rush of relief as he grasped Joe's hand. There was confidence and authority in every line of his brother's muscled body, a vigor that followed him through a room. Whatever Willi Dobler might say about the simplistic thinking of the *quintessential American*, Joe slept well at night, untroubled by doubt. He rarely second-guessed his decisions. Jack envied him that basic certainty. He realized he'd missed it—and Joe—over the past few months.

"I hear you saw the war," he said, as they stood together in Rose's salon.

Joe handed him a drink. "Better than that. I saw Madrid fall."

It was easy to listen to his brother talk about the weeks he'd spent in Spain, from the Republican internment camp he'd visited on the border, filled with depressed and defeated Loyalists, to the cellar of the Franco safe house he'd camped in during those last days in Madrid. The Spanish Civil War had collapsed into partisans of every stripe fighting their old comrades, the cause and the goals equally confused, the desperation to survive reducing political theories to so much blood on the ground. Franco, to hear Joe tell it, had won in the end because of discipline—in the chaos of the final battles, a strong leader would inevitably prevail.

"All those Italian and German warships bombing Barcelona didn't hurt either," Jack commented.

"They certainly did not," Joe agreed. "Fascists hang together. And they aren't afraid to pull a trigger."

Irony was lost on Joe.

He didn't ask much about Jack's recent trip through Europe and Jack was profoundly glad of his brother's disinterest. He'd decided to ignore the immediate past as he did his perpetual illness. If he could suggest to his family that he was in high spirits and had never felt better, maybe even he'd begin to believe it. And because of the flurry surrounding Eunice's debut party, his luck held: He barely saw his parents. This, too, was a relief; he was afraid of what he might say to J.P. and he had nothing at all to say to Rose.

There would be dinner for thirty in the dining room that night, a dance for two hundred in the ballroom upstairs. The Duke of Marlborough was coming. Baroness Ravensdale. Nancy Astor. The Duchess of Northumberland. Jack dug out his tails and white tie, immaculately pressed and ready, and put them on. Around five o'clock he found Eunice seated before her dressing table, in a peach-colored dress designed by Paquin; it was her first couture gown and she wore it like a newborn she was terrified of dropping. Eunice was shy and nervous, ardently Catholic; she slept badly, and if awakened in the night, could wander sleepless for hours. They all handled Eunice like a piece of blown glass.

He set a square florist's box on the dressing table. It held a white rose corsage. She smiled at him uncertainly.

"Is that for me?"

"Who else, kid?"

"You're so good to me, Jack. I don't deserve it."

"Sure you do. It's your night."

"I'll probably spend most of it in the bathroom."

She blinked and looked stoically at her reflection, her fingers struggling with a string of pearls she was trying to put on.

He was disturbed by the tears in her eyes. He pulled up a chair, flipped the tails of his dinner coat, and sat down next to her. When he touched her back the skin was goose-fleshed. "Scared?"

"Terrified," she breathed. "I'm not like Kick. Nobody'll want to dance with *me*. You have a dance card, you know, and you have to check to see whether it's filled for each dance. If it's not, you go up to the bathroom so nobody knows. Mother will *die* if I'm a flop at my own come-out."

He made a mental note to fill up her card. "Here—let me help you with those."

She gave him the pearls and he slid them around her neck, suddenly aware of the childish jut of her shoulder blades, emerging from the back of her dress. "You eighteen yet?"

"In three weeks," she said glumly. "But you turned twenty-two, didn't you? Where'd you spend your birthday?"

"Prague," he said, remembering the twenty-ninth of May. "I was in Prague."

"Good party?"

"I've had better," he said with effort. "Heck—*you* weren't there, kid."

She smiled brilliantly and dove into a drawer of the dressing table. "I didn't forget your present."

It was a Sacred Heart medal, strung on dark blue ribbon she'd chosen herself. "Wear it beneath your shirt, Jack," she urged. "It'll help."

"With what?"

"Whatever it is you're hiding."

His fingers twitched convulsively, and the medal skittered to the floor. He bent to retrieve it. Combing the carpet was preferable to meeting his sister's eyes.

"I've never seen you so sad," Eunice said. "You look like someone died. Is Prague a terribly lonesome place?"

FROM MOSCOW HEYDRICH had turned south to Bucharest, then Turkey, where he spent nearly a week in Istanbul. It made sense, Jack thought: the Turks controlled the Bosporus—which meant access to Russia's Black Sea—and they'd held it against the British in the last war. Heydrich would have to buy Turkish friends before the next war started.

Jack radioed Roosevelt again from the roof of the Istanbul consulate the morning after he arrived. Although Kitty Walker had never heard the tantalizing date of Heydrich's planned invasion, she insisted it was to begin with the seizure of Danzig, throttling the Polish navy before a ground attack from the west. Then Russia would strike from the east, and Poland would be forced to fight on two fronts. Without the promised help of Britain and France, the Poles would fall fast and fall hard. Jack figured Roosevelt needed to know.

He gazed at the bridges of Istanbul for twenty-three minutes before the President replied. He spent another sixteen minutes decoding the message.

Is this Nazi-Soviet deal signed? Roosevelt asked.

Jack had no idea. Rather than disappoint FDR, he packed up his radio. The following day, he was on the roof again. He'd seen Diana and had news for the President.

REINHARD HEYDRICH AND HIS entourage traveled in a fleet of black cars, his personal favorite being an open black Mercedes with a long, sleek bonnet and a prominent chrome grill. The license plate was instantly recognizable—SS-3, the letters elongated and sharp like the Nazi insignia. Heydrich swanked in the backseat, his arm thrown royally over Diana's shoulders, while a minion drove. In a hired taxi, Jack found it easy enough to follow this spectacle through the narrow streets of Istanbul. That day, a little before three o'clock in the afternoon, the Mercedes pulled up in front of the Beyazit Gate of the Grand Bazaar.

Jack had wandered alone through the vast market complex the previous day, hands in his pockets, the curtain called Boredom or Death rustling stealthily behind him. He was heartsick and restless; he hadn't come within touching distance of Diana for weeks. The memory of their encounter at the Metropol haunted his sleep. By night, he yearned for her; by day he feared for her. He distracted his darting mind by conducting interviews with the earnest functionaries at the U.S. consulate. But of what use was a senior thesis if he failed to secure the stolen account book? In late afternoon he abandoned his work and found his way into the bazaar.

The ancient souk sprawled over fifty-eight streets and held thousands of shops; traders had bargained beneath its arched ceilings for five hundred years. It was, Jack thought, a postcard from Byzantium, the lost world of Suleiman the Magnificent, and for a while the colors and scents transported him: cardamom and bitter orange blossom; tobacco bubbling in hookahs; the mustiness of rolled wool rugs and the brown coal smell of open braziers. The bazaar stank of goats and unwashed humanity and occasionally attar of roses. A man gestured at carpets and a boy offered alabaster; when Jack ducked down a quieter path through the labyrinth, an aged crone tried to sell him her daughter.

He hunched now in the back of his taxi, wondering what Reinhard Heydrich was buying this morning.

The Gestapo chief handed Diana down from the Mercedes and a phalanx of guards closed around them, their uniforms black as night. The Spider was not among them; presumably he still suffered the effects of his gunshot wound. Jack paid off his driver while the group passed through the Beyazit Gate; then he got out of the car and strolled slowly after them.

It was easy enough to keep the party in view—they attracted a swarm of hagglers young and old, a bobbing circle of fezzes that impeded Heydrich's progress and brought his pace to a crawl. Jack hung back fifty yards as Diana and her pack progressed through the bazaar. He was careful to keep a scrim of bodies—tourists and locals, bewildering in their array—between himself and those Nazi eyes.

They passed bustling *hans*—courtyards given over to a single trade—and a mosque, one of two within the market. They passed fountains trickling water over cerulean tiles, stalls filled with fan-

ciful glass lanterns, and cloying piles of Turkish Delight. Jack
watched as Diana stopped short before a display of embroidered
silks, murmuring as her fingers stroked them; Heydrich was unmoved. He grasped Diana's arm—Jack could almost feel the im-
print of his thumb on her flesh—and she was borne along in her
lover's tide. As she turned away from the silks, however, her gaze
swept back along the way she had come—and caught him.

He went hot, then cold. All his senses screaming.

Nothing in her face betrayed her. Nothing but the quick
duck of her head, the same movement she'd made once in a restaurant in Moscow. Would Heydrich feel her sudden awareness
through his fingers on her arm? He was making, Jack saw, for a
particular *han*—a private rug dealer whose name was embla-
zoned in gold-leaf Turkish script over his caravansary doors.

Jack came to a halt near a coffee vendor. Heydrich and his
coterie walked into the rug-dealer's courtyard and were momen-
tarily lost to view. Jack pointed to a cup and motioned with his
hands; the vendor nodded and began to prepare his brew, steam
hissing through a copper vat. Jack's nerves were jumping. He
dropped some Turkish coins in the vendor's lined palm.

How to talk to Diana?

She was surrounded by Heydrich's palace guard. But she
would be thinking of him. She would be thinking—

Jack drained the last of his cup and handed it to the vendor.
Then he wandered toward the rug-seller's *han* and glanced into
the courtyard. There was no sign of the Germans, who had presumably gone inside the dealer's showroom. Jack had watched
the drama played out before: the offer of tea or coffee, or for the
lady, a sweetened fruit juice; the unfurling of precious carpets
before the buyer's discerning eye. Heydrich was known as a con-
noisseur—of food, of music, of violence. He might be engaged

some time, fingering the knots and patterns, bartering down his price.

Jack scanned the old wooden buildings that lined the courtyard. They were as closed and secretive as Ali Baba's cave. He could not get near her. But Diana would be thinking—

He walked back to the silk vendor's stall. Bolts of brilliant fabric overrun with twisting vines and flowers were propped against the walls; a narrow aisle between led deeper into the shop.

Twelve minutes later she found him there.

"How did you get away?" Jack breathed. His hand was on her elbow but the fabric seller was watching them. He could not draw attention. Could not take her in his arms in the middle of the bazaar—

"I told him I felt faint. It's bloody hot in that rug shop, darling. Like a Turkish bath! The man has a fire going in May. I threatened to swoon, so Heydrich sent me into the courtyard with his lapdog Ernst."

Jack glanced around. "Where's your leash?"

"Hopelessly lost somewhere in the bazaar. I sent Ernst in search of ice. That should buy us a quarter hour."

He clutched her wrist urgently. "Run away with me. Right now. We'll lose them in this labyrinth."

She shook her head. "You're wasting *time*. Now listen to what I must tell you."

HEYDRICH NOT AUTHORIZED to sign Nazi-Soviet Pact, Jack radioed to Roosevelt from the consulate rooftop. *Ribbentrop to negotiate further details with Molotov, but delayed by pressing business in Italy. Ribbentrop has signed Pact of Steel, repeat Pact of Steel, with Count Ciano. Pact furthers German-Italian alliance and in-*

cludes secret side agreement requiring both countries to defend each other in time of war. Expect disclosure soonest. CRIMSON

The next day, May twenty-second, Jack took in the headlines over his breakfast of fruit and pastry.

Count Ciano and Joachim von Ribbentrop had just announced their cozy pact. With Mussolini as ally and Stalin waiting in the wings, Hitler's snare around Europe was pulling tighter.

FROM ISTANBUL HEYDRICH made for Vienna, with its Gestapo network firmly in place and its glorious opera house where *Tannhaüser* played. It was obvious even to Jack that Heydrich had descended on the city solely for *Tannhaüser*—he stayed four days, and went to the opera each night. Jack went twice just so he could see Diana across the expanse of the theater. She was ethereally thin, and there were lines running from her nose to the corners of her mouth.

He debated invading the ladies' room in the hope of finding her, but there was no Kitty Walker in Vienna to bar the entrance. He walked right up to Diana in the opera house bar instead, as Heydrich was handing her a coupe of champagne.

Heydrich's full lips—so strange and sensual in his narrow face—lifted slightly at the corners.

"Mr. Kennedy," he said, in precise English. "The . . . second son." He pronounced the adjective as if it were an insult. "Does your father know you waste your time pursuing another man's woman? Go back to London, Mr. Kennedy. She doesn't want you."

Jack almost threw his drink in Heydrich's face but Diana's stricken look stopped him. Instead, he summoned a sneer for the

Gestapo chief's benefit. "Mrs. Playfair has made her feelings abundantly clear, Herr Heydrich. I can only hope she tires of you less quickly than she did of me. Forgive me for disturbing your evening."

He bowed and left them—left the opera house and *Tannhaüser*. Jack was lucky the Gestapo chief thought it was all about love—that he dismissed him as an irrelevant boy. Diana was less fortunate. At the opera the next evening, when he saw her across the lobby, she moved with the stiffness of a whipped greyhound. There was a beaten look about her eyes. It was clear whom Heydrich had punished for Jack's pursuit.

Jack drank himself senseless with guilt afterward.

THEY MET FOR THE LAST TIME in Prague on May twenty-ninth, his birthday, in the middle of the Charles Bridge.

It was Diana who found Jack, not the other way around. She gave him no warning and she did not come alone. The White Spider walked beside her. Completely recovered, by all appearances, from his brush with death.

Jack watched them come, two bright figures skimming past the blackened statues that lined the bridge. It was dusk and the Spider's blond hair glimmered; Diana's white face floated like a magnolia, drowned in a bowl of water. There were people strolling everywhere on the bridge, one of the last days of May, a perfect spring evening. At home the first of the season's sails were rising in Nantucket Sound. Here, the trees dotting the Vltava glowed acid green against the gathering dark.

The Spider's hand was on Diana's arm, and Jack guessed there was a knife pressed into her side. They stopped short a yard from where he lounged against a parapet.

"Hello, Jack," Diana said in a stranger's voice. "I've come to tell you to go back to London. This game is beyond tiresome— and we're all fed up."

"Really?" Jack nodded at Obst. "Did your friend here tell you to say that?"

"He didn't have to."

No, Jack thought. All he needed was a blade in her ribs.

"I'm here to protect the lady," Obst said.

"Then you'll have to do a better job." Jack drew the Luger from his pocket and pointed it at the Spider. "Let her go," he said quietly, "or I'll shoot you in the other lung, asshole."

For an instant Obst's face was wiped clean of all expression; and then something animal flooded into his eyes, a hunger for violence. He hadn't known who'd shot him in Danzig. Now he had a score to settle, a need to kill.

"Oh, for God's sake," Diana burst out. "Put the gun away, Jack. I'm not leaving Heydrich!"

"Diana," he said urgently.

She threw up her hands in fury. "You're such a *child*. Very well—" She stepped in front of Obst, shielding him with her body. "If you won't listen, you'll have to shoot us both."

"Jesus," he muttered. *"Diana—"*

"Go *home*, Jack."

"Come with me."

She laughed. "You make me look ridiculous."

He took a step toward her.

She held her ground, ignoring the Luger's muzzle, her eyes angry and bright. She was wearing a light spring frock, something he remembered vaguely from Switzerland, weeks ago. He leaned forward and tried to kiss her.

She recoiled, as if from an adder's lunge, and slapped him.

The crowds strolled by, oblivious. Lovers had been parting on the Charles Bridge for centuries.

"Let me put it plainly," she muttered. "I'm not interested in little boys. Not when there are men around."

Every line of her body screamed contempt.

Jack slipped the gun into his pocket.

As he did, Obst pulled back his fist and slugged Jack, hard.

He hadn't been holding a knife after all. She'd brought him along of her own free will.

"God, how I despise you, Jack," Diana said bitterly.

He doubled over, his abdomen screaming, and sank to his knees. Ignoring the stares of the other people on the bridge, Obst kicked him in the face. Jack fell against the railing, his nose streaming blood, and vomited into the river. Diana and Obst were already walking away.

HE DROVE WEST THAT NIGHT out of Prague. By mid-June he was back in Paris, where Carmel Offie fussed over his exhausted body and the lamentable state of the rented car. Bill Bullitt claimed him for a time and Jack was content to drink champagne and regale him with tales of Spaso House. Bullitt was the first ambassador to Stalin's Moscow and the parties he had thrown at Spaso were legendary among diplomats.

Offie summoned LaSalle and his needles full of DOCA; he coddled Jack with private cables and interviews with French officials, who seemed as bewildered as the British by the mess they were about to receive.

At night, Jack drank in a series of glittering boîtes. Alcohol played havoc with his system but it dulled the pain he could not locate, the void where Diana had been. He did not know whether she'd deliberately hurt him to send him away—whether everything she'd said on the bridge was a lie—or whether he'd been duped by her all along. What was the truest thing about Diana? Her love, or her hate?

IT WAS A QUESTION HE ASKED himself all the way back to London.

Now, as he looked at his sister Eunice, exquisite and fragile in her Paquin dress, he came to some sort of answer.

"Prague's the loneliest place on earth, kid," he said. "Would you save me the first dance?"

FORTY-FOUR. DEDUCTIONS

"DO YOU THINK THE BOY KNOWS?" Sam Schwartz asked.

Roosevelt rubbed the back of his neck thoughtfully. "I'd be astonished if he didn't. I asked him to track this down, after all. And he's given us every lead we've followed."

A sheaf of paper lay between them on the desk. Handwritten, not typed, in Schwartz's careful script. The Secret Service man had done his work thoroughly and well. A certain charity's tax records had been laid as bare as a filleted salmon. Daisy Corcoran's deep-pocket donors might have given anonymously to the Little Sisters of Clemency, but those same deep pockets couldn't resist taking the charitable deduction on their individual tax returns. Weeks of patient cross-checking among the IRS files had yielded a crop of names. Joseph P. Kennedy's headed the list.

"He may have donated in all innocence," Schwartz suggested. "With no idea the charity was just a Nazi front."

"That's what he'll claim," Roosevelt said with a studied lack of emotion.

"He's Catholic. They're nuns."

"—run by Göring's banker. Who just pressed Kennedy to ask me for a billion-dollar loan. Too cozy a coincidence, Sam." He ran his eyes down the list of names, marveling at the effrontery of it. Two-thirds of the near-defunct American Liberty League had ponied up funds for the Little Sisters. So had a prominent Pennsylvania politician, a famous aviator, and the highest-paid lawyer in Manhattan. All were pillars of their communities. All would be shocked to be branded Nazi sympathizers. And all were apparently quite comfortable with the idea of buying a presidential election. They would argue, of course, that they were just supporting a Catholic charity; and he had no hard proof otherwise. But Roosevelt noted that most of the donors were Protestant. No wonder they'd given anonymously.

"Jack will think his father never knew it was a Nazi front," Schwartz persisted. "Do you want to destroy the boy's respect for him, sir?"

"If Joe Kennedy is a traitor? Perhaps it would be for the best. Jack doesn't seem the kind of fellow who enjoys living a lie."

Schwartz's lips compressed.

Roosevelt wrestled his chair in the direction of the bedroom. He considered his own sons. Jimmy, in particular—who was so frighteningly weak. Jimmy, who admired Joe Kennedy's charm and street smarts and ability to make money hand over fist—and had gotten them all into trouble because of it. When the press discovered the President's son was importing liquor from Scotland with his "partner" Joe Kennedy, there'd been more than a whiff of scandal. Jimmy had actually moved back into the White House with his entire family—supposedly to support his Old Man, but in fact to regroup and lick his wounds. Roosevelt would bet on the probability that Jimmy figured somewhere in J. Edgar Hoover's files.

But if somebody tried to tell Jimmy that his father was no good—a traitor, a rogue, a nasty piece of work—how would he feel?

Jimmy would hate the messenger. And he would never speak to the man again.

God have mercy on my soul, Roosevelt thought. *I sent Jack off to hunt down his own father, and made it sound like hero's work. He must know his father stabbed me in the back and used German money to do it. Now it's impossible for him to keep faith with both of us. That's why the radio's full of Hitler's alliances and I've heard nothing about Wohlthat or the charity network in weeks. He's waiting for somebody else to hang Joe high. Not him. Never the Black Sheep.*

Roosevelt had no desire to alienate Jack Kennedy. He had plans for him.

"Very well, Sam," he said. "We won't mention this. Yet."

FORTY-FIVE. LAST DANCES

JACK MIGHT HAVE CONFRONTED his father with Daisy and her account book, or the dead hatcheck girl, the next morning when he reported for work at the embassy. He might have asked him about Göring. Who approached whom. Whether Dad volunteered the Little Sisters of Clemency's charity network as an ideal vehicle for collecting treasonable cash, or whether exploiting the nuns was purely a Nazi flourish. But he didn't have the chance. His brother Joe was lounging in the armchair opposite the ambassador's desk. Joe idolized their dad. Jack had no intention of destroying him in his brother's eyes; and Joe wouldn't believe him, anyway.

". . . should have been allowed to show them around," his father was saying irritably. "The King and Queen of England make their first visit to the United States, and Franklin side-steps me completely! Goes over my head to issue the invitation—then *forbids* me to travel with the royal party! As if I didn't know Bertie and his wife better than he does! They've had us to stay at Windsor. It's goddamn insulting."

"He's just a tired old man, Dad," Joe offered. "It's obvious. Time to head back to Hyde Park and make way for the new fella."

"You said it."

Jack leaned in the doorway. Dad was working in his shirtsleeves and his thumbs were shoved into his waistcoat. He was supposed to be a risk-taker. A brilliant tactician. Only to Jack this morning, he looked like any other unscrupulous bastard blinded by ego and desire.

"He's running again," Jack said casually.

"Who is?" his father demanded.

"Roosevelt. If that's who you're talking about."

"Bullshit," his father said immediately.

"He can't," Joe burst out.

"There's no law against a third term."

"That doesn't matter!" Joe flung himself out of the chair. "It's *un-American*, Jack. Don't you know your history? They'd never let Roosevelt do it."

"Who's *they*? The Democrats? Republicans? Or the Nazis?" Jack looked innocently from his brother to his father. He thought Dad's eyelids flickered. "Hitler has everything to lose, way I see it, if FDR stays another four years."

"Wrong." His brother planted a forefinger in Jack's chest; he'd always been physical when it came to debate. "*We* lose."

"The Kennedys?"

"*Every* American! If Roosevelt's reelected, we're all going to war. Nobody wants that."

"I do," Jack said quietly.

"Like hell." The faintest amusement tinged Joe's voice. "You won't pass the physical, my friend. You'll get a nice, cushy desk job somewhere, while I'm soaking in a trench. *Oh, my stomach*," he whimpered in falsetto. "*Oh, my crapper. It hurts when I shit.*"

"That's enough." Their father held up his arms. "Nobody's going to war. This'll all be over by August."

"Care to bet on that?" Jack asked.

"How much money you got?" Joe retorted instantly.

"A few pieces of worthless property in Central Europe will change hands," their father persisted. "The Germans will go home happy; and people like Churchill will have egg on their faces. And come next November, we'll get a new broom in Washington for a change."

"And you're the clean sweep," Jack concluded wearily.

"Well . . . if it's what the American people *want* . . ." His father bared his teeth. "I've never been one to shirk my duty."

"Oh, Christ." Jack rubbed his eyes fretfully and turned to leave. "I can't listen to this anymore."

Joe gripped his shoulder, halting him in his tracks. "Have some respect, Jack. Dad knows a lot more about politics than we do. He'd make a great president."

"Who told you Roosevelt was running for a third term?" his father demanded.

Jack shrugged. "That's the word at Harvard. Has a guy named Helmuth Wohlthat contacted you, by any chance?"

J.P.'s expression was suddenly watchful. "What business is it of yours?"

"We met in Val d'Isère. And had quite the conversation. What'd he ask for this time, Dad? Something only the Führer could love?"

"Jack, what exactly are you insinuating?"

He met J.P.'s gaze squarely. "Everything you could possibly imagine."

His father's face reddened. He opened his mouth, then closed it again.

"They never ask just once, you know," Jack said. "They come back again and again. Until you haven't got a thing left to barter, or a shred of self-respect. And it's not just about you, Dad—it's all of us you're gambling away. My life. Joe's future. You always said he'd be president of the United States if you didn't get there first. Keep dancing with Hitler, and it ain't gonna happen."

"What are you *talking* about, Jack?"

The expression of shock in his brother's eyes might have been comical, if it hadn't struck Jack as so sad. Maybe he ought to take Joe aside and explain exactly what he'd learned on his own fact-finding mission through Europe. But Joe would demand proof before he'd believe a word against their father. Jack had no proof of J.P.'s treason. That was hidden for all the world to see in Daisy Corcoran's account book.

He watched his brother's move from surprise to anger. Then Joe shoved him back against the office wall.

"*Apologize* to Dad."

"I can't," he said. "I've done nothing wrong."

They stared at each other, tense as tomcats on a back alley fence. Joe's fists were balled up at his sides but he would never use them, not against Jack, not here. There was the faintest tinge of uncertainty in his gaze and it sharpened the edge of sorrow deep in Jack's gut. People he loved were going to be hurt by what he knew. Not just Joe, but Teddy and Jean and Kick and Bobby. Even his mother, he supposed.

"Jack had too much to drink last night." His father's voice was savage but calm. "He's hallucinating. And he'd better get out of my office right now, before I throw him out."

"Sure," Jack said tiredly, opening the door and backing out. "But let me know when you've got your story straight. You're going to need one, Dad. For Wohlthat and his bosses. And Roosevelt, of course. If you want to run it by me, I'm always ready to listen."

He stayed away from the two Joes as much as he could, after that. His services didn't seem to be needed at the embassy, and Kick was happy to drag him along on her summer ride.

It was a relief for Jack just to be with her. He never had to explain his moods to Kick or tell her what he was really thinking. And she didn't ask. They'd spent too many rainy days together as kids, in the basement of the Hyannis Port house, watching B movies on their dad's screen over and over, until they could mimic Cary Grant and Mae West in *She Done Him Wrong*. They were both wild at heart and restless as hell, always ready for a jitterbug or a game of touch football; but unlike Jack, Kick had a healthy body.

"It's my consolation prize, kid," she said as she watched him cut the DOCA into his calf one afternoon, "for not having your brains."

It was true she wasn't much of a student. She was talking about going to Sarah Lawrence back in Bronxville, but if she did, it wouldn't be for the classes. Jack didn't attempt to explain to her the strategic importance of Danzig or the complications of his recent life. He said nothing about Diana Playfair or the Heydrich-Enigma he'd helped to steal or, God help him, the specter of their father's treason. Kick would have found all of it incomprehensible. Worse, if he'd shared his worries, she'd have been burdened with something like sin. So much unhappiness in Jack's life would weigh on Kick's. She'd go in search of a confessor, and that was the last thing Jack wanted.

So he kept his secrets and went out with Kick's friend Sally Norton, the wellborn British deb he'd rescued from the Serpentine back in March. Sally was as unlike Diana Playfair as any girl could be, honey-colored and lean, with aristocratic bones and an upper-class drawl. Though she was polite to Jack in the most English of ways, it was obvious she had eyes only for Billy Hartington. Jack's charm had never been so wasted. He kept Sally occupied, however, which was a favor to Kick and the Protestant

Prince. The four of them frittered away night after night drinking champagne at the 400 Club.

There was a feverish atmosphere in London, this final summer before the war. Everyone figured the Luftwaffe would level the city in a matter of weeks, that civilian casualties would be in the hundreds of thousands, and that they were all going to die, as Billy put it, "as soon as the balloon goes up." So they danced the big apple and stayed out until dawn and drank deep whenever fear grasped their throats. Jack saw the willful stupidity of it all, but he was returning to America soon, to Harvard for his final year of college. He had no right to sneer at his English friends. Besides, he had failed. Heydrich had the means to blackmail a significant chunk of the Anglo-American elite, which might guarantee England's downfall. The span of their lives might be weeks or months. Why not die happy?

One morning in late June, Jack's Spee Club roommate, Torby Macdonald, showed up at Prince's Gate, dying for a summer in Europe. He brought a letter from Bruce Hopper that began with *Mon Brave* and ended with *Cheers* and asked, in between, if Jack had ever gotten to Moscow. Jack wrote a reply full of remorse and Spaso House and his observations of Molotov. He said nothing of a possible Nazi-Soviet Pact.

July set in with unusual heat. Torby planned a trip to Paris and Jack figured he'd go along. He was continually restless, the fog called Boredom or Death hovering just over his left shoulder. The image of Diana's white face above the piers of the Charles Bridge stabbed like lightning through his mind. He wondered where she was. How she survived. If she survived.

And then one night, when he thought he couldn't bear the not-knowing any longer, an unexpected voice fell on his ear.

"Fancy," Denys Playfair murmured, nursing a cigarette between his beautiful fingers. "Jack Kennedy in the flesh. The Terror of Happy Households. How do you get on, pet? And what the *hell* have you done with my wife?"

THEY WERE STANDING ON the west terrace at Blenheim Palace, gazing out over the Duke of Marlborough's magnificent water parterre, lantern-lit in the twilight, while a waltz swirled in the Long Library behind them. The Duke's daughter, Lady Sarah Spencer Churchill, was the same age as Eunice and the two girls had met while sitting out dances in a bathroom. The vast and bewildering palace, the thousands of acres of parkland, the allées of ancient trees and the casual assumption of power that Blenheim represented seemed unreal to Jack, like something out of *Young Melbourne*. He was remembering a different night on the outskirts of Danzig, the flames in the wood and the smell of burning flesh, when Denys Playfair spoke.

He turned. "You haven't heard from Diana?"

"Not in a month. Beginning to give me the willies. You?"

"We last spoke on the twenty-ninth of May," Jack said carefully. "In Prague."

"And it's the seventh of July. She ought to have been back for Ascot but sent her regrets instead." Playfair offered him a gold cigarette case. "Smoke?"

Jack took a Woodbine and allowed Playfair to light it. The tobacco stung his throat. "You know she's with Heydrich." It was not a question.

"So she said. He seems to allow her the odd letter. I'll wager he reads them before they're posted."

"And you can live with that?"

"No choice, old chap. She's lived with Willi for donkey's years."

Unexpectedly frank, from the exquisite Denys.

"Look, you've probably gathered that Diana is nobody's fool," Playfair said. "I owe her my continued reputation and my peace of mind. I never grudge her the least amusement."

"Heydrich's not funny. He's scary as hell."

"But she's doing her bit," Denys said evenly. "In an unofficial capacity."

"By sleeping with the Gestapo?"

"If you must. Yes."

"He hurts her, you know. She looks like hell."

Denys studied his fingernails. "I wonder, Jack, if you've time for a private chat? I was sent to fetch you, actually."

He followed Playfair's perfectly tailored form back through the French windows and out of the Long Library, down a series of corridors lit solely by candles, up a short flight of steps, and into an altogether different wing. He was thoroughly lost but Playfair seemed at home in the Duke of Marlborough's palace. He tapped lightly on a paneled door and threw it open.

Two men stood in a small, high-ceilinged room before a small fireplace with a cheerful fire. One of them was Colin Gubbins. The other was Winston Churchill.

He had been born at Blenheim, Jack remembered. The Duke was his cousin. Of course he'd attend Lady Sarah's come-out. But what on earth was Gubbins doing here?

"Colonel," Playfair was saying as he lounged across the room. "Winston. I don't know whether you're acquainted with Jack Kennedy? The ambassador's second son."

Jack forced himself forward and extended his hand. "Sir. It's a pleasure to see you again."

Churchill rolled a cigar between his lips, set down a glass of champagne, grunted, and touched Jack's fingers. "Indeed. You've kicked about the world since we last met, eh? A year ago, I believe. Your father's Independence Day celebration."

"Yes, sir."

"M'mother was American, you know."

"Jenny Jerome. The toast of New York."

Churchill glanced at Gubbins. "The colonel tells me great things about you. He says you've got nerve and intelligence, and your heart's in the right place. Glad you fell in with Gubbins; couldn't do better in a tight spot."

"He's landed me in a few," Jack said.

Churchill grunted again. "Sit down, sit down."

Jack sat. So did Gubbins and Playfair. Churchill paced instead, his words directed at the floor. "Danzig. You were there, Gubbins tells me. When the Heydrich-Enigma, as we're calling it, was lifted by the Poles."

So it was Churchill Gubbins reported to; Churchill who ran the shadow world behind Neville Chamberlain's back.

"*Lifted* is an understatement, sir. Half the woods and most of our hair were on fire."

Churchill glowered at him. "The colonel's friends in Polish Intelligence have informed us the new machine is damnably complicated, and the codes it produces virtually unbreakable. Moreover, they are well aware that time is short—that Hitler is likely to invade in the next few weeks—and the whole cipher-breaking effort will be buggered by the Nazis. They've asked us to get the Enigma to London. *To you from failing hands we throw the torch*, what? It's entirely down to Gubbins's work with the Polish Intelligence johnnies, of course."

The Partisan Leader's Handbook, Jack thought idly. He'd asked Gubbins that night in Danzig what the Baker Street Irregulars got out of ambushing a Gestapo truck. The colonel had suggested it would eventually be the machine itself.

"So when he suggested *you,* Mr. Kennedy," Churchill concluded, "naturally I listened."

Jack's thoughts came back to the fire-lit room with a start. "Suggested me for . . . ?"

"Fetching the thing," Churchill barked. "From Warsaw. Gubbins will go along, of course, although not *with* you. Just in parallel, as it were, to keep an eye on it all."

"I'm headed to Paris in a few days," Jack attempted. "Not Warsaw."

"You have two weeks to get yourself to Poland," Churchill ordered, as if Paris had not been mentioned. "Take a friend along, for cover—but lose 'im before you cross the frontier. It could get tricky there. Place is filthy with Germans, our Polish friends say."

"You want me to *lose* my friend," Jack repeated, thinking of Torby. "Just open the car door and hope he rolls clear?"

"Kinder, surely, to put him on a train," Playfair murmured.

"Gubbins will manage the actual exchange of the machine with the Poles," Churchill continued, as though neither of them had spoken, "but *you'll* carry it out. You're American and you've got a diplomatic passport. Can't do better than that, where Germans and borders are concerned."

I've heard this before, Jack thought.

He wanted to ask Churchill if he'd sent Diana to watch him, on his previous journey through Europe, *just in parallel, as it were*, or whether Churchill knew that his own name was on a certain Gestapo list. But the curtain called Boredom or Death had suddenly vanished, and for tonight, that was all Jack needed.

"Tell me," he said, as Churchill poured him a glass of champagne, "what you want me to do."

TWO WEEKS LATER JACK checked into the Polonia Palace Hotel, at the intersection of two fashionable streets with—to him—unpronounceable names. Nobody knew Jack was in Warsaw except Torby, whom he'd sworn to silence and then abandoned in Paris. Torby was a thoroughly nice guy who played football at Harvard when he wasn't sprinting around a track. Like all of Jack's friends, he'd fallen in love with Kick, and he'd spent his final days in London alternately proposing marriage to her and glowering at Billy Hartington whenever he appeared at Prince's Gate. It was a relief, therefore, to hustle Torby by boat train across the Channel, where he could drown his passion in a good Bordeaux. Within two days they had met some friends from Harvard on a summer tour of Europe, and Jack could leave Torby in their hands without much guilt.

He rented a small blue Citroën and made his way slowly through the woods and fields of Bavaria, beguiling his nights at beer halls in Bayreuth and Nuremberg and Regensburg. Bavaria was Hitler country but far less intimidating than Berlin, which Jack avoided. It felt like Heydrich's turf, and he dreaded seeing Diana.

As he drove, he tried his father's case in his mind—and found the man guilty. But so what? Did his terrible knowledge *require* him to expose Dad to Franklin Roosevelt? Or merely to confront J.P. with the truth? What if Jack made it clear to his father that he expected him to act with honor, not cowardice?—To stand up to Heydrich's blackmail, and damn the consequences?

Dad would snarl and call him insane.

A half hour before he crossed the Polish border, Jack came to a decision. No matter what kind of man his father was, no matter how traitorous his behavior, Jack could not be the one to destroy him. All his life, Dad had taught him that he was a Kennedy— and they stood together, the Kennedys, against all comers. If Dad caved to Heydrich's pressure, and did whatever the man asked in order to save his skin, Jack would keep silent. While Dad sold out the President.

Never mind that his decision disgusted him. He didn't have much future anyway. The intervals between his bouts of sickness grew shorter with every passing week; he'd just been buying time with George Taylor's pellets. Not even the new box from Mayo he'd found waiting for him in London could keep him going forever. He wouldn't live with the disgrace very long.

And with luck, he'd never see Franklin Roosevelt again.

TEN DAYS AFTER LEAVING TORBY, he reached the outskirts of Warsaw.

The Polonia was the city's most glamorous hotel. To stay any-where else would look suspiciously unlike a Kennedy. Gubbins arrived separately and took a room under the name of Harris; his card proclaimed him a dealer in Scottish tweeds. Jack applauded the man's mordant humor.

They studiously ignored each other in the Polonia's break-fast room and its nightclub, where blond Polish girls danced for a glass of champagne. Jack bought the prettiest a drink and watched her mentally weigh his American passport against the wallet of a German Luftwaffe colonel sitting alone in the corner. An exercise in geopolitics. The Aryan flyboy left with the girl on his arm.

Jack killed three days waiting for some sort of sign from Gubbins, walking in the Old Town and drinking vodka at night, listening to turgid Polish jazz and trying not to think about what would happen when Heydrich put the screws on his father. Roosevelt's voice was constantly in his head, cajoling and nudging him—the voice of conscience. He'd brought his radio in its special suitcase but he'd left it in the boot of the car. He had nothing further to encode. Or to communicate.

He wished he'd been a better spy, the kind Roosevelt had wanted—*an independent thinker with his own brand of guts*—but in the end he'd failed at this job, too, not because of his lousy body, but because of his divided soul.

TUESDAY MORNING, THE TWENTY-FIFTH of July, he woke with a jolt from a dream of Diana. He lay breathless under the single sheet, heart racing and penis erect, hating her for owning him so completely. There was a film of sweat on his brow and he knew it wasn't from summer heat. He was feverish again. An infection, probably, in the latest gash he'd cut in his leg. He'd gone through both thighs and one calf and was rapidly running out of muscle.

What was the time? What had wakened him? Some spectral sound. He glanced at the bedside clock and saw that it was only a few minutes after five. Light was seeping through the sheer curtains, the early dawn of a north European summer. The damp from the Vistula rose from the streets and clung to his curtains, which bellied exhaustedly against the open window. It would be a hot day. Jack, however, had chills.

He shook his head, trying to clear it.

The strange sound came again; a faint dragging and bumping. Someone was in the corridor outside his room.

He sat up cautiously and swung his legs over the side of the bed. He was dressed only in boxer shorts. He slipped his hand under the pillow and grasped the butt of the Luger.

He crossed the carpeted floor as silently as possible and hesitated by the door. Whoever was beyond it tried hard to control his breathing, but it emerged in short, violent gasps. Jack positioned the Luger as he reached for the doorknob, prepared for somebody to kick his way in.

"Jack." A soft, insistent whisper.

He stopped dead, recognizing the voice; then as quietly as he could, he opened the door.

Gubbins was crumpled in the hall, his face dead white and his trousers soaked with blood.

Jack shoved the Luger into his boxers and dragged the colonel inside.

"NOT THERE," Gubbins gasped as Jack tried to help him sit down on the bed. "Bathroom. *Tile.* Easier to clean."

They hobbled to the bath and Gubbins sank down onto the toilet. Jack thought for an instant he was going to faint—the man's eyes rolled back in his head—but then Jack slapped him hard on the cheek and he came round, grinning like a drunkard.

"Good show. Whiskey?"

"None in the room."

"Flask," Gubbins muttered. "Breast pocket."

He reached into the man's jacket and found the flat silver bottle. He unscrewed the cap and tipped it to Gubbins's lips.

"Where are you hurt?" Jack asked. His own head was swimming and he shook it again, damning himself for weakness.

"Leg." The colonel motioned to his left thigh. "Didn't hit the femoral. Flesh wound. But . . . lost a spot of blood."

There was a black hole in the fabric of Gubbins's trousers, just visible among the welter of dark brown stains. Jack was familiar with blood and shit and wounds and pain, but the colonel's customary neatness, his perfect tailoring, made this carnage more alarming. "You need a doctor."

Gubbins shook his head violently. "Wrap a tourniquet around it."

He was speaking more clearly; the short-term effect of alcohol, Jack thought. He glanced again at the oozing hole in Gubbins's leg. How much blood did a man have in him? *Tourniquet.* One of his shirts. . . .

Hurriedly, he set the Luger on the floor and dashed to his closet. Like all his clothes, the shirt could do with a laundering, but he figured it was better than nothing. He tore at the seam with his teeth and managed a single long strip of fabric. He knelt down on the cold tiles and began clumsily to help Gubbins out of his clothes.

He was a swart, muscular, hairy little devil. He leaned heavily on Jack's shoulder and stumbled for balance. Lifted one foot clear of his trousers, then the other, more difficult because the leg was sticky with blood. Jack thrust the trousers away and eased Gubbins back onto the toilet. He began feverishly to wrap the tourniquet above the wound.

Gubbins was drinking again. Jack waited until he'd swallowed and said, "What happened?"

"Gestapo. No business being here. Polish sovereign territory. Tell that to Heydrich."

"They shot you? Where?"

"Bit of woods south of the city. Don't think they *knew* it was me, per se. Fired at random on our little party."

Fear knifed through Jack. "They knew about the Enigma?"

"Shhhh," Gubbins muttered. He closed his eyes, as if he were about to swoon.

"Did they get it?" Jack grasped the man's shoulder, his mind filled with shadows, darting through flames. "Colonel—*the Enigma*. Where is it?"

"Poles." Gubbins's eyes opened again and he concentrated on Jack. "Handoff aborted. Nothing else to do. *Sauve qui peut* and devil take the hindmost. I think we all got clear. Hope to God the machine did."

Jack stared at him. "You don't *know*?"

Gubbins shook his head slightly.

"Is there someone I can . . . contact? Somebody who can tell us?"

Gubbins scrabbled for his hand and gripped it hard. "Over to you, old son. You'll have to manage it."

Jack, with his blurred vision and his spiking internal heat and a body no one could depend on. He reached for Willi's Luger. Focused on the narrow steel barrel. *He must focus.*

"Your baby, now," the colonel said. And fainted.

TWENTY MINUTES LATER, Jack opened his door and admitted the British embassy, in the form of a man named Forsyte. It was nearly six o'clock in the morning and the hotel was quiet.

"We've told the front desk you're a bit of a fusspot, Colin, with chronic heart trouble," Forsyte said briskly, "and being a British national unacquainted with Polish doctors, you called your embassy for help. Reynolds and Magnus have a stretcher waiting in the hall. We'll load you on, cover you to the chin, and carry you right out the Polonia's front door. Seven minutes by van to the embassy and Dr. Graham."

"Splendid," Gubbins whispered. He had opened his eyes when Jack doused his face with water, but they could all see he was fading fast.

"Mr. Kennedy—you'll collect Colin's kit from room 617?" Forsyte was holding out a key. "There's a good chap. Leave it with the bellman. We'll send for it later."

Jack took Gubbins's key and watched as Forsyte quietly opened the door to the corridor and admitted the two other men, who quickly lifted Gubbins onto the stretcher. It was done with a faint air of disapproval, as though the colonel was a tiresome schoolboy being forcibly returned to his Sixth Form Master. *How like the British,* Jack thought. *Even the Irregulars.*

As they were about to leave, Gubbins reached for Jack's arm. *"Listen,"* he said.

Jack leaned close.

"74-39-51-00. Do whatever they tell you."

FORTY-SEVEN. ESCAPE AND EVASION

HALF AN HOUR LATER Jack went downstairs and ordered breakfast, as though he'd never heard of a fusspot named Harris who dealt in tweeds. Fortified with coffee and some sort of Polish sweet roll made with currants, he went out into the street and found a public telephone.

He dialed the number he'd memorized. 74-39-51-00. A male voice, heavy with cigarette smoke, answered in Polish.

"My name's Kennedy," he said. "Gubbins told me to call."

There was a pause. Then a series of metallic clicks. Then the same voice said, "You are where, Kennedy?"

Jack glanced through the phone booth's windows. "Three blocks from the Polonia Palace."

"You will walk to Castle Square. You will find taxi stand. You will take number 52 taxi, yes?"

"Why—" Jack attempted, but the line had gone dead.

He stood for a second in the protective womb of the booth. Could the voice be trusted? What if Gubbins's friends were in the hands of the Gestapo? What if he was walking into a trap?

The Luger in his blazer pocket felt heavy. He patted it twice and, taking a deep breath, stepped out into the street.

CASTLE SQUARE WAS IN the Old Town, the medieval heart of Warsaw not far from the river. The streets running within the fortified walls were abrupt and narrow and all led to the same place; a few cars heaved past St. John's Cathedral and loitered in Queen Anna's corridor. The castle itself was massive and magnificent, a big-shouldered building that suggested Paris rather than Poland. Uniformed guards stood at attention near the entrance; Jack wondered idly if they were armed. A raised flag announced that the President was in residence.

He ambled diagonally across the square toward the marketplace, conscious that it was summer and that half the population of the city was gathered among the vendors' stalls, prodding beets and potatoes with blunt fingers. The taxi stand was near the market. Five black cars were huddled against the curb, leaving a narrow space for traffic to pass; a market truck blared its horn.

Jack let his eyes drift casually over the taxis, looking for number 52. It was fourth in line.

He'd draw attention if he walked right up to it. He turned his back and examined a display of cheeses set out on a table. The names scrawled in Polish with a bit of chalk meant nothing to him, but he grinned at the white-haired woman who offered him a slice of something pungent and hard, and slipped it into his mouth. He glanced over his shoulder at the taxis as he chewed. Number 52 was now third in line. That's when he saw him.

The Spider.

He was dressed in plainclothes, a light summer suit, leaning against one of the vaulted arches that formed Queen Anna's corridor. He was turning the pages of a newspaper, but Jack doubted

Hans Obst could read Polish. How long had the Spider been following him? From the moment he left his hotel?

And then he understood. Obst was there because Jack had been set up. He was the fallback plan if Jack did not get into the taxi. Blocking the most obvious direction Jack would run.

He turned to the old woman and fished in his pocket for coins. She took her time wrapping the cheese in a sheet of newspaper. Jack's belly roiled with the familiar disease. Chills ran up his legs and fluttered in his fingertips. He smiled idiotically at the crone and felt the Spider's eyes bore into his back. He could not get into the taxi. He could not run. There would be other men in other suits with other newspapers, posted around the marketplace; but he must somehow get back to the Polonia. He needed his car and his radio lying hidden in the boot.

The Enigma, said a voice in his head. Not Roosevelt's, this time, or Gubbins's—but Winston Churchill's. *To you from failing hands we throw the torch.*

He shoved the statesman's voice as far from his consciousness as he could and willed himself to concentrate on the problem at hand. The problem of survival.

He strolled deeper into the crowd, the cheese in his left hand, the butt of the Luger in his right, masked by his coat pocket. There were carved dolls on a table. Blown glass on another. Sausages dangling from a scaffold. Trussed birds. Trussed rabbits, eyes shining like polished stones. Crucifixes and rosary beads carved from wood. Eunice would like some rosary beads. Her Sacred Heart medal was sticky with sweat, inside his shirt.

Women draped in black shuffled by, brushing against him, the obvious Westerner, the obvious misfit. *Obvious.* He was obvious. He had a target on his back. Impossible to know who was following him. He hadn't been trained in this, the detection of surveillance. Gubbins had said something about stopping to look in shop windows, scanning his reflection for what didn't fit, but there were no shop windows here, only claustrophobic crowds. His panic ground up a notch and spots exploded before his eyes.

He pushed past a man with a massive gut pouring vodka into tiny glasses, and stepped out abruptly into the street. He'd reached the end of the market.

He balanced there wildly for an instant, like a fox flushed from cover. To the left, an archway into a narrow passage. A bolt hole. A dead end. To the right, a blond head with a flat stare and a faint smile, walking briskly toward him—

A car screeched up, cutting him off at the knees. *Taxi number 52.*

"Get in," the driver said in guttural English. "Get in, before they kill you."

He thrust open the back door.

Jack had no choice. He fell onto the seat. The door slammed closed as the taxi roared away.

THEY DROVE IN SILENCE and at a ridiculous speed, turning so often from boulevards into side streets that Jack only guessed where he was when he glimpsed the river. It disappeared almost immediately again and he was heading away from it—crossing back over it—diving under bridges and scuttling along waterfronts, crossing to the west, heading out of the city, doubling back and ending abruptly at the Central Railway Station.

"You want me to get on a train," he said stupidly, thinking of all he'd left at the Polonia Palace. The driver merely shook his head and pulled over near the station's front entrance.

Jack's car door was abruptly yanked open. He reared back from the stranger standing there. A slight, birdlike figure in a dirty raincoat. A newsboy cap on the black hair.

"Mr. Kennedy."

A gravel voice. It had answered the telephone earlier. "Please. You will come with me?"

Jack waited for the gun to emerge from the raincoat pocket, for the pretense of politeness to dissolve.

"We've met before, you know," the man said. "Near Danzig, in the dark. You were with a man who painted in oils."

Jack got out of the car.

He was led swiftly to another one, a tin can of indiscriminate make, and shoved into the passenger seat.

"Look behind you," his driver said. "See the bag?"

A carpetbag, his mother would call it—brown and squat and made of some heavy material.

"What you are looking for is inside. When I let you out, you will take that bag and you will hail a taxi. Do not get into the first one that stops or even the second. Tell the driver of the third that you wish to go to the Central Railway Station. When you get there, buy a ticket. Vilnius is still safe. Or Budapest. I mention these cities because they are not Berlin, which is the easiest route to the West. It will be watched. *Do not go to Berlin.* The border search alone would kill you."

"I have a diplomatic passport." That was why he had come. Why Gubbins needed him.

The Bird Man barked with laughter.

"I left a car at the hotel," Jack said.

"Do not go back to the hotel. You know that members of the Gestapo were in the market?"

"Yes."

"Well, then." The sharp face darted toward him. "I assume that Mr. Kennedy is not a fool."

"They know about the Enigma? That you've got it, and you're trying to pass it to us?"

The man shrugged.

"If they already know you're trying to crack this new machine . . ."

"They'll invent another. *Yes.*"

"So—"

"—Why bother to go on?" the Pole asked. "Because we do not *know* that they know. Because it is all that we have. Because if I allowed myself to ask and answer that question, Mr. Kennedy, I would have shot myself long ago. And there really would be no hope for honest men in Europe anymore."

The tiny car swerved to a halt. Jack grasped the carpetbag and was actually pushed out onto the sidewalk.

The tin can pulled away.

AS HE WALKED, Jack stopped to rest his arm—the carpetbag was quite heavy, as though it held a load of his books—and occasionally studied his reflection in plate-glass windows, which were numerous in this part of town. He saw furniture displays and mannequins wearing women's clothes, shoe shops and pastry store windows. No Aryan killers smiling their secret smiles, backward in the glass.

He considered opening the carpetbag to check what was inside, and rejected the idea. He might draw attention, and he'd had enough of that for one day. He was debating his options as he walked. Car versus train. Budapest versus Vilnius.

By the time he found his third taxi, he'd made up his mind.

"Polonia Palace," he said, as he got in.

FORTY-EIGHT. THE PRICE IN BLOOD

YES, MR. KENNEDY was indeed a fool, Jack thought in anguish. He should have taken the Bird Man seriously and been halfway to Budapest by now.

SHE WAS SPRAWLED on his ravaged bed in a light summer frock, her black hair spread over his pillow. The dress was torn down the front and her legs were parted and one high heel was dangling from her right foot. The left was bare. It was clear the Spider had enjoyed his time with Diana. But perhaps enjoyed, even more, leaving her for Jack to find.

He had cut her open from neck to navel with side journeys along her arms and across her inner thigh, and around the delicate curve of each breast. The face he'd left intact so that Jack would be forced to look at her, forced to know how completely he'd failed her. Diana did not look back. Her black eyes stared at the ceiling instead. Her mouth was open in a scream.

Taking it all in, Jack swayed in the bedroom doorway, the carpetbag dropping to the floor. The smell of blood was rank with July and the humidity rising off the river. There was blood all over the bed and arced across the wall; blood in deep black gouts on the thick carpeting. Blood impossible to hide or wash away.

He stumbled toward Diana, mouthing obscenities. Tears salty on his lips. He knew that he *must not touch her* but he gathered her up anyway, held her close, desperate to knit together the brutal slice in her skin, the ravaging of bone. He had not known she was in Warsaw. He should have known, from the mere fact of the Spider standing in Queen Anna's corridor. He smoothed her hair with his fingers and cradled her. Groaned her name. She would never hear him say *Jesus, I loved you.*

He should have stayed in Prague. Or taken her with him. He should have shot the Spider dead on the Charles Bridge and pulled her along, racing for home, Heydrich and his blackmail be damned. What sort of man left the girl he loved with sadists and knives? His trembling fingers traced her cheekbone while a knot inside him unraveled—guilt, refusal. *Hatred.* For Heydrich and his butchers. For himself, who'd delivered Diana into their keeping.

He laid her on the pillow and her head rolled sideways toward the wall.

She had died screaming, Jack thought. Why had nobody come?

The Spider must have stuffed a gag in her mouth.

He brought her here as if to see Jack—and then took out his knife. She had known exactly what he would do to her. And then had watched him do it. Screaming.

Jack's pulse began to throb.

Heydrich had known. He'd ordered this—*Jack's punishment*, for escaping them in the market this morning. Diana left like a sick present in his room.

His room.

He lurched upright and forced himself to look at her. There was no crouching spider cut into Diana's breast, no killer's calling card. What Obst *had* left was a razor.

Jack's flat steel razor with the ebony handle, presented by his father six years ago. When he'd finally had enough beard to shave.

It lay on the sheet beside her delicate fingers, her blood smeared over its blade.

Nothing in the room would point to anybody else. He was alone with a corpse he'd have to explain. Blood all over his shirt and jacket, now, trailing down his pants. His razor was lying next to her body. It would make a perfect story.

He stared around him wildly. The Enigma still sat in its bag by the door, where he'd left it. *And the door was wide open.* He lunged to close it before anyone saw.

As he crossed the room, his foot struck something lying on the floor. Diana's evening purse. The one he'd bought her in Danzig.

He reached for it, his hand shaking. It was a small beaded thing in platinum and steel; he held it quickly to his nose, searching for her scent. Pain clawed at his chest. She'd carried it with her even during the day.

The open doorway leered. He set down the purse, dragged the carpetbag inside his bedroom, and kicked the door closed. He leaned against it a moment, trying to breathe. He did not have much time. Heydrich would send somebody, soon, to make sure his props had done their job. And to catch Jack—with blood on his hands.

Jack tore off his clothes and bundled them into the hotel's laundry bag. The butcher's smell was suddenly overwhelming and he gagged at the rusty smears all over himself; he dashed into the bath and scrubbed his fingers in the basin, standing like a sick child in his underwear, retching. Then he stared at himself in the mirror. The hollow sockets around his eyes, the prominent bones of the leprechaun; a face for comedy, not tragedy. It looked like a killer's face to him now. Frantically, he soaped his chest and arms, then hid his face in a clean towel.

After an instant, he steadied himself. Threw on a clean shirt and his second pair of flannel trousers. His breath was coming rapidly and he could no longer look at the bed. He shrugged himself into a spare jacket. He should pack his things. But he could not think straight and he was wasting time. He reached for his loafers and realized the soles had blood on them. *He'd left footprints in the carpet, for chrissake.* Back to the basin, and the swirl of pink down the drain. He shook the shoes frantically, rinsed them twice, and shoved them damply on his feet.

He tucked Diana's evening purse in his left pocket, with his passport and wallet. The Luger went into his right. He took the carpetbag in one hand and the laundry sack of bloodied clothes in the other. Tried to stop the juddering of his mind.

He was nuts to think he could pay his bill and drive fast, right out of Poland.

He opened the bedroom door.

Oh, Diana, I would have died for you, he thought, looking at her for the last time. *I'm dying anyway.*

Forgive me.

He shut the door behind him.

He wouldn't get far. They would close the borders. He'd be hauled back to Warsaw on a murder charge. The whole world would hear about it. *Kennedy Son Stabs Married Lover.*

His dad was going to kill him.

Fuck his dad.

"Ah, Mr. Kennedy."

He glanced vaguely at the man strolling toward him down the hallway. His fingers felt for the Luger in his right pocket.

"I popped round for Harris's things—he's being sent out on

a diplomatic flight this evening—but the bellman says he knows nothing about them. Do you still have the key?"

It was the Englishman he'd met that morning. Foreskin? For*syte*. It seemed a thousand years ago.

Jack blinked at him stupidly. "I'm sorry. I . . . I forgot." He slapped his pockets. "*Jesus*. I think I left the key in *there*. On the dresser."

Forsyte peered at him and frowned. "I say, old chap—are you unwell?"

"I'm a mess."

He reached back and opened the door.

Forsyte hesitated an instant, then stepped inside.

Jack slumped against the wall, cradling his head in his hands. There was a burning in the back of his throat.

From his room, the sudden in-drawing of breath and then silence. As if seeing Diana's body had turned Forsyte to stone.

Jack felt a hand on his shoulder.

"That's Diana Playfair," Forsyte said softly.

"It *was*."

"Lock the door and come along with me."

Jack did as he was told. He followed Forsyte down the hall to a service stairway and then up two flights to the sixth floor, the carpetbag banging against one leg and the laundry against the other. Forsyte must have found Gubbins's key on Jack's dresser because he pulled it from his pocket as they neared room 617. He bundled Jack inside.

"Sit down."

The room smelled and felt like Gubbins. It made Jack want to cry. He sank into a chair.

"Did you know her?" Forsyte asked. He perched on the edge of the bed like a consulting physician.

"I loved her."

"But you didn't *kill* her, I take it."

He shook his head dumbly.

"Know who did?"

"A man called the White Spider. He works for Reinhard Heydrich."

Forsyte whistled softly. "And Heydrich framed *you*. Joe Kennedy's son. Nice publicity stunt, that."

Jack glanced up. "You know my father?"

"Of course. I'm from Foreign Office." Forsyte rubbed at his nose with one finger. "Do you mind me asking, Mr. Kennedy—exactly how *old* are you?"

"Twenty-two. And it's Jack."

"Have you contacted your ambassador here? Mr. Biddle?"

Jack shook his head. He knew and liked Tony Biddle, but he'd deliberately avoided him on this trip. It was secret, and anyway Biddle would want nothing to do with smuggling a stolen German code machine out of Poland.

"Where were you today?" Forstye asked.

"All over Warsaw."

"*With* anybody?"

"A few taxi drivers."

"Any you could name?"

Jack hesitated, thinking of the Bird Man, then shook his head.

"Blast," Forsyte said succinctly. "Not a terribly good alibi, I'm afraid."

"Maybe somebody downstairs saw Diana come in with Obst."

"Obst?"

"The Spider."

"Nobody will have seen him take her to *your* room, I can tell you that. He'll have been damn careful. Picked the lock, I suppose?"

"He's good at that."

"Hotels are never difficult," Forsyte offered.

Gubbins had said the same thing. Jack remembered, suddenly, standing in the Spider's room in Danzig in total darkness, waiting for him to come through the door. *I should have killed him when I had the chance.*

"I'll go down and tell the manager," Jack said wearily. "I'll tell the truth, even if nobody believes it."

"You'll do nothing of the kind."

He stared at Forsyte. "*That's my room.* They know it. I can't pack my bag and run. I'll never make the border."

"True," Forsyte agreed. "We'll have to handle things a bit more diplomatically. Mrs. Playfair's a British national. She's an Irregular, isn't she? One of Gubbins's people?"

"I've never known for sure," Jack said. "She was doing something . . . in an unofficial capacity."

"Rumor has it. Are you one of Gubbins's people as well?"

Jack looked at him. "I guess maybe I am."

"*Right,*" Forsyte said quickly. "We'll go straight to Colin's friends in Polish Intelligence. They'll pull rank, pop by the hotel with a few of their johnnies, and get the place tidied up. Nobody the wiser. We'll send Diana home on a train tomorrow—I imagine Playfair will like to have the body."

Send Diana home on a train.

He had a sudden image of her adjusting a hat, her gloved hands working with a pin, the sleeves of her frock fluttering.

Playfair will like to have the body.

He would have to tell Denys how his wife had died.

"Jesus God," he said, feeling the burn in the back of his throat again. "She'd never have left England if it weren't for me."

"Don't flatter yourself," Forsyte said briskly. "She was the sort of girl who did exactly what she wanted, all the time; and she paid the price, I'm afraid. Damn shame, of course. Nobody *likes* to see a nasty end."

A damn shame. A nasty end. That would be Diana's epitaph among the Foreign Office—while to Jack, it was something akin to Lear. Ashes and bitterness. *Howl.*

THEY BROUGHT HIS LUGGAGE, neatly packed, to room 617. Gubbins's friends were removing all trace of Jack's presence—his fingerprints from the bath, his footprints from the carpet. His bag full of bloody clothes. Polish Intelligence had suggested to the Polonia management that someone had committed suicide in a room upstairs. The manager was anxious that the mess be handled without the slightest disturbance to the Polonia's guests.

"Give me your money," Forsyte commanded.

Jack opened his wallet.

"One of these chappies will settle your account. He'll have your car pulled round to the *side* entrance, not the *front*, mind— and you're to take the stairs down, not the elevator."

"The place is being watched?"

"Of course it's watched," Forsyte snapped. "Heydrich's people did this for a reason, Jack. They're waiting for all hell to break loose. We'll have to hope they haven't recognized our Polish friends entering the lobby, or they'll know their dirty game has gone awry. This is still a sovereign country, so they can't *formally* intervene—but I should not expect them to give up. As soon as you walk out of this hotel, they will be hunting you. I don't want to know why."

He paused, then said diffidently, "Have you thought of what to do next?"

Jack rubbed at his eyes. The lids felt dry and itchy, something to do with tears. He had failed to get the DOCA into his system this morning and he knew he would regret that later. But for now, he had to think. Forsyte had asked the critical question.

How to get out of Poland—and take the Heydrich-Enigma with him?

He had gone through too much—he had lost too much—to forfeit the prize now.

He was tempted to ask for a seat on the plane that would carry Gubbins out that evening; but he was not a British subject, and Forsyte had already done enough for a relative stranger.

He could hand over the brown carpetbag, and tell Forsyte to put it on the plane with Gubbins. But Forsyte had said he was *Foreign Office*, not "one of Gubbins's people," a deliberate distinction Jack could not ignore. Forsyte knew nothing about the Heydrich-Engima. He was part of Neville Chamberlain's official apparatus, the creaking machinery of the British Empire—not the Baker Street Irregulars. If Forsyte *opened* the brown carpetbag and looked at its contents—what in God's name would happen?

Nothing good, Jack felt certain.

Your baby now, Gubbins had said.

Churchill was counting on him to succeed.

So were the Poles, who were industriously covering his bloody tracks.

He met Forsyte's gaze. "It's safest if you have no idea what I do next."

FORTY-NINE. THE RAILWAYS OF CENTRAL EUROPE

WHEN HE REACHED THE BOTTOM of the six-storey stairwell, he exited into a narrow alley devoid of life. He was reminded, incongruously, of the Waldorf-Astoria and a freight elevator opening into a deserted garage. There was no Casey or Schwartz to offer Jack a comb. A car waited, rear door open—but it was not Jack's blue Citroën. It was the tin can he'd occupied early that afternoon, and behind the wheel was Bird Man.

"Lie down," the gravel voice ordered, as he heaved his heavy bags into the car. "Do not move until I tell you."

He did what the man asked. The car swung away from the curb. To his surprise he felt it move at a leisurely pace, weaving sedately in and out of traffic. It was possible, Jack thought, that Bird Man thought speed would attract attention.

"What will happen to my Citroën?" Jack asked the seat cushion. He was keeping his head down.

"After it has sat for too long, someone will break into it and steal it," Bird Man said indifferently.

"Want the keys?"

"Unnecessary. You will wish to report the theft when you reach home. The keys will be proof of your innocence, then, to those who care about such things."

From his tone, Bird Man cared about very little. That he bothered with Jack was due entirely to the brown carpetbag.

Ten minutes, perhaps a quarter hour passed, the car turning and accelerating, the spans of bridges visible from the corners of his eyes. His head was spinning muzzily and he wondered if it was the car, or his illness. Had Gubbins's friends packed his bottle of DOCA?

"You may sit up now," Bird Man said, "and tell me where you wish to go."

The casualness of the words was jarring. Jack had assumed he was in Bird Man's hands, that he would be directed in his eventual salvation, as he had been all day.

He sat up. "Where *I* wish to go?"

"Indeed, yes. The aerodrome? The train station? Or your embassy, perhaps? I will undertake to deposit you on Mr. Biddle's back doorstep."

He stared at the man's head, narrow and bristling under its slice of newsboy cap; the harshness of the profile. Sallow skin and a hooked nose. There was no plan. It was up to Jack to save himself.

He ruled out his embassy immediately. The United States was officially neutral—and Jack Kennedy, proud possessor of a diplomatic passport, had stolen a German cipher machine. He could not begin to explain the Irregulars, or his private act of war, to Roosevelt's official envoy, however much he liked Tony Biddle, or yearned for a good glass of Bourbon in the safety of the man's dining room.

He would have to take this journey alone.

"It's a long flight from Warsaw to London," he suggested. "Where would a plane touch down, do you think?"

"Berlin, first," the Bird Man said. "And your journey would undoubtedly end there. I do not advise flying west."

Trains, Jack thought, presented the same problem. The rails led to Germany. Or Austria. Or the Czechoslovak border. All bristling with gray uniforms. "You suggested Budapest this afternoon."

"Which is also west," the Bird Man concluded tranquilly. "But from Buda one might get to Ljubljana. And from there, to Trieste or Venice . . ."

Jack tried to think. *Where the hell was Ljubljana?* Croatia? No. Slovenia. He would have to look at a map. But it would not be a hub of air travel, wherever it was. He had a vague idea Trieste was a port. If he could reach it, he might board a ship. Sail the Adriatic. Make a tour of the Mediterranean. Forget that Diana's butchered body was clacking home, by slow degrees, across all the train lines of Europe.

He would never forget.

"There is a night train to Budapest," Bird Man said. "I have taken this train myself, several times. It departs Central Station a few minutes after nine o'clock. It is now half past five."

"That's a long time to wait." He could see it all: a lonely table in the station dining room. Himself, choking on the food. Watching as the wolves in uniform gathered and circled. He would never reach his compartment. They would slit his throat and toss his body from the train. *Ambassador Kennedy, we regret to inform you that your son, John Fitzgerald . . .*

They would seize the Heydrich-Enigma. All the desperate cipher-breaking work would be lost.

"You cannot wait so long," Bird Man agreed. "So I will drive you to Katowice."

"Katowice?" Jack repeated, startled.

"At half past eleven, the Buda train stops at Katowice. The Gestapo will never look for you there, at such an hour. We will take the back roads. It will require some time."

The man, Jack saw, was holding out a flask. A gesture of comradeship that reminded him of Gubbins. There was probably a section on "Flasks, Sharing of," in *The Partisan Leader's Handbook*.

He tossed back a burning slug of vodka. Bird Man had a plan.

KATOWICE WAS THE CENTER of Upper Silesia, an industrialized, nineteenth-century town in a part of the world that, like Danzig, had changed hands too many times to count. Katowice had been Bohemian, Hapsburg, Prussian, and Polish; but many of its inhabitants spoke only German.

Jack shrugged off his faint edge of panic as he stood on the deserted platform in the central train station. Many people spoke German. It was one of history's occupational hazards. That did not make them automatic Nazis. But he glanced continually over his shoulder nonetheless, at the two silent men smoking cigarettes in the humid night. One leaned against a lamppost—the platform was flooded with light—and the other paced irritably, his hands in his pockets. Was he holding a gun? The Luger was still in Jack's pocket. His suitcase and carpetbag rested on the platform, ready to be grasped if he had to run. Only: How to run and fire the Luger at the same time? He didn't have three hands. He would have to leave the suitcase behind. Bird Man, he thought, would have been useful as a bag carrier; but Bird Man was already on his way back to Warsaw.

He had dropped Jack at the curb fifteen minutes before, after a tortuous night journey through the winding roads of the Silesian Highlands. The Eastern Carpathians were not far distant, and the terrain was rugged. The tin can bucked and snorted up steep grades, threatening to stall and leave them at the mercy of any passing stranger. With a giddy sense of fatalism, Jack *expected* the car to break down—he *ought* to be marooned in a Carpathian Hell for the sin of Diana's death. But in fact, the tin can rolled into Katowice later that night with time to spare.

He shook Bird Man's hand with awkward formality, aware that he would never know the man's name.

"Listen to me carefully," Bird Man said. "The train stops again at Bratislava. A man will board there. *English.* He will enter your compartment. Although it will be the early hours of morning he will make conversation. He will use the word *irregular.* You are to answer something—it does not matter what—with the word *Harvard.* Understand?"

"Bona fides."

"Correct. This man will have a brown carpetbag exactly like yours. He will place it on the rack above your head. When you leave the train in Budapest, *take his bag.* Not the one you carry now. That is clear?"

Abundantly, Jack thought. The choices presented back in Warsaw had been mere distractions. There had always been a plan—Gubbins's plan. Baker Street was happy to use Jack as a courier out of Poland, particularly as the colonel himself was *hors de combat,* but they had no intention of allowing the Heydrich-Enigma to reach an American embassy. Churchill wanted the device in British hands. They would take the prize from him before dawn.

Jack didn't mind in the slightest. After Bratislava, the only thing he'd have to save would be his own neck.

The Budapest train chugged to a halt in front of him. Five carriages, one of them a dining car. He would sit in *there*, Jack thought suddenly, until the Englishman boarded. There would be comfort in the presence of waiters. Nobody would kill him with a fork in his hand.

He reached for his bags, trying to disguise the effort it cost him now to lift the heavy Enigma. The men on the platform moved in behind. He waited for one of them to stick a muzzle in his back. But they ignored his existence and he was allowed to board.

"How long to Bratislava?" he asked the waiter who led him to his table. Nobody was following him. Jack felt light-headed with relief. The waiter looked at him uncomprehendingly; he did not speak English. Jack asked the question again, in his bastard French.

"*Ah.* Six hours." The waiter glanced disapprovingly at Jack's luggage. It ought to have been left in a compartment. Jack placed it on the seat beside him, instead. "You wish brandy? Cognac?"

"Black coffee," he said. He glanced at his watch. The Englishman would appear sometime around five-thirty a.m. He would need to stay awake. He would have to settle his stomach. "Have you got any ice cream?"

WITH POINTED INDIFFERENCE to the waiter's annoyance, Jack stubbornly held down his table as the night hours passed. He slipped *Young Melbourne* from his suitcase and reread certain passages. Caroline Lamb and Lord Byron. The Ministry of All the Talents. Perceval's assassination. *Imagine that,* he thought. A nutcase shooting down the Prime Minister, in broad daylight.

When the typeface began to blur before his eyes, he called

for more coffee. He badly needed to use the bathroom and he'd have liked to have gotten a DOCA pellet in his leg, but he couldn't leave the carpetbag unattended or carry it everywhere with him. He would draw too much attention. Patrons drifted in and out of the dining car: a few couples, a few men, never a single woman. *Diana,* he thought. He could see her sauntering through these midnight cars alone, elegant and unapproachable. She'd have taken a table a few seats away, backlit by the hushed lamps, a cigarette holder in her gloved hand. He missed her acutely in the small hours of morning. The typeface blurred again.

When a few early risers bound for Bratislava made their way down the aisle, calling for breakfast, Jack put his book away. He had already settled his bill. He gazed out the window through the gray light, seeing branch lines and switches, the detritus of rail yards, the hint of red tile roofs somewhere beyond. Abruptly they entered a tunnel, and the scene went black. In the flick of an eyelid, they emerged again. Bratislava station, lofty overhead, and the train slowing now to a halt.

He shoved his window upward and leaned out, craning to glance down the platform. At least two dozen people disembarked from the train; dazed-looking women with hats jammed on their sleep-mussed hair, a few children clinging to their skirts; and men, all of them discernibly *Mittel* European. It was something about the clothes, Jack thought. Not just the quality, but the style and cut. That fellow, for example, in the worn heather tweeds and the soft hat, waiting to board the train, would never be mistaken—

Would never be mistaken for anything but an Englishman.

He was an island of calm in the milling crowd of disembarking passengers, content to wait until the platform cleared. He was smoking a pipe and twitching desultorily through a newspaper. Middle-height, middle-aged, as unremarkable a figure as Colin Gubbins. Which to Jack, fairly screamed *Irregular*.

The platform gradually cleared. Few passengers were boarding the train for Budapest at such an early hour. Jack watched as the Englishman folded his newspaper, tucked it briskly under his arm, and reached for the brown carpetbag at his feet. In a leisurely fashion, he sauntered over to the train. The conductor mounted the steps ahead of him. Jack caught the sudden expulsion of steam and air from the locomotive; they would be moving in a minute.

Then a pair of stragglers dashed down the platform and leapt for the train. They—and the Englishman—were lost to view as they pushed their way aboard. Jack withdrew his head from the window to collect his things, when a sudden flash at the edge of his vision drew his gaze around.

The Englishman was down—curled on the platform in a fetal position, his arms clutched to his abdomen. His face was a rictus of pain. His hat had rolled off. He'd been pulled from the train car's steps and tossed to the ground. And the train was already moving.

"Hey!" Jack leaned out the window. "Stop the train!"

There was something protruding from between the Englishman's fists—the haft of a knife . . .

And the carpetbag was gone.

"Hey!" Jack shouted again. But the slow chug of the engine pulled the cars inexorably forward, the platform was slipping back, the Englishman was staggering to his knees, supporting himself with a single splayed hand, and nobody understood Jack's English, or the panic that was driving him to grab his bags and thrust his way through the dining car. He was on the verge of running, fear screaming in his ears, but he knew that he must

look natural, now; he must not be noticed. The waiter was taking a young girl's order. She was speaking German. Was he surrounded by enemy agents? Was she glancing at him as he passed, taking mental notes for the use of a killer?

The dining car was the train's last—it was backed by a high-railed observation platform where passengers could take the air or smoke. He thrust through the door that led to it and stepped out on the swaying platform. They were still in Bratislava's rail yard, clacking along at moderate speed, surrounded by branching lines, by signal lights he could not hope to understand, all the usual train traffic of a busy weekday in a largish city; but there was nothing for it—he would have to jump.

He glanced ahead. A train was coming in the opposite direction, on the line immediately to Jack's left. He calculated the distance and his own strength; tried to calculate the other train's speed. Then he shrugged and hurled both his bags off the platform. They fell away behind. He imagined the lawn at Hyannis Port, a game of Touch, his brother Joe tossing a long pass a few yards away. He leapt sideways, body arcing like a diver's, arms outstretched; and cleared the neighboring track with seconds to spare. He rolled over in a ball, gravel railbed painful in his back and legs, and felt a *whoosh* of heat as the incoming train thundered past him.

It would block his exit from anybody gazing out of the Budapest train.

With luck, his hunters would still be looking for him. Compartment by compartment, car by car. Carrying the bogus brown carpetbag.

The brown carpetbag.

He vaulted to his feet and half ran, half stumbled, back along the tracks to where his luggage lay. Fell to his knees and scrabbled at the buckles. If the Heydrich-Enigma had been damaged in the drop—

He pulled open the carpetbag and stared inside.

A heavy wooden case, with a hinged lid. The case had splintered slightly at the corners from impact, but it was still intact. He pried off the top. The Enigma looked like a typewriter. For a long moment, Jack thought it *was*—thought they'd all been had, from Churchill to Gubbins to Bird Man on down. Then he saw the strange second set of buttons ranged above the typewriter keys and the drums at the back, and realized he would never be able to tell if it was damaged or not. That was a job for an engineer. He shut the lid, and snapped the carpetbag closed.

A train whistle blasted in the distance. He glanced up, jolted into awareness of his surroundings. Gray light was giving way to the August dawn, and he was hunched like a beggar in the middle of the Bratislava train yard. With another train bearing down on his tracks.

He stared into the single engine light as it grew larger, a bald and blazing eye, then he rose to his feet and grasped his bags. He began to pick his way across the branching lines, carefully and with great effort. His legs were trembling—from the fall or his sickness or simply because he'd been hunted—and his arms were aching. There was an embankment in the distance, perhaps a football field away. If his luck held, he would reach it.

FIFTY. CLIFF-DIVING

"**COME ON, TEDDY.**" Joe's shout drifted up from the distant surf below. "Don't be such a coward!"

"What if you don't *catch* me?" the little boy yelled back. His voice had risen an octave, as if he were close to tears. "What if I hit the rocks?"

"I'll catch you, for Pete's sake."

"You didn't last time!"

"Just jump already!" Joe was fed up.

Jack rolled over on his towel and squinted into the sun. His baby brother was silhouetted at the top of Eden Roc in a half crouch, his bare toes gripping the gravelly edge. As he watched, Bobby ran up with a war-whoop, arms outstretched to push. Teddy gave a shriek of terror and ran back to Jack.

Bobby grinned. *"Baby."* He jumped over the edge.

There was a splash far below and the sound of Joe cursing. Bobby's drowned laughter.

Teddy buried his head in the towel between Jack and Kick, who was propped on her elbows above the Hotel du Cap. She was sunning herself while the boys hurled themselves into the Mediterranean. Girls didn't attempt suicide in a two-piece in the South of France, but Jack suspected Kick would give anything to dash herself on the rocks, just to know she could still *feel*. She was in exile this August, torn from Billy as he was about to celebrate his twenty-first birthday. *The Marquess of Harting-ton's Coming of Age*. A party for five hundred at Chatsworth. Three days of ceremony and fireworks, fetes and champagne. Every debutante in England was at the ancestral home of the Dukes of Devonshire—except Kick. The Irish Catholic American upstart.

She was heartsick and furious and didn't bother to hide it. While Jack had been in Poland, rumors of Kick and Billy's engagement blazed through the London papers—and the *New York Times*. The Kennedys issued denials on both sides of the Atlantic, but the Duke of Devonshire issued his *first*. Rose took this as a deliberate insult to her daughter; it was well-known the Duke despised Catholic girls on the catch for wealthy peers. Billy apologized for his father, but Rose was implacable. She declined Billy's invitation to Kick, carried her off to France, and said *she would never see Billy again*.

Kick stopped eating. She moped around the Domaine de Ranguin, the Kennedys' rented château, with its rose gardens and olive groves and glorious views of the sea. She was wan and listless and hollow-eyed. The threat of war was nothing compared to the threat of losing Billy.

Joe was still yelling from below the cliffs. Jack grabbed Teddy by the shoulders and swung him high. "Let's cannonball right over him," he whispered. "*Promise* I won't let you go."

Teddy crowed. Jack ran for the edge. He soared out into air with his kid brother's body held tight against him.

Waiting to feel something.

Anything.

———

HE'D KEPT THE DIANA RECKONING at bay during the crazed twenty-four hours after her murder. As he stumbled across the train yard in Bratislava, he'd thought only of surviving. It was clear to Jack that the Germans had learned, somehow, of the existence of the brown carpetbag and the Englishman intending to receive it. Had one of the Polish partisans talked? Had Bird Man been arrested and tortured? Jack couldn't know. He could only think frantically about how to get out of Bratislava before his killers learned he wasn't on their train.

He might have contacted the British consulate and turned over the carpetbag. He might have walked back to the station and waited for another train to Buda. But he was shaking with fever and adrenaline and so he chose the most obvious path. He hailed a taxi and said, "Airport."

It turned out to be the one word of English even a Bratislavan knew.

The field had a wind sock and a single runway and a shelter that might as well have been a bus station. No planes had yet landed, Jack guessed, that morning. Three people were waiting inside, their gazes uncomprehending when he tried to ask them about flights. He dragged his heavy cases into the single john, locked the door, and camped on the toilet for a quarter hour, his trousers down around his knees and a DOCA pellet in his shaking fingers. He felt like a hunted animal run to earth.

When he left the bathroom, a red-headed girl in a sober dirndl had taken up a position by a desk and was stamping tickets. She spoke French. When he asked, she agreed that there was a flight to Budapest. It would leave at noon.

Jack glanced around. "What are all these people waiting for?"
"The flight to Ljubljana," she said. "Eight o'clock."

It was already seven-thirty.

He bought a ticket to Ljubljana.

By lunchtime, he was dozing in a second-class compartment of the Ljubljana–Trieste train.

He dined on the ferry from Trieste to Venice: some sort of fisherman's stew pulled from the Adriatic, dotted with garlic and what he suspected was squid, washed down with raw red wine.

He found a room in Canareggio not far from the Santa Lucia train station, and the following night he slept in Rome. It was easy enough from there to fly to London—if you were a Kennedy, with cash in your pocket and a diplomatic passport. He had not seen a German soldier in days.

Seventy-two hours after he'd thrown himself off the Bratislava train, Jack walked into the lingerie shop off St. James and handed the brown carpetbag with the Heydrich-Enigma to an unflappable Matilda. She told him Gubbins's leg was mending nicely.

It was only later, as he made his way exhaustedly with Torby to his parents' summer idyll in the South of France, that the misery of Diana's murder broke like a massive wave in his mind.

HE AND TORB HAD ARRIVED in Cannes a few days ago, and found the whole family pretending to have a fabulous time. The air of gaiety was murderous. News bulletins came hourly over the radio his brother Joe kept tuned to the BBC: Czechoslovakia was in lockdown, with nobody but Germans allowed across the borders; Czech political figures were rumored to be dead or in hiding; Hitler was accusing the Poles of ever more fantastic atrocities against Germans in the Polish Corridor. They'd heard this kind of talk before. Everyone in Europe knew it was a prelude to invasion.

Jack noticed his dad snapped off the radio whenever he passed through the salon. He played golf relentlessly; he was on vacation. He was determined to have a good time. Nothing was happening in London—Chamberlain had adjourned Parliament, despite Hitler's rising frenzy, because the British Parliament *always* adjourned in August. Hitler could keep until September.

"You look like hell, Jack," Kick said when she ran down the limestone steps in a halter dress to meet him when he arrived. She pecked Torby on the cheek, utterly destroying him. "What did you boys *do* in Paris?"

That's right; they were supposed to have been in Paris all this time.

"Burned the candle at both ends, kid," Jack said lightly; but he recognized the haunted look in his sister's eyes. He guessed she saw it in his own. They were both heartsick.

They both smiled for Torby.

When they went into the house, his mother was waiting at the bottom of the stairs. "You're so pale, Ja-ack," Rose declared. "You look *ill*. Get over to Eden Roc and lie in the sun."

So he lay in the sun. It didn't matter what he did anymore. Diana was dead, her martyrdom meaningless, because the account book was still in Heydrich's hands. Jack's father was faithless. Jack had failed Roosevelt. He'd failed himself. He might as well dance the night away and lie to his friends about the way he'd spent his summer. Anything to avoid thinking.

"Fuck the thesis," he told Torby drunkenly one midnight as they lingered on the château's terrace long after everyone else had gone to bed. "Fuck Harvard. I'm gonna drop out and wander the world. *Write* for a living. Beholden to *nobody*."

"Except your old man," Torby said drily. "Costs a lot these days, to wander in the style you do."

Torby knew Jack pretty well and he figured something bad had happened in Poland—but he thought it was about some girl. Torby was twenty-one and could imagine nothing worse than being kicked out of a warm bed. He waited for Jack to tell him about it, and when Jack said nothing about blood or knives or a secret machine smuggled off a train, Torby kept his distance. It was the chief reason Jack loved him. That studied Yankee indifference.

HIS SKIN FIERY WITH SUN and the salt of the ocean still stinging his eyes, Jack moved through the evening crowd at Eden Roc. He wore light linen trousers and a summer jacket Rose had brought from his closet in London. His hair had turned gold in places; the leprechaun bones were flecked with freckles. His mouth wore the usual grin; it kept people at arm's length, now, instead of drawing them in. He held a gin and tonic in his hand.

He jitterbugged with Marlene Dietrich's daughter, who interested him less than Marlene herself; but the star's household was already crowded and he lacked the energy to compete. She'd taken several suites at the Hotel du Cap, as she did every summer. She talked loudly in French about how much she hated the Nazis, whirling her cigarette holder and glaring through the smoke with slitted eyes. Her legs were tanned and gleaming and crossed at the knee; her self-presentation superb. Her husband formed part of her entourage and so did her lover, the writer

Erich Maria Remarque; she moved, it was said, between the two men's suites. Amid so much glamour the daughter was wasted— a shy girl with dark hair who looked nothing like her mother. Jack had trouble remembering the daughter's name and so did everyone else, who perpetually called her *Darling*. He kept glancing over her head at the shifting group around Marlene.

His brother Joe was talking to her. So was his father. J.P. could never resist the pull of a star. But it was the third man in the group that grabbed Jack's attention: a dark-haired figure with perfect tailoring and beautiful hands.

Willi Dobler.

Not in London, but in Cannes. He was lighting Marlene's cigarette, and the mere sight of the flame spilled a cascade of memories through Jack's brain. It seemed years since the conspiracy of taxis, the exchange of brittle confidences.

The music ended in a clashing blare and Jack took the Dietrich girl in hand, piloting her through the crowd to her own people. Marlene exclaimed over them, in English this time, as though the script required her to act like a mother. Jack bowed and muttered something to Remarque about *All Quiet on the Western Front*, but his eyes were on Dobler. When he moved toward the bar, he knew the German was following.

He took his drink away from the dance floor, out toward the rocky shingle that ran down to the water. He needed space and the sound of waves if he was to talk to Willi.

"Hello, Jack," Dobler said as he came up with him. "You're looking well. Perhaps it is impossible to look anything else in the South of France, during Europe's final summer."

He stood at his ease as Jack sipped his drink, the tonic cool in his throat. It was choked and stinging again, as it was whenever he thought of Warsaw.

"I failed her, Willi," he said. "It's my fault and there's nothing I can do. I have to live with it for the rest of my life."

Dobler smiled faintly. "Since when did you take up knives, Jack? I know who's responsible. So does Denys."

Jack took another pull on the tonic. "Bullshit. We're all responsible. My father, who sold his president for thirty pieces of silver. You and Denys, who let her do your dirty work for you. Me, of course—I beat it out of Prague when she needed me most. And Heydrich—*fucking Heydrich*, who decided to teach me a lesson, and used Diana to do it."

"Is that what you think?" Dobler said slowly. "That Diana died . . . to teach *you* a lesson?"

"Heydrich set me up. That was the point."

"More a case of killing two birds with one stone. I thought you knew that. Forgive me—I didn't realize you believed it was all about *you*, Jack."

Jack drained his glass and tossed it viciously onto the rocks. "What the hell do you mean?"

Willi frowned at him. "You've allowed guilt to cloud your judgment."

"You bet I have." He laughed hollowly. "Let me tell you about Catholics, Willi. Nobody does guilt like us—*nobody*. We've made a cult of the thing. We fall on our knees and let it bleed us dry. I could confess all day long about the sins of Diana—but there's not a priest on God's earth who could absolve me, and none I'd listen to if he tried."

He stared past the German to the Hotel du Cap, the terrace with its string of lanterns, the swirling couples on the floor. He imagined it in flames, a doomed truck in Danzig. He did not want to go back inside. He walked farther down the beach in his stiff shoes, his hands clenched in his pockets.

"There's been a lot of talk about Diana's murder around the Abwehr," Dobler said. He was following him. "People are trying to make sense of it. Heydrich lost his temper. We think Diana crossed him—that she caused him so much damage he killed her. Tell me, Jack: What kind of damage could Diana do?"

Jack stopped short and stared at the ocean. He could feel Dobler halt several paces behind him. The sheer simplicity of Willi's words settled in his mind like stones dropping through a pool of water.

"The account book," he whispered. "*She got the account book.*"

"Very good."

"You actually think she stole it from Heydrich?" Jack asked.

"I think it's certain."

"That's insane." Jack twitched impatiently. "If she did, where is it?"

"Heydrich must not know. It's clear he hasn't used the list of names. There's been no arm-twisting or blackmail."

It was true; Jack had been watching his father, waiting for the unmistakable signs that the Old Man was caving to Nazi pressure. He'd seen nothing but golf. And more golf.

"Given that we're mere weeks from hurling all of Europe into war," Willi mused, "I'd have expected Heydrich to act. He should be forcing your father, for instance, to secure those American loans. Or approaching Mr. Churchill with the demand that he stand idly by while Neville Chamberlain stumbles. But I understand even the effort to thwart Roosevelt's third term has faltered completely. Why, Jack? Can you explain it?"

Jack turned to look at Willi, waiting for his next words.

"The account book is gone. And with it, Heydrich's greatest weapon. Diana took it."

A surge of feeling swept through Jack's gut. Emotion so

ragged, he clenched his jaw against it. She was still gone. Her blood all over his hands.

"She died without telling him where it is," Willi persisted. "Not even the knife got the truth out of her."

Screaming. She died screaming.

"You thought it was to punish *you*." Dobler grasped his shoulder and shook him. "Let yourself off that hook. She died in pain—because she made the choice."

The lights from the lanterns wavered and blurred. The damn salt in his eyes, again.

"We've got to find it, Willi," he whispered. "The account book. We owe her that much."

"Wouldn't it be safer, Jack," Dobler said gently, "to let sleeping dogs lie?"

HE HAD NEVER PARTICULARLY CARED about what was safe.

He left Kick and Joe and Torby and his father at Eden Roc and grabbed a taxi back to the château alone. He needed silence between himself and the momentous things Willi Dobler had said. Silence to consider this faint hope: that Diana had died for something much more important than a sick college kid from Boston. Jack wanted to believe it. It would ease the guilt he carried in his pocket. Fingering it like a piece of the true cross.

High up in his bedroom, he watched the night slip past without the comfort of sleep. Moonlight paved a road through the open French window as the hours wore away. Diana might just walk down that glimmering path and sit beside him on the bed, her cold fingers tugging at his hair; so he stayed alert, watching the moon as it shifted across his floor. When it slid up the far wall and disappeared, he turned restlessly under the single sheet, his nude body damp with fever.

Dobler was right. She'd taken the account book. Where was it now?

If she'd left it among her things, it was lost to them—Heydrich had probably dumped her clothes and luggage in a trash bin weeks ago. But no: he'd have searched Diana's belongings first; he'd be desperate to recover his prize. And he hadn't. As

Willi said: There was no hint of behind-the-scenes blackmail in these last crucial weeks before war.

"Come on, Diana," Jack muttered. "Tell me the truth. Where'd you hide Daisy's records?"

It's the only place I'm allowed to go alone, she replied.

A bathroom?

He could not begin to search the women's lavs of every gilded cage she'd used over the past three months.

She was still trying to steal the book when he deserted her in Prague; he was certain of that. She would never have stood by and watched the Spider kick him in the teeth if it was already in her hands. She'd have run to Jack that day, instead of walking deliberately across the Charles Bridge.

So she'd lifted Daisy's records from Heydrich's special strongbox sometime between Jack's birthday, the twenty-ninth of May, and the day he'd found her dead in Warsaw—the twenty-fifth of July. As soon as Heydrich discovered her treachery, he'd turned on her. The interrogations and the manipulations began.

He thought of Diana's sightless eyes on the bed in Warsaw and shivered.

Where'd you hide it, sweetheart?

She'd taken her last clues with her, into the silence of that final scream.

And yet—had she?

He sat up in his airless room.

There was one thing she'd left behind.

The evening bag he'd bought her in Danzig.

Steel and platinum, and totally inappropriate to carry in the daytime. Even as he'd stumbled toward her body, obscenities streaming from his mouth, his mind had snagged on that minor detail. He was enough Kick's brother to know the purse was all wrong, that it should never have been in her hands, much less lying on his hotel-room floor. He'd dismissed his doubt as soon as he'd tucked the bag into his pocket. Grateful to have something, anything, of Diana to remember.

She'd known she was going to die. She had brought the evening bag deliberately, and left it for him to find. Trusting that the Spider would never notice.

He swung out of bed and went to his armoire.

He'd emptied his jacket pockets long ago. The evening bag lived beneath his handkerchiefs, piled carelessly in a drawer. His fingers found the beaded surface, slippery as caviar.

A blue dawn was breaking. Birdsong rising in the woods. His sleepless mind felt like somebody had bludgeoned it and his thumbs fumbled at the purse's catch.

Inside, a few coins and notes.

A red lipstick, French.

Her cigarette case.

He opened this and sniffed the tobacco. Nothing of Diana in its scent.

There was a gambling chip from the casino in Monte Carlo; a small crucifix without a chain; and a book of matches from the Metropol in Moscow—the last time they'd made love.

She'd kept the purse to keep *him* with her. A pocket-sized Jack, for when the fear grew too much.

He turned the treasures over like a magpie. Fingering the bones. Then he turned to the bag itself.

It was lined in black silk, trapped by the steel frame. At the bottom, however, the lining's seam was visible. And it had been opened in one corner, then neatly re-sewn. . . .

Jack dashed into his bath and found his new razor. He cut a

slit in the lining large enough for his index finger and thrust it frantically through the silk. *Nothing.* His heart sank. Then he felt the edge of the flimsy cardboard scrap, tucked into the edge of the frame between the beading and the lining. The Spider had been too stupid to look for it.

His thudding pulse slowed. Carefully, he pulled the cardboard free.

It looked like a ticket from a hatcheck girl.

Praha Hlavni Nadrazi, it said, with a number stamped beneath.

Jack closed his eyes and blessed Diana.

Daisy Corcoran's murderous account book was at the Left Luggage counter in Prague's main railway station.

AN HOUR LATER, he walked into his father's bedroom to find J.P. dressing for another round of golf.

"The Duke and Duchess of Windsor arrived in Cannes yesterday," he told Jack with immense satisfaction. "Wallis loves a good game. And my handicap's lower than the Duke's."

"He used to be King of England, for chrissake. Aren't you *supposed* to let him win?"

"Pretending to lose is un-American," Joe snapped. "Come along and make a fourth. I'll show you how it's done."

"I'm driving to Prague today," he said. "I'm not sure when I'll be back."

His father stopped fussing with the buttons of his plus fours and squinted up at Jack. "Driving to Prague? Just like that? Are you out of your fucking *mind*? The borders are closed. Nobody's getting into Czechoslovakia—or out. Do you even *listen* to your brother's radio?"

"I need you to send a cable to Embassy Prague alerting them I'm coming," Jack persisted.

"There *is* no Embassy Prague." His father's voice was a lash. "Carr left six days after Hitler marched in."

Wilbur Carr was the ex–U.S. ambassador.

"There are still people there," Jack said patiently. "I've seen the cables. The chargé's named Kennan."

"George Kennan?" Joe Kennedy hooted with laughter. "You'll get a lot of change out of *him*. No flies on George. He's an egghead of the first order, and hates political appointees' guts. The last thing he's going to do is babysit some college kid—much less *my* college kid."

"You've got to wire him. And I'll need a diplomatic letter of safe passage to get through the border."

"Not on your life," his father said flatly. "Your mother'd never forgive me. It was bad enough when Joe went haring off to the Spanish Civil War, but at least *he . . .*" he paused.

"Yeah?" Jack prompted, when his dad fell silent. "At least he could take care of himself? At least he didn't get himself killed?— What exactly do you want to say?"

"At least Joe's a *man*," his father fired up. "He's not going to fall over in a dead faint the first time he's a few miles from a doctor. Hell, send *you* into a battle zone, Jack, and you'll come home on a stretcher—and not because you took a bullet for anybody, either. Stay here and work on your tan."

Rage flooded through Jack—a rage that crashed against his self-control and overcame it in a cascade of anger and disdain. He shoved his father hard against the bedroom wall. Joe's head snapped back and his breath left his body with a sharp grunt. In another second he'd grabbed Jack's shoulders and pushed back.

Then they were grappling in the middle of the room, Jack's teeth bared in a furious snarl, his fists driving into his father's chest, his words coming as hard and fast as a spray of bullets.

"Look, old man, I know what you did and how you did it. I know you funneled thousands of dollars into the nuns' charity, from donors all over Europe and the U.S. I know the Nazis used it to buy the next election. I know you're a traitor."

Joe went still, staring at him. "That's a lie."

"You want power so badly, you'd sell your soul. Even to Hitler. Loyalty means nothing to you."

His father's fist slammed into his jaw. "Watch your mouth, you little—"

"There was a time I'd have covered for you"—he tasted blood and stepped back, shaking off the blow—"because you're *my father*, because we're Kennedys and we stand by each other. But too many people have died, Dad. You've lied and lied while Daisy Corcoran's throat was slit and Katie O'Donohue got a knife in the heart and Diana . . . *Diana* . . ."

"Who the hell is she?" Joe demanded.

"A woman I loved. Your friends sliced her to pieces."

"I know nothing about that." Joe's lips were set in a thin line and his gaze was dead, but he'd stopped swinging now. "I got Katie a job at the Stork Club, sure. Took her to dinner once in a while. Had a few laughs. But I wasn't there the night she died."

"You made sure of that, didn't you?" Jack's voice dropped. "*Deniability.* What you don't know, can't screw you. You'd stand in front of Roosevelt himself and swear you're a choirboy."

"Damn right," Joe retorted. "Prove me wrong, smartass."

"You were just unloading a few charitable bucks on the Little Sisters of Clemency," Jack suggested. "That's the story, isn't it?

Taking a tax deduction? But I know better, Dad. Because Daisy Corcoran kept records of every donation she got. And how they were used."

For the first time, his father's assurance faltered. "That's impossible. Daisy wouldn't be that stupid."

"You fool—she was murdered for the account book. Everybody in Europe seems to know it but you. Reinhard Heydrich got his hands on it. You know who Heydrich is, right? Head of the Gestapo? He thought Daisy's records were immensely valuable. Imagine the names on that list. All the people Heydrich can use. And the ways he can use them."

"Blackmail." Joe had gone white. He groped for a chair and sank into it. "Jesus. Are you suggesting he'll come after me?"

"Why not? You gave him the screw to turn. You've got Neville Chamberlain's ear. And Roosevelt's. You're a man of influence, and Heydrich needs influence. If England refuses to back its pledge to defend Poland, and doesn't lift a finger when Germany invades, Heydrich's happy. If England surrenders in a few months instead of fighting to the last man, the whole war's a walk in the park for Hitler and his friends. Question is, Dad—what will you say to Chamberlain and Roosevelt when they come to you for advice? The Gestapo's script—or your own?"

"How can you ask?" his father spluttered. His face was mottled with shame and anger. "I've got no choice. Not if Heydrich has that book. Not if he means to—"

"—Tell Roosevelt you paid to bring him down?" Jack stepped toward him. "Tell the President yourself, Dad, and take the consequences. There's always a choice. You can go further down the Nazi road of lies and fear. Or you can choose to be a man of honor."

There was a silence.

"I need time," J.P. said. "How much time, Jack, before Heydrich moves?"

"I can't tell you that."

"Why hasn't he tried to break me already?"

Jack hesitated. "We think it's possible somebody stole the account book. We think it's in Prague."

"We?" His father scrutinized his face. "How do you *know*, Jack?"

"Thesis research."

Joe's mouth twisted. "What the hell am I going to do?"

Jack crouched down beside him. "You're going to send a cable to Kennan at Embassy Prague. So I can find the account book."

He wondered for a fleeting instant if they'd ever looked at each other honestly, without the flash and bravado that passed for Kennedy closeness. Father and son. The tycoon and the also-ran. The ambassador and his ne'er-do-well son. Jack stared through the owlish glasses, into his father's eyes, and saw something he'd never seen there before. Fear.

Joe looked away quickly. "You think I'm a monster," he said. "But I did it for *you*, Jack. For all you kids. I'd do anything to make your lives better."

Better.

Jack felt suddenly hollow. There'd been a time in his life when he thought his father was the greatest man in the world.

"I'll find the account book before Heydrich does," he said. "Just send the telegram. Old man."

FIFTY-TWO. NAME-DROPPING

PRAGUE WAS NEARLY six hundred miles from Cannes, and given the politics of the moment, the only plausible way to get to it was by car: driving east through the top of Italy to Innsbruck, then across Austria to Vienna and Bohemia. The Germans had closed the Czech border to trains and planes and automobiles. Jack drove anyway.

He reached Czechoslovakia four days later. A long line of traffic was exiting toward Vienna: dusty cars piled high with household goods and children, overheating in August. Nobody was going the opposite way except Jack. He slowed to a halt as he reached the checkpoint; he was alone with an impressive clutch of gray uniforms, maybe ten altogether. And the Germans would be on the lookout for him. He'd been in Gestapo territory from the moment he crossed into Austria yesterday; the name Kennedy would have hit Heydrich's desk within an hour of his passport being stamped. Jack had weighed the risk and calculated his odds. If the Gestapo wanted to ask him about a bloody hotel room in Warsaw, they could haul him in any time they liked. Jack was a far better bargaining chip for Heydrich than a vanished account book. On the other hand, snapping up one of the Kennedys—and an official diplomatic envoy at that—would spark an international incident and an American outcry. It was simply a matter of how far the Gestapo wanted to push.

To his surprise, he was allowed to sleep unmolested in Austria and depart in the morning for the Czech border. He suspected that Heydrich was content to have him watched for a while. And see where he ran.

He was thinking about these things as he rolled down his window. Trying to calm his thudding heart and ignore the sweat starting out on his brow. The border guard was saying something to him in German. He offered his passport. The man shook his head and pointed the muzzle of his Mauser at Jack.

"*Sprechen Sie* English?"

The guard frowned, glanced away, and motioned to another soldier standing in the doorway of the kiosk. He trotted over.

"The border is closed," the second man said firmly.

"I'm on a diplomatic mission to the American embassy in Prague."

"There is no American embassy in Prague."

"You and I both know that's not quite true." Jack handed the guard his father's typed message declaring him a special envoy. "That's a guarantee of safe passage."

The German scanned the single page. Was Jack imagining it, or did his eyes linger on the name Kennedy? "Your passport."

Jack handed it over.

"Who do you wish to see at this embassy that does not exist?"

"The American chargé d'affaires. Mr. George Kennan."

The guard studied him in silence for several long seconds. His companion muttered something low in German. To Jack's imagination it sounded like *Let's kill him now.*

The man holding his passport grunted and went into the border station. The other one leveled his rifle again. Jack nearly reached for the sky, but lit a cigarette instead. He adjusted his sunglasses. Offered the soldier a smoke. The German did not respond. Neither did he move his gun. The muzzle was trained on Jack's left temple. A few of the other Germans milling aimlessly around the kiosk came up and stared; he saluted jauntily.

The soldier with his passport was on the phone. Talking to Prague? Or Berlin? As Jack watched, he replaced the earpiece on the cradle, depressed it several times, and lifted the earpiece again. So *now* he was calling Berlin. Or Prague.

After an eternity, the operator on the line rang back with the trunk call. The soldier listened, spoke a few words, nodded at his unseen interlocutor, and hung up.

"Mr. Kennan is coming," he told Jack as he emerged from the kiosk. He did not return Jack's dip passport.

"From *Prague*?" Jack asked, startled.

"Yes. He will escort you. It is required."

"How far away is Prague?"

The guard wrinkled his nose. "Perhaps two hundred thirty kilometers. He will be several hours, I think. You will pull the car to the side of the road and remain with it, yes?"

KENNAN WAS IN A WHITE RAGE when he showed up, three hours and twelve minutes later, in a black car with a driver. Jack was in no better mood—the sun was blazing down on the border crossing, he had no water, and a few of the German soldiers were lounging on the hood of his car, guns dangling. He'd tried to read a book—Ray Buell's *Poland—Key to Europe*—but the subject seemed far too academic for his life at the moment. He thought of Diana and wondered if she'd been consumed by fear as she died—if it had overwhelmed her, controlled her mind, as it sometimes threatened to control his. He knew he had a tendency to idealize Diana now that she was dead—to believe that all martyrs died nobly. A Catholic fallacy, perhaps. But he could not forget her silent scream. The memory made him miserable.

"You're John Kennedy?"

He'd expected a man his father's age, but Kennan was only in his midthirties. He had a round face, large and eloquent eyes, and a balding pate. The anger was visible in the compression of his lips and the way he spat out his words.

Jack had gotten out of his car as Kennan approached and they faced each other like gunslingers. The sun beat down. He thought of mentioning they had a friend in common in Bill Bullitt—Kennan had worked for Bullitt in Moscow—then decided against it. Maybe Kennan hated Bullitt, too.

"Call me Jack," he said. "You're Mr. Kennan, I take it?"

The chargé swept him with his eyes. "What are you—*fifteen*? Jesus Christ."

"I'm twenty-two. I'm sorry you had to drive all the way out here—"

"The *hell* you are." Kennan's eyes were blazing now. "You Kennedys don't give a rat's ass about anything but yourselves. Do you realize this is an occupied country in a state of war? That there's no official American presence? No trains, no planes, and no cars allowed in or out? That we're scrambling every hour just to keep ourselves out of the Gestapo's hands?"

"Yes. I do. And I'm very grateful."

"—And in the middle of this *fucking* chaos, I get a cable from *Joe Kennedy*, who doesn't know his ass from a hole in the ground, telling me to meet his idiot son."

"I understand you're angry. You don't have to be offensive."

Kennan smiled tightly. "You waste my time, kid, I can be anything I want. Now tell me what the hell you're doing here."

Jack swallowed. "Research."

"*What?*"

"A fact-finding mission." Kennan was supposed to respect scholars. "I'm working on my senior thesis. At Harvard."

Kennan swore under his breath and turned toward his car. "Go back to Vienna, Mr. Kennedy. I've got better things to do than babysit a spoiled brat."

"You might want to check with President Roosevelt first," Jack suggested, his voice lower.

It was a huge gamble. He had no idea whether Kennan would call his bluff. Or whether Roosevelt would back him up if he did. It'd been weeks since he'd sent the President so much as hello.

Kennan stopped dead. *"Roosevelt?"* he repeated.

"Yes. He's aware of my trip. You might say he . . . sent me."

"Oh, shit." Kennan looked him over with loathing. "So you're one of *those*."

"One of what?"

"FDR's freelancers. His amateur specialists. His little *friends*." The chargé's voice was heavy with contempt. "A deadweight and a pain in the ass, at a time when I need both about as much as I need a hole in the head. Look, Mr. Kennedy. I can't send you packing. You've made that abundantly clear. But you gate-crash Embassy Prague, you get twenty-four hours. No more, no less. And *none* of my people are at your disposal."

"Thank you," Jack said.

Kennan ignored him. He nodded once to his driver. "Make it good with the Krauts, Charlie. Kennedy—*follow us*. And God help you if you lose your way."

FIFTY-THREE. AGENT PROVOCATEUR

ARRIVING AT EMBASSY PRAGUE in the heart of the Malá Strana—the ancient red-tiled Lesser Town that knelt beneath the sheer escarpment of Prague Castle—was something Jack would never forget. Prague was painful for its memories of May, when the border was still open, when he'd lost Diana forever on the Charles Bridge, but during that trip he had hugged the opposite bank of the Vltava, the trendier Art Deco districts of coffeehouses and trams, and left the dreaming Baroque splendor of the castle and its neighbors alone.

Schoenborn Palace, as the embassy was called, was four hundred years old. It had been built on the ruins of an even older building destroyed by the Swedes during the Thirty Years' War. Four distinct wings enclosing three green courtyards spread out from the deceptive little gate letting onto Tržiště Street; the palace had more than a hundred rooms. Some of the ceilings were thirty feet high. From its windows, the castle walls and the spire of St. Vitus Cathedral were visible.

As he followed Kennan's car through the gates and parked within the palace's encircling arms, he knew that he had shut out Heydrich's killers for the night; but he would have to leave the embassy in the morning, and the Gestapo would be waiting for him.

He'd invaded their territory.

The long delay at the border and the longer drive back to Prague had given them time. They would know how to use it.

"DAVID ARMSTRONG," the commercial attaché said, as he shook Jack's hand. "Long day? Want a drink? Food's a crapshoot, under the circumstances, but alcohol's plentiful. The palace has cellars, and successive generations of ambassadors have stocked 'em."

George Kennan had barely acknowledged Jack as he strode into the embassy, being far more intent on a brief of the situation since he'd left Prague that morning. But before he completely ignored the ambassador's son he'd ordered Armstrong to show Mr. Kennedy his room, and make sure he had what he needed.

"I'd love a drink," Jack said.

"Will rye suit, or do you prefer Bourbon?"

"Either. Both."

"I like a two-fisted drinker."

Armstrong showed Jack to his room. It was clean and spare. A window overlooked the gardens, blowsy with August.

"Meet me at the foot of the stairs in twenty minutes," Armstrong said, "and I'll hand you a glass. If you're not too tired, there's a place down the street that does a good beef stew. We'll have to hurry. Curfew."

"I thought only Germans got beef in Prague."

Armstrong grinned. "So it's probably horse. Or mule. But the food's not the point. It's been weeks since I've talked to anybody from outside. I'd like the view from London."

"I'd like the view from Prague," Jack replied.

"Ah, yes. The senior thesis."

"Kennan told you."

"He told everybody. At the top of his lungs. You're persona non grata here, Mr. Kennedy, and don't you forget it."

"Then call me Jack," he said.

ARMSTRONG'S CAFÉ WAS sandwiched into one of the tiny buildings that lined the quarter, a narrow but deep room that was airless in August. The only available table was in the back, near the kitchen, where the smells and the heat were most intense. Privately, Jack thought the celebrated stew was made of goat, not horse. He toyed with it while Armstrong talked about his reassignment. He was headed to London himself in two days.

"It's taken a few weeks to figure out the protocol," the commercial attaché explained as he poured a glass of raw red wine for each of them, "but the Czech government-in-exile has set up shop in your dad's neck of the woods, and State doesn't want to burden him with a second job. They're relocating most of the Prague staffers to London, so we can liaise there with our old friends."

"An embassy-in-exile. Will Kennan be ambassador?"

"He'd like that," Armstrong said with a smile, "which is why he's running such a damn tight ship as chargé now. But I don't think he's senior enough. Not the kind of guy who makes a statement to the Germans. For that, Roosevelt'll want one of his friends. Tony Biddle, for instance, if the Nazis run him out of Poland in a few weeks."

"You leave Wednesday?"

Armstrong nodded. "Part of the legation's advance guard."

Jack's heart thumped painfully. "Kennan said the airport was closed."

"Depends who you pay."

Naturally. He filed the fact away in a corner of his brain, in case he needed to leave Czechoslovakia fast. How much would it cost to save his particular hide? Probably depended on whether he had to pay the Czechs, or the Gestapo.

"Tell me something, Jack," Armstrong said. "Why is Neville Chamberlain still in power?"

"I thought he was grouse-shooting in Scotland."

"I suppose that's as good a way as any to ignore Poland."

"How long do you think they've got?"

"—before the Panzers show up?" Armstrong glanced at his watch. "Hitler likes to invade on Fridays. Catches people like Chamberlain off guard, just as they're closing up shop and heading to the country house for the weekend. But it's already Monday and there's no smell of war in the air, so I'm betting on *next* week. First of September."

"Five bucks says it's this Friday," Jack offered.

"Done," Armstrong said. "I'll collect when we're both back in London."

There was a commotion at the café door; Jack glanced over his shoulder and saw three Germans.

One of them was Hans Obst.

Diana's butcher was hanging behind his two companions, who were loudly demanding a table. He wore a Gestapo uniform tonight and his blond hair shone with virtue. The Pride of the Aryan Nation, in search of Jack Kennedy and a free meal. It was a foregone conclusion the Gestapo didn't pay.

"Time for the check," Armstrong said, with a glance at the Germans. "Those guys are unpredictable, and they're already drunk."

Jack was staring at the Spider, a whistling in his ears. His body flooded with heat, then with cold. *Standing there. As though he'd never sliced into her heart—*

"Jack?" Armstrong shook his arm. "You all right?"

He didn't answer immediately, his mind sifting the possibilities. Dobler was in Prague—*Dobler was in this restaurant*—because he was following Jack on Heydrich's orders. There would be no mistakes this time: Jack was supposed to die. Which made the likelihood of getting Diana's stash out of the train station pretty remote. The Gestapo would follow him and corner him there, by the Main Train Station's Left Luggage counter.

"Sure I'm fine," he told Armstrong. "Is there a back way out of this place?"

The attaché looked at him strangely. "You short on cash, or something?"

"No—*no*. I just can't walk past those guys."

Armstrong did not glance at the Gestapo. Instead, he rose and tossed some currency on the table, purposely screening Jack with his body.

"You'll have to go through the kitchen. The doors are fifteen feet behind you, to the right. The kitchen opens onto an alley. Move casually or you'll draw their eyes."

"Thanks."

Jack shoved back his chair and slouched toward the kitchen doors, his chin tucked into his collar and his hands in his pockets. Waiting for gunfire or a shout in German.

The doors swung violently open and a waiter skirted Jack neatly, an oval tray held high over his head. Jack ducked through the opening and the doors swung closed behind him.

The kitchen was tiny and sweltering. Heat struck him in the face like a blast wave. A single range with three pots bubbling on its burners was against the far wall, a triad of ovens beneath. A chef in a dirty white jacket stood before it, surrounded by three waiters and a woman Jack recognized as the hostess, arguing loudly in Czech. None of them turned to look at him as he slid by. The door to the alley was open to the August night.

He stepped out, his breath coming in gasps. He glanced left and then right, forcing himself to *think*. They had walked down Tržiště Street from the embassy toward the river. If the alley ran parallel to the street—and why should it not, except that the quarter was a thousand years old and never built on a grid?—the river would be on his left. Therefore, he should turn right to head back toward the embassy.

He turned right.

He had gone perhaps fifty feet, stumbling on the cobbles in the blackout darkness, trying not to breathe too loudly though his heart was racing, and listening for some sound, any sound, that might betray a waiting enemy. There was a fainter darkness ahead of him that suggested an opening in the narrow alley, as though it ran into a wider lane. He stepped carefully toward this gray area, navigating the piles of garbage that punctuated the back lots of Malá Strana.

And then suddenly there was a nerve-tearing screech and an indistinct form rocketed over Jack's shoulder.

He cried aloud in shock, his nerve ends jumping, and pressed himself flat against a wall. The Luger already clutched in his right hand.

It was only a cat, foraging in the garbage. *Only a cat,* he told his thumping heart.

"Jack."

He glanced to the end of the alley, and the man waiting there. Obst?

"Hey, Armstrong," he said, pocketing his gun. And stumbled toward him.

FIFTY-FOUR. THE DECOY

"I CABLED SECRETARY HULL," Kennan said as he stopped Jack in the embassy's foyer the next morning, "and lodged my official complaint. I told him I had better things to do than babysit Joe Kennedy's kids. His answer came this morning."

"I'd like to hear it." Jack bounced a little on the balls of his feet, his hands thrust in his trouser pockets. Hull was no fan of his father's. He expected the secretary's language would be choice and abusive.

"Please offer Mr. Kennedy every possible assistance," Kennan recited scathingly, *"per the orders of the President."*

There was a brief silence.

"I guess I'm just *one of them*," Jack said.

"Oh, believe me, you are." Kennan's eyes snapped with dislike. "So what possible assistance can I offer you today, Mr. Kennedy?"

"Von Neurath."

"*Konstantin* von Neurath?" The chargé was stunned. "The Protector of Bohemia?"

"Well—only Hitler calls him that, you know. The Czechs have saltier names for him. I'd like to interview the guy."

Kennan's face flushed. "And you think I can just pick up the phone and get you a slot?"

"Personally, I doubt you've got that kind of clout, George," he said apologetically. "But Hull seems to think otherwise. And Roosevelt certainly does."

For an instant he thought Kennan was going to punch him. But the chargé merely thrust his face dangerously toward Jack's, before he wheeled and went into his office. The door slammed. Jack grinned and saluted it before he strolled down the hall in search of Dave Armstrong.

HE FOUND THE COMMERCIAL ATTACHÉ packing up his office for London. Jack was glad he'd taken the time to eat with Armstrong last night, and not simply because the man had saved his life. Armstrong was good in a tight spot, and he had something Jack thought could be useful: a plane flying out of Prague tomorrow.

"Think you'll be searched on the tarmac before takeoff?" he asked as he glanced around the chaos of the attaché's office.

"By the Gestapo? I doubt it," Armstrong said. "We're neutral diplomats, Jack. And if they touch our commo equipment, I can tell you we'll put a bullet through their brains. Why?"

"Would you do me a favor, and take something home for me?"

"To London?"

"Sure. You'll get there long before I do." He made a show of fishing through his wallet for Diana's claim stub, and handed it to Armstrong. "Only I haven't got the package, exactly. It's at the train station. So you'd really have to be a pal, and pick it up."

Armstrong studied the ticket in bewilderment. "You're asking me to quit packing and run all the way over to the Left Luggage counter? What the hell is this about?"

"My mother." Jack studied the attaché's office; crates were strewn everywhere, filled with files and mementoes. He slid a photograph from a manila sleeve. A dark-haired girl in a head-scarf and sunglasses smiled at the camera. Armstrong was no fool: the real subject was behind the girl—some kind of factory. Munitions, probably. On the Slovak border. Maybe where the Germans had developed the Heydrich-Enigma.

Jack whistled appreciatively. "Say, she's a looker, Dave. Anybody I should know?"

"Barbara Casey, Smith '37," he replied, harassed. "Look, Jack, I'm busy. I've got the entire office to pack, not to mention my clothes. The plane's scheduled for eight a.m. tomorrow."

"My mother," Jack persisted, replacing the photograph in its sleeve, "was wandering around the world this winter. Cairo, Jerusalem, Istanbul, Athens—and then she got this sudden call from my dad about a command performance at the Pope's Coronation. Dropped everything and flew to Rome, in the middle of March."

"Is that a fact?"

"It is. Very Catholic, Rose—big fan of the Pope's. Had him to the Bronxville house when he was just a cardinal, and never used the chair he sat in again. Put a rope across it, so our mortal asses wouldn't sully the great man's seat."

"Jack—"

"Point is, Dave, she parked some things in Prague on the way. In mid-March. And then a few days later Hitler took over Czechoslovakia! Can you imagine? Bit of a facer for Rose—"

"So she sent you back here with a letter of safe passage," Armstrong said, "to pick up her stuff. I get it. Go to the train station yourself."

"Can't," Jack said diffidently, "because Kennan just got me

an interview with Konstantin von Neurath. The Nazi Protector himself. And Kennan's booting me out of Prague as soon as my interview's over. I'm under orders to vamoose before the curfew tonight. So if you could be a pal. . . ."

Armstrong glanced at his watch and sighed. "This wouldn't have anything to do with those Gestapo guys you were running from, would it?"

"Mother's the toast of London, you know," Jack said, ignoring his gambit. "The hostess with the mostest. I'll get her to invite the entire Czech government-in-exile to dinner, Dave, and seat you next to my sister—she's a swell girl. Whole world's in love with Kick. Has to beat off the boys with a stick."

"Whereas you just use that gun you hide in your pocket."

Wordlessly, Jack met his gaze.

Armstrong threw up his hands. "All right. I'll do it."

Jack pressed the Left Luggage ticket into his palm. "Thanks. I'm grateful. More than you know. And Dave—"

Armstrong was slipping the ticket into his wallet.

"—If I miss you this afternoon—if for some reason I don't make it back—take the stuff to London, on the plane tomorrow."

"Why wouldn't you make it back?" Armstrong asked.

But Jack was already gone.

AN EMBASSY CAR DROVE HIM to the Protectorate headquarters, which turned out to be Prague Castle. Word of his appointment had been relayed to appropriate channels—a black Mercedes pulled away from the curb near the embassy, and followed Jack quite obviously up the narrow streets of the Malá Strana. He hoped to God it was the Spider behind him. Jack was bait this morning, a decoy in the service of Diana and all she'd died for;

his sole purpose was to lead the Gestapo in the opposite direction from Dave Armstrong and the Main Train Station.

As they passed through the wrought-iron gates at the top of Loretánská Street, and entered the First Courtyard, he asked his driver if he'd wait.

The man shook his head. "The Krauts get suspicious if you loiter with intent. Think there's a bomb in every glove box. I'll be back in an hour."

A soldier in gray stood ready to conduct him to Von Neurath; Jack had no choice but to follow. There was a Second Courtyard, and beyond it, a third, with the fantastic medieval gyrations of St. Vitus Cathedral. The soldier turned right in the middle of the Third Courtyard and made for a much smaller building—the palace. At the entrance, Jack was frisked.

One guard looked on while another patted down his shoulders and rib cage, feeling for a holster. They even ran their hands down his trouser legs and prodded his ankles, searching for a knife. He'd expected that. He wasn't stupid enough to call on Hitler's man in Prague with a Parabellum in his pocket.

He'd tucked the pistol inside his boxer shorts, butt in the crease of his groin and muzzle along his inner thigh, using a first-aid bandage he'd scrounged from the embassy medical kit that morning. He'd found a diagram of the maneuver in Gubbins's *Art of Guerrilla Warfare*.

The soldiers were too squeamish to frisk his balls. A pair of pleat-front gray flannels and the tails of his jacket helped disguise any bulge; he simply looked like a healthy bit of manhood. Which he liked to think he was.

He handed the guards his passport and waited. And then he was walking down the vaulted corridors to Von Neurath's office.

He tried to remember what Professor Bruce Hopper had

taught him about the man. An old-school career diplomat in his high sixties, a respected ambassador who'd risen to be Foreign Minister—until he fell out of Hitler's favor. Von Neurath believed in diplomacy, not war; and his lack of enthusiasm for the Nazi regime had cost him his career. Von Ribbentrop—a rabid Aryan expansionist if ever there was one—replaced him as Foreign Minister. Prague was a retirement post. The end of Von Neurath's personal and political road.

He rose from his desk as Jack entered the vast room, a portly, white-haired figure. The ruins of a once-handsome face.

"Mr. Kennedy," he said, in excellent English—he'd been ambassador to London once—"what a distinct pleasure to welcome you to Prague. I have met your father, you know. Yes, indeed." He ought to have bowed or thrown out the Nazi salute, but instead he shook Jack's hand warmly. "Please, sit down—and tell me how I may serve you."

IN THE END THEY TALKED for over an hour and a half, while the business of the Protectorate went unfinished outside Von Neurath's doors. Jack started with lebensraum and the Polish Corridor and ended by simply talking to the man. He was reminded of Willi Dobler. The two Germans shared a certain quality of despair. They knew that they, and the country they loved, were doomed.

"I have enjoyed our talk," the protector said, "as I have enjoyed nothing in recent weeks. Remember me to your father."

"I will, sir."

There was a man waiting for him outside—not a soldier, this time, but one of Von Neurath's aides, a nondescript fellow in civilian clothing.

"I'd like to visit the men's room before I leave," Jack said.

"The WC?" The aide hesitated. "Of course."

He led Jack to a small public powder room adjacent to the protector's office. Jack locked the door behind him, dropped his trousers, and untied the Luger from his inner thigh. Having the thing shoved in his crotch for over an hour had been damn uncomfortable, but it had served his purpose; nobody would search him for a weapon on the way *out* of Prague Castle. There were five bullets left in the magazine. It would have to be enough.

He snicked off the gun's safety while the toilet flushed. He slipped the Parabellum into his breast-coat pocket.

The sound of his heels echoed on the stones as he followed his keeper. They reached the sun of the First Courtyard. It must be nearly noon. Plenty of time for Armstrong to have reached the train station on the far side of the river.

He thanked Von Neurath's aide, who shook his hand, bowed, and turned briskly away. Jack moved toward Castle Square and the gate.

No embassy car was there.

But Hans Obst and his Mercedes were.

"Your man came, Mr. Kennedy, but as you were detained past the designated hour, he did not stay," he told Jack, with all the familiarity of long acquaintance. "I assured him that the Protectorate would be happy to deliver you to your embassy."

In a hearse, Jack thought. He stood on the step dividing the First Courtyard from the square and stared at the killer by the open car door. He could feel the presence of half-a-dozen uniformed figures behind him; another three in the black garb of the Gestapo flanked Obst. Blood throbbed thickly in his ears. Even with a gun in his pocket, the odds were not looking good.

"I'll walk, thanks," he said, and stepped off the step.

Instantly he was seized from behind and hustled, legs dangling, straight to the Mercedes.

The Spider smiled as Jack hit the passenger side door, hard.

"It's no trouble, Mr. Kennedy," he said. "Please—get in."

FIFTY-FIVE. THE HOP FIELD

THERE WERE FOUR OF THEM in back: Jack and Obst and two others on the jump seats. The fifth man drove.

The Mercedes shot out of the castle gates and hurtled down Loretánská Street. Jack was dimly aware of the Loreto Church flashing by and then the car wheeling around a curve past the Strahov Monastery and its grounds, the red tile roofs of the Lesser Town rippling past the windows. Somewhere to the left was the embassy and Armstrong packing his things, maybe whistling as he did it. Diana's parcel sitting on his desk. Jack hoped to God it was on that plane tomorrow.

The man opposite him slid a Mauser from its holster and casually unlatched the safety. Like Obst, he was probably in his midthirties, crows-feet at the corners of his blue eyes, hair beginning to thin; a police-state veteran indifferent to murder. He stared at Jack as he leveled the gun, as though he were counting down from a hundred before he pulled the trigger.

Obst was turning his knife absentmindedly in his right hand, over and over, the way a drummer twirls a stick. He was lounging easily against the car's cushions, thighs spread, black boots gleaming. The third Gestapo man was no older than Jack. He was stuck facing Obst, but kept glancing at Jack, then glancing away. He must have a gun, too, but he wasn't playing with it. His pose was as rigid as Obst's was relaxed.

Nervous, Jack thought. *Vulnerable.*

It helped to think of something. To pretend to plan. Yes, he had a gun and he might get off a shot and take at least one of them with him—but that would be the end. He'd figured on facing the Spider alone, and got the entire web instead.

Waves of fear washed over him. He breathed shallowly as though he'd just returned a punt. He hated fear, hated betraying it to Obst. *So he was going to die.* He'd expected it for years. He knew it could come any day, even without warning. He just thought he'd die in a hospital bed, his white blood cell count trickling away. Not from a bullet to the brain.

It was the knife he feared most. Something to do with Diana. So to shake loose his fear and take control of the situation—*control of the situation?*—he started to talk. See what the famous Kennedy charm could do.

"I guess you boys passed my embassy about a mile back."

"The United States embassy is closed," Obst said indifferently. "So is the Czech border. *We* closed it, Mr. Kennedy. But you ignored that, as you have ignored every attempt to save you."

"Save me?"

"From yourself." Obst glanced at him and smiled. "Smart men mind their own business. But I think you are not very intelligent. And perhaps not very much of a man."

"Because I don't get my kicks carving up women?"

They had left the city behind surprisingly quickly and the car was running south, beside the Vltava River. The road was lined with trees, and beyond them, open fields. *Bohemia.* The fields must be planted in hops. The place was famous for its beer. *Pil-*

sner. From Plzeň. Did they use hops in Pilsner or just barley? He had no idea.

"Diana was my business," Jack said conversationally. "Did it make you feel like a man, Obst, when you cut into her body?"

The boy sitting across from the Spider glanced imploringly at Jack. *Don't excite him,* the look said. *It'll be worse.*

"Did it get you hard? Is that what it takes—sticking your knife in a woman while she screams? You couldn't have her any other way, could you, Obst? Diana knew you were shit."

He was goading him deliberately; he wanted the Spider to lose control and make a mistake.

"That whore," the Spider said absently, fingering his knife. "She was no pleasure to kill. A Jewess, you know. Your black-haired bitch usually is. But yes, she screamed when she died. You know what she screamed, Mr. Kennedy? As I drove my knife into her cunt?"

No. No—

"She screamed for *Jack.*"

His movement was involuntary—a convulsive clenching of the fists as he swayed toward the Spider—but the guy with the Mauser was ready and the gun was suddenly pressed against Jack's right temple and his head was pinned to the cushions of the car. The circle of the muzzle on his skin was simple and cool.

"Not in the car, Klaus," Obst said, bored. "The mess."

The mess.

That's what he was to them.

Not Jack Kennedy, failed choirboy; not the Black Sheep, or the kid lost in his brother Joe's light; not the best friend Kick would ever have; not the wiry skeleton incandescent with energy, or the crack sailor tipping his keel in Nantucket Sound; not Roosevelt's man with his own reckless brand of guts. Just *the mess*.

He supposed that's all he'd ever been, really.

The big car slowed and then veered bumpily onto the verge of the road, turning into an unpaved track between two fields. *Hops,* Jack thought, as the gun muzzle drifted away from his temple and hovered two feet from his face. The car pulled up between the tall rows of blond grain and the engine died there.

In the silence, everyone seemed to draw breath.

Jack looked at Obst. Fear surged through him. *Why?* He'd expected to die every day. But he wasn't done, yet, with life.

"An accident would be easiest to explain," Obst was saying, "to the people at Schoenborn who will eventually look for you. A car crash, for instance, or a sudden fall from a height. But then we thought . . . how much more useful if you were an unfortunate victim, Mr. Kennedy, of the idiot Czechs who insist on fighting us? The ones who hide in the woods. The ones we will hunt down like rabbits and shoot once your body is found. Because of course, the Führer will never stand for the murder of a neutral ambassador's son. A price will have to be paid. And the Czechs will pay it."

Jack glanced around, as if a band of Gubbins's partisans might materialize from the fields. But the hops remained inviolate and lonely.

"You will have been tortured, of course"—Obst lifted his knife and smiled into Jack's eyes—"and then dispatched by a bullet to the base of the skull. You'll be begging for it, by the time we shoot."

The boy sitting opposite him made a faint sound, like retching.

"Hubner, here, possesses a Czech pistol," Obst said, glancing at the boy. "He took it from a dead partisan only yesterday. Now it will be found by your body. But Hubner has not used the gun yet. Have you, Hubner?"

The boy shook his head.

"This is to be your baptism, then. A baptism by fire. Get out of the car, Mr. Kennedy."

The man called Klaus waved his pistol toward the hop field and pulled at the passenger door's latch. He slid out first, holding the door ajar with one hand, the other trained on Jack.

Take one, he thought desperately. *At least one.*

He bent double as he slid out of the car, right hand in his breast pocket, and came up with the Luger firing right into Klaus's face.

The man spurted backward, his head blooming hideously. He fell on his back. Jack dove for the ground and rolled clear of the car door.

Obst was hurtling out of the other side of the Mercedes, his knife raised. Hubner would be behind him with his gun. They'd both come around the car's back end any second. Jack crouched behind the open car door, using it for cover. But the fifth man—the driver—could exit behind him. If he stood up and made a run for it—tried to reach the cover of the hop fields—he'd be shot in the back.

He was cornered. But he would die fighting, not screaming.

His eyes darted frantically along the Mercedes's body. The acrid smell of a rubber tire, overheated from the August road, filled his nostrils. He thought of Gubbins. *The Art of Guerrilla Warfare.* At least he could make the sons of bitches *walk* back to Prague. He stuck the Luger against the tire and pulled the trigger.

The bullet shot through the rubber and into the Mercedes's undercarriage.

A jet of flame seared Jack's face. The rubber was burning. He lurched back, right into the path of Hubner's gun.

He saw the kid's terrified face and his shaking hand as he tried to aim. He saw Obst barreling right behind him. Jack scrambled to his feet and bolted for the hop field.

A bullet sang by his left ear. He could hear Obst swearing and he waited for the knife in his back.

Then there was a soft *thump*, like a cornice of snow folding in on itself. Jack was picked up off his feet and tossed into the hops, a leaf blown by the wind.

He landed hard, stalks crumpling beneath his face and body.

His conscious mind left him, on an echo of laughter.

FIFTY-SIX. THE LAST LETTER

A BAPTISM BY FIRE. Obst had been dead right.

When Jack came to, the smell of roasting beer was heavy on the air. The hops were burning.

He forced himself to his knees, trying to shake sense into his head. Stared at his hands, which were filthy and scratched. He was braced on a crushed bed of grain. He shook himself again and saw the Luger, lying where he'd dropped it. As he grasped the butt the memory of the man named Klaus and his bloody face surged into his brain.

Obst cursing, and the boy with the gun.

The Mercedes.

He turned and saw it. A writhing mass of curling steel. The air around it shimmered with heat.

He'd shot the tire, and taken out the fuel tank.

There was another smell underlying the beer, now, the smell of burning flesh. He did not want to see what had happened to Hubner or Obst or the driver whose name he'd never learned. He wanted to get away. He stumbled forward into the hops, pushing blindly against the grain, driving himself deeper in a direction he vaguely thought paralleled the dirt track through the fields.

An eternity later, he stepped onto asphalt. The river flowed beyond it.

There were hops in his hair and his nose and his trousers were burned away at the ankles. His shoes were singed. His hands would not stop shaking.

He pocketed the Luger and glanced to the right and left. They had come from the left. He started walking back to Prague.

HE HAD NO IDEA what time it was when he reached the crossroads. He could not read the signs and it wouldn't have mattered if he did. It was simply a crossroads on the way back to Prague and there was an inn that served beer.

Pilsner Urquell.

For the rest of Jack's life, the smell of beer would be the smell of death.

He asked for water in English nobody could understand.

The man and woman behind the bar looked apprehensively at his blackened trousers. He glanced around the pub; there were no apparent Germans, none in uniform. He took the publican aside and said one word: *Gestapo.*

It required no translation.

He was given water, and the publican himself put through the call to the American embassy.

It was Armstrong, eventually, who came for him.

"YOU'RE TELLING ME they dragged you off for questioning? Right from Prague Castle? You're a *diplomat.* From a neutral country."

George Kennan's back was turned and he was staring through his office window at St. Vitus Cathedral. As usual he was angry, but it was a grim anger this afternoon, not a white rage.

"The Gestapo didn't check my passport," Jack said.

"What happened?"

"There was a car accident."

"And?"

"The car burst into flames. I managed to crawl out."

"The Germans?"

"No idea," he said.

Kennan wheeled and stared at him.

"How can you *not know*?"

"Sometimes it's preferable."

They studied each other for an instant.

"Jesus Christ," Kennan said softly. "Five Gestapo guys are dead in a field, and you don't have a *story*?"

"Sure I do. You just heard it."

"The Castle's going to come down on us like a ton of bricks."

"I don't think so," Jack said. "It wasn't an official interrogation. There won't be a record of it anywhere." He thought of something Willi Dobler had once said, and repeated it for Kennan's benefit. "The Gestapo simply forget the people they torture and kill."

"Torture and . . ."

Kennan was incredulous.

"Look," Jack said. "They offered me a ride to the embassy. Everybody at the Castle heard them. And I'm *here*, aren't I? What happened after they dropped me off is hardly our business."

Kennan considered this. The doubt in his face was a lesson to Jack, one he was glad he'd learned early in the war. There were the Gubbinses of the world, who rode the wave of chaos without questioning why it existed; and there were the Kennans, who were outraged by the wave, and filed official complaints even as it drowned them. Both had their place, Jack realized; and the war would decide who survived.

Personally, Jack was sticking with the Gubbinses.

"We've got to get you out of here," Kennan said. "I'd send you on the plane to London tomorrow, but that means another twenty-four in Prague. It's too risky, under the circumstances."

He glanced at his watch. "It's just past three o'clock. If we leave now, we can reach the Hungarian border by six. You don't want to go back to Austria—make for Budapest. I'll escort you as far as the border."

"Thanks," Jack said. Weariness flooded his body and he wanted nothing so much as to bathe and sleep and have a drink— but Kennan was right. He couldn't risk the plane and he had to get out of Prague immediately. He'd be lucky to make Budapest.

"Pack your things," Kennan said, "and meet me in the court-yard in ten minutes. There'll be hell to pay if I'm not back by curfew. And Kennedy—"

Jack turned at the door. "Yes?"

"Don't ever darken my legation again. *Any* legation I happen to run."

"Got it," he said.

HE STOPPED BY ARMSTRONG'S office to shake his hand, wish him well, and retrieve Diana's parcel.

"I thought it'd be bigger," Armstrong said. "Your mother travels light. What's so important about that envelope, anyway?"

Jack pried open the gummed manila flap with a letter knife and slid the small black book into his hand. "Her address book. The lifeblood of every ambassador's wife. She's been completely hamstrung since she left this behind. Can't write a thank-you note to save her soul."

"Seems an odd thing to leave at the Prague train station," Armstrong observed.

"Rose Kennedy is a very odd woman."

There was something else in the envelope—a single folded sheet in Diana's handwriting. With a twist of the heart, Jack tucked the letter into his wallet. He would read it later, in Budapest, if he got that far.

Kennan was honking.

"See you in London," he told Armstrong, and ran down the stairs.

KENNAN HAD BROUGHT CASES of Pilsner Urquell for the German soldiers working the checkpoint at the Austrian border—the kind of goodwill bribe that Jack would never have thought him capable of making. But it turned out to be useless. The same English-speaking guard who'd held him up for hours the day before ran his eyes over Jack and said simply, "We have received word from Prague Castle."

Kennan swallowed, his eyes flicking away from Jack. "Indeed? What kind of word, may I ask?"

"*Reichsprotektor* Von Neurath sends his regards, Mr. Kennedy. He wishes that you may return to Bohemia in happier times." The soldier handed him his diplomatic passport, clicked his heels, and thrust his hand in the air in the Nazi salute. "You may proceed."

The light faded as he skirted the hip of Austria and drove toward the Hungarian border; but nobody followed him and he met no resistance as he entered Hungary. It was, for the moment, an entirely sovereign state without the menace of German border guards. He pushed on, and reached the embassy a few minutes after ten o'clock that night. Kennan had wired ahead, so that they were expecting him in the grand old building on the Pest side of the river; a room and a plate of sandwiches was waiting. After he'd finished them, he drew a deep breath. He felt precarious and yet safe. He had nearly died today, but the account book was in his hands.

So was Diana's letter.

My dear Jack,

As you see, I've got the account book. I won't bother with how. I'm about to take a train from Prague to Warsaw and have excused myself to the Ladies'. You know it's the only place I'm allowed to go alone.

I will hand this letter with the account book to the first likely girl who walks through the door—with enough cash to persuade her to leave my envelope at Left Luggage, and bring me back the ticket. Is there so much goodness in this bloody world, do you think?

Heydrich has a plan for launching the war. He means to take a clutch of condemned criminals, dress them in German uniforms, and truck them across the Polish border. They're to be shot in the lorries before they arrive, and their corpses strewn about to suggest they've been attacked by Polish forces. Hitler will claim the Poles started the war and he had every right to invade. Heydrich calls the plan Operation Canned Goods. He's immensely pleased with himself.

He means to tell the prisoners they've been freed, of

course. Poor bastards. They're due to die the first of
September.

I know you're an honourable man, Jack, and will see
that the information reaches the right people in England—
before September 1st.

I should like to tell you how dreadful it felt, to walk
away from you that day in May, on the Charles Bridge;
how bitter and brutal these months have been. I only hope
you've found it in your heart to forgive your—

Diana

HE SAT FOR A WHILE, in uncharacteristic stillness, on the edge
of the bed that night. She had not escaped the train, and Heydrich had discovered her treachery far more quickly than she'd
hoped. Ever the sadist, he'd toyed with Diana. Jack knew
that now.

He means to tell the prisoners they've been freed, of course. . . .
Had Heydrich told Diana that Jack was in Warsaw? That she
could return to her lover, no strings attached?—And then ordered the Spider to slaughter her in his bedroom at the Polonia
Palace?

Heydrich would enjoy the bait-and-switch; her farewell in
utter ignorance; the promise of freedom that turned to murder.
But even as Diana went off in her summer frock to the unimagi-
nable horror of her death—part of her had known. *Poor bastards.*
They're due to die. . . . She'd brought that incongruous evening
bag, with the Left Luggage ticket hidden inside.

He refolded her last letter and placed it in his breast pocket,
close to his heart. He was increasingly doubtful of the existence
of any God; but he hoped it was a vengeful one.

FIFTY-SEVEN. DIVIDING ALLEGIANCE

TAP, TAP. TAPTAPTAP TAP.

The man lying in the iron bed had no idea what had awakened him. It had been so long since Morse code had broken the stillness of the presidential bedroom.

Tap. Taptap. Tap.

Jack, he thought, as his eyes flickered open. *Jack.*

He forced himself to a seated position and reached for his glasses. It was just after six a.m. on Wednesday, the twenty-third of August; the air was humid and still. Seven years in Washington, and still he could not abide the heat. His mind flew to Maine and the fog off Campobello, the fall that would already be coming into that country, the water temperature of the Atlantic hovering somewhere around forty-eight degrees; and then he reached for the wireless receiver he still kept beneath his bedside table, and set it on his knees.

He picked up the pad and pencil at his elbow.

The message would be repeated. He positioned his hand over the paper, and waited.

SEVERAL HOURS LATER His Majesty's ambassador to the United States stood in the Oval Office. The President would have preferred to have spoken to Neville Chamberlain, but the man was unreachable during his holiday. And Churchill, he thought wistfully, was not even in the Cabinet. Lord Lothian—the British ambassador—was as close as he could get to the reins of British power.

"You're sure of this?" Lothian said. "It's to happen in a *week*?"

"So my information says," Roosevelt replied.

"You're certain the man can be trusted?"

Roosevelt smiled savagely. "The intelligence was obtained directly from a member of Reinhard Heydrich's inner circle."

Lothian's brows drew together. "May one ask by *whom*?"

"One may ask," Roosevelt agreed genially. "One is unlikely, however, to receive an answer . . . I attempted to reach Mr. Chamberlain earlier, but I was told he was unavailable. Fishing in Scotland. Can that really be true?"

"It *is* August," Lothian said fretfully. "One would think the Führer would be decent enough to respect the *conventions*."

"A man willing to murder several truckloads of convicts in order to launch a war has no interest in the standards of British decency."

"Still. A *week*. The first of September! Parliament won't even be seated yet!"

"You could recall your members today," Roosevelt snapped. "*Prepare* them." *Good Lord,* he thought. *No wonder Hitler's rolled Chamberlain. The man's useless.*

"In the middle of August?" Lothian snorted. "No, no, Mr. President—the Führer may not understand the sanctity of the Long Vac, but we do things very differently in England. Very differently indeed."

"Ah," Roosevelt said. He studied Lothian speculatively. He was the eleventh marquess of his line; a man about Roosevelt's age, with a womanish air. Like Chamberlain, he appeared perpetually aggrieved. "I thought you should know."

"Obliged to you," Lothian retorted.

There was a soft knock at the door and Sam Schwartz stuck his head into the room.

"Begging your pardon, Mr. President—"

"What is it, Sam?"

"A cable from Moscow."

Roosevelt took the single sheet of paper and scanned it. Then he glanced at Lothian, who was waiting to take his leave.

"The Nazis and the Soviets have just announced the signing of a non-aggression pact."

Lothian's face lightened. "Jolly good. At least *someone's* renounced war!"

"Hitler and Stalin," Roosevelt said. "Allies!"

It took a moment for this to register with Lothian. "—But Communists and Fascists *despise* one another."

Roosevelt looked at the nobleman in disbelief.

"They both like Poland," Sam Schwartz murmured, as if he were reminding Lothian of a school lesson. "They'll butcher it between them. One from the east, the other from the west. The country will cease to exist. Have you read Raymond Buell's *Poland—Key to Europe*? It lays out the whole thing."

Roosevelt met Sam's eyes over the head of the British ambassador. "And there's not a damn thing I can do to help. *Yet.* Thank God your government has pledged to stand by the Poles, Lothian."

The ambassador reached for his hat. "Serves the bloody fools right, I say—starting a war in August! I shall urge Chamberlain *not* to lift a finger!"

"That's advice he's always willing to take," Roosevelt replied.

HE HAD SENT THE ENCODED MESSAGE from the roof of the American embassy in Budapest at lunchtime, borrowing a commo kit from one of the State department clerks who made a hobby of shortwave radio. He let the guy watch him work the Morse key, in return for the favor.

"Who's it going to?" the man asked.

"Can't tell you," Jack said. "Don't ask what I'm typing, either."

"Don't have to," the guy replied with amusement. "I know Morse. You're sending complete gibberish."

Jack grinned ruefully and said it didn't matter—he just wanted to see if a buddy at Harvard could receive his message, and it was a fine summer day up here on the roof, with a great view of the Elizabeth Bridge throwing her arms across the Danube.

He'd made his choice of allegiances somewhere in a burning hop field. The evil Hans Obst so casually represented was impossible to bargain with. It could only be fought with every weapon he possessed.

He slept better that night than he had in weeks.

A SENSE OF URGENCY, an awareness of the swift passage of time, propelled Jack across Europe to France, where he dropped his rented car in Paris and took a flight across the channel to England. He reached London on Monday, the twenty-eighth of August, and took a room in a cheap hotel near Victoria Station.

Early on the morning of the twenty-ninth, he jumped a train rolling south into Hampshire and, after a brief taxi ride from

Edenbridge, presented himself at Chartwell, Winston Churchill's country house. Churchill received him in his bath.

"You're the only person I can give this to," Jack said as he handed him Diana's letter. "I'm sorry it took me so long to reach you. I couldn't trust the news to anybody else." *Except,* he thought, *Roosevelt.*

Churchill pulled the stub of a cigar from his mouth. A bit of ash and a spurt of water trailed across the sheet of paper, instantly blurring the blue ink and Diana's handwriting. Churchill was round and porcine in his tub. Jack kept his eyes fixed on the wall above his head as the statesman read.

"Poland?" Churchill grunted. "The first of September? We've *heard.*" He returned the letter to Jack and sank deeper into the hot water. It spilled over the tub's rim in a gentle cascade and pooled at Jack's feet. "Your admirable president had some foreknowledge of events—and the sense to heed it. He spoke to our ambassador, and our ambassador sent a thick-headed cable back to Whitehall—which the *right* people as well as the *wrong* seem to have read. Parliament has been recalled."

"Good," Jack said.

Churchill scowled. "That's from Denys Playfair's lady, I expect."

Jack nodded, suddenly unable to speak.

"Grand girl, Diana. *Top-hole.* I assume we owe our measure of preparation—lamentable though it may be—to you both."

"You owe it to Diana," Jack said.

Churchill growled. "Saw the notice in the *Times.* 'Suddenly, in Warsaw.' Knew what *that* meant. Hand me the whiskey and soda siphon—there's a good chap."

Jack obliged, leaning awkwardly over the tub.

Dripping, Churchill mixed two drinks in glasses waiting at his elbow, and offered one to Jack.

"Dulce et decorum est pro patria mori," he said solemnly.

It is sweet and fitting to die for one's country. Wilfrid Owen had called it the old lie, and Jack knew in his heart that it was. But he drank to Diana anyway.

"BACK AT LAST," his father said distractedly when Jack finally put in an appearance at the embassy in Grosvenor Square that afternoon. "All hell's broken loose. Everybody's talking war instead of sense. Poor Neville's had to cut short his holiday. And if ever a man needed one—"

"So I hear."

His father surveyed him irritably. "You look lousy. When's the last time you cleaned that suit?"

"Can't tell you. My other one got . . . damaged."

"You seem to have given Kennan what-for, anyway. He's been howling at Washington for the past week."

Jack smiled faintly. "He's got no love for the Kennedys."

"Then the hell with him," Joe said brusquely. "Did you find that account book?"

Jack glanced around. At least four members of his father's staff were darting in and out of the ambassador's office with pieces of paper, phone messages, the latest rumors from Berlin. None of them seemed to be listening to the second son.

"Yes," he said quietly.

"Give it to me."

There was a pause. His father's eyes were very bright behind his spectacles. His expression offered no quarter.

"I can't."

"You damn well *can*, and you damn well *will*."

"I don't have it anymore."

"What?" An unaccustomed panic in J.P.'s voice.

"I sent it to Washington. In the diplomatic pouch from Budapest. It should hit Roosevelt's desk in a couple of days."

His father surged to his feet, swaying slightly. "Tell me you're joking. God *damn* you."

"I'm dead serious." Jack walked deliberately to the door and turned. "You see, Dad—it was Roosevelt who asked me to find your network, months ago. And for maybe the first time in my life—I delivered."

WHEN SAM SCHWARTZ USHERED Ed Hoover into the oval-shaped room on the White House's second floor that rainy September morning, Roosevelt was busy with his new album—the one for stamps that would soon be obsolete. The State department had sent over some beauties from Poland. Along with the contents of the Budapest diplomatic pouch.

"Mr. President," Hoover said.

Roosevelt glanced at the little man over his spectacles. "Edgar. Good of you to come. Please—make yourself comfortable."

Schwartz left them alone.

Roosevelt concentrated on his tweezers. The delicate edge of the stamp. Patience was required, but also precision; a swift or clumsy hand destroyed the effort. He found that Jack Kennedy's young face was hovering just beyond the range of his vision. The gift in the Budapest pouch, and the raw emotion in the letter that accompanied it, had taken Roosevelt's breath away.

Hoover's high-pitched voice broke through his thoughts. "I have some information for you. About Hans Thomsen."

"The German chargé?" Roosevelt released the edge of the stamp. *Perfect.* "You're going to tell me he plans to pay off the entire Pennsylvania delegation to next summer's Democratic convention. Or is that William Rhodes Davis? No matter. The real point is the Philadelphia delegation. I suspect we can persuade them to take the German money, by all means—but vote their consciences. Which by next summer, will be mine to command."

Hoover was frowning at him. Roosevelt could discern the rapid movement of the FBI director's mind: from surprise to disbelief to calculation. He had already figured out that the President had more than one source of information. He would move immediately to pinpointing it. Hoover did not tolerate rivals.

"But I didn't summon you here to discuss the Germans," Roosevelt continued, pushing his wheelchair away from his stamp table. "I've found a curious thing in my Pullman, Edgar— or rather, Sam Schwartz and his people have. It seems I've been *bugged*."

"Is that so, Mr. President?" Hoover hunched slightly, his neck disappearing into his collar. He stared out from the carapace of his clothing like a turtle from its shell. "I'd like to send my boys over to look at it. Just to verify that Schwartz knows what he's talking about. Where did he find the thing, and why does he consider it a . . . bug?"

"In my portable telephone. And it's a wiretap of some kind. But you needn't verify it, Edgar. I know what your boys will say. Vincent Foscarello has explained that already."

The wheelchair rolled to a stop barely two feet from Hoover. Roosevelt's knees were splayed directly opposite his guest's. An enforced intimacy. An invasion of space. "We had to ask ourselves, you see," Roosevelt continued, "who had access to the phone. No foreign government that we could think of. No obvious Bureau man, helpfully appearing on every train platform. So Schwartz and I were forced to accept that the device was installed—and maintained—*by one of us*. Someone we trusted. A *friend*."

Hoover pressed backward into his chair. His ruddy complexion had drained to chalk, but he was grinning still, like a death mask.

"It's terrible, that kind of knowledge," Roosevelt said thoughtfully. "It eats away at trust and reason. One suspects every face. Schwartz, for instance. I actually took it upon me to suspect *Schwartz*. I suspected each and every friend, from Morgenthau to Hopkins to Berle. I suspected Miss LeHand. And my own wife. God forgive me, I even suspected *my son*." He kept his gaze on Hoover. "I know, you see, how much Jimmy likes and needs money."

The Bureau chief's eyes glistened a little.

"But then Sam sat back and considered his own people. The ones who shadow me, day in and day out. He told me you'd attempted to buy them, Edgar. Sam's a good leader of men. He makes a point of understanding the ones who work for him. Their troubles. Their passions. Their . . . vulnerabilities."

"Foscarello's a skunk," Hoover said dispassionately. "He's got—"

"—a gambling habit that would beggar Howard Hughes," Roosevelt agreed. "And you took advantage of it, didn't you? To commit a crime? You threatened to get Vincent fired. To trumpet his sins to the Treasury department, to his boss, even to me . . . unless he did you a favor. A small thing. A device hidden in the base of my telephone."

Hoover's grin faded. "Foscarello may have installed that bug. *Sure.* But you have only his word he did it for me. The word of a skunk, against mine."

"Very true," Roosevelt agreed. "I suppose a court of law would settle the question, however, were I to have you arrested. A court of law could establish the manufacture of the device and its probable origin. And I could have you arrested, Edgar—I most certainly could. For breaking the surveillance laws and possibly, even, for treason. Sam Schwartz is standing by now, with a warrant."

Hoover looked at him shrewdly. He was unfazed. "I wouldn't advise you to do that, Mr. President. The consequences might be . . . unfortunate."

There was a slight pause. A slight humming, as of a distant aeroplane, in the background. Hoover's eyes strayed to the sitting-room door, but it remained firmly closed.

"You refer, of course, to your files. And everything in them," Roosevelt said wisely. "The secret files you keep on innocent citizens, for your own edification and pleasure."

"No one in power is innocent," Hoover replied.

"Not even yourself," the President agreed. "I'm willing to concede the point. Which is why I would propose a bargain, Edgar. One that may prove of equal value to us both."

Hoover's neck emerged slightly from his collar. His pink mouth pursed.

"You keep your job and your professional reputation. In return, you hand over the files you've amassed on my family, my cabinet, and my guests in my private Pullman. You hand over the file on Miss LeHand."

"I can certainly ascertain whether such files exist," Hoover said slowly, "and if they do—and were compiled in violation of federal surveillance laws—I would certainly ensure that they were destroyed . . ."

Roosevelt shook his head. "Not good enough. I shall have to summon Sam. He can search the entire Bureau with impunity once he takes you into custody."

He wheeled his chair around.

"Wait!"

Roosevelt glanced back.

"All right." Hoover swallowed. "All *right*. You get the files."

"Excellent," the President said softly. He reached for some papers on his desk. "I took the liberty of compiling a list of the ones I expect to find on my desk by this afternoon."

The FBI chief glanced over it. The faintest expression of pain suffused his features.

Like parting with his children, Roosevelt thought. *I have taken hostages from J. Edgar Hoover.*

"Oh, and Edgar," he continued, "—there's one other thing you could do for me, if you'd be so good."

"Yes, Mr. President?" Hoover said woodenly.

"This second list." Roosevelt handed him a compilation of names culled from Daisy Corcoran's account book. "I'd like you to start watching *these* people, if you please. Wiretaps, surveillance, whatever quasi-legal methods you deem necessary. They're dangerous Fascist subversives in the pay of the Nazis. I believe the FBI claims the right to monitor subversives?"

"Ever since you gave it to us, sir," Hoover replied. "After the affair of the American Liberty League. May I ask where you got these names?"

Roosevelt ignored the question. He flashed his dangerous smile. "No secret files this time, Edgar. I expect detailed reports on my desk each week. That will be all."

AFTER THE BUREAU CHIEF had left, the President rolled over to his desk and reached beneath it. Schwartz had obliged him recently by consulting with Wild Bill on a technical matter—and had installed a recording machine that could be operated from the President's desk. From now on, Roosevelt would capture his private conversations *himself.* He flipped off a switch, and the faint sound of a distant aeroplane abruptly fell silent.

One name he had not included on the Subversives List was that of J. P. Kennedy. This was not because he regarded the man with compassion, or cared about his public reputation, or hoped to shield his son. Jack had made it quite clear, in the letter he'd included with the account book, that he understood the depth of his father's perfidy.

Roosevelt would keep Kennedy's name, and all the evidence that damned him, like a pilfered jewel in a private safe. He now possessed the power to control the man for the rest of his life. And he refused to share that with Hoover—or anybody.

EPILOGUE

BRUCE HOPPER WAS READING a newspaper, a pipe gently smoking in his hand, when the light was blotted out by a figure in the doorway. He tossed the paper aside.

"Well met, *mon brave*. We'd almost given up on you."

"Better late than never," Jack said.

He'd flown across the Atlantic on the Pan Am Clipper, several weeks late for the start of term; it was nearly October, his senior year at Harvard, and he was already behind.

"Take a seat," Hopper suggested. "You look tired."

"If I had ten bucks for every time I've heard that, Professor . . ."

He waited until Jack threw himself into an armchair, then got up and closed the door.

"I read about the *Athenia*. You did good work there."

Jack laughed abruptly. The Germans had torpedoed the ship two hundred miles off the coast of Ireland on September third—the day England declared war. The *Athenia* had been filled with people fleeing to New York, some three hundred Americans among them.

Hitler accused Churchill of deliberately sinking the ship, to make the Nazis look bad.

Joe Kennedy sent Jack to Glasgow in the middle of the night to meet the American survivors. It was good to put some distance between himself and Jack. They weren't speaking, and Rose was beginning to ask inconvenient questions. The *Athenia* was the reason he was late for school.

"You got those survivors home on an American vessel," Hopper persisted. "Even if it *was* without a military convoy. I read it in the paper. *Schoolboy Diplomat Urges American Transport for Athenia Heroes.*"

"They were terrified of being on another British ship." His eyes slid over to meet Hopper's. "Schoolboy, huh? The London papers said I was eighteen."

"You look that young sometimes." *And sometimes,* Hopper thought, *you look a thousand years old.*

Jack shrugged. He seemed curiously indifferent, and very far away. "The *Athenia* was as much my dad's job as mine. He paid for hundreds of transatlantic telegrams to the survivors' families, did you know that? The State department wouldn't authorize the expense. They didn't get it—that these people were feeling abandoned by their government, in a war zone. They'd been *torpedoed* in the North Atlantic, for chrissake. But Dad understood." There was a short silence. "He knows what it means to worry about your family."

"He should. His own means the world to him," Hopper said mildly. He tapped the ashes from his pipe bowl and settled back in his chair. "You don't want to be here, do you?"

"It's just hard to see the point." Jack thrust himself from the chair and began to pace restlessly between the bookshelves, his fingers running lightly over the volumes bound in dark leather.

That quickly, the impression of malaise was gone and the crackling energy Hopper remembered filled the room. "Dad sent us all home. No choice and no argument. Joe's in law school. Kick's been bundled off to college. Her boyfriend's British, so he's already enlisted, and God knows if they'll ever see each other again. Which would suit my mother just fine. But Kick *hated* being sent back. She says we look like cowards. Running at the first sign of danger."

"Which is how you feel."

Jack shot him a glance. "Nobody's *safe* anymore, Professor. Nobody will ever be safe again."

"You never thought you were."

"I know I'm always on the edge of dying. But I want to be *doing* something."

"Then write your thesis."

"What the hell good would that do?"

"It might rouse American opinion," Hopper suggested. "Most people still think this is a *European war*, Jack. That it'll never touch us. You know better. You know it's coming. Whether we like it or not."

"Even the Brits tried to deny it was really happening," he mused. "It took Chamberlain *two days* after the tanks rolled into Poland to declare war! You know how many Poles died during those two days? Churchill said—"

He broke off, and looked at his shoes.

"So you met him."

"We met. Yes."

"And he said?" Hopper prompted.

"—That Neville refused to bomb Berlin while the Nazis were fighting in Poland. *It wasn't cricket,* apparently, to attack from the west, while the Germans were fighting in the east. *Like shoot-*

ing a man in the back, Chamberlain said. *Not* the act of a gentleman."

"—And Winston?"

Jack grinned. "Nearly broke Neville's pencil neck."

Hopper didn't laugh. "But the Poles are still dying."

"While the rest of us stand around and watch."

Hopper rose, and grasped Jack's shoulder. "*Write your thesis.* An analysis of the months leading up to war. Have you got a title?"

He shrugged. "*Why England Slept.* That should make most Americans yawn."

"People will listen to you. You've been there. You've done your homework. And you're Joe Kennedy's son."

"A lot of people hate my father," Jack said.

"But they know his name. You can use that," Hopper insisted.

Jack hesitated, then lounged over to the door. "I don't really have a choice, do I? I've got to get out of here somehow. See you later, Professor."

Hopper stared after him, a frown between his eyes.

Patience, mon brave, he thought.

This war will find each of us, soon enough.

AUTHOR'S NOTE

Jack 1939 is a work of fiction—a speculative recasting of Jack Kennedy's twenty-second year. It was inspired by a photograph I happened to glimpse a few years ago: Jack on a street in Germany during the summer of 1937, wearing clothes he'd probably slept in for a week, hair tousled, head thrown back, mouth open in a grin. He was juggling fruit for the camera. He looked like a wild and free street busker without a care in the world; he was also rail thin, the bones of his face dangerously prominent. I had forgotten completely that he had ever been so young. The image haunted me for weeks. I wanted to know more about that boy.

I began to read everything I could regarding Jack Kennedy's childhood and experiences during World War II. For those readers whose interest in the period has been sparked by this story, I would recommend, in no particular order, Michael Beschloss's *Kennedy and Roosevelt: The Uneasy Alliance* (New York: Norton, 1981); Nigel Hamilton's *JFK: Reckless Youth* (New York: Random House, 1992); Robert Dallek's *An Unfinished Life: John F. Kennedy, 1917–1963* (Boston: Little, Brown and Company, 2003), which is particularly valuable for its survey of medical records and issues; Will Swift's *The Kennedys Amidst the Gathering Storm: A Thousand Days in London, 1938–1940* (New York: Smithsonian Books, 2008); Laurence Leamer's *The Kennedy Men: 1901–*

1963: The Laws of the Father (New York: William Morrow, 2001); Doris Kearns Goodwin's *The Fitzgeralds and the Kennedys* (New York: Simon & Schuster, 1987); Richard J. Whalen's *The Founding Father: The Story of Joseph P. Kennedy* (New York: New American Library, 1964); Amanda Smith's edition of her grandfather's correspondence, *Hostage to Fortune: The Letters of Joseph P. Kennedy* (New York: Viking, 2001); and, of course, John F. Kennedy's *Why England Slept* (New York: Wilfred Funk, 1940). There are myriad books on the subject, as there are on related topics—J. Edgar Hoover, Franklin Delano Roosevelt, Winston Churchill, the Mitford Sisters. Colonel Colin McVean Gubbins surfaces in numerous histories of the British Special Operations Executive, and his *Partisan Leader's Handbook* is (remarkably) available through Amazon.com. The Göring to buy the 1940 election is discussed in Joseph E. Persico's *Roosevelt's Secret War* (New York: Random House, 2011).

Throughout the months of researching his senior thesis in 1939, Jack wrote letters—many to his friend Lem Billings, others to his father that have been subsequently stolen, lost, or destroyed. *Jack 1939* is roughly faithful to his actual itinerary: he was in Val d'Isère when I suggest, and in Moscow, Danzig, and Prague at about the times I send him there. George Kennan's memoirs mention Jack, whom at the time he viewed as "an upstart and an ignoramus," at the Czech border in August 1939; it was particularly fun to imagine those two in a room together. I chose not to mention Jack's trip to Palestine in May 1939, although his letter to his father from Jerusalem is one of the few from the period that survive. The location didn't fit with the fictional world I'd invented—and this book is, after all, *fiction*.

The picture of Jack juggling is part of the collection of the John F. Kennedy Presidential Library and Museum, where one can also find such things as Jack's stained and much-stamped passport from 1935; his beloved Wianno Senior yacht, *Victura;* and the telegram Frances Ann Cannon sent to the *Queen Mary* on February 25, 1939. The fact that the telegram exists is wondrous to me—Jack must have kept it in his pocket or wallet throughout the crossing and for the rest of his life. A testament to love and loss, if ever there was one. Many of the Kennedy Library's collections are open to the public; others, such as the Billings correspondence, are closed collections requiring permission for access. I am grateful to Maryrose Grossman of the Audiovisual Archives, and to Stacey Chandler of the Reference Staff, for their assistance. Open items (including the Cannon telegram) may be viewed online, for those who cannot travel to Boston.

Throughout the process of writing this book, I was unflaggingly supported by my agent of nearly twenty years, Raphael Sagalyn, who read numerous drafts and offered—along with his staff—invaluable suggestions. He placed the resulting manuscript in the care of Jake Morrissey at Riverhead Books, whose editing was masterful and whose enthusiasm for both Jack and this author are sustaining. I'm also grateful to Mr. Morrissey's assistant, Alexandra Cardia; to copy editor Diane Aronson, who fact-checked the entire manuscript with verve and tact; and to publicist Glory Plata, who helped shepherd the story to the public. It goes without saying that any fault in the resulting novel is entirely mine.

Francine Mathews
Denver, Colorado
December 2011

Francine Mathews is the author of more than twenty novels of mystery, history, and suspense. Her historical thriller *The Alibi Club* was named one of the fifteen best novels of 2006 by *Publishers Weekly*. A graduate of Princeton and Stanford, she spent four years as an intelligence analyst at the CIA. She lives and works in Colorado.